MW00574541

ONCE MORE UNTO THE BREACH

Jeffrey Cook

WRITERPUNK Press

Published in the USA by Writerpunk Press
Layout and typesetting by Lia Rees
Cover designed by Elizabeth Hamm and Thais Lopes

Fonts used: PASTELARIA by Misprinted Type
Kingthings Trypewriter by Kevin King
Rafale by Suleyman Yazki/Svet Simov/Vasil Stanev
Cardo by David Perry
SENANG BANYOL by Adien Gunarta
Angst Dingbats – ✇❀✿◙⊕ – by Angst

Copyright © 2015 Punk Writers
All Rights Reserved

ISBN: 978-0692560495

This book is dedicated to all the readers who give indie authors a chance, including those in this volume. Thanks also to the following:

Editing and proofreading: Rachel Brune, Tabitha Davis, T.J. Ford, Carol Gyzander, Andrea Stafford Hintz, Voss Foster, H James Lopez, Ken Rodriguez, Rie Sheridan Rose, Christopher Saldaña, J. Sarchet, Janice Stucki, K. M. Vanderbilt, D.j. Wilson, Mary Zemina.

Layout and cover design: Elizabeth Hamm of Lizzie Belina Designs; Thais Lopes of Magic Editorial Design; and Lia Rees of Free Your Words

Also a big shout out to the others who offered help, and particularly anyone who helped but was inadvertently left off the list.

"*We can no other answer make but thanks,*

And thanks, and ever thanks."

All profits from this book go to support PAWS animal shelter and rescue in Lynnwood, WA. PAWS is a champion for animals – rehabilitating injured and orphaned wildlife, sheltering and adopting homeless cats and dogs, and educating people to make a better world for animals and people. http://www.paws.org

paws.
people helping animals

Foreword
Thank You Readers

Tarry a little…

WHEN WRITERPUNK PRESS set out to publish our first anthology, we had to decide what to do with any profits. After the inevitable jokes ("Well, if we don't sell any books, we don't have a problem! Ha!"), a decision still needed to be made.

We settled on donating the proceeds to a charity and chose PAWS, a non-profit animal shelter and rescue that has helped over 200,000 animals since its doors opened in 1967.

So, it is with great pleasure we announce that the first six months' sales of *Sound & Fury: Shakespeare Goes Punk* have added up to a donation large enough to fully fund a large dog kennel at PAWS, an accomplishment that would not have been possible without the support of readers and fans like you!

We at Writerpunk Press offer our sincerest thanks for your help in making this dream a reality.

But just who is Writerpunk Press?

J. Sarchet

Introduction
Who We Are

We know what we are, but not what we may be.
— Hamlet, Act 4, Scene 5

IF YOU BROUGHT all of us into a room, you might be surprised at the collection of people before you. You'd see people from all over the world and a range of ages. Then, if you asked us to introduce ourselves, you might be further surprised at the variety of occupations. Web designers. Truck drivers. University students. Cashiers. Freelance dilettantes.

Still, these words describe what we do and not who we are. We are daydreamers, world-builders, star-gazers, and boundary-pushers – the kind of people that sit around and ponder *What if?* We're the kind of people who like to imagine new worlds and explore alternative histories.

Writerpunk is an international community of authors, illustrators, bloggers, poets, artists, graphic designers, and readers from all walks of life who are fans of cyberpunk, steampunk, dieselpunk and associated genres. Some of us have read, watched, and listened extensively within the punk genres while others of us are stepping through the looking glass for the first time. Some are commited to their craft full time while others approach it as a hobby. Some have published works and others still are penning their first drafts.

There is one thing we are not: static. The community continues to grow, to evolve, to be redefined. Who knows what we may become?

But now, in this moment, we know who we are: We are writerpunks.

And we are proud to present to you our second anthology. *Sound & Fury* was well received on Amazon, and is still available there; we consider it a successful maiden flight. With experience at the wheel and the wind of inspiration at our back, our little airship is set to rise higher. Join us on the voyage! (And visit www.punkwriters.com for updates.)

J. Sarchet

Preface
The Origins Of Punk Literature:
Steampunk, Cyberpunk, Dieselpunk,
Biopunk and more

*"Personally, I think Victorian fantasies are going to be the next big thing,
as long as we can come up with a fitting collective term ... like
'steampunks,' perhaps."*
– K.W. Jeter, 1987

IN THE PREVIOUS VOLUME of *Shakespeare Goes Punk*, I attempted to give a loose definition of punk literature, and what differentiates it from mainstream science fiction and fantasy. I started out as a steampunk author, and still attend a lot of local steampunk events. When I attend conventions and speak to people who are relatively new to these various subgenres of science fiction, the question that usually follows "What is steampunk?" is "How long has steampunk been around?" or something similar.

The roots of steampunk date to the science fiction of the 1800s: H.G. Wells, Jules Verne, and others. They were just writing science fiction true to their times, but the subgenre still uses many of the ideas they set into motion.

A number of works in the 1960s took their inspirations from Wells, Verne, and other science fiction of the 1800s. Disney – and a few others – borrowed visual cues not from the actual look of the Victorian era, but from the sepia-tone photographs of that time. The television show *The Wild Wild West* and Disney's adaptation of *20,000 Leagues Under the Sea* both have the look and feel of steampunk works. Meanwhile in literature, books like Keith Laumer's *Worlds of the Imperium* and Ronald Clark's *Queen Victoria's Bomb* were being written. Some people would consider these works to be steampunk, but they didn't self-identify as any kind of subgenre of literature.

For the first of the punk genres to self-identify as a subgenre of science fiction and a literary movement in its own right, we need to get to the mid-1970s and cyberpunk.

John Brunner, William Gibson, Bruce Sterling, Pat Cadigan, Neal Stephenson, and Philip K. Dick are among the earliest cyberpunk authors. Cyberpunk differed from a lot of the science fiction of the era and before by emphasizing atmosphere over everything. A lot of the work, in particular, was a response to the utopian science fiction of the times, which featured space travel and technology that improved the life of the common man. In contrast, while the technology was often no less impressive, cyberpunk took place in dystopian settings, and tended to focus on crowded urban environments instead of far-flung, exotic worlds. A common motif of cyberpunk was the low-life versus the corrupt elite – often in the form of corporate entities. The works of George Orwell, hard-boiled detective fiction, and film noir are often cited as influences by the listed authors.

Bruce Bethke coined the term in 1980 for his aptly named short story, "Cyberpunk," but the term was quickly taken for use in describing the works of Gibson, Dick, and others. Bruce Sterling, in particular, championed the movement in his fanzine *Cheap Truth*. By the time Philip K. Dick's *Do Androids Dream of Electric Sheep* was adapted into the movie *Blade Runner* in 1982, and William Gibson won most of science fiction's biggest awards with 1984's *Neuromancer,* cyberpunk was a fully recognized subgenre of science fiction, with its own tropes, proponents, and critics.

Steampunk is the second "punk" genre to self-identify as such, and it emerged from the writings of three authors who cited Philip K. Dick as a particular influence. While many of the early works later adopted into the genre were written in the 1960s and early '70s, the first group to identify what they were writing as similar, non-mainstream, and a literary movement in its own right, were K.W. Jeter, Tim Powers, and James Blaylock. Jeter's *Morlock Night* (1979), Blaylock's Narbondo series, and Powers' *The Anubis Gates* all echoed similar themes, and were published around the same time, leading to comparisons between the three, and eventually leading to Jeter coining steampunk as the collective term for a derivative of cyberpunk in a letter to *Locus* magazine.

William Gibson and Bruce Sterling, again, had a major hand in giving the subgenre an identity with their novel *The Difference Engine*. Published in 1990, the book didn't just tell its story, but set out to build a world and explain its aesthetic. Moving from a successful use of Babbage's Analytical Engine in 1824, the world of the novel's Victorian era had changed drastically, adopting a lot of the visual cues we now associate with steampunk.

Eventually, the term "punk" was added for numerous technologies that helped define particular eras. None have been as successful as cyberpunk and steampunk, but a number have become accepted. Dieselpunk has been regularly applied to works that mostly center around World Wars-era technologies, with their own noir style applied to the look, and plenty of era mad science included.

Teslapunk imagines the electrical era of Nikola Tesla and Thomas Edison, with their inventions, and those of similar innovators, writ-large upon the world.

Biopunk looks to the future, but instead of the cybernetics and internet advances of cyberpunk, derives its defining look and feel from unintended consequences of bioengineering. Nanopunk is an overlapping subgenre which examines the impact upon society of using nanobots in the human body – whether for good or ill.

Outside of technology, some derivatives using the name "punk" use other elements as their defining characteristic, from which they draw the defining style that shifts them from works of typical adventure science fiction or fantasy, and deems them punk. Splatterpunk is one such appropriation of the punk title, being applied to horror films that take a great deal of license in the name of style, or have horror tropes as defining background elements of their world. Elfpunk is another, drawing fantasy creatures into the modern world, and pitting them against very modern threats.

Not everyone agrees on all of these variants, and only time will tell which will become literary movements of their own, and which may fade. But for the time being, with the explosion of steampunk culture in the early 2000s, there's no shortage of authors, filmmakers, crafters, cosplayers and so on making their mark on the world of "punk" today.

Jeffrey Cook

People To Blame, Part 1
The Writers

JEFFREY COOK is quickly becoming a Steampunk veteran. He is the author of the emergent Steampunk *Dawn of Steam* trilogy. (*Dawn of Steam: First Light, Dawn of Steam: Gods of the Sun,* and *Dawn of Steam: Rising Suns.*) He has had Steampunk stories published in the anthologies *Steampunk Trails 2, Avast Ye Airships, Free Flowing Stories,* and *A Cold Winter's Night.* In a much less steam-powered vein, he is also the author of the YA Science Fiction-Mystery *Mina Cortez: From Bouquets to Bullets,* and the first book of the Fair Folk Chronicles, *Foul is Fair,* co-written with his normal editor, Katherine Perkins.

He lives in the wilds of Maple Valley, Washington now, but after a start in Boulder, CO, he moved all over the United States (and a little bit of Canada). His mother insists he's wanted to be an author since he was six years old, but he didn't get his official start until 2014. In addition to the novels and anthology projects, the life-long gamer has contributed to Deep7 Games out of Seattle, WA. When not reading, researching, writing or gaming, he is also a passionate football fan. (Go Seahawks!)

http://www.authorjeffreycook.com/about.html

KATHERINE PERKINS is Jeff's co-writer on *Foul is Fair* and a lot of other stories and edited his first trilogy with all the pedantry of someone who's taught both grammar and history. She lives in Mobile, Alabama, with her husband and one extremely skittish cat. She was born in Lafayette, Louisiana, and will defend its cuisine on any field of honor. When not reading, researching, writing, or editing, she tries to remember what she was supposed to be doing.

ROZENE MORGANDY was born in Lamaline, Newfoundland in Canada. She now lives in St. John's, Newfoundland with her husband and two cats. This will be her first time contributing in an anthology and publishing her work, although she has been writing since she was in her early teens. When not writing, talking about writing, or reading, Rozene enjoys playing a variety of video games, watching TV shows, and spending time with her husband and friends.

Writer and playwright, JANICE STUCKI, experienced the joy of having her late 70s-era themed play, *Tropical Depression*, produced for the NYC stage in the summer of 2014. This was followed up with another successful production in the summer of 2015 with *Fight or Flight*, a short play telling the story of two very anxious recruits during an aerospace training program who have more than their careers at stake. Janice has also published short stories in various small press publications, was a regular feature article contributor for a parents' magazine, and has some pretty awful poetry that is certainly unpublishable to her credit. Janice's inspirations for her creative endeavors whether twisted, schmaltzy or wondrous are shaped by her childhood loves which include dinosaurs and dragons, Marguerite Henry and Ray Bradbury, and *Star Trek* and *Get Smart*. She lives in the midst of hard-core suburbia in northern New Jersey with her family and their stubbornly adorable mixed-breed rescue hound, Mellow. Mixing the fantasy world of nanopunk with one of her favorite plays by Shakespeare has been a crazy and rewarding experience and Janice is thrilled to be a part of this anthology.

www.facebook.com/selenalunaproductions

CAROL GYZANDER writes under her own name, even though few can spell or pronounce it (think "GUYS and her"). She was a prolific reader of classic science fiction and Agatha Christie mysteries in her early days because when you move every two years, you're the perpetual new kid and have lots of time on your hands. But she became adept at people-watching in order to fit in at each new school, and followed this up by studying anthropology – the study of people and their culture – and lots and lots of English literature at Bryn Mawr College. Now that her kids have flown the coop, she has gone back to her early loves with an amateur detective novel and more science fiction in the works. She wrote a cyberpunk version of Macbeth for Volume I, and has followed it in this one with "Hank," the prequel set in the same world. She was also the Managing Editor of this book. See what else Carol is working on at:

www.CarolGyzanderAuthor.com

ESAIAS MAYO is an undergraduate biology major currently residing in Florida. A robust mixture of coffee and literature comprises his lifeblood. Raised in a military household, he is no stranger to travel and being raised on the road has greatly influenced his love for the adventurous aspect of science fiction. His love of fiction is matched only by his love of poetry. For a glimpse into his mind, follow his Twitter:

@A_Road_Scholar

People To Blame, Part 2
Editing, Design + Related Mischief

CAROL GYZANDER was the Managing Editor of this volume, and was responsible for commissioning the many small projects involved and monitoring their progress. She also submitted the cyberpunk story "Hank", and her biography can be found in the writers' section.

J. SARCHET was born on the day before yesterday with holes in her shoes and crying the blues. No, wait. That was the Scarecrow from *The Wiz*. Well, despite her mysterious origin story, J. has been writing all her life. In fact, she often remarks that she likes words more than most people (present company excluded, naturally). The first story she ever wrote was scribbled in a small spiral notepad and stashed behind her family's piano for safekeeping. Although she has spent most of the last 26 years filling notebooks with stories and not letting anyone read them, more recently she has begun sharing her work with others. Though she has seen the most success as a poet, she has also written one-act plays. Currently she is hard at work on a speculative fiction novel she hopes to self-publish. When it is completed, J. won't be hiding it behind a piano, but rather shouting the news from the rooftops.

An aspiring writer and lover of both steampunk (especially corsets) and the Bard (especially *Macbeth*), T.J. FORD has found this rather a fun project on which to work. In between rescuing dangling participles and saving serial commas, T.J. is a mind-body therapist with bicoastal practices in New York City and in Portland, Oregon, where she lives with her food-scientist husband and their increasingly deaf cat Scamper. In her spare time T.J. has a penchant for running long distances of 20 or 50 or 100 miles, preferably on the trails of the Hobbit forests in the Pacific Northwest.

LIA REES is a free-spirited admirer of all things visual and arty. She has a particular fondness for grunge, industrial and the less twee side of rustic. For several years she has been working with authors, turning manuscripts into professional and beautiful books, and creating posters and publicity graphics. Lately she has branched out into website customisation, T-shirt design, marketing advice and music videos! At present living in London, she plans to cross the Atlantic as soon as she can; there's a bearded American anarchist waiting for her, and a crazy crew of writer friends. Her business, Free Your Words, lives nominally at FreeYourWords.com but is mainly carried out via Facebook. She likes sharing her designs and other people's art at her Facebook page, The Wayward Eye.

www.facebook.com/LiaWayward

ELIZABETH HAMM of Lizzie Belina Designs collaborated on the cover. Born in California, raised in North Dakota, and probably never going to get a proper tan, Elizabeth has been interested in the graphic, video, and written arts since she could form tangible memories. Closing in on finally finishing a dual degree in Broadcasting and Multimedia Studies, she continues to combine the two worlds together along with her love of writing. Being creative and passionate about the world of fiction brought her to volunteering her growing knowledge and time to design the cover of this book. In her spare time, she writes novels, shoots short films, and does her own video news program weekly. Elizabeth can be reached at lizziebelina@gmail.com for all things cover design, graphic design, or video.

THAIS LOPES of Magic Design Editorial was also involved in the cover design.

The cat will mew, and dog will have his day.

As You Like It

Katherine Perkins
+ Jeffrey Cook

THE NEW BOSS was not precisely the same as the Old Boss.

Of course, that made a certain degree of sense, since Boss Frederick had driven the Old Boss, his own brother, from the Factory, old personal and professional arguments finally having come to a very threatening climax. He'd seen enough reason – or just spoiled his own daughter enough not to deprive her of her best pal – to keep the Old Boss' daughter, Rosie, around. He hadn't sent her off in the small caravan of trucks and motorcycles that had sped away, friends of the Old Boss who weren't safe from the hostile takeover of the business. Not that Out There would be safe. Now, Boss Frederick owned half the town, in its towering tarnished silver and smoke. The other half wasn't worth owning, though the Foreman's family had some investments in parts.

The Foreman was new, too. The old Foreman, who'd been close with the Old Boss, had been spared any trouble in Frederick's takeover on account of being on his deathbed at the time, and then he had passed. Frederick had given the Foreman's oldest son, Oliver, the job. Oliver had quickly fallen into the rhythm of what he did and didn't have to do. His brother Orrie disagreed, and standing there, five feet nine inches of solid muscle, had found the opportunity to disagree once more.

"It ain't right, Oliver. I want to go to school. I want to be Somebody."

"Well, you'll have to settle for being Somebody's little brother."

"Dad said you were supposed to look out for us."

"I sent Jacob to school. Not like he can haul boxes."

Orrie snarled. It wasn't that he'd objected to being in the warehouses. He'd thrived there – heavy lifting, engine grease, and all. The men liked and respected him. He didn't mind a hard day's work, and he was always up for tossing a few heavy boxes in the back of his own truck and spending time on the road by himself.

What Orrie objected to was the same thing that caused Oliver to be considered ideal for management at the factory: the very concept of slotting people into boxes, like specialized machines filling packages straight off the assembly line. Oliver was the oldest; he'd be in charge. Jacob was small and delicate and bookish. He'd been shipped off, gotten out of the way. And Orrie, who'd hungered for any knowledge outside the Factory's cut-rate assembly line of a school, was destined – by his brother's casual judgement – to haul boxes.

"I'm not a damn workhorse!" Orrie shoved his brother into the wall. "It wasn't your call! Dad wrote a will, didn't he?"

Oliver stared at him blankly, ignoring being pinned. "Are we going to pretend any law gets enforced in this town without the boss saying so? Usually saying it to me?"

Orrie let go of him and backed off. "Yeah, well, to hell with you. There's a prize fight tomorrow. Should be enough to get me a start in school."

Orrie stormed out. Oliver watched him go calmly, and then made a few calls.

A pair of trombones played relatively soft and slow as several women in rust-colored coveralls lined up in front of the ring. When the entire brass band, augmented by flashing colored stage lights, began to blare along and accelerate the tempo, the girls peeled off the coveralls. The showgirls' dresses – if they could be called dresses, with that amount of cloth – were covered in silvery sequins. The overalls were kicked off into little heaps before the kicks became higher, the dance number culminating with a little singing:

It's be-en a long day!
We hope you're doing well!
So lay down your troubles

And lay down your money
And just wait for the bell!

"Well, that was quite a little number! Lots of ... um ... spectacle tonight!" Cecily and her halo of golden curls bounced in her seat as they all waited for the fight. Her lacy white dress bounced with her. Rosie, in a simple dress dark enough for practically mourning, slouched slightly in her chair. Cecily noticed, and her bouncing slowed to a stop. She set a hand on her cousin's and smiled broadly when Rosie looked up.

Rosie met her eyes, but her lips remained tight. "Sorry, Cecily. This is the biggest smile I can fake right now."

"It's... it's going to be okay, Rosie. We'll... we'll get your dad back someday. Maybe when we own the factory."

"In about 30 years," a quiet voice said from behind them. "I'm looking forward to seeing the first time anyone in your family tried to come through on a deal." The man in the patched suit smiled a thin, dry smile.

Cecily turned and shushed him. "What if Dad heard you?" Boss Frederick was seated just a little down the front row, absorbed in conversation with various associates. "Mr. Litmus, you're going to get yourself thrashed."

"No," said Mr. Litmus. "One of those guys is going to get himself thrashed. Most of the money says that'll be the youngster."

"That's too bad," Cecily said, frowning.

Rosie surveyed the ring, watching how each fighter conducted himself, and nodded a little. "Here's hoping there's no serious injuries."

"You girls really like being the first in your family to say something, don't you?" Mr. Litmus asked with that thin smile again. "What do you think people in this town come to see Charger Thompson for?"

There was no question who the crowds favored. Charlie 'Charger' Thompson was playing up to the crowd, and they were eating it up. It made sense. He was the ring veteran, and Orrie had little business being in the ring with him. He also had some questionable connections that helped to market his fights, a reputation that helped intimidate some of

Charger's opponents. At the very least, some of his fights had made a lot of money for various 'associates' of Orrie's brother.

As far as Orrie was concerned, the disparity in their renown was just fine. Old Adam, who'd been close to his father, had agreed to serve as manager. That was all the support he needed just yet. It got him entered in tonight. That should do it.

The dancing girls hadn't really been much of a distraction for Orrie. Nothing against them, but no matter the shine and polish, he could tell a bunch of tired girls going through the motions just to get through another night when he saw them. He saw them a lot in this town, people who felt trapped. He wasn't going to be trapped. He was getting out.

Once the lights were right again, he took the opportunity to assess the older fighter, watching how he moved, looking for any sign of weakness aside from overconfidence. He didn't see much, but given Charger's record, he also hadn't expected to.

The pair touched gloves and listened to the referee's spiel on the rules. All the while, Charger tried to stare him down, but Orrie wouldn't budge. They returned to their corners, getting last-second instructions from their managers. Orrie turned down water, refusing to take his eyes off of his opponent.

As soon as the bell rang, both men moved quickly to the center of the ring. Charger, true to his reputation as a fierce puncher, came out swinging. Orrie evaded the first flurry, but fell for a feint and took a hard shot to the side of the head, staggering back. He managed to steady himself before being fully trapped at one edge of the ring. He almost bought a second feint but got his guard up in time, as he realized he wasn't going to be able to stand up to the cagey veteran for long.

Resolving to outsmart his opponent instead, he started circling, fighting defensively and making his opponent chase him. Whenever he could, he readied himself to block a couple punches and let Charger start another series of hard swings. Then he'd move again, after throwing a quick counter or two to urge Charger to keep coming after him.

The crowd booed, and the taunts and calls for him to quit running and to stand and fight started raining down. Orrie ignored them, and continued feigning leaving an opening again and again before darting back, while keeping track of the time as best he could.

Finally, he saw what he was looking for. Charger put everything into a hard cross, leaving himself wide open, having gotten used to his opponent fleeing the hard punches. Orrie ducked his head back, avoided the fist by a narrow margin, then stepped in again, landing a hard jab to the older man's face. When the quick shot startled his opponent as much as he'd hoped, he followed up with another jab, then another. He went on the full offensive, throwing punch after punch while not letting Charger find his balance again. With seconds to go in the round, he finally landed a combination of jabs and an uppercut that put Charger on the ground. The bell rang seconds later, stopping the referee's count, though Charger was starting to get up anyway.

"Wow," said Cecily, clutching Rosie's hand. "This is sure exciting."

"Yeah," Rosie replied. "He's good at what he does."

"Yeah," said Mr. Litmus, leaning in from behind them. "He really is. God help the kid."

 Cecily didn't hear him, her eyes fixated on the young fighter. Rosie glanced down the row at her uncle, who was frowning. Granted, a great deal of the people in the audience were frowning, but her uncle was a special case. Rosie knew people who'd upset her uncle, and she was still wondering if she'd ever see them again.

Orrie returned to his corner, breathing hard, but in much better shape than his opponent appeared to be. He nodded to his manager's instructions and accepted the offer of water. At some point during the break, he found he was having trouble paying attention to Adam. His vision started to blur a few moments later. The bell rang before he was able to explain to his manager how he felt. Feeling disoriented and dizzy, he struggled to his feet, moving back out into the ring unsteadily.

At first, he attempted to keep his former strategy in mind, but he wasn't able to react to Charger's punches in time. He took a beating in the early seconds, and found himself on the mat. By the time he regained his senses, he heard the referee counting six. He fought back to his feet as quickly as he could, barely beating the ten count. He assured the referee he was okay to continue and prepared to face his opponent's onslaught.

This time he managed better, though he still couldn't dodge and move. Instead, he just got his hands up, defending his head as best he could and absorbing punishing blow after punishing blow. When he staggered back against the ropes, he found that he could put his weight against them and let them absorb part of the force of his opponent's blows, as long as he stayed covered up. He still nearly fell repeatedly and didn't manage to throw a single punch. Despite that, when the bell rang, he was still on his feet.

Something was wrong. Rosie could tell. And as another round ended, she realized, and she stood, unintentionally dragging Cecily, who was still clutching her hand, up with her. She ran to the old man at the corner. "Drugged. He's been drugged. No water."

"Oh gosh, is that what happened?" Cecily asked.

"Has to be. He didn't have any water before the match started. He did between rounds."

Fortunately, Rosie was earnest enough – and her reasoning adequate – that the man listened to her and didn't try to insist on water when the struggling fighter returned in terrible condition, but still standing. It was impressive. Rosie was, in fact, impressed. She was also determined not to see the cheaters win if she could be of any further assistance.

As Orrie staggered back to his corner, Adam got the cuts on his face patched up as best he could, with help from, for some reason, a pair of girls. Pretty girls – was that the Boss' daughter? Or niece, or whatever? She was something. Though he still had some trouble focusing, his head started to clear. As it did, a plan began to form.

When the bell rang, Orrie feigned still being as unsteady as he had been last round. He put his defenses up again, luring his opponent in close while Orrie backed off. As soon as he saw an opening, though, Orrie put everything he had into a hard left cross, just as Charger was preparing to unleash a new combination to finish him off. Caught in mid-swing, Charger staggered. Orrie followed up as hard and fast as he could, throwing hard punches and just hoping to connect with enough of them to keep backing up his opponent towards the corner.

Without water, and after taking the beating last round, he knew he was running out of time. His patient strategy wasn't going to work. If he didn't knock out his opponent this round, or if he gave Charger any time to recover from underestimating his young challenger, the match wouldn't last much longer. When Charger did try to fight back, Orrie took the punches as best he could, focusing on putting all of his limited concentration into offense and hard punches.

With time winding down and the punches starting to blur his vision again, he managed to land a new combination – two jabs and an uppercut – dropping Charger to the ring floor. He was forced to step back, almost falling over himself when the referee pushed him away, while the referee counted. Orrie needed to grab the ring ropes to stay on his feet, the drugs and punishment taking their toll, but he managed. Charger tried a few times to get to his feet, nearly doing so at eight, before he lost his balance and fell back to the mat for the final count.

Barely able to see or stand upright, and booed by the crowd, Orrie was still declared the winner, with his manager rushing out to help him stay upright while the verdict was announced.

Arm upraised, with a glaze in his eyes, Orrie called out, "There we go. Can somebody give me my ticket out of this life now?"

"Absolutely," announced Boss Frederick, rising from his front-row seat. His daughter looked on in consternation. "You have until midnight to get out of town."

As they walked home, Cecily was sad, and Rosie was raging.

"Other people rig the match, might even have wanted the guy dead, and *he* gets run out of town! It's insane!"

"I just don't understand," Cecily muttered.

"I think I do, is the trouble. All the right people bet against him. That makes his refusing to lose a problem."

"But Dad–" Cecily began, but her cousin looked her in the eyes. "Okay, yeah, I can't say that doesn't make sense." She was silent for a while. "He seemed like he was going to be okay, though?"

"He seemed like he wasn't going to let anyone see him flinch, and wasn't going to waste time."

"Yeah. He's… he's quite a guy."

"He really is. I just really hope nobody heard Old Adam feeling all awful and offering to try to help. Not a half-blind old man's fault that somebody switched the bottles."

"Why did Orrie turn him down?" Cecily asked, her curls bouncing again as she canted her head to the side. "Why was Orrie looking at Dad's bodyguards when he talked about Old Adam's grandchildren?"

"Because he was concerned. Even just getting his head back, Orrie's not stupid."

Orrie indeed wasn't stupid, and he wasn't wasting any time as he climbed into the old truck. It had served him well over the years. It was big enough to handle a few boxes, and had enough power that he could surprise most folks who wanted to race – especially after he refitted the engine himself. It wasn't like Oliver's toy cars, like a lot of his friends had, with way too much engine for the frames, made for nothing but speed. All of those broke down easy, needed way too much fuel, and spent half their time in repairs. The truck, while it had seen better days, just kept going.

The wilderness was dangerous but Orrie figured that other people had managed, and with some work, he would too. The truck would serve as shelter for a bit until he got his bearings, and maybe if he got out of the way and stopped antagonizing Oliver, Jacob might have an easier time of it whenever he came home from school. With Oliver's temper and bad-seed nature, he doubted it, but right now, it was all he could do.

As soon as the truck passed city limits, half a dozen headlights turned on behind him, and even over the growls and rattles of his own truck, he could hear the roar of souped-up cars coming to life behind him. Oliver couldn't be content to just see him turned out of town; he and his friends had turned out to see Orrie off. More than likely, he figured, if they got a chance they'd try to run him off the road to steal the extra tanks of fuel he stored in the back. They hadn't been able to touch it when the truck was locked safely away on Factory property, but outside city limits, and especially as an outcast, he was fair game.

There was no way he was going to outrun Oliver and his friends: their cars were nothing but speed and power. Orrie knew all of them, Oliver included, had included nitrous injectors, for sudden bursts of speed. It was intended for the races, on which those who could afford it – and some who couldn't – bet their cars or large sums of cash. Oliver had picked up quite the car collection before everyone stopped racing him entirely, and he just got a share of the weekend's take from the bookies.

Orrie's truck, however, was bigger than any of them, and on rougher territory, they wouldn't last long. No one was going to chance their expensive toys breaking down because they couldn't handle fractured, sunken roads and loose gravel.

Orrie pushed the engine, picking up speed and trying to focus on the road ahead, instead of the growing glow of headlights behind him. He moved to the middle of the road, to make himself harder to pass safely, and egged all the speed he could out of the aging rig.

The glow increased in intensity faster than it should have, the dim light reflecting off his rear-view becoming a bright flash. One of Oliver's friends, either trying to prove himself, or just overeager, had hit the nitrous right away, shooting ahead of the others, weaving side to side to try to figure out a good way to come up alongside Orrie. Orrie kept the truck moving, trying to keep the car cut off, until it gave up passing and just rammed into the back end of the truck. Orrie jolted in his seat, but kept control. Then a bump came again, and again, as the lead tried to disrupt his control. Knowing that the driver had to act quickly since the nitrous was hard on the engine, and he'd have to slow way down before much longer, Orrie tried to time the crashes of the car's grill into the back of the truck, and then slammed on his brakes. The car barreled into him far harder than the driver had intended, and the hood buckled under the impact with the heavier truck. When Orrie hit the gas again, the truck was moving; the fancy muscle car wasn't.

The others didn't even slow down to make sure their friend was okay, weaving around the stopped car in pursuit. While they obviously weren't that concerned for their friend, Orrie knew it was even more urgent to stay away from them – he'd destroyed one of their expensive toys, and worse, shown them up.

Since he'd had to slow down, they were steadily catching up, alternating who was in the lead. Those times he did look back, the only brightly painted car that he never saw take the lead was his brother's. He was pretty sure Oliver would be hanging back, letting the others take the risks and wind resistance for him, to let his car last as long as possible, and he'd catch up when he needed to. He'd won a lot of races through better strategy.

Orrie didn't even slow down at a fork in the road, briefly running on two wheels with a sharp turn before the truck righted itself. The faster cars mostly handled the turn fine, but one turned too sharp and ran off the road, upended in a ditch. Orrie couldn't help but grin at the sight in his rear view, before turning full focus on the road ahead. Two down, four to go, but he still had a lot of road before anything that he'd consider safe, and the four were gaining. Orrie tried to urge more speed out of the truck, risking some overly tight turns.

At one, he nearly got spun when one of the pursuing vehicles hit the back end, and Orrie fought with the wheel to stay on the road, throwing all his weight into not getting rolled. He regained control of the truck, but the pursuing cars were right behind him now. He moved quickly side to side, trying to prevent anyone from getting alongside, succeeding for a time. Eventually, he drifted too far left, cutting off one car while another hit the nitrous and rocketed ahead, pulling up to his right.

Orrie yanked the wheel back the other way, barely staying on the road when the sides of the vehicles hit each other. A second car slammed into him from behind, trying to jar some of that control, and he ended up having to fight with the wheel again as the pair of cars tried to shove him off the road. The sloped ground and sunken thickets of briar made it uncertain how far a drop that'd be.

This time, the car running behind him didn't drop back at all, continuing to push him along. Any attempt to hit the brakes resulted in screaming brakes and the smell of burning metal. The muscle car continued to push him along, while the other kept trying to slam into the side and shove him left. The teamwork almost succeeded before the road widened in a spot, and Orrie gained just enough room to pull left then jerk the wheel back hard, slamming into the other car. The other car might have the bigger engine but Orrie's truck was a lot heavier, and once it got some momentum behind it he was able to drive the colorful car sideways. He kept cranking the wheel until the encroaching car was only half on the road, threatening to drop off into the ditch – at least until it crashed into a stump hidden in the tall grasses off the road. One more down.

The car that had been trailing used the distraction to pull ahead of him, taking off with a sudden burst of added speed, and then slowing, trying to nearly match speeds so when Orrie ran the truck into him, it would have minimal impact. Then the driver hit the brakes, trying to slow him down. Though they kept moving, pushing the car was letting the last two catch up rapidly, until Orrie could clearly see his brother at the wheel of the trailing car.

Unable to speed back up, and seeing more cars closing in, Orrie did the only thing he could. He braked hard for a moment to get some separation from the car ahead of him then hit the gas just as hard, yanking the wheel around and intentionally jumping the road. Gravity took over as he rolled down the hill, with the metal frame and weight of the truck crunching a path for him through the thickets. His seatbelt bit into his waist and shoulder hard. Broken glass added to the effect when the windshield and one of the side windows exploded in, somewhere through the third roll.

Buried deep in the thicket, the truck came to a halt upside-down. Had Orrie had a passenger, they'd have been crushed as part of the car collapsed in. As it was, he wasn't entirely certain he was going to survive. He was pretty sure his shoulder had been pulled out of joint, and he wasn't sure how badly he was bleeding from numerous cuts. But he was alive and able to move. He undid the seatbelt, almost screaming when impact with the roof of the car jarred his shoulder. He slowly crawled out through the missing front windshield, and looked through the bramble towards the road at the top of the slope. He was fairly certain his brother didn't see him, but the three remaining brightly colored cars were all stopped, with figures moving, looking down the hill.

He crawled away from the ruined truck and through the briars, finally dragging himself up to a place to rest and pop his shoulder back in. He'd survived, but no thanks to Oliver. Apparently failing at rigging the fight had either shown him up enough in front of the new boss, or maybe cost Oliver enough money that he'd been willing to go to extremes to make sure that Orrie's exile stuck.

The cleaning fans whirred slowly and softly around the two blonde girls as they stood on the roof, Cecily grasping one hand around Rosie's and the other on the railing as she peered in the distance. "What are those flashes of light, down at the edge of the smoke?" she asked, confused.

"Probably an ambush," Rosie said drily, not looking confused at all. She shifted a little, almost as if trying to stand between Cecily and the rail – and whatever had happened in the distance.

"Oh gosh! Should somebody tell Dad – oh." Cecily frowned and dropped hands as she turned away. "That might not help, huh?"

"It really won't help," Rosie said, slowly walking with her. "I'm sorry to say it again, Cecily, but your – what's this?"

'This' was a paper stuck to the door of the girls' penthouse atop the silvery tower.

'EVICTION NOTICE:' it read. *'ROSIE DUKE HAS 24 HOURS TO REMOVE HERSELF FROM ALL FACTORY PROPERTIES. CECILY, IF YOU'RE READING THIS, JUST THINK ABOUT HAVING YOUR ROOM TO YOURSELF AGAIN, PRINCESS.'*

Silence reigned at first, as they walked back towards the elevator with the note.

"Well...." Rosie at last said quietly. "Guess I need to get myself a bike."

"A bike?" Cecily said in consternation. "You think you're getting out on a bike? We're taking the Hornet! Or maybe one of the trucks."

"There's no way to – what do you mean, 'we'?"

"What do you mean, 'What do you mean?' Dad's kicking us out."

"Your dad is kicking ME out."

"So he's kicking us out. I don't see what's so hard to grasp here – oh hi, Mr. Litmus."

The man in the patched and pocketed coat was groaning. "Yes, yes, because a pair of lovely young ladies who have never worked a day in their lives are exactly what's needed Out There." He started to follow them as they paced back toward their room. He was still groaning. "The types you get Out There are going to think this is a dream come true."

"Hey, my dad's out there!" Rosie began indignantly, but quickly caught herself. "You're right, Mr. Litmus. Do you have any scissors?"

"Of course I have scissors," he said, automatically reaching into his coat and handing her a pair.

She then handed them to Cecily as they entered the penthouse. "Cut it. All the way, like a boy's."

"Seriously?" Cecily set the scissors aside for a moment as she started to, very hesitantly, undo Rosie's heavy blonde braid. "Can I at least make you look like a good-looking boy?"

"Seriously. And good-looking's fine. Just cut enough of it no one's mind goes straight to 'girl.' Clothes and dirt'll have to make the difference. Then I'll do yours."

Cecily bit her lip. "I… I don't want to cut my hair off. When it's my turn just … make it look less fabulous."

Mr. Litmus sighed. "Guess I'll start siphoning the gas out of everything in the garages."

"Huh?" Cecily looked up from cutting Rosie's hair.

"Slow down their start once they get the word you're with us. Plus we get to take extra cans of gas."

"What do you mean, 'us'?"

"Let's not get repetitive, kid," the scruffy man said, rolling his eyes as he walked away, pulling a coil of dark rubber out of his coat.

There was a pond, far enough out into the wilderness that no water flowing from the town had ever happened to make it there; nothing from the towering Factory, barely a dot on the dusky horizon, had ever been dumped near it. The water was pristine.

Somewhere on the edge of the darkness was a shot.

And soon, a red truck was running down the overgrown highway with a deer spitted on its grille. The wind mixed blood with paint and rust as the old man at the wheel threw his head back and laughed.

"To hell with the suits and the shiny shoes, boys. This is the life."

"You got it, Boss."

"Sometimes, bad luck is the best luck you can get, if you work it right."

"Couldn't pay me to go back, Boss."

"Going to be good eating tonight, too," the older man continued. "We've got to be careful, though. A little conservation. Don't want to run through the poor devils until there's nothing left."

That got a grin. "The college boy is sure you're trying to, Boss, being a murderer and all. Y'know, the one who showed up in camp half-starved, but wouldn't even touch the kill. 'I'm a vegetarian.'"

The grin was answered. "That boy's a lot of fun. Going to get himself killed, but a lot of fun."

"Well, he's getting a proper start on it. Now he's gone walking to get away 'before people manage to ruin everything out here.' The real funny part is, he ended up walking towards town."

The man who once owned half the city looked out in the far, far distance to the trail of smoke. "Good luck to him finding anything people haven't ruined thataway."

Just outside the edge of town beyond the final way station was another truck, one of the factory's, speckled with grease and dirt and leftover chips of white paint. The insides, however, had been kept running smoother than most anything in town, and that was why it had been chosen. Various parcels of cargo were tied to the walls of the truck bed, and the broad, flat expanse still had plenty of room for more than one to sleep.

"Well, Alice, Gary, you can take your filter-masks off now," Mr. Litmus said.

The girls peeled the masks off. They'd been useful just in case of surprisingly well-informed way station guards, as well as the fact that they'd been through some of the worst of the smoke. Cecily fidgeted with her new coal-black curls, loose and frizzy from the dye Mr.

Litmus had given her. The chemicals had somehow removed the bounce. Her dress hung down in a way she wasn't used to, either. It was one of Rosie's long, simple dark ones, onto which Mr. Litmus had sewn patches.

"So," Rosie began, running her fingers through her short, neat blonde hair. "This is it." She fidgeted a little in her own borrowed clothes – apparently, Mr. Litmus had owned more than one outfit to wear under that ever-present and ever-patched coat. Rosie's frown as she looked out the window changed to a different kind of frown. "What about my voice? Does it give me away?"

"Well, it'd give you away to me, 'cause I know you really well," Cecily admitted. She smiled, thin at first, but soon getting her usual chipper expression back. "But you're already all low and contralto. You'll just sound a bit young, really."

"Oh good," Rosie said. "And we probably still look related, so we'll say I'm your brother."

Cecily giggled.

Mr. Litmus, Rosie eventually noticed, though he had his eyes fixated on the road as it bent into the dead and briary undergrowth, was quietly drawling out a low little song.

> *The poison wind will kill us, but our neighbors kill us faster.*
> *I must say I find people our most natural disaster.*
> *We burn from fire, choke on exhaust, and this as well is true:*
> *It's better to have loved and lost than wake each day to you*

"That's... that's kind of awful, Mr. Litmus," Cecily said. "I've never heard a song like that before."

"It's not the kind that gets pressed onto records these days," Litmus said. "Not surprising, though it's a shame. People should have more advance warning in this life."

Orrie was walking alone. He hadn't slept, between the pain of his injuries and wanting to put real distance between himself and town. It wasn't the fear for his life, for there was no fear in his eyes. It was the need to put the place, which made such a stark contrast between luxury via select opportunity and abject poverty, as far behind him as he could.

He wasn't afraid of the pain or the blood. He'd survived, and would continue to do so for as long as he could manage. He might have been afraid for the girls who'd helped him out, but they were too well-connected to end up in any trouble, surely. His guardian angels in nice dresses – he certainly didn't hold against them that they weren't on the road in the night. It was funny that anyone in the Duke family had given a damn what was happening to him in the first place. But families were funny, he knew too well.

He wasn't afraid of Oliver and his friends, either. He just wanted some distance from the fact that his own brother had tried to run him down. He wasn't afraid of the wilderness; at least no one was purposely standing in his way.

Fear didn't hit his eyes until he saw the slight figure sprawled in the undergrowth, a cheap gray suit ensnared in the brambles.

"Hey, are you okay – Jacob?" Orrie nearly threw himself into the brush. "Damn it, Jacob!"

"Orrie? Wha?" The teenager looked up blankly.

"I should be asking you! What are you doing here? And when's the last time you ate?"

"Purple," Jacob replied as he lost consciousness.

The next morning, Mr. Litmus wasn't in the truck when the girls awoke. Rosie and Cecily worried and went looking.

They found the raggedy man walking in the company of a small, dark woman in clothes far more ragged than his. Strips of rough leather were wound decoratively around her throat.

"Hello, girls. This is Audrey," he said, a new tone in his voice.

"Mr. Litmus!" Rosie said, scandalized.

"Oh, don't worry. She's not that kind of girl." They'd never heard him laugh before. "Not that kind of girl. In a place like this! When you'd think there's nothing to prove!"

Audrey placed her hands almost exaggeratedly on her hips and rolled her eyes.

The raggedy man held up his hands. "Don't get me wrong, beautiful. I think it's great. You just don't know what it's like – man, I love that you don't know what it's like!" There was a manic look at that, as he started to try to explain. "In the city, self-respect is tied to fashion and just as expensive. Sure, plenty of girls still do, but the attitude of men with any insect authority to 'slum prudery' is – sorry, kids, sorry. Shouldn't talk like that around ladies' ears – or Gary's either."

Rosie appreciated that whatever had gotten into him, he at least was trying not to out her.

Cecily, who hadn't even entertained thoughts of impropriety until they were denied, was clearly mortified and trying to assuage what she assumed must be Audrey's mortification. "Aw, gee – fellas these days, huh? Nice to meet you. I'm Alice, and this is Gary. That's an interesting choker."

Audrey nodded with a small smile.

"No need to be shy. We're all friends here!" Cecily said cheerily.

Litmus laughed again, that touch of something bitter not out of his tone, but watered down. "She's not shy."

Small, callused dark fingers moved the leather strips on her throat, revealing light beige lines across her skin.

"Near as I can tell between some of her friends and Audrey's corroborations," Litmus said, "Somebody once didn't take so well to her not being that kind of girl." Litmus seemed unsurprised by this, but stared at the small scarred woman admiringly. "But I'm told I should see the rat himself now."

The girls were horrified.

"Oh gosh." Cecily shuddered. She looked to Audrey hurriedly. "Sorry, it's not that – I just –" she looked at Mr. Litmus almost tearfully. "Does life get that cheap here?"

"Here? Kid, not all the lives in the city are as expensive as y– the ones in the penthouses."

"Oh. So... so... You said Audrey had friends?"

"Yeah, couple of kids about your age. Got themselves a goat's milk racket going."

"Goat's milk? And that's a racket?"

"Is out here."

That was when a shout of frustration rang out from the other side of some trees. The source soon strutted out into the clearing.

She was a bit too curvy to have classic good looks. The long, red-gold locks with just a bit of curl were there. And the dress would have been that classic, checked summer dress look but on her, places were just a bit too tight, and in others, much too tight, or short, or low. Attractive, certainly, with enough wear and tear on the dress and the rest to be a local country girl and just enough bad intentions spelled out in the fit of it all to be trouble.

The figure following her also faced barriers to classic good looks. He simply faced many more, and generally had a face like a puppy that had just been kicked.

"Cheese is not that hard," declared the redhead. "It damn well isn't. You're fine enough with the goats and the milking and fine enough with the adding up. I don't see how you can never manage the cheese."

"It's just that you're so much better at it than I am. It seems better to let you handle that part. I'd only muck it up."

"Here's an idea: instead of just planning around the fact that you're useless, why not just stop being useless?"

Rosie raised an eyebrow before clearing her throat – in a properly sophisticated-but-boyish fashion, of course. Maybe the backcountry beauty queen wouldn't be quite so harsh if she realized people could hear her.

The girl looked over – and promptly stepped a little closer, ignoring the boy's attempt at apologies. She extended a hand. "I'm Phoebe. And who are you?"

Rosie shook it. "I'm a little frightened to get into a conversation with you," she said drily. "Do the goats worry that Mommy and Daddy are fighting so much?"

"Me and Sylvester are business partners," Phoebe said hurriedly and emphatically. "Although unfortunately for business and other things, he doesn't have his own truck or anything." Sylvester's face somehow found even further places to fall.

"I think any kind of partners should be able to talk a little more civilized than that," Rosie remarked.

"If you're using words like 'civilized,' you're not from around here."

"You're right. That's not appropriate of me. 'Friendly,' maybe. Or 'human' might do. Hi, I'm Gary," she added, because even amongst the cutting remarks, they were still shaking hands.

"Nice to meet you, Gary."

"This is my sister, Alice. That's... well, that's Mr. Litmus. So where do you all live?"

"Cenaggie," Phoebe answered, having somehow managed to nod to the raggedy man and the dark-haired girl without removing her eyes from her target.

Alice blinked. "What on earth is that?"

"Central Agricultural Camp," Sylvester started to explain. "Been at what's now the edge of the woods ever since–"

Phoebe interrupted him. "There's a dance tomorrow."

Sylvester stopped the history lesson and nodded. "There is. In fact, Phoebe, I was hoping you might do me the honor of–"

Phoebe interrupted him again, still looking at Gary. "Just a small one. Things're pretty quiet this weekend with Mister Duke and his men off deeper into the hunting grounds."

"So Boss Duke is in Cenaggie, normally, but not now?"

"Mister Duke, yeah. He's only Boss to the latest batches of city folk."

"Makes sense."

"It's not far at all. We'll wrap up a few issues with the goats and some horrifically ruined cheese and see you there." Phoebe swept away, with Sylvester following after her forlornly.

Litmus watched. "Boy, a pretty face'll turn anyone into a damn fool."

"You don't know how right you are, Mr. Litmus," Rosie said quietly.

"I never do, Kid."

'Leave No Food Out. Much is Not Healthy for Bears, and Neither Are You.' The empty campground in the woods was full of helpful little signs – as well as bear ropes, water casks, sealed food stores, and, best of all, places to sleep. Someone had clearly built the place to last and not to rust – perhaps the builders had once been familiar with the Factory and its environs and wanted to avoid its example. Orrie assumed as much as he lay his younger brother on the makeshift bed in the wooden shelter.

He then used a little of the first aid materials on the worst of his cuts before lying down himself, finally letting unconsciousness overtake him.

He awoke to the sound of munched granola and very loud sighing. "What's the 'Saint John of the Locusts Universalist Church,' anyway?"

"I don't know, but they helped save your hide, Jacob." Orrie had occasionally tried to call his brother Jake, but it had never worked. The kid was the least Jake-like of anyone ever to be named Jacob. "Why aren't you in school?"

"What was the point?"

"The point was to get out. You get an education, and you're not stuck–"

"We're all stuck, Orrie. Life is a process of being stuck. All of human society is just this puppet show, and the strings are slowly strangling us."

Now it was Orrie's turn to sigh.

Elsewhere in the backcountry, at the far more populated Cenaggie camp, where crowds were forming in the wide spaces between the rows of aluminum shacks and reinforced tents, music was playing. This consisted mostly of a violin and a few empty jugs. Also empty was the cask. A pair of young men, by their clothes one a refugee from the town, one born nearby, rolled in its replacement. As they set it on a table, they looked around. "Anybody got a–"

"Of course," Litmus interrupted, removing the tap from his coat and boring it into the cask.

By the time the drinks were flowing again, and he'd found Audrey, she was standing in front of – and constantly stepping backward from – someone who had clearly seen the drinking festivities as a marathon and had been training in advance.

"Come on, girl, don't be like that," he said, showing obviously great courage in the face of Audrey's body language, expression, and constant movement away from him.

Litmus tapped him on the shoulder. "Excuse me, kid. What's your name?"

"Billy."

"And how old are you, Billy?"

"25."

"Okay, that's definitely old enough."

"For what?"

"Do you know what happens when you drop potassium cyanide into sulfuric acid?"

"…No."

"So you wouldn't know the antidote for such effects either."

"…No?"

"Interesting. Are you familiar at all with spring-loaded daggers?"

"…Not really."

"Do you know what sort of things can be done via strict attention to human nerves, even if you can only work with the ones in the feet?"

"Look, guy, what's this about?"

"This is about three facts: that you're bothering the lady, that I have far less patience than the lady, and that I can kill you a hundred and fifty ways."

As the guy backed away, Audrey stood looking at the raggedy – by City standards – man, her hands on her hips and an eyebrow raised.

He shrugged and smiled sheepishly. "Too much?" he asked.

Meanwhile, the music was starting up properly – for a given cultural concept of 'properly.' It certainly was starting up in earnest – and dancers were lining up.

Rosie was still getting the sense of the place, standing beside Phoebe. Sylvester approached, his arm reaching to tap the redhead on the shoulder. Suddenly, Rosie felt her own arm clutched.

"Why, Gary, I would love to dance!" Phoebe proclaimed.

"What?" But Rosie was already half-dragged out among the dancers by the time the thought processed that Phoebe had loudly accepted an offer that hadn't been made in order to avoid Sylvester.

Amidst the lively sound of the violin and the varyingly deep notes of the jugs, a rich voice started to talk-sing loudly. And Rosie was in the uncomfortable position of dancing in these circumstances.

The gents circle 'round now, and ladies whirl.
And they'll retell the oldest story soon,
Beneath the sunsets, stars, or daytime moon:
It all can boil down to Boy Meets Girl.

The instructions that followed throughout the song helped, although Rosie had to keep reminding herself that she was among the 'gents.' It was, generally, terribly awkward, but after some initial stumbles, she rapidly improved – and managed not to be nervous every time movements switched around.

The violinist and the caller continued to conspire, putting all the interweaving circles, lines, stars, and any other shape of couples through their paces. As things progressed, Rosie was almost a little smug as she managed to adjust more easily to the more complex arrangements, keeping her eye on everything as she swung around her partner. The 'glass-winds,' strings, and words seemed to get faster and faster in places – all the more contrasting when the people of the countryside had seemed to have a slower way of talking. By the end, Rosie had to admit to herself that it was quite a workout.

Afterwards, they caught their breath. Rosie was glad that she was wearing heavy boy's clothes and, if her chest was heaving slightly, had never had much to heave. She didn't need to be given away on top of other embarrassments.

Phoebe, for her own part, seemed not to worry about straining any buttons. Eventually, she spoke. "That turned out nice."

"Yes. Lovely. Thank you," 'Gary' managed.

"The end was better than the start."

"You got me off guard… but that wasn't all that was wrong with the start."

"I had to. Sylvester steps on feet."

"I never said you owed him a dance."

"Oh, good. Yes, I would love to have the next with you."

"You realize that is not the same as asking?"

"Whatever works."

"You might want to occasionally stop and think."

"About what?"

"About the fact that other people are people."

Phoebe actually stopped for a moment at that. And then something caught her eye, and she looked quizzical. "Gary, why's your sister staring at the guys who just walked in?"

Rosie looked at first to Cecily and was fortunate to see she wasn't panicking, just staring. She followed her cousin's gaze to … oh.

Orrie was trying to shake some errant dust and leaves out of his long brown hair and factory-issue clothes.

Rosie stepped in front of Cecily slightly, trying to help her feel less awkward. As she did, she was hit with the smile. Oddly serene yet straightforward, it didn't seem like the smile of someone who'd recently been run out of town to wander the wastelands.

"Sorry, I'm a mess," Orrie said good-naturedly. "Was clearing out a lot of the brush over by the church grounds before we headed this way. I'm Orrie, and this is my brother Jacob." He extended a hand and Rosie was relieved to not have hers completely crushed. Firm though the shake was, Orrie wasn't out to make it a contest with the younger guy. Jacob just glowered.

"Gary. My sister's Alice. Welcome to Cenaggie, I guess."

Orrie smiled some more. "Thanks." He looked around. "Quite a little party you've got going."

"No credit to us," Rosie said. "Alice and I just got here yesterday."

"Everyone's been lovely, though," Cecily said.

"She's got a funny sense of lovely," Jacob muttered to his brother. "This place is full of people. Which kind of prevents anything's being lovely. And they haul around animal corpses."

Cecily looked at the younger man, then whispered to her brother, "Does he want to be Mr. Litmus when he grows up?"

As she was only slightly better at whispering than he was, Jacob caught some of that. "Mr. Litmus? The sardonic handyman who dresses like a tramp? That guy's great. He knows what a sick and sorry world this is."

A strange brittle laugh floated over the gradually resuming music as Litmus and Audrey danced by.

Jacob frowned.

"So, Gary," said Orrie. "Have you found out yet how a guy can pull his weight around here?"

"Still trying to sort that out. Animal herding seems to be a thing."

"Maybe I can pick that up," Orrie said. "I'm hoping I'm a fast learner."

"Hoping?"

"Never had much chance to find out before. Always hoped to fix that. Part of how I ended up getting myself run out of town."

"Lousy place to be anyway," Jacob interjected. "Of course, so's anywhere."

"Yeah, well, I might be lucky to be alive. Had some help there, on one occasion." Something changed in Orrie's smile.

"With what?"

"Not getting who-knows-what beaten out of me while out of my mind on poisoned drink. Unfortunately, had to deal with some other garbage afterward on my own."

"Help from whom, then?"

"These two girls. Rich, classy girls. You fellas should have seen them."

"So we're talking about girls now?" Rosie said, feeling awkward.

"They were angels."

"You were drunk."

"One of them... I think I want to marry her."

"You were real drunk."

"Well, I'm never going to see Miss Duke again, so education and love both out of the picture, just like that."

"Hey, never say never." Rosie gave him a friendly punch in the shoulder – then had to shake her hand out a little, because punching muscle that solid was uncomfortable. "And definitely not that love's out of the picture when you don't know what the picture is, or what love is."

Orrie glared. "I think I know how I feel. She's beautiful, and she helped save my life."

"Yep. People were trying to kill you, more ways than one. Your blood was pumping. You weren't thinking straight. If you hadn't been run out of town as soon as the drugs wore off and the fighting stopped, the two of you might have grabbed each other and done what came naturally before you came down … and were just two strangers."

"Hey, she's not that kind of girl."

"Orrie, you can't possibly know what kind of girl she is. Not for sure. If you ever uncross all your stars and see this Miss Duke again, the two of you are going to have to get to know each other. So let's practice. Pretend I'm a girl."

Orrie looked at the figure in front of him for a moment. "No offense, pal, but I think I can manage that."

"None taken. So, I'm your Miss Duke. Come on."

Orrie coughed. "'Scuse me, Miss Duke. I can't afford much or anything, but I was hoping maybe you could–"

"Wait," Cecily interjected, having stood watching a little behind Rosie as Orrie took Gary's hand. "I, um, want to help too. Why are you leading with what you can afford instead of what you want to do?"

"The girl's family owns half the City, Alice. She's used to a certain style, and it can't be handled by anything I have in my pockets, which is literally all I've got."

"Alice has a point, though," Rosie said, her eyes switching back between her cousin-as-sister and Orrie. "Any girl from a family with that kind of money was brought up to think talking about money is vulgar. 'Cause only vulgar people have to pay attention to money. People who can pay for anything don't have to pay attention. Not that that's a great plan on how to raise somebody, because you're left with girls who just sort of float through life until something goes wrong and they have to stand there realizing that they've never really thought about how the bills got paid."

Cecily winced a little at that. Then she cleared her throat. "So… um… anyway, don't start by knocking yourself. You shouldn't knock yourself. Please."

"Yeah, Orrie. You don't have to be unrealistic, but it's not wrong to lead with your strengths. Come on. Let's try again."

Back in the town, Boss Frederick was sending out his Foreman, because his daughter was missing. The city had been scoured with no sign of her. And after she and Rosie had squealed and fretted over

45

Orrie, Oliver had 'damned well better find your brother and bring back my little girl.' And so Oliver tried to map out the direction in which Orrie's car had crashed. He started packing up his car.

That night, Rosie and Cecily lay alone in the smallest of the aluminum sheds.

"The music was nice," Cecily said.

"Yes, it was."

"It was almost nicer, with just a violin and some leftover dishes, than a whole brass band."

"Yeah. Realer, in some ways. Cecily, I wanted to say I'm sorry,"

"I've told you, none of this is your fault."

"I mean about the 'lessons' with Orrie. When I talked about rich city girls not paying attention, I meant myself the way I used to be. Then I realized you might think I was talking about you."

"I – okay, it was a little uncomfortable. But I know you didn't mean me any trouble. Besides, there's a lot of uncomfortable going on. We need to get used to it."

"There sure is," said Rosie. Then, after a long pause. "Orrie's a heck of a guy."

"Yeah, he is."

Some days passed. The goatherds and former-city-dwellers worked together, the former instructing the latter in some aspects of the business, and 'Gary' occasionally instructing anybody who would listen on decision-making, conversational skills, and empathy. As Litmus volunteered his truck to carry various things with Audrey along for the ride, Gary and Alice would spend a great deal of time 'coaching' Orrie before Phoebe would try to get Gary alone. She had, nevertheless, been listening to all the advice on consideration and self-awareness and did not drag anyone off – whether for conversation, dancing, or other activities – without agreement. And nervous though Rosie was, Phoebe always got that agreement.

Mr. Duke returned to Cenaggie, but Rosie didn't seek out her father before he made another brief trip to negotiate with gasoline traders. She wasn't sure why she didn't try to catch him. She just didn't. She was okay being Gary for a little while longer.

Orrie was particularly eager to contribute. Early on, he was hindered somewhat by his injured shoulder, but he attempted to get right into clearing brush and carrying firewood. He could keep quiet, but he couldn't quite police his expression.

"Are you okay?" Cecily asked.

Rosie glanced over. "Yeah, something looks wrong."

"I'm fine, Gary," Orrie said through gritted teeth.

Gary grinned. "Would you lie to Miss Duke?"

"That's not relevant right now. If I'm going to take care of myself and Jacob, I can't have people thinking I can't pull my own weight."

"Of course you can pull your own weight," Cecily reassured.

"You just can't go putting weight on the arm," Rosie added drily. "Not until you do something about it. Mr. Litmus, come take a look at this."

Mr. Litmus sauntered over. After an examination of the arm and shoulder, with which Orrie was uncomfortable in more ways than one, Litmus frowned. "I can brace it, but I'd need more metal than I have on me." He seemed particularly disappointed in this. "And somewhere to work."

Phoebe chose this time to step up. "I know a jalopy scavenger with some workspace," she said with a smile. "And a three-wedge-a-day cheese habit."

"Excellent," said Litmus. "Let's get to it."

Orrie started to object, but Cecily looked at him and said, very quietly, "Please. Let us help. The countryside isn't completely devoid of civilization."

Orrie sighed. "Or maybe it is, Alice. In a good way."

And eventually, when the joints of that arm were wrapped in a metal bracer whose colors suggested an old car, Orrie became even more interested in pitching in, mostly by hauling buckets and crates, but attempting to learn other things. One day, when all the work he could do was done, and anyone who could show him anything new about the business was preoccupied, he crouched thoughtfully by an oak tree. Taking out a small knife from among Litmus's supplies, he started carving a heart into the bark.

Just as he was about to add initials to the center, a quiet voice spoke up. "Thinking of Miss Duke again?"

He turned, rising. "Hi, Alice. Yeah, I was. Gary'll probably get on my case."

"Gary doesn't – we don't mean any harm by it."

"Oh, just the opposite, I'm sure. Don't worry, it's nice to feel looked out for. Never really had a lot of that 'til those girls decided I needed help."

"You're good at it, though. With your brother, I mean."

"Thanks. I can take your word as an expert on taking care of brothers."

She laughed. "It's more the other way around."

"Oh yeah, I know how Gary always steps in front so you don't have to deal with anything that looks tense. But when things are calmed down, you two work well together. Not saying Gary needs too much help, being such a smart guy. Smart enough to appreciate having his sister always there to help."

She smiled. "Yeah. Thanks."

"Have you two always been like that?"

"Well... yes, we pretty much always have. Growing up without any mom around – the epidemic years back, you know – it was just the two of us a lot." Cecily petted an approaching goat as she reflected sadly. It was true. Her mother and Rosie's had both slowly succumbed. "What about you? Jacob's quite a character."

"He is. We lost our mom in the epidemic, too, and Dad was always working, like most people's parents. Wasn't quite just the two of us, though. We have an older brother, but ... I don't know. Might be some of where Jacob's pessimism comes from. Oliver likes keeping control without taking up much responsibility. So I had to be responsible for me and for Jacob a lot."

"Well, sounds like you did just fine – oh!" Cecily blinked slightly as she noticed the goat, which apparently had run out of briar and dandelions and was eating the loosest bark it could find. This happened to be the bark that Orrie had been carving into.

There was a contralto chuckle. "The little guy's eating your heart out," declared Rosie as she approached. "Well, I'm done helping with the cheese, so we can help you work on talking to girls again. Practice is better than pining." As if reminded by the word, Rosie looked over her shoulder as she said 'pining.'

Sylvester was standing just behind Phoebe, taking deep breaths before tapping her on the shoulder.

"I wanted to let you know," he said. "We're doing well enough that I think I can make one of the ex-city folk an offer on another truck, maybe talk to the gas traders."

"That's great, Sylvester."

He smiled nervously. "So I was thinking maybe once we get it, you and I could celebrate, take a drive...."

"That's ... Sylvester, you know Gary and I are together now, right?"

"Oh, okay, yeah. But..." He looked hopeful. "Maybe, someday, with things improving, you and I might have a chance?"

"Um." Phoebe looked at his almost panicked desperation. "Like I said, there's Gary. Otherwise–"

"Phoebe, hold on," Rosie interrupted. "You need to think about this. You can't say things just to say them. Not at these stakes. And you don't know all the information. You don't know everything about me or that we'll work out. This – you and me – can't be a crutch. Don't tell Sylvester you'd be with him if not for me unless you're absolutely sure you mean it."

"I'm actually trying not to be rude, for once. I thought that was a good thing."

"There's a difference between being rude and saying what needs saying."

"Okay." Phoebe looked at Sylvester. "I'm sorry, Sylvester, but I just don't feel that way about you. I don't think we'd work well going out together."

"Oh."

Orrie broke the awkward silence. "C'mon, man. Alice and I'll help you haul some milk. We can talk about the new business plans." He and Cecily flanked the deflated goatmonger and led him mercifully away.

***

Orrie continued to work at whatever he could, often later than those who'd been born to it. One day at dusk, he heard the baying of wolves on the hunt, and at first, was prepared to give them a lot of room. The very human shouts that carried over them, however, got his attention. He scooped up several rocks, and went running towards the noise.

Oliver had run out of places to run, backed up against some rocks. He'd managed to pick up a stick, waving it around to ward off the wolves. Every time he'd back one away, another would close on the other flank, wearing him down. He couldn't turn to climb, or they'd be on him in a second. Orrie came upon the scene from higher ground, and, without hesitation, threw the first rock, bouncing it off the flank of one of the wolves. It yelped and spun, trying to find the attacker. Another rock hit home, stinging another of the pack in the shoulder. When Orrie struck a third, drawing its attention, Oliver finally struck home with a swing of the branch, leading the target to yelp and back away.

There were a couple more attempts to close in, and, eventually, they caught the scent of the person throwing the rocks, but couldn't find an easy way to get up to him. A couple more accurate throws convinced them to stop trying.

With their prey still armed and rocks coming in from above, the pack gave some ground. It was enough time that Orrie was able to find a branch, lowering it to within his brother's reach. Oliver scrambled out of the wolves' reach before they managed to figure out Orrie couldn't hold the climbing branch and pitch rocks at the same time. They spent a few moments at the base of the rocks, looking upward at the pair, then almost as one turned and raced into the woods in search of easier prey.

"Where did you come from?" Oliver asked, staring at his brother.

"That way, same direction we're both going. Might even be some dinner left."

"I don't need your charity."

"You needed my rescuing."

"I'd have figured it out."

"Right, because you never need help with anything. Fine. Now come on, let's go get you something to eat."

"First, you explain what you did with Miss Duke."

Orrie blinked. "What I did with Miss Duke? Not a thing. I don't really know her. Which makes her an even more stand-up girl for saving me from, well, you."

"So you know that was me, and–" Oliver nodded toward the brace on Orrie's shoulder. "You can't be stupid enough not to know what happened after was me, but you expect me to believe you still just want to get me dinner?"

"Yeah. Because I'm not you."

"And you didn't have anything to do with the Boss getting sore at me, or my car breaking down?"

"Your car didn't stand a chance if you brought it out here. If I wanted to cause you trouble, all I needed was the real smart technique of staying away from wolves. Oliver, come on. We can talk more when we're in camp. And we'll need to talk more."

"I can make my own way."

"No," Orrie said firmly, "Not out here. You can't. I thought the same. And then I found people who showed me otherwise. Now, Jacob and I – did you ever even check up on Jacob? Well, we've got something like family."

Oliver sneered. "Sure, because you never fit in at home."

"But you did, right enough. Come on with me. You can sleep in camp, and we'll figure out getting you back there tomorrow."

"I'll make my own way back. I'll find…" he trailed off, glaring at his brother mistrustfully. "…what I'm looking for, and I'll go back."

"That's a real bad idea, Oliver. You won't make it. But I won't stop you."

"Good, and goodbye."

Orrie shook his head, and headed back to camp.

Oliver, looking around, once his brother was out of sight, took up the idea from his brother, and filled his pockets with throwing rocks. He then made his way in the opposite direction.

The rocks had done wonders in dealing with the wolves. They merely annoyed the bear.

***

Orrie reported the encounter with a matter-of-fact serenity to the others. Jacob sighed, shrugged, and lamented the ways of the world.

"I still wonder why he was asking about Miss Duke," Orrie quietly admitted. "I hope she's okay. Nice girl and all."

Alice looked exceptionally uncomfortable, as did Gary as he subconsciously put a foot in front of hers. Litmus was amidst offering some distracting commentary when he was tapped on the shoulder.

"What is it, Beautiful?"

Audrey handed him a small slip of cardstock.

"Some sort of wild, rustic calligraphy," Litmus said, staring at the card. He read aloud, "'*Anybody can have a fresh start. We count as anybodies.*' Did you write this?"

Audrey shook her head, grabbed the card, and turned it around in his hand.

"Okay, got some sort of grasshopper on it."

"A locust," Sylvester said. "It's a prayer card from the church just a ways 'round the edge of the wood."

"Yeah, we were at their shelter," Jacob said.

Litmus blinked. "So you want a preacher, Audrey?"

She nodded as she took his hand.

"What, like, to get married?" Jacob rolled his eyes. "Surely a guy like you's not going to go in for a charade like that."

"Kid, it's my charade, and I'll advise you not to rain on it. Or call me Shirley."

"You know …" Phoebe said. "Might not hurt to save the preacher a little time, make it a double wedding."

Rosie froze slightly.

"I'm not trying to force it," Phoebe added. "I'm wanting to discuss it."

Rosie swallowed. "Yeah, I get that. I–"

Suddenly, Cecily spoke up. "Gary, we need to see Mr. Duke. He should be on his way back to Cenaggie, from what everyone says."

"Yeah. Yeah, we do."

"Just the two of us."

"Yeah. Mr. Litmus, please give us a ride. We need something from your truck, anyway."

"Okay, kid."

"Don't worry, Audrey," Cecily said. "We'll have him back to you soon. Go ahead and send word for the preacher if you want."

There was much confusion for the next hour or so, until the two trucks approached: the formerly white one driven by Litmus, and the formerly red one driven by the former Boss.

When the trucks stopped, each driver got out, and so did Rosie and Cecily, cleaned up, the latter in her bouncing lacey white dress, the former in her long, dark one.

The Old Boss smiled. "Everyone, I'd like to introduce my daughter, Rosie Duke, and my niece, Cecily Duke."

Everyone stared a little. Phoebe stepped up.

So Rosie stood there in her dress and took a deep breath.

"Okay, let me be clear," Phoebe said. "You're smarter than me about plenty of things. Plenty. Your advice about how to think through how I'm treating people? Not totally unwarranted. But I'm not stupid. Did you really think I didn't figure you probably had lady parts under there somewhere? Sure, you could pass with all the people who are just city-folk rejects, but you've seen those of us born and bred out here. Do you really think clothes and haircuts say the same drown-out-all-the-rest things to us as they say in the city? Ain't how it works. So, if it turns out you want to be called Rosie, that's fine. If you want to wear a dress, okay. The pastor of St. John of the Locusts doesn't give a damn who's what or in what."

"Really? He doesn't give a damn?"

"Doesn't even hold with damnation as a concept. Man's totally damnless."

Rosie blinked. "Well then. If no damns will be given..."

They were both in dresses when Rosie kissed her.

Orrie, meanwhile, stepped up and took Cecily's hand. "...in my defense," he said with a sheepish grin, "With the drugs and all, the angelic-looking golden hair kind of drowned out everything." And then it was just the usual grin.

"I guess I can see the problem there," Cecily said cheerfully.

"I know I haven't had a proper talking-to-your Dad or anything…"

"Yes," Cecily sighed. "Well, in the circumstances…" She trailed off, starring into the distance. Driving through the dust was a limousine.

When the limousine finally stopped, Boss Frederick got out, preceded by one bodyguard and followed by three more toughs. As the group approached, it was Cecily, with Rosie and Orrie on either side, who met him first.

"This doesn't have to be a fight," Frederick said. "I'm just taking Cecily and going home."

Cecily stepped a little in front of both of her defenders, to look at her father squarely. "I'm glad you're here, Dad."

"Great. Let's get going."

"You've made it to my wedding. The preacher'll be here any minute. And then we can talk about whether you're prepared to negotiate my coming home."

"Wedding? I don't think so." The Boss gestured to the men, who moved as one.

Orrie moved to run interference, catching the first man with a quick jab that caught him off guard. The three started to circle, looking for an opening, while trying to goad Orrie into a mistake. Orrie feigned distraction, looking right. The man on his left moved in to try and take advantage of Orrie's injured left shoulder, exactly as Orrie had hoped. Punching with the arm still hurt, but not nearly as bad as it hurt the surprised man, who'd seen no cause to keep his guard up, when Orrie backhanded him with his metal-encased arm. There was a strangely satisfying sound of steel ringing off of skull, and the thug hit the dirt and stopped moving. It was enough to goad the final two into more caution.

The pair circled warily, feinting and trying to find an opening. Orrie finally lunged back, but only managed to get a quick jab in, bloodying a thug's nose but leaving him upright. The swing left him open for a moment, letting the other hired thug grab hold of him, trying to pin him for his remaining friend. Orrie smashed his elbow back into the man's gut, knocking the wind out of him, and pulled away just in time – so when the opportunist did swing, he smashed his fist into his friend instead. Before the thug had figured out what had gone wrong, looking at his friend staggering after getting hit by an ally, Orrie landed a right cross to his jaw, putting the man down.

The final thug, the one who'd tried to grab him, went down more easily, leaving himself wide open while he tried to catch his breath. It was only when the third assailant went down that Orrie realized he'd lost track of the bodyguard. "Cecily?"

As it turned out, he needn't have worried. While the man had, in fact, gone for Cecily, when he tried to grab her, Rosie had caught hold of his arm. That left Boss Frederick's most expensive muscle wide open to be knocked out by the Boss's own daughter, swinging a tree branch at his chin.

All three turned to look at Boss Frederick, suddenly left to negotiate alone.

Cecily spoke up first. "I'm not a hostage. I'm an adult. I'm also the only heir you've got. So you and Uncle are going to work out your differences, and you're going to apologize to Orrie and to Rosie. We're all going to come home together. Or I'm sorry, Daddy, but you're going to grow old alone and never see your grandchildren."

Boss Frederick looked at his brother's men, only just called for and still hanging back. He realized his position but wasn't done yet. "I can get more men out here." He stepped back toward his limousine – and found a man in a raggedy coat sitting on the hood.

Litmus leaned over and whispered a few things. Since he was actually fairly good at whispering, nobody managed to catch any of it until the end. "But then, what kind of man would possibly carry around anything like that in his coat?"

Silence reigned for a long time, as the Boss looked nonplussed. Finally, he sighed, looking back to Cecily. "I guess you're going to need that kind of negotiation when you own the factory."

"When Rosie and I own the factory," Cecily said. "But thanks."

As the preacher arrived to begin the triple wedding, Sylvester sighed. "Don't girls like Nice Guys?"

Rosie sighed in turn and turned to him. "I know it's lousy, but the right girl isn't just going to get handed to you if you don't do anything stupid, Sylvester. They're not door prizes. People aren't. Relationships aren't. You're a good guy and you're learning. Keep at it. Maybe it'll help you with girls. Definitely it'll help your self-respect. There are options. You've got some head for numbers and ... natural stuff. Develop it further. Talk to Jacob about school."

Orrie smiled wryly as he listened to this. "School...I was ... do you think...?"

"Yeah, of course I do. Won't have a cousin of mine saying he gave up on his goals, right Cecily? Don't let him."

"You sure we should be going back at all, Rosie? It's ... it's pretty messed up. I didn't always want to see it until it hurt people I knew. I mean Dad is willing, sure, and Orrie's brother is settled, but there's still a lot of mess."

"Yeah. We need to go back. If everyone who's got a chance or an idea or just any kind of gumption at all ends up wandering the wilderness, nothing is ever going to get better. It's not. So we go back, not to just live The Life, but to fix it. We're going to make the city work for everyone, eventually. No quick guarantees."

"You're being very realistic for a bride coming off a whirlwind romance."

"Speaking of which," Phoebe speaks up. "We talked of passing earlier. I'm never going to pass for City. No more than Audrey."

"I know I'm asking a lot. As to passing, you don't have to. You're with one of the future Bosses."

"So you're going to use the fact that things are unfair to make things more fair?"

"Like I said, no quick guarantees. But I know we can do this. Please."

Phoebe took her hand. "Right. We're in."

Clockpunk Sonnets

18

Shall I compare thee to women of elegance?

You are more lovely and an epitome of what is perfect.

Time warps the beauty in women of flesh

And the curves that they use to seduce men disappear, losing them their false respect.

Beauty is variable in the world of the living

And for eternity, it does not last.

Even the most fair maiden's allure will fade away

With barely a hint of the glowing skin of their past.

But the harshest winter will never cause your porcelain skin to fade to grey

And your clockwork heart will never cease to tick along matching my heartbeat.

Nor will death ever steal you from my side

Because you will live eternally in the realms of my adoration.

So long as men can breath or eyes can see,

So long lives this and this gives life to thee.

The Tragedy Of Livingston

Janice Stucki

Dramatis Personae

CJ Livingston, governor and presidential candidate

Mark, friend and campaign advisor to CJ

Sandy, casino worker, later representative of the common people

Junior, casino worker, later representative of the common people

Don Whist, presidential opponent to CJ

Valora, mother to CJ

Virginia, wife to CJ

Valerie, friend to Virginia

Moderator

Audience Member 1

Audience Member 2

Senior Advisor to Whist

Media Advisor to Whist

Casino workers, CJ's campaign supporters at headquarters, audience members at press conference.

Scene: Atlantic City, NJ and the neighborhood; CJ's house in Livingston, NJ and the neighborhood; Simi Valley, CA Ronald Reagan Presidential Library; Moorpark, CA CJ's West Coast Campaign Headquarters; Bedminster, NJ Whist National Golf Club

ACT I

Scene I: Atlantic City. A Street.

SANDY and JUNIOR enter along with a small group of fellow casino workers. The mood is angry and desperate. They are dressed in well-worn clothes; already talking over each other in an attempt to be heard

SANDY: Before we go any further, are we all in agreement that he can't keep ignoring us?

All: Yes!

SANDY: You're resolved that we will do whatever it takes?

All: Yes, resolved!

SANDY: No more talking about it then! Let's go!

The other casino workers leave. SANDY and JUNIOR stay behind a moment

JUNIOR: But Sandy, I think maybe we need to discuss—

SANDY: Discuss what? They've always thought we're just poor casino workers and that's the way we should stay. And now? Now CJ wants to close down all of AC for good. Just cut us off from the mainland, why doesn't he? Our livelihood is just not worth anything to his kind. I say this not because we have so many other reasons for revenge but because we are literally going to die here.

JUNIOR: Yes, but would you especially call CJ to the carpet for all this?

SANDY: Him first. Absolutely. If he hadn't been leading the charge against AC maybe we would find our footing again. And that after he was the advocate for our city at the start. Nice how he can just double back on that, isn't it?

JUNIOR: But what about some of the good he's done for the state?

SANDY: Seriously? Well I might be able to commend him for some of his deeds if he wasn't such a blowhard. He can say he does this for love of country and state, but honestly, he's just always doing it for his own damn pride. And pleasing that mother of his. What a mama's boy.

JUNIOR: But you know he can't help it, Sandy. You consider it a flaw in him but it's really just his nature.

SANDY: But not his *true* nature. If he wasn't full of nanobot shots puffing up his ego even higher I think it might be different.

JUNIOR: That could be true.

SANDY: *Could* be true? No question about it. And only the precious higher class can get botshots? Nice. Don't they think we would all like to have superior health, strength, and smarts?

JUNIOR: No way they're going to put any money into tailoring the right botshot to give each one of us, anyway, so no point in even thinking about it.

SANDY: Well they sure didn't mind using us for the clinical trials though, right? Anyway, let's not stay here wasting our breath while the rest of the workers are already on their way. To the Convention Center!

As they turn to leave, enter MARK

JUNIOR: Well hello, Mark. You've always been a friend of the common people. Why aren't *you* the man entering the race?

MARK: You flatter me. Where are you off to in such a hurry? I'm not wrong in sensing there's some tension, some problem here?

SANDY: Oh come now, your sort is well aware of our problem if by *problem* you mean our preference for survival.

MARK: My dear friends! We're honestly here to help you. You must know that.

JUNIOR: Help us? How so? What we need is food on our plates. CJ would rather pretend that AC no longer exists than to save our jobs so we can put bread on the table.

MARK: To achieve what you want from CJ you'd be best to not make yourselves enemies. I would take a step back.

SANDY: I'm sure you would. Unfortunately, we can't afford to do that. We need to feed our families and not weeks from now. Let's go. CJ's just about to have that live feed from the Convention Center.

MARK: I was just on my way there myself.

SANDY: I hope you're aware that we have no choice but to go and make ourselves heard today. If he intends to shut down all of AC he must face those that will suffer.

JUNIOR: Hurry…let's go. We don't want to be late.

Scene II: Atlantic City. Outside the Atlantic City Convention Center.

CJ stands outside the Convention Center. Mark, Sandy, and Junior approach him

CJ: Well if it isn't my two favorite rogues! Still claiming you speak for every man? Still scratching that damn itch of yours so hard that you're making yourselves bleed?

MARK: CJ, quiet, I think it best if you give them a listen. The common man is still the voting man.

CJ: Yes, I suppose. For now. So, what is it this time? You know there's nothing I can do but shut down all the casinos. Atlantic City's time is over. You've had your chance.

SANDY: All we want is to have a small voice in what you're planning for AC. Last time we spoke of having five representatives—that you may choose—who can speak for our needs. Well how about at least two? Junior and myself? This isn't an unreasonable request, is it?

CJ: It would only be reasonable if there were cause to hear what the needs are of you casino workers.

MARK: CJ...careful....

JUNIOR: You must think us so foolish to try to keep this dying city alive. This is where we live. This is how we pay our rent, feed our children. You seem to think we have no right to have a voice in what goes on here.

CJ: I would say that is spot on.

SANDY: Wow. I would guess then, Governor, that you probably have a nice size nanobot dashing around in you today, am I right? You're as flaunting as a peacock. Feeling quite invincible like nothing can touch you? I think if you heard the voice of the casino workers you would realize that we're well aware of what makes you so tough. You can shoot whatever combination of enhancements into your arm you like. Go ahead and mainline every single one of them. We're not impressed. And if you continue to ignore us, I think you might do well to sleep with one eye open.

CJ: Is that a threat? You know, I have heard for many years now the voice of you common people. The main problem is you can't seem to understand your place. And really, you just don't know when it's time to leave the party, do you? That time is well past. Now, I'm going inside to make my speech. Great things will be coming. You can stay out here and listen on the jumbotron if you like.

MARK: CJ, could we not get these two good citizens tickets to go inside?

CJ: I'm afraid not. The Convention Center doesn't allow dogs.

CJ goes into the building. MARK follows, his eyes avoiding SANDY and JUNIOR

Scene III: Livingston. A Room in CJ's House.

Enter VALORA and VIRGINIA. They are carrying a bottle of wine and wine glasses. VALORA opens the bottle as VIRGINIA rifles through a stack of records that sits next to an antique phonograph

VALORA: I would be singing at the top of my voice right now if I were you. You should really express yourself better, Virginia. No one can see how proud you are of CJ. If he were my husband, he would know how thrilled I am that he's planning to run for the highest post in the country.

VIRGINIA: I am proud. It's just that…it's that…CJ was a different man before the botshots. He always had a strong political drive, but he was a man who cared more about me…more about our children.

VALORA: Nonsense! And there is not much wrong with putting power first—he *loves* his country. And the injections are what he's entitled to! Why shouldn't he avail himself of them if they'll make him stronger? Make him more able to fight with his quick tongue? He'll need every trick in the book come this election. Don't you think the others will be sticking needles in their arms or any damn place to compete with the rest? You know they will! My dear, how do you think that a man such as CJ rises to this position? This is where he is meant to be. What he is meant to do.

VIRGINIA: But there is talk that too much botshotting can be deadly. So what if he dies, how will you feel then?

VALORA: Let me tell you honestly that I would much rather have a son die nobly for his country—and striving to become head of this great land of ours is truly that—than have him home safe while he has attempted nothing.

Enter VALERIE, rushing in

VALERIE: Hello, ladies! What are we drinking?

VALORA: Pour yourself a glass. Enjoy.

VALERIE: No one ever has to ask me twice! Say, Virginia…I was planning on taking a jitney down to that new shopping complex. You know the one I went to last week?

VALORA: Not that awful one with the live cashiers? Such a crazy idea. I hear it takes forever to get out of there! Live people instead of scanners. Silly.

VALERIE: I like the live cashiers. They're not efficient, but it's fun. So anyway, Virginia, how about it?

VIRGINIA: I'm not really up for it right now.

VALERIE: Why not? You're acting too much like a housewife, my friend. You need to get out in the air.

VALORA: She hates it when CJ is campaigning. And she's worried about the debate with Whist.

VALERIE: Oh, she has nothing to worry about. That idiot doesn't stand a chance.

VALORA: Truer words were never said.

VIRGINIA: It's not the debate.

VALERIE: What is it then?

VIRGINIA: I'm worried about all the botshots CJ is taking. I think it's too much. I wish he would just come home and stay for a while.

VALORA: That time will come, but it won't be soon. Anyway, Virginia, you should go. It will do you good to get out of the house. But first, a little more wine, ladies?

Scene IV: Simi Valley, CA. Ronald Reagan Presidential Library.

CJ and WHIST approach the dais. They meet in the middle of the room and shake hands. They converse quietly before taking their respective positions

CJ: I come here to fight with no one but you.

WHIST: Really? In all honesty, I believe we hate alike. Our fight is really not with each other but rather with those standing here who don't even deserve to have their voices heard by the common people.

CJ: Looking around at our competition, I can say that I mostly agree with you. Not really sure who is going to be eliminated from this primary debate today.

WHIST: With Eagleton and Lartius already eliminated, I'm thinking today has Jones getting the thumbs down.

CJ: Very possible. I only know with the ratings we are creating it isn't going to be you or me.

WHIST: Amen to that, brother.

CJ: But to be fair, we need to be the same. Are we both equal today? Have you had an enhancement?

WHIST: How could you even ask? If I were to come here today as a natural man, I could possibly lose to any of these pathetic candidates. And you would have me finished off easily.

CJ: If only it were so.

WHIST: Ha! So may the best man win?

CJ: Always.

Scene V: Moorpark, CA. CJ's West Coast Campaign Headquarters.

CJ and MARK enter the room for the first time after CJ's most recent debate. CJ's staff jump up in excitement

All: CJ Livingston! The man of the hour!

CJ: Hello, all! That was quite a hot debate in more ways than one! I think I need to wash up. I'm sweating to death. But first I want to thank you all for your support and for your praise.

MARK: It certainly is clear that we won *that* debate!

CJ: Yes, we did. And the four debates before that!

MARK: You know I heard Whist's advisor call you a devil. But Whist wouldn't have any part of that and instead even *he* praised you as 'the boldest man he ever met.' Even Whist is a fan!

CJ: I'm starting to have some pity on that fool.

MARK: How are you feeling, old friend? You're not looking that well. You're not doubling up on the botshots, are you?

CJ: I need to do what I must to compete, Mark. Don't worry about me. It was hot as an oven in that library. I'm fine. So, aren't we supposed to be celebrating now? Have we no champagne here?

MARK: Of course. Off to the showers with you and we'll pop some corks as soon as you're ready.

ACT II

Scene I: Atlantic City. A Boardwalk Restaurant.

MARK, SANDY and JUNIOR are seated for a meal at an oceanview boardwalk restaurant

SANDY: Thank you so much for meeting with us, Mark. We appreciate the gesture.

JUNIOR: And the free meal.

MARK: The meal is my pleasure. And the meeting is only right. I know we all need to weigh in on this matter. I can tell you in secrecy that the debate judges tell me that we shall have news tonight.

SANDY: Good or bad?

MARK: It depends on who you're truly rooting for. Whose side are you really on?

SANDY: You know which side that is. For the side that'll make us all equal again. Whichever side that will stand up for the common people and abolish the laws that are keeping us living like dogs.

MARK: Well now you're speaking like a true Democrat.

SANDY: You know my argument isn't with CJ's side. I'm not for any party or any candidate. I'm hoping that justice can be brought back to our state—to our country. If that's with CJ in office then good for him, but if it's not—.

MARK: It will be. Look. CJ has already agreed that he will consider your need for representation in the future of Atlantic City talks.

SANDY: Consider? That means nothing more than 'forget about it.'

MARK: I think you would be wise to not give up hope.

SANDY: If I had, I would not be sitting here right now. I would have already thrown myself off that crumbling Steel Pier out there.

MARK: If CJ says that he'll consider your people having a voice in the talks, then you can bet that he is taking your concerns seriously.

SANDY: If that's true, then I think I know why.

MARK: Because for all the faults you believe him to have, he is foremost a generous man?

SANDY: Generous! Is that what this would prove? That he's generous? This is something we are entitled to! Our livelihood and the very culture of AC is something that should be a given. It is not being 'generous' to give us respect and chance at a life. We are due that as human beings!

MARK: Perhaps 'generous' was not the word I meant.

SANDY: Oh, I actually think it was.

MARK: You know me better than that. I'm not a man to put others down.

SANDY: Maybe not out loud, Mark, but can you deny that you think we are a *different* class of people? Anyway, you must know that truth be told the only reason CJ would hear our concerns is because we'd be a nice group of voters to support him. Our numbers are large and there are others in the outlying areas that would vote the way the casino workers vote. And you know the common people tend to vote on our recommendation. It's the only power we have but it's a big one. Our support would be *hugely* helpful. I'm no fool. I know his reasons.

MARK: I can't say that your vote wouldn't help. Of course it would. But CJ doesn't suck up to any group just for votes.

SANDY: Oh, please.

JUNIOR: Say, this makes me wonder. Mark, how can a man with integrity such as yours stand in allegiance to CJ?

MARK: All right. So what are his weaknesses that the two of you claim he has in abundance?

JUNIOR: He tops all others in boasting, I can certainly say.

MARK: Having pride does not make him a bad man.

SANDY: Having a body full of super DNA to improve the weaker man underneath certainly doesn't make him a *good* man.

MARK: So you're saying that his pride is false? That without the botshots he would not care about the state? About the country?

SANDY: I think he may have been a good man at one time. But what he's doing to his body has turned him into a wolf. A wolf that smiles and then preys on the common people—the lamb.

MARK: Such a lovely allegory you have going on here. Now CJ's a wolf? How exactly does he prey on the average citizen? Is he looking for a Little Red Riding Hood to devour, too?

JUNIOR: You make fun of us, but you know there is truth in what we say.

SANDY: And why is it that you don't care for the enhancements, Mark? If they're the God-given right of the upper class, why haven't you offered your arm?

MARK: This discussion is not about me.

SANDY: Ah, deflecting like a true politician. Are you sure you don't aspire to a higher position if CJ gets elected?

MARK: It seems you don't know me, yourselves, or anything.

Enter VALORA and VIRGINIA

VALORA: Oh my, Mark! What are you doing here?

MARK: Lovely ladies! I'll get some chairs. Please sit with us.

VIRGINIA: I think we're just going to grab some takeout—

VALORA: Nonsense! We can certainly sit for a bit. Who are your friends?

MARK: This is Sandy and Junior. They represent some of the good people who work in these establishments.

VALORA: Casino workers?

SANDY: Do you see, Junior, how she can barely contain her disgust?

MARK: Oh, Sandy, don't start.

VIRGINIA: Please…don't misunderstand my mother-in-law.

VALORA: Oh. He is not misunderstanding. He's quite right. I don't have much love for the people of this decrepit place.

VIRGINIA: Valora. Don't.

JUNIOR: Oh. I thought I recognized you two. You're CJ's mother and you're his wife.

SANDY: Yes, and that does explain so much in itself.

VIRGINIA: Stop, please. This has been a very trying time. We're just taking this little weekend away to try to relax a bit.

VALORA: Yes, and celebrate that CJ is coming home! The debates have gone so well. He's exhausted. The fatigue shows on his face and he said he's had tremendous pain as of late in his left arm and shoulder but I suppose that's just a touch of bursitis. Either that or maybe it's from raising his arm waving to the adoring crowds! It's so glorious. We have worked so hard for this!

VIRGINIA: Oh, please, Valora. Enough.

VALORA: And again you fail to excite when your husband is praised. You should have a drink and celebrate.

MARK: Yes, no more talk other than about the good things that are to come. Let's hail the waiter – another round for all!

Scene II: Livingston. A Room in CJ's House.

VALORA and VIRGINIA sit at the breakfast table drinking coffee

VALORA: My dear, you should be giddy as a schoolgirl this morning.

Soon CJ will be walking through that door.

VIRGINIA: Yes, I'm happy, but I'm worried. He's late.

VALORA: What? Do you think the limo coming back from the airport has driven off the parkway?

VIRGINIA: Of course not! And please don't joke like that!

VALORA: You would be better to stop worrying and go put some makeup on. You look horrid. He doesn't deserve to come home to such a lack of enthusiasm.

VIRGINIA: Always with such compliments. I suppose it's because you save every last one for your precious son?

VALORA: Look, silly girl, your husband!

Enter CJ, looking weary

VALORA: My dear CJ. What is it?—soon, Mr. President, should I call you? But oh, sorry, your wife!

CJ: Oh, honey, cat got your tongue? And why the tears?

VIRGINIA: CJ, I've been so worried!

CJ: I know…and I do look quite wretched, don't I?

VIRGINIA: All is fine now though, right? You're home. You need some rest, some healthy food.

VALORA: Yes, I'll make your favorite dinner tonight.

VIRGINIA: I thought I would be cooking dinner tonight.

VALORA: Nonsense! Only I can cook CJ's steak and potatoes just the way he likes it.

CJ: Ladies, you're both amazing cooks. Why not cook together rather than fight over who shall treat me to my favorite meal?

VIRGINIA: No, no way. That's not going to happen.

VALORA: CJ, why don't you sit down? I'll make you some fresh coffee and then off to the market I go.

CJ: Where are the children?

VIRGINIA: They're all at the beach today.

VALORA: Even knowing you would be coming home today, she let them go. I told her they should be home to greet you.

CJ: It's a beautiful day, Mother. Why shouldn't they enjoy themselves? You know how hard I've worked rallying the state to put up the money to replicate that seashore. The cost of that Simisand is exorbitant! It's a gain for all if my children spend their allowance down there.

VIRGINIA: See, Valora? You aren't *always* right. Darling, can I get you something to eat?

VALORA: Of course! But not too much. We don't want him to spoil his appetite.

CJ: Actually, I'm not hungry. The coffee's enough.

VIRGINIA: Nothing?

VALORA: He said nothing, Virginia. Leave it.

VIRGINIA: I think I know what this means. You've been double dosing, haven't you? Maybe even triple dosing? You know how those botshots kill your appetite. You have to eat, darling. It's even harder on your body if you don't.

VALORA: Let him be. He knows how to take care of himself.

VIRGINIA: No, apparently he doesn't or he wouldn't have ended up in the hospital last year.

CJ: Enough, please, from both of you. I'll eat every single scrap of that wonderful hearty meal tonight. Promise.

VIRGINIA: You're burning the candle at both ends, darling.

CJ: Pray now no more. I have to do what I must to keep up. A natural man could not keep this kind of schedule and fight these opponents with a clear head and you know it.

Scene III: Atlantic City. Gardner's Basin.

SANDY and JUNIOR walk on the grounds of the long-ago shuttered aquarium; waiting for a meeting with CJ and MARK

JUNIOR: I suppose if he needs our voices, it might be in our best interest to not deny him.

SANDY: We have the power to do it. Now that he appointed us as the representatives for the common people we hold the key to help him win. But only if CJ comes and gives us the offer we also deserve – the right to keep our city, our jobs alive – then we can also tell him of our noble acceptance of his needs – to win the election. But only if that's the arrangement.

CJ and MARK arrive

SANDY: How I see you have dressed for the occasion. No blazer and bow tie for you today? And what about your straw boater? Aren't you afraid of this blistering sun? But what a lovely cotton shirt you have. And nary a stain on it.

CJ: I felt I could dress comfortably to meet with friends.

SANDY: Friends? Well, we hope to find you our friend.

MARK: Come now. Let's not get off on the wrong foot.

SANDY: No, honestly, I like *this* man. Natural and real. I so prefer him this way.

CJ: How perceptive. You're saying you can tell that I come here today without the benefit of an enhancement simply by my choice of clothing?

SANDY: Oh no, not just your clothes. Although not dressing like a pompous ass is a bit of a giveaway. It's everything else. The way your posture is relaxed, your eyes clear and focused. You seem like an actual human being.

CJ: You always make me laugh, Sandy. Very funny. You're just a little jealous because you'll never know the pleasure of feeling that kind of health. Like every cell of your body is in glorious unison.

SANDY: Is *that* what it feels like? So how do you feel right now?

CJ: Exhausted.

SANDY: Welcome to our world. So, why did you come here without your precious enhancement?

MARK: Look, this is not important. Come on now, enough useless chatter. Shall we take a walk along the inlet?

CJ: Yes. Let's go. So…have you decided to support me in the upcoming election?

JUNIOR: Wow! No time is wasted!

CJ: Would you rather that I dance around or get right to the point?

MARK: Since the sun already is getting unbearable I think it would be best to move this along, don't you?

JUNIOR: Of course. Continue.

SANDY: CJ, I think it fair to say we need a bit more information from you before we can say who we will back in the election.

CJ: I understand.

SANDY: Not quite sure you do. If you did, I think you would have tried to court us months ago. Certainly way before you struck the deal to close down AC at the end of this year.

CJ: But what would you have me do? Businesses are running away from Atlantic City—or as you folks insist on calling it *AC*—in droves. And look around you here. It's a damn ghost town. We have tried many things to improve income. The virtual funhouse at the pier? That oceanfront gigamall? Do you know what those improvements cost? And they made no revenue! What more do you think I can do to save this dying city? It's merely an eyesore now. I know it sounds harsh but you need to walk away. Need to find another livelihood.

SANDY: Another livelihood? You know I have to stay within my career assignment. I'm a gaming supervisor, same as my father before me. Do you think I'll find another job when that's all I'm allowed to do?

CJ: There are other casinos.

SANDY: Only in Vegas and the damn Poconos. All the other states shut down their casinos when they couldn't make it either and you know it. Nobody's hiring.

MARK: You can blame the Ninth Reform for that.

SANDY: Yeah, well, when you stupidly regulate everything you should expect some problems, right? And then when the Reform Movement tried to bring some sanity back they start with trying to make gambling illegal? What sense does that even make? Like that was more evil than drugs and prostitution? Glad it didn't take hold but it ruined the industry.

MARK: The casinos weren't making money back then anyway.

JUNIOR: Because the common people *have* no money, that's why.

SANDY: Yeah, always comes back to the money. Who cares about the starving? The homeless, right? But come on…AC is different, don't you get it? AC was a beauty back in its day. Don't you remember seeing movies with those sparkling casinos along that glittering sea? Everything so shiny and posh. It was never just about the gambling. It can get back to that again. AC deserves the chance.

CJ: What would you have me do?

SANDY: Give us a little longer?

MARK: I fear it's hopeless.

SANDY: The same could be said for CJ winning the election.

CJ: I see what you're saying. There is a bargain to be struck?

JUNIOR: We hope so.

CJ: So…let me get this straight. You want me to amend the call to close your dear city…and you want me to offer some financial support? Oh, I'll see what I can do. But…only through next year. It's merely a delay. You must know how this will end.

SANDY: Like the election, I know not.

MARK: You will give your support likewise?

SANDY: If he has done right by AC he shouldn't be denied any honest man's voice.

CJ: Again, is that a yes?

JUNIOR: Yes, you have our votes, CJ!

SANDY: And we pray to God that you deserve them.

ACT III

Scene I: Atlantic City. Resorts Casino Hotel.

CJ and WHIST, the last two candidates standing after the Republican field has been slowly whittled down from the debate eliminations, hold a press conference at the urging of WHIST. A MODERATOR, MARK, SANDY, JUNIOR, and other AC workers are in attendance as are the media who are broadcasting live. CJ and WHIST speak quietly to each other before it begins

WHIST: Atlantic City is truly suffering right now. I did so well there right before it crumbled for the last time. It's such a shame.

CJ: What's truly the shame is that how this place votes, so votes the country. The masses trust these casino workers.

WHIST: Yes. A bit ridiculous. The common people put so much faith into these useless losers knowing what's right for the country. Can't they just think for themselves or is that too much work?

CJ: Well what can we do? If the country has their voices then we must make sure we have their ears.

WHIST: We?

CJ: I meant to speak for myself of course.

WHIST: Oh, I see. For a minute I thought you were suggesting that we work together.

CJ: Pray tell, how do you think that would come about? You would be willing to be my running mate?

WHIST: Heavens, no! The other way around, my friend.

CJ: You use those words very loosely.

WHIST: Again, we find ourselves baring our teeth.

CJ: Be quiet. The light's gone on. The microphones are live.

MODERATOR: Welcome all. We are broadcasting live from the beautiful Resorts Casino Hotel. We will give each candidate three minutes to give a speech, which should include key highlights of their plan for the country. After that time, there will be a short Q&A session. Who won the coin toss?

CJ: I did.

MODERATOR: Please step up to the podium and let us know when you're ready.

CJ: I'm ready.

MODERATOR: The timer is being set…go.

CJ: As you are all aware, I have been in service to the state for most of my career. I have improved the lives of many of the common people by creating jobs, giving them the chance at a better life—

AUDIENCE MEMBER 1: Your idea of a better life! Try living on what I make as a teacher and now with no pension!

MODERATOR: Oh, come now. Already? We will have none of this. Please refrain from commenting or you will be removed. There will be ample time for civil-tongued questions after. Mr. Livingston, additional time will be added to the clock for that outburst.

CJ: Thank you. As governor, I have improved the state's roadways and increased the safety of our multi-level overpasses. I have helped to remove gang warfare from most of our city streets. I have made our sole use of wind and solar energy a reality. I have increased our focus on making a serious attempt to save the planet, while still making the reduction of taxes a priority. As your president, I would continue to do all this and more. Instead of talking about it, as past presidents have done, I will squash the terrorists that plague our country and reinstate Death to Hate—the only immediate and sensible solution to our overpopulation of terrorists within our country. When I am elected president, you will be able to lay down on your pillow at night knowing that you are being protected 24/7. And you will enjoy a life on a healthy planet with all the comforts that every American deserves. I most welcome any and all questions after Mr. Whist speaks. I thank you for your time and thank you for your votes.

MODERATOR: Thank you, Mr. Livingston. Mr. Whist, please let me know when you're ready and I'll start the clock.

WHIST: I've been more than ready listening to this pointless drivel.

Laughter from the audience

MODERATOR: Please, Mr. Whist. I expect to admonish the people in this room, but would hope not to have to quiet you.

WHIST: So sorry. As you are aware, I have a hard time not saying what I think.

MODERATOR: Are you ready now?

WHIST: Yes, my apologies. Please start the clock.

MODERATOR: And...go.

WHIST: I think my record speaks for itself. I have arranged many real estate and business deals that have cost an incredible amount of money, which fortunately I have at my disposal. These deals improved the cities they were in and therefore, improved the lives of the people living in these cities. Just as I can win any deal, I can provide a winning chance for our country to be great again. I feel the people of this entire country deserve to have me going to bat for them. And that is what I will do with all the power I have. Because that is what running the country is really about. Not who you know in the political arena, but who you know in the real world who you can count on. I have many important people I can count on. You can be sure I will keep you safe from the terror that plagues us and you will have plenty to eat. I will keep the terrorists and other outsiders who don't deserve to be in this country away from our borders permanently. That is my promise. And unlike past presidents, if I win your heart, I will never break it. And I always come through on my promises. Thank you for your time and for the good of this great country, I hope you make the right choice.

MODERATOR: Thank you, Mr. Whist.

CJ: I'm sorry but you call my speech pointless drivel? You didn't even say anything!

MODERATOR: Please. Now, thank you both and let's open up the floor to questions.

AUDIENCE MEMBER 2: This question is for Mr. Livingston. You know there are still some who oppose the Death to Hate initiative. How would you explain to them that merely photographic evidence and witness testimony is enough to put a person to death in under a month's time?

CJ: Well, I would ask them first if they have ever known someone who was killed in a suicide car bomb or that was found lifeless after a mass biological warfare attack. If not, I would tell them how that act against a loved one would rip their world apart. I believe that people who question the need for the initiative, question it because they have fortunately been dealt a blessed life. They didn't experience these horrific losses. Unfortunately, too many of us have. If there is video and eyewitness testimony to such a heinous act, why should any more time be taken wondering what to do with such a human being? Thirty days is enough time to make sure that at least that particular person's reign of terror is over.

WHIST: Would it be alright if I also weigh in on this question?

MODERATOR: Of course.

WHIST: I say why wait a month? These degenerates don't deserve that much time. I believe the only thing wrong with Death to Hate is that it's not quick enough. I say bring back the firing squad and have it done in less than a week's time. These scum don't deserve to take one more breath.

Applause from the audience

CJ: You have a way with words.

WHIST: Thank you. I'm not like you, CJ. I don't filter what comes out of my mouth.

CJ: Obviously.

MODERATOR: Another question?

SANDY: This question is for Mr. Livingston.

CJ: Hello, Sandy. Glad you could make it.

SANDY: Thank you for the invitation. CJ...I mean, Mr. Livingston, in your speech you say all the wonderful things you will do for the country. But as you are still the governor of this state, can you tell the audience what your plans are for the improvement of AC?

CJ: The particulars are still being discussed, but great things will be coming to this city.

SANDY: That is what we have heard, but no formal plans have been made?

CJ: As I said, they are in the works, but I'm not at liberty to give exact details at this time.

SANDY: When do you think you will have the details, Mr. Livingston?

CJ: I can't yet say.

SANDY: Very interesting. And oh so vague.

CJ: Is there more to your question?

SANDY: I guess not, but let me just say this—don't assume that you know who your friends are, Mr. Livingston. And your answer shall remain a poison where it is.

CJ: So dramatic.

MODERATOR: Another question?

JUNIOR: I would like to direct this question at Mr. Whist. You claim to be a good candidate because you are a shrewd businessman. As a voice of the people, I believe it takes more than a history of good transactions in real estate to be a good president. If you were elected, what would be your plans for the improvement of this city?

WHIST: That is a wonderful question and I thank you for posing it. I would first and foremost be a great listener to the people of this wondrous place. As you well know, I have much experience here and Atlantic City is very close to my heart. I would do all I could to bring her back to her original standing and beauty. I would treat her with respect.

JUNIOR: That is what we want to hear. Thank you so much, Mr. Whist.

CJ: But again…he is not really saying anything! He hasn't offered any plans for this city.

SANDY: And neither have you!

CJ: This is ridiculous. I have done so much for this city. I don't have to justify myself to the likes of you people.

SANDY: Oh, there it is. You should listen to the words you choose. 'Likes of you people.' You would do better to court the likes of us or else you will find yourself not even back in the governor's seat but back shuffling papers.

CJ: Ha! You are better to turn your attention to me, than this oily flatterer!

WHIST: I have been nothing but forthright.

CJ: Well you are certainly right about the 'nothing' part. You are like a weed in this campaign and you're growing out of control!

MODERATOR: Gentlemen, we had wished the tone of this discussion to stay civil. And fortunately, our time is up. This concludes our brief press conference. Thank you all for coming and for watching at home.

CJ walks out of the room with MARK

MARK: I think they've turned on you, CJ. That did not go well at all.

CJ: If they do turn against me, then I think they might actually deserve Whist. When I think on it, they're the same. Inferior. Ignorant.

MARK: CJ, keep your voice down. Are you all right? Come now. Let's go.

Scene II: Livingston. A Room in CJ's House.

CJ and MARK are speaking to VALORA

CJ: Mother, do you agree with Mark that I should be more accommodating? Not so strong with these common people? You would prefer I be false to my nature rather than the man that I am?

VALORA: You are certainly enough the man you are but maybe ease up a bit in front of the media?

MARK: You have been too rough. Much too rough with the crowds, CJ. You must mend this rift or you may lose this election.

VALORA: I know that the crowd riles you up, my son. I have as little patience as you with these people but yet I use my anger to better advantage.

MARK: Well said, Valora.

CJ: So what must I do?

MARK: Apologize for starters. Then reassure them about their hopes for Atlantic City.

VALORA: Yes. You must go to the people with your hat in your hands and show them you're one of them.

CJ: But I am *not* one of them, Mother, and I can't pretend to be either. You would never want that. And with my hat in my hands? Even that would betray what I was saying because *they* could never afford such an expensive hat.

VALORA: Oh, CJ...sometimes you are too rigid. If I were you I could see the point here. If the common people turn against you, you're finished. You must do this to honor yourself, honor your country's chance at a great president. If you don't, that fool, Whist, will win and he will destroy everything. Mark my words.

MARK: It's true, CJ. But their hearts are yours and they will forgive you if asked.

CJ: So I have to tell them a lie? Tell them I was able to push through the extension on closing this city even though I couldn't?

VALORA: Yes. But it's not a lie. You simply must give them what they need to hear. Even if what you say is amended later, no one can blame you for that. You can't predict the future.

MARK: Certainly not.

CJ: So what I say today does not have to be true tomorrow? And you don't call that a lie?

VALORA: Oh, I beg of you, CJ. Your pride is going to kill me one day. You know what you need to do.

CJ: Ugh...well I will do it if I must. Mother, Mark, excuse me for a moment...

CJ pushes himself away from the table and leaves the room

MARK: I don't think he's looking very well lately.

VALORA: He'll be fine. He just needs to get through these next few weeks.

MARK: Did he just leave us to give himself a botshot?

VALORA: Maybe. I don't know.

MARK: You don't know? I would more say that you don't care as long as your son, the obedient politician, does what you tell him to.

VALORA: Mark, that is certainly not fair.

MARK: Oh, isn't it? You have made him incapable of making a single decision on his own, Valora. He lives to make you proud.

VALORA: And what is wrong with that?

MARK: What is wrong with a grown man living up to his mother's insanely high expectations? And at the opposition to the better sense of his wife and friends? Well, I would say there is much wrong with that. But this is not my concern. My concern is CJ's health...and this election. And I would say that both are on very shaky ground right now.

VALORA: He's fine, Mark. You worry needlessly, especially about the election. There is no way Whist will be the victor. And the opposition is weak. CJ has this.

MARK: Valora, I will put this as simply as I can. He may not make it to the end of this if we don't intervene. The injections are going to kill him if he doesn't stop.

VALORA: Oh, Mark, really. This kind of talk is unnecessary.

MARK: Wake up, Valora! Your son is wearing long sleeves campaigning in this blistering heat because he doesn't want anyone to see his veins. I am sure he is filling himself full of these botshots everywhere now. That doesn't alarm you? It damn well should.

VALORA: Mark, enough. He's strong. He knows he needs this to win the election. He'll cut down afterwards. Don't you think that idiot, Whist, is also injecting like mad?

MARK: Believe it or not, that man is pumped up on pure ego. I'm sure he is doing some botshots but not to the extent CJ is.

VALORA: Alright...quiet now, here he comes.

CJ enters the room

CJ: Mother, I've decided to go back to Atlantic City so you need not worry. I'll go and win their hearts and their votes. You'll never distrust my tongue again. You'll be proud of what flattery I can dish out to those people.

MARK: Now CJ, be careful. I hear they are prepared to sling more strong accusations your way other than about the closing of Atlantic City.

CJ: Let them accuse me of whatever they can invent about me. I will answer with my record.

MARK: Yes, but tread lightly. Try not to be so heavy handed in your wording. Just try to be a bit mild, if you can.

CJ: Well, mildly it be then!

ACT IV

Scene I: Atlantic City. The Stockton Casino Hotel Cocktail Lounge.

CJ and MARK are already seated at the bar, drinks in front of them

MARK: Well that was truly a disaster.

CJ: Was going pretty well in the beginning.

MARK: Yes it was. You were calm...some might even call it 'mild'...telling them that their voices were heard and that their city was on a path to healing.

CJ: I was trying.

MARK: But not quite hard enough.

CJ: What right did Sandy have to ask for written proof of the extension? He has no rights to have proof of anything. Ungrateful lowlife.

MARK: And you are doing it right now. Every time you turn on that arrogance you dig yourself in deeper.

CJ: They're not equal to us, Mark. I find it hard to pretend.

MARK: We had this worked out, didn't we? And really…telling them that you reject that the common people should have any authority over anything at all? Didn't we go over this with your mother at your house? You've just put the nail in your own coffin.

CJ: You're saying we can't turn this around?

MARK: You're exhausting me, CJ. Honestly, I don't know. The new numbers come out tomorrow. I wouldn't be surprised if you're way below Whist now. You may have given him a huge lead that you'll never catch up to.

CJ: Mark, actually, I am starting to think I just don't care. If these common curs are what this country is full of, maybe I don't want to govern them.

MARK: CJ…what are you saying? You haven't had enough to drink to talk like that!

CJ: No, I mean it. I'm so tired of this game. Politics…it's like war, isn't it? A hostile lying battlefield. Who needs this? I'm sick of even you…this city…I feel like turning my back on it all. You know, I hear there's a world elsewhere.

CJ gets up and storms out, just as VALORA and VIRGINIA enter the lounge

VALORA: My son, where are you going?

CJ: Leave me alone, Mother!

VIRGINIA: Heavens!

CJ: Just call me a lonely dragon—I seem to be feared and talked about all over the place.

VIRGINIA: A lonely dragon? What are you even saying? How much have you had to drink, darling?

VALORA: Let him be. He just needs some rest. Some privacy.

CJ: Yes, that's right. Mother always knows best.

CJ pushes past them and exits the lounge

VIRGINIA: But where is he going? Do you think I should follow?

VALORA: No. As I said, let him be, Virginia. Mark, we heard what happened here. Those undeserving people – bastards all!

MARK: I know...it was truly awful. I only hope he's not taking another injection right now.

VIRGINIA: I should go after him.

VALORA: No! I told you, let him be.

MARK: Well, I don't even know what to say about this anymore. Is it all hopeless? It has truly been one very long day. I'm starved. Ladies, will you have some supper with me?

VALORA: Not for me, Mark. Anger's my meat. I really have no appetite. It's a long drive so we should head back to the house. I'm sure CJ will be coming home soon. Virginia, let's go.

VALORA and VIRGINIA leave

Scene II: Bedminster. Whist National Golf Club. Main Clubhouse After Hours.

WHIST opens the locked door to the clubhouse to see CJ standing there

WHIST: CJ Livingston! Well, come on in.

CJ: Well, I'm glad to hear *you* can say my name. It's a name unmusical to the common people's ears right now.

WHIST: Yes, it does seem that way. You're definitely persona non grata in Atlantic City.

CJ: Not just there. All of the media are calling me a traitor. Haven't you heard?

WHIST: Yes, I have. And thank you by the way. But CJ, why did you want to meet with me?

CJ: I was thinking…maybe it *is* time for us to set our differences aside. To collaborate. Unify for a stronger chance at locking this up?

WHIST: Interesting. I am sure you still have a modest amount of fans. What are you suggesting exactly?

CJ: Let me be right up front, Whist. I do this not out of hope, you know how I feel about you. No, I do this in mere spite.

WHIST: Spite? That doesn't sound like you.

CJ: It's me all right. I gave those lowly commoners my life's blood. I worked tirelessly for this state and that is the way that they thank me? Kill my chances at presidency?

WHIST: You just don't quite know how to play the game, do you?

CJ: Oh I do know how. Now. I see the way they want to play it.

WHIST: Come on, CJ, you seem a bit unsteady. Come in. Sit down. Have a scotch? Tell me what you've been planning.

CJ: I've been thinking…you had a potential deal back a few years ago…the one with the Chinese that was so hush-hush?

WHIST: How did you hear about that?

CJ: That's not important. Anyway, that deal would all but have removed Atlantic City from the map, right? Just brilliant selling the whole damn thing from Absecon down to Scull Bay to them. They were going to put up some ocean wave energy converter station on the boardwalk, right? A nice wave farm right along the coast. Sounds great in theory, but horrendous in practice. You'd have to pay off the EPA but I suspect that's not a problem.

WHIST: It does concern me that you heard about that. Yeah, well that would have been a sweet deal. I know they're still interested too. You gotta love the Chinese. They don't care about popularity.

CJ: Would definitely put every one of those casino workers on the street. And not even an Atlantic City street.

WHIST: Look out Brigantine.

CJ: That would teach them not to betray me like they did.

WHIST: So you're suggesting that we go to the press with this new deal? Why exactly would I do that?

CJ: No, of course not. I'm not saying we should say anything now. I think we should maybe allude to running together? Strengthen our forces?

WHIST: Here we go again. Since you are the underdog at present, you'll be the running mate, right?

CJ: Fine. I don't care. But once we get in, we're going to make this Chinese deal our first priority. I'll show those ungrateful bastards.

WHIST: I'm going to seriously consider this, CJ. Your motivation frightens me a bit, but I think I like that. With our star power together we can blow the Dems out of the water.

CJ: No doubt. Good God…I'm so exhausted.

WHIST: I can see that. What about a little enhancement to go with that scotch?

CJ: I didn't bring any with me.

WHIST: I meant one of mine.

CJ: Yours? I'm not sure I can take one of yours.

WHIST: Of course you can. If we can put it in our bodies it must be safe. Come, I've dreamed of encounters like this between you and me. It will bond us and make our union stronger.

Scene III: Bedminster. Whist National Golf Club. Pool Complex.

WHIST is relaxing poolside at his golf club. He is speaking to his SENIOR ADVISOR

SENIOR ADVISOR: Sir, I think you should take the media more seriously. CJ is winning the hearts of the people over you.

WHIST: The public is so fickle. Why do you think he is back in their good graces?

SENIOR ADVISOR: Word is that they think he's the stronger candidate. More integrity. Media reports that the common people are pushing for him to shake you off. I told you, Sir, I wished you had not joined in commission with him.

WHIST: Anyway, watch, you'll see, he is really doing himself in. Don't you see he is getting thinner every day? He may talk prouder than anyone I've ever met, but his body is growing weaker, his nerves more itchy, his words more chaotic. It won't be long.

SENIOR ADVISOR: And what will happen then?

WHIST: Then? Well then, I'll meet with the Chinese and close this deal once and for all. Nobody cares what happens to the institution of Atlantic City and I own most of the real estate. The other property owners will be falling all over themselves to sell to me and get out from underneath this mess.

SENIOR ADVISOR: But what about the public? Bad press selling to the Chinese.

WHIST: Oh, I'll blame it on CJ of course. I'll make sure he signs all the legal documents. The public will know from his anger towards them that it was certainly him to barter this deal. And once he is gone I will have all the riches but none of the fallout.

SENIOR ADVISOR: You really think that's the way it will play out? Just wait for him to fall on his face?

WHIST: Before this is over, CJ will come to realize he should have stayed a faithful servant to the state instead of trying to win against a champ like me.

ACT V

Scene I: Bedminster. Whist National Golf Club. Main Clubhouse Dining Room.

MARK comes to visit CJ at the golf club. WHIST is also present. They are seated in the luxurious dining room about to order dinner

MARK: Your mother and wife are eagerly waiting for you to return to them, CJ. It's been too long and you look like hell.

CJ: Dear old friend, I miss them as well, but I must strategize here with Whist to win the election.

MARK: Win the election with him? CJ, don't you remember what you used to think of this man? Let me see your arms. He's going to kill you, you know.

WHIST: Mark, I'm sitting right here and a little respect for your host would be nice. You just can't accept that CJ has come to appreciate my expertise, can you? It really is as simple as that.

MARK: You are telling me that you haven't been manipulating him?

WHIST: Of course not.

MARK: Whist, where has he been getting his botshots from? He's been staying in one of your suites and hasn't been home for weeks. What the hell are you injecting him with?

WHIST: Calm down. Ask CJ. He feels fine. We've just been focusing on election strategy.

CJ: I'm okay, Mark. You need not worry.

MARK: Oh, I most certainly do. You can't keep doing this. The man I know prides himself in his strength. You are becoming a mere shell, CJ. And what you are planning for that poor city is just wrong and you know it. I beg of you, please reconsider.

CJ: Mark, I think you should probably leave now. We have much to do here.

MARK: You aren't thinking of anything else, are you? Very singular focus. Just botshots and planning your next move. This isn't a game, CJ.

CJ: No…it's a war.

MARK: There is no war.

WHIST: I think CJ said you should probably leave.

MARK: So, you really want me to go, CJ? Then I'll not meddle. I thought there was still time but I'm afraid you'll never hear me now.

Scene II: Bedminster. Whist National Golf Club. A Cottage Accommodation.

VALORA and VIRGINIA enter CJ's cottage at the golf club. CJ is slumped on a couch

VIRGINIA: Oh my Lord, my husband!

CJ: I know…these eyes are not the same as when I last saw you.

VIRGINIA: No, they're definitely not. You're not looking good, CJ. Let us take you home to see the doctor.

CJ: To a doctor? Better to let the pebbles on a hungry beach fillip the stars.

VIRGINIA: What?! I said, what? What does that mean, darling? You aren't making any sense!

CJ: I sometimes feel like that worthless pebble—

VIRGINIA: You aren't worthless—

CJ: That worthless pebble that can elevate itself to the mighty height of the stars just by flinging itself—

VIRGINIA: Oh, CJ, no more, no more! You are frightening me with this talk! You need to stop this and come home. Leave this Machiavellian man who has such a terrible hold over you.

CJ: No man, nor woman, has a hold over me. Enough.

VIRGINIA: What I meant was—

VALORA: Should we be silent and not speak? Do you want us not to say what you must hear for your own good? I still know you are the son of mine who cares deeply for his country. Who knows that only *he* can properly rule it—run it. You have so many wonderful ideas, CJ, but leading this great land with this man is not one of them. You must break away from him before your name becomes synonymous with the destruction of our country.

CJ: Mother, what would you have me do?

VALORA: I would have you speak to the common people. Tell them that Atlantic City has its extension. Give them something to believe in. Faith in you again. And you must cut all ties with Whist.

CJ: Aligning with him has given me strength. He helped me when *they* turned on me. Why should I turn on him now?

VALORA: Oh my son, how can you think that he did this for any other reason than his own gain? How far gone are you? You're not being honest and that's something new for you. What you're doing is without honor. It's not a noble thing. You don't seem to care how your family feels. Unlike you. You don't care when you see Virginia cry? You no longer hope to make a better land for your children? You're playing for the wrong team now, CJ. You'll discredit us all and ruin all you have strived to achieve. If you stay with this fool, you will not become the victor in this election. And your family will have to hide our heads in shame with the name you have disgraced.

CJ: Oh, Mother, Mother…what can I say? Talking like that almost makes me want to cry…You, this country, Virginia, the children…all mean the world to me. Of that I hope you always know. Perhaps I have lost sight of what I hold dear. I know that you have always seen with clear eyes when mine have sometimes clouded. I can't believe it when I say I think that with your words alone you may have won a happy victory for Atlantic City. I won't turn my back now. I will get back on track, I promise to, and I suppose it best be by myself as the sole candidate.

VALORA: I knew you would see the light! Please now, before any more time is wasted. We'll leave and wait for you at home. Go and pack your things. Tell Whist you're forging ahead without him.

Scene III: Bedminster. Whist National Golf Club. Main Clubhouse After Hours.

The SENIOR ADVISOR and MEDIA ADVISOR enter the clubhouse to find WHIST pacing anxiously

SENIOR ADVISOR: What's the news?

WHIST: Nothing good. I suspected that bastard didn't have the tenacity to continue with this.

MEDIA ADVISOR: How can we help you? There must be something we can do to get him back.

WHIST: I should have never taken him in like that in the first place. I should have left him out there—banished. This is the thanks I get? I welcome him in and he takes the lead. I become his follower, not his partner. He has such a patronizing manner. And now, he changes his mind so I'm to be glad about it? Oh, wait, I hear him coming. The proud victor. Or so he thinks. I'm surprised he doesn't have a marching band with him to announce his magnificence.

SENIOR ADVISOR: I'll get the door.

SENIOR ADVISOR opens the door and CJ enters

WHIST: Well hello, traitor.

CJ: Traitor? How now?

WHIST: Honestly. You decide that you'll go it alone without even consulting me? Changing your mind about our deal? Dear 'boy', you are a measureless liar all the way around. You seem more bent on betrayal than being my ally. And what changed your mind so easily? Your wife's tears? No, never that. More the pleading smile of your holy mother.

CJ: Sure, cut me down. Criticize my mother. It doesn't matter. I told you from the start I wasn't doing this for any other reason than revenge. But now I see how that thinking was wrong. And you fed that disease in me, didn't you? You can't deny it. And as far as your campaign? You very well know that without me you would again be floundering. You're weak. Your numbers were always way below mine, and sure they rose a bit when I was kicked in the gut, but it took for *me* to come to *your* campaign for your numbers to really soar. Your numbers would never have been that high without me. Alone I did it – 'boy'!

WHIST: You unholy braggart!

WHIST attacks CJ and during the scuffle, CJ falls and hits his head against the corner of a stone column knocking himself unconscious

SENIOR ADVISOR: He's not moving. Is he dead?

WHIST: That would be too simple. Check his pulse.

SENIOR ADVISOR: It's faint. But he's not dead.

WHIST: Damn. Arrogant bastard can't even do that right.

MEDIA ADVISOR: What do we do now? Should we call an ambulance?

WHIST: No. Let me think for a minute. That Atlantic City deal has to go through.

MEDIA ADVISOR: What exactly are you suggesting?

WHIST: I think you know.

MEDIA ADVISOR: I surely hope I don't.

WHIST: He already signed the papers. We need to finish this.

SENIOR ADVISOR: How can I help?

MEDIA ADVISOR: Are you crazy?

WHIST: We can botshot shock him. It might be a kindness actually. He's half-done already. Has been working on it for weeks. Months.

MEDIA ADVISOR: Some would say thanks to you.

WHIST: Some would say that, huh? I hope I can still count on you to back me? You don't want to be left without a media post during this election.

MEDIA ADVISOR: As you know, having a post in the media means I have always been able to look the other way.

WHIST: And he's such an insolent villain! He has stirred my anger more than any man I've known. Even laying here unmoving he provokes me. We'll finish this now.

WHIST goes into another room and comes back with a lethal botshot which he shoots into CJ's arm as he is still unconscious. WHIST stands next to his body, looking down on him quietly for a time and thinking. He feels CJ's pulse, which is still

WHIST: How can it be so quickly...my rage is gone. How I wish that I could feel something like sorrow but that is not me I suppose. I will miss our heated talks. He was the closest to my equal that I have ever met. I do try to learn from the past, while I plan for the future focusing exclusively on the present. I believe if he had lived he would thank me. He was not the man he wanted to be. By having him end this way—his honor, and mine, untarnished—I have provided him a lasting position in our country's heart. He shall have a noble memory.

Clockpunk Sonnets

105

I refuse to submit to my passion being mistaken for madness

Nor that I worship the creations of my own hands

Since I toil away at but one mechanical fabrication

And shall, til death steals me away.

You are the pinnacle of my achievement today, tomorrow the apex

Your spark of barely-life wonderfully constant

Because you exude constancy, unlike the variables that are this world.

I know that my every action will yield a definite result as I tinker with you.

You may be looked upon as a monstrosity

But I know that it is through the work of creating you that I see beauty.

The turning of your gears;

The tick of your mechanical heart;

The supple bend of your cool metal;

They all express the range of beauty.

These things never seen in nature,

And have been nonexistent until I glance at my wonderful clockwork beauty thus.

Blast The Past: Fae And Far Between

Rozene Morgandy

Act I, scene i

THE ECHO OF A GUITAR backed by drums filtered through the halls. The music crept through Tiernan's mansion from the auditorium, where he and his fiancée sat together previewing Pirro's entertainment selection for their wedding reception. However, Harlequinn's long sigh and the way she cradled her cheek in her hand were tell-tale signs that she wasn't impressed.

He ordered the music to cease and dismissed the band. If it wasn't good enough for Harlequinn, it simply wouldn't do. He turned to look at his bride-to-be and saw her frown, which could only mean one thing.

"I need to kill something." She pushed herself out of the chair and began pacing the room. "How is it that we have so many people under our rule, but not one band that's worthy of the fame they've achieved?" She stalked toward the stage. "I just want to dance at my wedding! Is that so much to ask?" She stormed up the steps, muttering, "I can't dance to this…this tuneless pop music!" Kicking the microphone over, she watched as it crashed to the floor, causing a sharp squeal to echo throughout the room.

Tiernan smiled and approached her. "Now, now, darling, do try to compose yourself. You wouldn't want to be on the wrong end of my sword again, would you?"

As soon as she turned her attention toward him, the twinkle in his eyes became apparent. The familiar beating of wings fluttered in her chest. Huffing indignantly, she wrenched her gaze away from his, but only to hide her smile. It was both embarrassing and thrilling that he knew how to get under her skin. It'd been how he won her love in the first place – out on the battlefield, proving his worth. That was her kind of foreplay.

"Really, Tiernan, can't you wait until our honeymoon?" she asked coyly, twining her fingers through her blond locks that traveled down her bodice in erratic braids.

It was their running joke. As they'd already consummated, there was no point in playing at abstinence. Harlequinn did love to hold that threat over his head – playfully, of course.

He caught her wrist in his hand, a grin plastered on his handsome features. "Don't get too feisty, Love, or I might have to cut this audition short." He snaked his free hand around her waist and pulled her against his chest. The rosy tint blossoming across her cheeks was delicious. He loved catching her off guard.

Before Harlequinn could reply, the sound of Pirro clearing his throat killed the mood. She cast him a withering look and pulled away from Tiernan. "What?"

"Apologies, your grace, but the next band is ready." Pirro's voice cracked and he fidgeted with the sleeves of his white jacket.

Rolling her eyes, Harlequinn stepped down from the stage and collapsed back into her seat. She crossed her legs, glancing toward her fiancé as he followed suit. When the doors didn't open, she flicked her gaze back toward Pirro. "What are you waiting for?"

"There's one thing I should mention," Pirro added, and the pause between those words and his next only served to emphasize his hesitance. "They're…fairies."

"What?" Tiernan snapped, rising out of his seat. "What are they doing in my house? Execute them immediately!"

It was no secret that Tiernan hated all things supernatural. Fae experiments had corrupted the world and turned it into a poisonous wasteland, and many humans had grown ill and perished from the toxins. The first generation exposed to the pollutants bore children who were changed for the worse. The current generation were either infertile or had evolved into abominable beings branded by a glyph birthmark revealed only by moonlight. Upon discovering this, most people had come to the conclusion that the Fae wanted to change mortal DNA and wipe out those who couldn't survive it.

Tiernan had seen the damage it could cause and how it tore families apart. His own family was ruined after his mother died while giving birth to a mutant, and his father had immediately ordered the disposal of the monstrosity. Afterward, he had proceeded to drink himself to death. He'd left the daunting task of saving the empire to his only living son.

Tiernan had rallied what remained of his people, destroying supernatural habitats to drive the Fae to extinction. He had vowed to save the last of humanity by any means necessary. Thus far, his campaign had been successful. Only a fraction of the Fae remained in smaller parts of the outlying forests, and things had been fairly quiet up until now. It seemed they were becoming bolder, however, having had the audacity to enter not just his territory, but his home! He would have to make sure the distasteful creatures suffered.

"On second thought, don't kill them. Bring them to my dungeon instead. I want to torture them before I allow them the comfort of death." When Pirro didn't move, Tiernan bellowed, "Did I stutter?"

"No, sir," Pirro quaked. "It's just that…well…"

"Out with it!"

"It's the king of fairies, my lord. He's come personally to offer entertainment for your wedding." He crumpled to his knees. "Please don't execute me, my lord! I tried to turn him away, but he wouldn't listen! He's right outside, awaiting an audience with you."

"Oh hush," Harlequinn chided. She appeared beside Tiernan as Pirro looked up with wide, frightened eyes. "We can't kill you. You have to plan our wedding." As Pirro scrambled to his feet, she focused her attention on Tiernan, her expression thoughtful. "Isn't it odd that the king of fairies would come here personally instead of sending a messenger?"

Tiernan scoffed, staring hard at the door that separated him from the Fae in question. "Who cares? Now is the perfect time for me to make an example of him."

Harlequinn sighed. It was all too easy to forget how pigheaded and short-sighted her lover could be, but he never failed to remind her. "Whatever the reason, I'm sure it's something altogether more interesting than auditioning to entertain at a wedding. Wouldn't you agree?"

Tiernan rolled his eyes. "Just say whatever it is you're insinuating, my sweet. You know how hints aggravate me."

"You really are a dolt." To her dismay, she got little reaction. He never cared if she insulted him, and he often took it as a sign of affection. "Fine. I mean, he must be coming to offer something more than just entertainment. Do you understand that, *darling*?" She emphasized the pet name, unable to stifle her sneer.

Tiernan watched her, his grin growing wider with each insult. Her scorn was one of the most attractive things about her. More important, however, she'd managed to pique his interest. What could this "king" want with them other than to kill them? The fairy was little more than a coward, and had never been present in any of the campaigns Tiernan led against his people. The supernatural had kept their leader well hidden all these years and yet now he decided to reveal himself? That in itself deserved at least an audience. "Pirro, bring them in. I want to see this…king of fairies." As Pirro immediately rushed toward the doors, he added, "But bring the guards after you do so…in case things get ugly."

Pirro did as Tiernan bid, opening the doors and then disappearing from the room as five prismatic-winged fairies entered. Four were carrying various instruments to use for their audition.

Tiernan glanced at each one dismissively until he locked eyes with one at the back of the group. The albino was dressed in leather – tight fitted pants, a jacket with silver spikes protruding from the shoulders, and a vest underneath that revealed his abdominal muscles. Medium-length white hair partially concealed the left side of his face, one jade-colored eye peeking through the fall of loose braids.

Tiernan stepped forward, as did the green-eyed fairy. He looked the creature in the eye despite his inhibitions; to do anything less would show weakness. "Welcome, your…majesty." He bowed, but it was all he could do to contain his laughter at the absurdity of it all. To think that this mutant considered himself royalty!

A polite but vicious smile spread across the fairy king's face and he nodded his thanks. "I am honored to meet you, your grace," he replied with equal amusement, bowing right back. "It must have come as a shock that I decided to visit unannounced. Your hospitality is most appreciated, Lord Tiernan."

Tiernan straightened, never taking his eyes off the fairy. "I don't believe we've properly introduced ourselves," he said with a tense smile. "You have obviously heard of me. However, I have only heard whispers of you." A swift elbow to his side caused him to cough, and he glared daggers at Harlequinn. "Forgive me, I nearly forgot to introduce my lovely fiancée, Harlequinn." He waved in her direction.

Harlequinn smiled, offering a courteous bow. Her braids tumbled down over her sapphire corset and white blouse. "Charmed, your majesty."

She rose, gazing into his one visible eye before glancing at Tiernan. How strange that their eyes were the same color. In all other ways, they seemed to be polar opposites. Tiernan's ebony hair pulled back into war braids, his dark complexion, and his black suit compared to the fairy king's white hair, pale complexion, and leather clothing made them seem like a yin yang symbol.

Curious, Harlequinn looked over at the Fae woman standing off to the side. She noticed how the violet bodice fitted against her and the way it flowed down into tattered strips of cloth that made up the skirt. It wasn't until Harlequinn looked at the woman's face that she saw the real differences that marked her as supernatural. The woman wore a relaxed mohawk that dipped down to conceal her right eye in splashes of red and purple. The left side was braided up into the mohawk, revealing the silver of her left eye. Unlike the king's, it lacked a pupil. She supposed that this ruler of the supernatural must have had a human parent. How else could he be such an oddity when compared with both factions?

The Fae woman arched an eyebrow at Harlequinn, as if to question why she was staring at her. Harlequinn blushed and tore her gaze away, looking to the fairy king instead.

"She is a beauty. You are a lucky man." The albino's mischievous gaze flicked from Harlequinn to Tiernan. "I am called Osiris." That smile stayed plastered onto his face, jade eyes locked firmly with the human king's matching gaze.

Tiernan's rage threatened to boil him alive, but he fought it down. "Indeed. It is a pleasure to finally make your acquaintance." He swiveled around and beckoned him closer. "Please, come this way and have your band set up while we chat."

"The pleasure is all mine," Osiris said as he stepped forward. He signaled for his companions to follow.

"I'm sure you know that it is not without risk that you are standing here in my private residence," Tiernan noted as he took his seat. "What would cause you to endanger the lives of yourself and your companions?"

The fairy's smile only seemed to grow wider. "I have come on behalf of my people to implore you to consider a truce. To prove that what I say is true, I have come personally to offer a wedding gift."

The Fae were not known for expressing emotions in a way Tiernan's people could easily identify. Osiris seemed sincere, however. This not only puzzled Tiernan, it intrigued him. One glance at Harlequinn told him that she felt the same. He couldn't help but wonder if it was a trap. The supernatural were known for their tricks.

"Oh please do tell," Harlequinn chimed in before Tiernan had a chance to work through his thoughts. "We've been having a dreadful time finding entertainment for the wedding reception." A smile crept across her face. "I'm interested to know what you have in mind, your highness."

"Please, my lady, Osiris will do just fine." The fairy king inclined his head respectfully. "As for what I have in store? Well, why explain when I could simply show you?"

Harlequinn clapped giddily. "Go on then!"

The Fae's shape distorted until it completely faded from sight. The guitarist started to play, followed by the keyboardist, and then fireworks exploded high above their heads. Osiris dropped down onto the stage, as if materializing from the brightly colored sparks. The drums picked up beat as he landed. He held out his hand, a guitar appearing in his grip. Once he started to play, the Fae woman stepped into view, mixing violin with the symphony. She started to sing in soft and low tones. Her voice caressed their ears with the melody, and heated their blood with the throaty overtones.

It didn't take long for Harlequinn to gain her feet, swaying to the beat. Just when she thought it couldn't get any better, Osiris backed up the lead singer with his own vocals, and finally, the symphony was complete. Even Tiernan had to admit they were good.

Once the crescendo reached its peak, the music started to die out and Harlequinn's dancing came to a halt. "Fantastic!" She giggled like an exuberant child, clapping. "They have to perform at our wedding reception, Tiernan. I will have no other band!"

"Do your best to restrain your excitement, my dear. We still don't know what his humble majesty wants in return, or if it will be within our power to grant." At the crestfallen look she gave Tiernan, he raised his hand to stop her protests. "I simply do not want you to get ahead of yourself. Of course I will hear him out."

Osiris stepped off the stage. "What I want is simple. Just a peace treaty, your grace."

"You can't possibly mean there are no strings attached," Tiernan said, his head balancing against his palm. "Such things are unheard of from your kind."

"Oh, but I do. The only strings attached will benefit you," Osiris answered. "I realize it may be hard to believe, but you know the state of our well-being. The war that has raged between us has torn the earth asunder, as well as our peoples. What can we hope to gain but more chaos if it continues?"

He paused. Then he snapped his fingers, as if a wonderful idea had just crossed his mind. "Let us show you that we mean to live in peace. What do you say? I will throw you and your beloved a party. I can have a boat – or two if you prefer – ready by tomorrow night. Only the best entertainment, food, and drink will be available to you and your guests. To make the deal sweeter, I will even offer entertainment for your wedding reception and your wedding if you like. If you're convinced that what I say is true, you'll agree to sign the peace treaty."

Osiris fell silent and Tiernan wondered if he was gauging their reaction. It sounded like a trap – an opportune time to slaughter them all, or worse, turn them into supernatural creatures. Then came the real deal.

"Did I mention that we may have a way of curing the infertility issues plaguing your people?"

Tiernan could hear Harlequinn's breath catch in her throat. He glanced at her, watched her lean forward, her wide eyes trained on the fairy king.

"Mind you, we haven't been able to confirm for certain that it will work. We obviously have no willing participants to test it just yet."

The words sliced through Tiernan's defenses. Surely they wouldn't offer such a thing if they didn't sincerely want peace? It sounded too good to be true. Yet these creatures did work in mysterious ways. How could he be so certain they hadn't found a way?

"No doubt you're wondering how and why we would do this. Could it be a ploy? A trap?" His eyes gave away nothing, that smile still frozen perfectly on his white face. "I assure you, this is no trick. I understand the blow my people dealt yours. It was an irreparable mistake, made before we had a grasp on how sci-magic worked. We had no idea how disastrous its effects could be. Though our people have no difficulty bearing children, we suffered greatly in other ways. The tragic miscommunication between humans and magical beings, for example. I want to dispel that by becoming your ally. I want our worlds to unite so that we can grow and recover from these events."

"What's stopping you from butchering the lot of us if I refuse?" Tiernan asked, his face hard.

"We are not so distasteful as to come into your home and act like common criminals," Osiris said dismissively. "Consider this a parley. You don't have to agree now. Contact me after you've seen for yourself that we're capable of playing nice at your party. Your servant – Pirro, is it? – has the information."

Before Tiernan could even consider the proposal, a commotion at the doors of the auditorium commanded his attention.

Edric, an old friend, had flung the door ajar and was struggling against the guards, his face red. "What is this nonsense? Let me through at once! Don't you know who I am? I led the attack on Oakhart Village!"

Tiernan arched an inquisitive brow, wondering why one of his lead military officers would need to make such a scene. "Let him through. He is a trusted friend."

The guards relaxed their hold on Edric and he jerked away from their grasp with a disgusted noise. As he strode into the auditorium, he dragged his daughter, Harmony, behind him, neatly ignoring her protests. Daemyn, a young nobleman in a well-made navy suit, was on his heels.

Behind them, a red-haired woman in a plain shirt and jeans struggled against the guards. "What the hell? Get out of my way!"

Her appearance answered Tiernan's silent question. This must be Lucinda, Harmony's current obsession. He'd only heard about her in passing from Edric, though never in good terms. However, it was a ruler's duty to hear both sides of all stories, and so he waved her through as well.

As Lucinda caught up with Edric, she wrenched his daughter's arm free and pulled her close. Harmony did not object, but seemed to melt into the contact, while glaring at her father.

Bewildered, Edric scowled at the commoner. "How dare you!" He leaned forward to grab his daughter again, but Lucinda was faster.

She shoved Edric away from them. "Get the fuck away from her!" The young woman wrapped a protective arm around Harmony's shoulder.

When Edric lost his balance and stumbled backward, Daemyn stepped in and helped him regain his footing. "You should learn to respect your betters!" Daemyn warned, shoving Lucinda hard. "And don't touch my fiancée!"

Lucinda lost her balance and fell to the floor while Daemyn made a grab for Harmony. She dodged, hissing, "I'm not your fiancée!" She kneed him in the crotch, watching dispassionately as he fell to his knees with a strangled cry, clutching at his privates. She twisted around to take Lucinda's hand and pulled her up. "Are you hurt, babe?"

"I'm fine." Lucinda smiled at her reassuringly.

There was a lasting tension even as the physical violence paused. Once all three of them were back on their feet, Lucinda and Daemyn eyed each other, daring the other to make a move. Before either could start another fight, Tiernan stepped between them. "Perhaps instead of wrestling in my auditorium, we can all address one another like adults?" He turned to his friend. "Edric, what brings you in the middle of my auditions?"

"My lord, it is good to see you. Congratulations on your engagement." Edric shook Tiernan's hand. "I wish that my visit was more of a festive nature." He bowed his head apologetically before raising it to make eye contact. "I found my daughter with this peasant you see beside her. They were partaking in…inappropriate behavior. Harmony doesn't seem to understand the importance of her betrothal to Daemyn." He cast a glare toward Lucinda. "And this woman seems convinced she has some type of claim over my-"

"Harmony has a right to choose who she wants to spend her life with. We all do!" Lucinda protested.

"The law clearly states that she is to marry whom I deem suitable. This affair needs to stop, else our family's name will be ruined!" Edric made a sour face and looked to Tiernan for approval.

Those few men and women who were fertile were highly sought after to continue the lineage of their people. As such, a new law had been ordered to preserve what was left of their population. Any children proven fertile through testing at puberty became the property and responsibility of the head of their household. Harmony's father, therefore, had the right to decide whom she would marry.

Nobles were always the first pick due to their many favorable qualities. Regrettably, Harmony had become enamored with a disinherited noble – a peasant for all intents and purposes – and a female, no less. Tiernan was torn on the matter. Their laws were put in place to propagate humanity. Lucinda was neither noble nor male, so offered Harmony nothing in the way of appeasing those laws. The idea of love lost its charm in the face of reality.

"I love her!" Harmony shouted, bringing Tiernan out of his thoughts.

"I own you," Edric spat. "You will marry Daemyn and have his children to continue our lineage!" He looked at Tiernan imploringly. "Please, my lord, make her understand."

Tiernan crossed his arms and sighed, allowing his eyes to fall upon the girl. She had strawberry blond hair with braids twisted throughout the lengthy waves. They fell down the line of her bare shoulders, finally settling on the red and black plaid dress. She reminded him of Harlequinn. It made him wonder whether or not his own children might have been this rebellious. Since Harlequinn was infertile, she was unable to give him an heir.

Since the discovery of the population's infertility crisis, their initial ventures into artificial insemination had yielded only abominations, so surrogates were the only sure option. While most men wouldn't be bothered by such a prospect, he wasn't certain Harlequinn's wrath was worth the trouble. He knew she would push hard for him to accept Osiris' offer.

Curiously, he glanced back, realizing that neither Edric nor any of the others had mentioned his company of fairies. Not a trace of them remained. Setting aside his confusion, he addressed the issue at hand. "Your father is correct, Harmony. The law dictates that you have a greater duty to your people than to your heart. As a nobleman's daughter, you must be willing to make sacrifices for the good of mankind. We can't ignore your disobedience."

"Oh, fuck you," Harmony retorted. "My mother was a whore, so it's not like my father put duty before himself."

"Harmony!" Edric looked around at the crowd of people, thoroughly mortified.

She flicked her gaze to her father and shrugged. "It's the truth. You all know it's bullshit. A child born out of duty will be more fucked up than a child born out of love. I'm proof of that." She glared accusingly at her father before turning her attention back to Tiernan. "So don't feed me your idealistic crap and expect me to say it tastes like cake."

Tiernan cleared his throat. "The situation is far from ideal, but that doesn't absolve you of your responsibilities. You're an intelligent woman. Surely you must realize that people make mistakes. That doesn't give you an excuse to be selfish. You can and should learn from the errors of others and use those lessons to be an upstanding member of society." When the girl scoffed, he pressed harder. "It doesn't matter whether you think the law is bullshit or not. The law still stands.

Should you go against your father's wishes, you will be held accountable for your actions."

"Is that a cowardly way of saying I'll be forced into solitary confinement and raped until I get pregnant?" Harmony countered. "That is the current law, right?"

He didn't have a better answer to her question. That was the current penalty if a fertile man or woman refused the wishes of the head of their household. As barbaric as it seemed, it was necessary. Ever since the birth of abominations had risen, most of the population had turned back to old faiths, condemning anything considered to be an alternative lifestyle. Their focus had to be on procreation. Same sex relationships had no place in their society when humanity was so close to extinction, save for liaisons out of public view. If what Osiris said was true, though, that law could be abolished altogether. Of course, he couldn't base any of his decisions on vague hopes.

"The fact that you can't even answer that question proves my point." Harmony's eyes were trained on Tiernan, challenging him.

"You are, of course, entitled to your opinions, but the focus of the law is to prevent the extinction of the human race. Until another solution is discovered, everyone is obligated to adhere to it," Tiernan replied.

"I'd rather die than be forced to procreate with that pig." Harmony clenched her jaw. "If I can't have Lucinda, then no one can have me."

"I'm certain I could change your mind about that," Daemyn purred into Harmony's ear. "One night with me and I doubt you'll look at another woman again."

"Keep telling yourself that, sweetheart," Her tone was sickly sweet to disguise the venom beneath. "I'm certain your ego is much larger than what's in your pants, anyway." She gave him a wink, watching as his sly smile soured.

"You shouldn't throw away your life so casually," Tiernan interrupted. "You're still young. Either you'll see that your father has your best interest at heart, or you will be forced into doing your duty. Unfortunately, there is no other option."

He allowed a moment for that to sink in before continuing. "Let me be clear, Harmony. If you and Lucinda continue down this path, the penalty is brutal. You will be confined until the gestation period has passed and you are ready to give birth. Your child will be taken from you and raised to become a contributing member of society. You will be doomed to a life of servitude until you've reached the age of infertility. Think carefully about what is more important. Daemyn is not only a suitable husband, but he would treat you and any children you have respectfully. In the meantime, you will be under house arrest until you've made your decision and Lucinda will not be permitted–"

"No!" Harmony cried, her eyes wide with the fear Tiernan had hoped to see. "I'll marry him!"

"What? Harmony, what are you saying?" Lucinda grabbed her shoulder and turned her so they were face to face. "I thought you loved me."

Harmony tore her gaze away from the girl, her hair hiding the guilt in her eyes. "I'm sorry. This hurts me more than you realize, but you know that I can't escape my duty, no matter how much I hate it."

Lucinda stared at her, mouth hanging open in disbelief. She stood there for several moments, as if willing her to say it wasn't true. Eventually, she regained what little composure she had left and walked out of the auditorium.

Daemyn slid his arm around Harmony's waist and pulled her against him. "I assure you, my love, you won't regret this decision."

She didn't seem to notice. Instead, she looked up at Tiernan, heartbroken. "Will I still not be permitted to see Lucinda, even though I've agreed to the marriage? I just...I need to make peace with my feelings."

Tiernan recalled how he and Harlequinn once hated each other. They had decided to meet on the battlefield to settle their differences. Harlequinn had insisted on it before she'd agree to marry him to unite their people. She'd been disgusted with his spinelessness in the wake of the supernatural chaos. He'd been provoked by her temerity. Upon meeting, they'd fallen in love with the other's ferocity and will to live. She'd helped him come to terms with the responsibilities that had landed in his lap upon the death of his parents. Had it not been for the necessity of uniting their people against a common threat, he never could have agreed to marry her. He was glad of those circumstances, but it didn't change anything for Harmony. Perhaps that was why he took pity on the girl now.

"If you like, you can see her under supervision."

"Thank you," she whispered and bowed low before turning to run out the door.

Neither Edric nor Daemyn seemed concerned with Harmony storming out right behind Lucinda. In fact, both looked rather pleased with the outcome. Now that Harmony had finally agreed to do as Edric wished, he seemed confident that she would uphold her word.

"Thank you, my lord. I am forever in your debt," Edric said gratefully, bowing.

"It was nothing, my friend." Tiernan laughed. "I'm sure Harmony will be happy with Daemyn." He knew better, but winked at the young man and grinned just the same. "On another note, Harlequinn and I have decided to have a bachelor party. We would love for you all to come and celebrate with us."

"I am honored to be invited, my lord, but I must decline. I fear I must arrange to have my daughter married before she changes her mind," Edric replied, straightening. "You know how women are."

"Nonsense," Tiernan waved a dismissive hand. Perhaps he could buy the star-crossed lovers some time. If Osiris' promise turned out to be genuine, he could abolish the law and Harmony could marry Lucinda if she wished. "How about they marry alongside Harlequinn and me? The wedding is in four days."

"I wouldn't want to impose."

"I'll hear none of that." Tiernan glanced over at his bride and she smiled approvingly. "See? Even Harlequinn thinks it's a fantastic idea."

"Well, if you're certain, how could I say no?" Edric grinned.

"Thank you kindly, my lord," Daemyn added, bowing as well.

"It's nothing. Just be ready for tomorrow night," Tiernan smiled back. It was far better to keep the nature of the party a secret until they could see it for themselves, or they might have thought him mad and refused to have anything to do with it.

Once Edric and Daemyn had excused themselves, Harlequinn finally exploded into excitement over the possibility of finally being able to have a child, along with the party and the wedding plans. While she was babbling about their future, Tiernan proceeded to secure it. Should Osiris' offer prove to be a ruse, he wanted to know beforehand.

He pressed the button hidden in the face of his watch and a dark form materialized before him. It first appeared as pixelated numbers, and then gradually focused into the solid shape of a man in a form-fitting black bodysuit.

Before speaking, the black-clad figure reached up to the side of his head to push a button. It activated a soundproof barrier that immediately surrounded them. "It's good to see you, Tiernan. Who am I killing today?"

Act I, scene ii

After fleeing from the auditorium, Harmony ran into her friend Hazelle. The girl looked heartbroken. As much as she would have liked to reassure Hazelle, however, she wasn't able to in front of Tiernan's guards.

"I need to tell you something, " Harmony whispered, keeping her head bowed while she addressed her friend. "Can we go somewhere private?"

Hazelle regarded her incredulously. Part of her wanted to disown their friendship after what she'd overheard. Harmony knew full well that Hazelle was in love with Daemyn. They were destined to be together, and it was only Daemyn's obsession with Harmony that had come between them.

She knew she was just average looking – brown curls, tanned skin and hand-me-down dresses. She couldn't compare to Harmony's fair hair and complexion. Despite that, she kept telling herself that it was just a phase. It had to be.

The entire time she'd been standing just outside the auditorium, Hazelle had been praying that there was a catch. Harmony wasn't the type to just switch sides, or roll over and agree to her father's wishes. When her friend agreed to the marriage, it was just another slap in the face, a cruel reminder of Hazelle's shortcomings.

"Please, Hazelle," she begged, taking the girl's hands into her own and giving them a squeeze. When the brunette nodded her assent, Harmony immediately pulled her friend down the hallway without another word.

"Where are we going?" Hazelle was having difficulty keeping up with the blond's pace. When her friend came to a sudden halt at the end of the hallway, Hazelle almost ran into her. "What's going–"

Harmony shushed her and shoved her back against the wall. She waited for what felt like ages before poking her head out to glance around the corner. Lucinda was sitting on the front steps of the mansion, looking utterly depressed. Harmony had to get her attention.

She glanced between Lucinda and Hazelle and said, "Don't ask questions. Just march out there like you're angry and follow my lead. Continue into the servant's quarters, then into the washroom, okay?"

Hazelle furrowed her brows, unsure of what this was supposed to accomplish. Harmony did have a lot to answer for, though. "Are you going to explain why you've suddenly lost your mind if I do this?"

Harmony nodded, and that was all she needed.

Hazelle headed in the direction Harmony had outlined. Seconds later, she heard footsteps running behind her.

"Hazelle, please let me explain!"

"Why should I? It's clear that you don't take my feelings into consideration." Perhaps this was meant to be a farce, but Hazelle couldn't deny how good it felt to say it out loud.

She would have walked away, but Harmony caught her arm and whirled her around. "It isn't like that. You're my best friend. I didn't want to hurt you."

"Bullshit!" Hazelle yelled, wrenching her arm from the woman and storming into the servants' quarters. She could hear Lucinda calling to Harmony not far behind, but she didn't look back. Once she reached her destination, she stepped into the washroom and attempted to close the door, but Harmony slipped in behind her.

Immediately, Hazelle dropped the act and crossed her arms over her chest. She stared at her friend expectantly. "So why are we in here? What's going on?"

Harmony shushed her again and just watched the door. When the pounding on the other side started, she opened it, grabbed Lucinda's arm and pulled her inside. She shut the door again and locked it.

"What the hell is going on?" Lucinda demanded.

The redhead was still completely in the dark as to why Harmony had suddenly decided to toss her aside for a man, let alone a homophobic nobleman like Daemyn. She could never understand what Hazelle saw in him, but now Harmony was apparently seeing it too. Or perhaps she was afraid of the consequences Tiernan had threatened her with? She'd known about the law previously but had fearlessly fought for their love up until now.

"Shut up and listen," Harmony hissed. "Both of you."

When they'd both quieted, she continued, "I'm not going to marry Daemyn." Both Lucinda and Hazelle immediately let out a breath they'd been holding. Harmony could see that the risk of putting a rift between them upset not only Lucinda, but Hazelle as well.

Hazelle didn't give either of them a chance to say anything before smacking the blond on the arm. "Why the hell would you say that if you didn't mean it? Don't scare me like that!"

Harmony rubbed her arm, pouting. "It's not like Tiernan gave me a choice. Would you have preferred that I was on lock down, unable to run away with Lucinda instead?"

That had the intended effect. They were stunned into silence.

Harmony placed her hands on her hips and smiled. She couldn't believe she'd managed to deceive them. "Oh, come on, you guys didn't actually buy that, did you?" She snorted. "It was just a ploy to get them to leave me the hell alone long enough to get out of here. Tiernan has no jurisdiction over the rebels – they're beyond Fae territory. If we cross through to the other side, Lucinda and I will be free. Then Daemyn will renew his engagement to you." The conflicted look on Hazelle's face caused Harmony to falter just slightly. "That is what you want, isn't it?"

"Well, yes, but…" Hazelle hesitated, meeting her friend's gaze. "It sounds dangerous. Are you sure the fairies won't kill you both if they catch you trespassing?" She wanted Daemyn to herself again, but Harmony's plan to run away made her nervous. She didn't want her friends murdered.

"That fate is no worse than what Tiernan has planned for me if I break the law." Harmony shrugged. "I'm willing to risk it if Lucinda is."

Lacing her fingers with Harmony's, Lucinda pulled her close. Their bodies fit perfectly together. "You don't have to worry, Hazelle. I won't let anything happen to her."

Harmony shoved her playfully and giggled. "Don't make promises you can't keep, hon'. I can take care of myself and I might have to save your ass while I'm at it." She reached down and squeezed Lucinda's backside, despite her protests. "It's worth saving, after all."

Hazelle rolled her eyes at the public display of affection, it just made her miss Daemyn more. Unfortunately, her friends often forgot that little detail. "Okay, I get it, you're dying to fuck each other," she interrupted before they could get too cozy. "Wait until you're on the other side, at least."

The couple parted reluctantly and Harmony turned her attention back to Hazelle. "We should make it look like I'm upset." She glanced at Lucinda, unable to keep the smile from lighting up her face as their eyes met. "You need to hide in here and wait a few minutes before you leave."

"Wait, how are we even going to pull this off?" Lucinda interjected. "The forest is across the water, and the water is beyond a wasteland. How are we supposed to make it through there unscathed?"

"Don't worry. I'll think of something." Harmony waved off her concern. "Hazelle will let you know when I figure it out." She twisted around and turned on the faucet, splashing water onto her face to smear her mascara and make it look like she'd been crying. Once done, she opened the door and exited the washroom, Hazelle following right behind her.

Lucinda listened to their voices fading into the background and sighed. She leaned against the wall, crossing her arms over her chest as she wondered how they were going make this work. It didn't sound like Harmony even had a plan. She'd do anything for Harmony, even follow her into a death trap.

When she opened the door, the girls were long gone and she didn't see anyone else. She stepped outside the small washroom and started for the exit. Once she'd left the mansion, she heard Hazelle call her name and she turned around, watching as the girl jogged down the steps.

"Hey, I just heard. I wanted you to know that I'm sorry it ended like that," she said ambiguously.

For a moment, she wasn't sure what Hazelle was referring to or why she would say something like that. Then it hit Lucinda that the girl was following Harmony's plan. "Yeah, me too," she replied back. An awkward silence passed between them. She couldn't think of what else to say up until she realized that, had it been true, Hazelle would be in a similar position. "Are you okay? I know how much you love Daemyn."

Hazelle dropped her gaze and looked to the side, raising her arms to hug herself. "I've been better, but it's not like she had a choice, right? As much as I love Daemyn, I can't hate her for choosing to marry him. We're still going to be friends."

"You're a better person than I could be." Lucinda sighed. "Anyway, I should get going." She turned her back to Hazelle and started down the cobblestone path.

"Tiernan has offered to have Daemyn and Harmony married beside them on their wedding day," the girl added hastily.

Lucinda stopped to glance back curiously. Had Harmony figured out a plan already?

Hazelle closed the distance between them before continuing. "They've been invited to a bachelor party tomorrow night. Apparently, it's being held on a boat."

Hooking her fingers into the belt loops on her jeans, Lucinda regarded the brunette. This could be their only chance to escape Tiernan's jurisdiction. She was curious about how it would work, given the ocean's current condition. She reasoned that it must be safe if Tiernan was willing to host a party on the water, however. Perhaps they could make their way to the forest from wherever the ship anchored. But how would she get on?

"My family will likely be invited as well," Hazelle commented casually.

"I'm not a noble anymore," Lucinda pointed out with a shrug. "So it has nothing to do with me." She had been disowned by her family when she went public about her bisexuality. Before the cataclysm, nobody batted an eye at differing sexual orientations, but now it was paramount that healthy human children be birthed in every generation. Though Lucinda was infertile, her parents had pushed for her to marry and have children via a surrogate. However, after meeting Harmony, she'd made it clear that she would never marry a man. For all intents and purposes, she and Hazelle were both social pariahs.

"I wanted to ask if you'd accompany me," Hazelle replied, rubbing her arm in a show of anxiety. "I thought we might offer one another support. It might be good to have each other to lean on, you know? Help us come to terms with the situation and move on…" She trailed off, her eyes trained on the cobblestone between them. "What are friends for, right?"

Hazelle's family had gone bankrupt soon after her mother gave birth to a supernatural stillborn. Since that unfortunate incident, most of the nobles viewed Hazelle as a defect. They feared that she would have stillborns as well, or worse, supernatural children.

Daemyn had been the only one to ignore the superstitions and paranoia of the others. He didn't seem concerned that a magic born child marred the lineage of her family. He had spent months attempting to win her affection, which had driven her mad with rage. She'd found it offensive that he wouldn't give up what she assumed was a prank. She thought that if she could get him to admit it, he'd finally stop tormenting her. She'd done everything she could to send him running for the hills, but he'd proceeded to shove her up against a wall, force his knee between her legs and show her exactly how he felt about her. She'd never been so turned on in all her life. They hadn't had sex that day, and the fact that he was willing to wait for marriage to please himself proved to her that he was serious about his proposal.

Until Harmony had moved here for her father's new position as one of Tiernan's officers. Then everything had changed.

"I accept your invitation," Lucinda said, breaking Hazelle out of her reverie.

"Lovely," she murmured. "See you tomorrow night, then."

Act II, scene i

The hum of Osiris' magicycle vibrated through his body. The wasteland he and his four companions traversed was marked by lifeless sand dunes spanning the edge of Tiernan's city, Nirvana, to an equally desolate ocean. The Fae's forest home, the only other inhabited site for countless miles, lay on the other side of the water.

The Fae had been driven away from Nirvana during the last war. The remnants of their home only stayed untouched due to the magnetic field they had erected, which wouldn't last much longer if Tiernan decided to march on their territory. Osiris could only assume the delay was because of the high amount of radiation that had seeped into the earth and the sea around the area.

The humans hadn't yet created portable energy barriers like the Fae. Tiernan protected Nirvana via a dome that kept out toxic air. He'd even burrowed through the ground to block infected soil with cement.

The Fae's methods were altogether more sophisticated. The thought made Osiris frown as his magicycle transitioned smoothly from sand to water. It hovered over the unnaturally bright green waves, leaving a trail behind it. Others hadn't been nearly so lucky.

The only life that remained in the sea, for instance, had been saved by the Mer people and their magic. However, it was inaccessible to those above the surface. Just crossing the water had proven to be a treacherous task. If not for his lead magician's brilliance, Osiris might never have been able to enact a plan to save his people.

Even as he observed the toxic water, he couldn't think of a way to cross it without the help of sci-magic. Tiernan was a crafty bastard, though. If there was a way, he would find it. The fairy king couldn't take that risk.

As Osiris was nearing the opposite shore just a few miles from the forest, a series of beeps sounded in his ear. He pressed a button on the side of his helmet to accept the call. "Have you learned anything of value?"

"Yes, your grace," came a reply rife with interference, but Osiris still managed to pick out what Revelin said.

"Good, give me a full report once you've returned. Don't delay." The fairy king ended the call. He couldn't afford distractions this close to home.

When the forest was in their sights, Osiris revved his engine, accelerating to hit the barrier at top speed. His companions followed suit and they left a sand storm behind them as they tore through the grains. Once they hit the flux, they were all pulled forcefully through the magnetic field and back into their homeland. If any of them had failed to hit the speed mark, they would have been repelled and torn apart. That was the risk they took whenever they ventured out of the safety of their habitat.

Sighing, Osiris powered down the magicycle and pulled the helmet off his head, shaking his hair out. He barely had time to hoist his leg over the side of the bike and steady himself before his wife dismounted her bike and came close. He expected a kiss, but she gave him a hearty slap instead.

Rubbing his cheek, he watched Tatiana storm past him. He could hear the other three band members snicker as they disappeared into the foliage. The king rolled his eyes. "Typical."

Tatiana was angry with him. He supposed it was understandable, considering how hard they had worked to keep him from harm's way. Though she'd accompanied him on the trip to Nirvana, her presence wouldn't have stayed Tiernan's wrath had things gone badly.

Despite his success in uniting all races of Fae, the elders had questioned Osiris's ability to make decisions related to war because he was a halfbreed. Unlike him, they could easily see past their own misgivings when it was necessary. Humans were inherently flawed and didn't share that ability in most cases. So, while he could be fickle like the others, his emotions were also capable of blinding him to the bigger picture. To avoid such complications, they'd sheltered him from the burdens of leadership.

That was probably a mistake on their part. Because of their coddling, he'd learned very little about human nature and his childhood had been fraught with terror. The humans had hated nothing more than someone like Osiris. Because he knew nothing of them short of their bigotry, he'd spent many nights hiding away in the Great Oak

Tree's branches, fighting sleep as he listened to Revelin's stories about the way things used to be.

Before the calamity all magical beings had lived beside nature, without human knowledge. However, as humanity's technology progressed and their populations grew, they had destroyed nature – cutting down entire forests, building over lakes, tunneling through mountains, and even poisoning the sea. It changed the way of life the magic folk had always known. They'd been forced to adapt to their new surroundings and come out of hiding.

Since humans had a tendency to be blinded by their emotions, their reaction to these new races was fear. Unfortunately, that fear had morphed into hatred. Many Fae had been exposed to violence and killed simply for being different. Those humans who were only curious wanted to treat magical folk as science experiments. That was when the Fae were first exposed to such a concept – science.

Taking what they'd learned, they created a new form of magic – one that could utilize the convenience of technology and science, improving both, enriching the quality of life for both humans and magical races. Instead, they widened the chasm between them with a chemical explosion that poisoned much of the earth with magically altered toxins. It had also created a new type of radiation. Though this disaster primarily impacted humanity, the Fae were not left unaffected. Forests withered and died, soil couldn't grow life of any kind, and wildlife suffered almost irreparably.

A new form of acid rain proceeded to poison lakes and rivers. It was a miracle that the Fae were able to salvage even one water source. Magic folk had imbued the lakes and rivers close to them with protection spells. Tiernan had built large barriers in the shape of pyramids to prevent contamination from the rain. It was only a temporary fix, though. If they couldn't purify the sea soon, the lakes and rivers would eventually run dry. At the very least, they would have to find a way to transport supplies from the Mer safe havens to above ground. First though, Osiris needed to take care of the competition for the water resources. Tiernan's hatred of the Fae wasn't the only reason he was dangerous. It was merely what spurred Osiris to take things into his own hands.

As if on cue, the familiar beeping started once more, taking him out of his thoughts. He turned his attention toward his wrist. It harbored a magically imbued device that could tap into airwaves and cyberspace, so his people could stay connected no matter the circumstances.

A hologram of Tiernan's face materialized in front of him. "Greetings," the man said. "I wanted to touch base with you about the party. One boat will do just fine, thank you. Please send me the details about how this will be arranged. I have also attached a gift to this message. I hope it serves you well."

Tiernan's face faded out of view, leaving a message window remaining. It prompted Osiris to accept or decline the gift.

"What is it?"

At the unexpected intrusion, Osiris instinctively turned and tried to throat punch the person who'd spoken.

Tatiana dodged. "Your reflexes are slow," she scoffed.

"Thank you for noticing." He returned his gaze to the message, considering his options. Tiernan was a ruthless human and it could easily be a trap.

"You're welcome," she chirped back, reaching out and pressing accept before he had time to stop her.

Pixelated numbers traveled down to the ground from the wrist tech. They expanded into a solid shape as they rose upward. Bare feet took shape. Within seconds, legs clothed in rags, a chest clothed in an old vest, shoulders, and a head could be made out. The numbers melted together and solidified into a young man, who regarded them in silence.

Osiris noted the strange spark of recognition in his eyes before the "gift" knelt down on one knee, bowing his head. "Greetings, Master, Mistress. My lord Tiernan has sent me to you as a thank you for your kind wedding present. How may I be of service?"

Osiris wasn't sure what to make of him. Unfortunately, he didn't have time to ponder it before Tatiana was all over him.

"Well aren't you just precious?" his wife cooed, lifting the man's chin up so she could see his face. "What are you called?"

"Isra, Mistress."

She cast a mischievous glance toward her husband and smirked.

"You'll be my new plaything," Tatiana decided, stroking his cheek with her fingers.

The more she spoke, the tighter Osiris' chest became with aggravation. Not only was she carelessly putting them in danger, but she was trying to use Isra as leverage – to make Osiris jealous, and to blackmail him into staying close to her. Sometimes he forgot how conniving she could be. And now, she was furious at him for putting himself in danger.

"He might be a spy, or worse," he protested, but she paid him no mind.

"Oh, do shut up. My decision is made." She grabbed Isra's vest in her hands and pulled him up. "Come and serve me, my sweet."

Osiris watched helplessly as Tatiana led Isra away, his hands forming fists as she winked at him. She was daring him to follow, but he had more pressing matters to deal with. He had to prepare a boat for the party and gather willing participants for entertainment and wait-staff, not to mention the rendezvous with Revelin.

Even with his frustrations mounting, he admitted to himself he was more bothered by the slave. Something about Isra wasn't right. The servant's eyes spoke of some underlying intention, an intelligence that didn't match the persona. There was little he could do about it until Revelin returned with his report, but at the very least, he could have the spy watch over Tatiana to ensure her safety. Despite how much she often angered him, he loved his wife. If only she was as forthcoming with her feelings. One of the many downfalls of being half human among Fae, he supposed.

Luck seemed to be on his side that day. The magnetic barrier shimmered. It immediately spat out Revelin from the other side. His magicycle whirred to a halt and he hopped off, pulling his helmet from his head with a face-splitting grin. "Top o' the morning, m'lord!"

"Report," Osiris demanded, crossing his arms over his chest. He was in no mood for childish antics.

"Ah, must be a lover's quarrel," Revelin said. "Tatiana still angry over your secret rendezvous with Lord Fuck Face?"

Osiris grimaced; Revelin had guessed right on the first try. He placed a hand on his hip to accentuate his impatience. "Report, please."

"Well, since you asked so nicely," the spy teased. "After Sir Pimp-a-Lot entered and you made your hasty retreat, I learned that women's uteruses are now traded for high end egotism. His unwilling prostitute is planning to run away with her lover through our territory tomorrow night. It just so happens that they were invited to the party you've so kindly offered to host for Lord Fuck Face and his faulty uterus." A thoughtful look flickered across Revelin's face and he raised a finger to tap on his chin. "Although that seems like a bad trade off to me. Not the party, but the faulty uterus. Last I heard, they usually want them to work properly."

Osiris arched an eyebrow, somewhat amused by Revelin's report. This particular fairy was indispensable to their plan. He'd hated to leave him behind in such a dangerous situation, though he'd known that Revelin could do it without any trouble. "You'll have to forgive me for putting you in that position, my friend. Had I stayed longer, things would have gotten messy."

When Osiris had been born, he'd been given a death sentence by his parents, or so he was told. Had it not been for the compassionate woman who had taken mercy on him, he would have died. Revelin's skills in espionage had made it possible to retrieve Osiris. He didn't like thinking about what might have become of the woman responsible for his survival. She had taken a great risk to her personal safety to preserve his life.

Revelin retrieved him and took him to Oakhart Village, where he was raised by the fairy elders. To everyone's surprise, he'd shown an unexpected amount of self-awareness and intelligence as a child. Since he was half human, he aged and matured far quicker than any full blooded fairy. He could relate to situations in ways many of them overlooked and was able to help them see the plight of both sides more clearly.

To give him a foothold with the people, the elders had arranged a courtship between him and Tatiana. She had been intrigued by him and he by her. Their relationship progressed from friendship to something deeply passionate in the span of months. Such things were common for fairies. Tatiana was no exception; she loved quickly and fiercely, and she liked the fact that he had no involvement in the war. She had wanted him all to herself.

Originally, he had wanted peace for all races, and so he'd asked Idris – his lead magician – to look into creating a cure for humanity's infertility problem early on. That had changed when Edric launched an ambush on Oakhart Village. That attack had claimed Osiris' Fae parents. Since that moment, he knew what he had to do, but he'd been forced to wait. The Fae were few now, so going to war with Tiernan's people had not been an option. Instead, he'd sent Revelin to Nirvana periodically to find an opportunity to strike. When the spy reported that Tiernan was in the process of getting married, Osiris knew that this was his chance.

"My lord? Have you lost yourself in that big head of yours?"

Revelin's voice cut through the haze of memories and Osiris blinked a few times, shaking his head. "Apologies. I was reminding myself of my motivations."

"No matter," Revelin said. "I knew you'd find your way back." He waved his hand in front of Osiris' face, grinning. "Do you have any orders for me, my lord? Perhaps you'd like me to go pinch Tatiana's nipples to kill the mood?"

Osiris looked at him blankly. Had he really been dazed long enough for the spy to wander off and return without him noticing? "No, I have other things in mind."

"Join them, perhaps?"

"No," Osiris snapped. "Shut up and let me speak."

Revelin's mouth snapped shut and he pantomimed choking on his own words.

Osiris rolled his eyes and turned his back to the man long enough to gather his thoughts. When he glanced toward Revelin again, the spy was laying on the ground, playing dead. Sometimes Osiris questioned his own sanity when dealing with Revelin.

Ignoring the spy, he began. "Tiernan has presented me with the gift that's currently serving my wife." He had to swallow down his distaste. "I don't trust his intentions. The man – Isra – is hiding something. He feigns being a slave, but there's an underlying self-awareness in his eyes that sets me on edge. I don't want him alone with Tatiana. In fact, I'd like you to administer the love elixir to them both when the opportunity presents itself."

Revelin opened his eyes and raised a hand, one finger pointing upward. "Done! Anything else?"

"I want Edric to feel the pain I felt when he destroyed my family," Osiris intoned. "Poison his daughter and her fiancé at the party. Use the new concoction the magicians have been toying with recently."

"Allow me to compliment you on the high quality of your evil genius today, sir." Revelin saluted from the ground. "I will do as you bid."

Osiris nodded, clasping his hands behind his back and started toward the foliage. "I'll also need you to gather an elite team to surround Tiernan and his fiancée during the party. At the appropriate time, they will come to understand the consequences of their actions. Their attempted genocide will be met in turn. Once I give the signal, you're to set the plan in motion."

"Understood. You've grown into an honorable man, Osiris. I would follow you to the ends of the wastelands and back."

Osiris stopped and turned to stare at him, having never expected to hear such sentiments from the joker. However, Revelin was nowhere in sight. Assassin, spy, and master of espionage he may be, but he was a damn clown underneath it all. Most would have thought the trickster had long gone, but he knew better. "None of this would be possible without you, Revelin. Thank you for saving my life that day."

"Oh, stop, you're gonna make me tear up!" Revelin squealed from behind Osiris, startling the fairy king.

When he turned around, he saw the spy fanning himself with a rapidly moving hand, and Osiris finally broke out into smile. He realized that may have been Revelin's goal all along.

Act II, scene ii

Revelin shot through the forest in a multicolored streak, dodging tree trunks and branches. He was heading toward the makeshift laboratory at the back of the wooded area. It was far from the rest of the residents to protect their dwindling population. They couldn't afford any more causalities from failed experiments.

As the building came into view, Revelin perched on a branch long enough to contact Idris. "Hello, hello. Special Agent Trickster here for pick up. Is it safe to come inside, or should I wait until I see smoke?"

"It would have been safer if you hadn't called while I was juggling five different vials," Idris grumbled. "Hurry up and get in here so I can get back to work. The portal isn't going to test itself."

Revelin disconnected the call without answering and dove off the branch. He zipped through the air in a spin until his feet hit the ground in front of the entrance. Upon entering, he raised his arm to announce, "Honey, I'm home!"

"What do you want?" Idris grunted, still tinkering with the frame of the portal conduit.

"Two love elixirs and two asphyxiation toxins to go, please." The spy grinned viciously.

Idris crossed his arms and gave him a sour look, tapping his foot impatiently. "What is the nature of the love elixirs? The concoction is different depending on who the recipients are supposed to fall in love with."

"Our subjects must fall head-over-heels in love with Osiris," Revelin replied while he danced around the room. He stopped long enough to lean against a table, sighing heavily as he batted his lashes. "Engineered love is so sweet!"

"Ah yes," Idris mumbled. He opened a cabinet and pulled out a tray of purple vials.

When the old fairy glanced up, Revelin was dancing a circle around him. Idris followed his movements for a few seconds and then scowled. "Oh, will you stop? How am I supposed to concentrate?"

The spy halted, unmoving while Idris held the vials out to him. "You inject these into the intended victim and that's it. When they wake, they will pledge their love to the king."

"Are you going to take these or not?" Idris barked. "I have to get that portal up and running by tomorrow night! I don't have time for your tricks."

Revelin grabbed two vials from the tray and placed them in a pouch on his belt, followed by the needles Idris supplied.

Rozene Morgandy

"Why, thank you," the spy said with a wink. He did love to tease the ancient magician. "And the poison?"

"Yes, yes give me a minute." Idris returned to the cabinet, and slid the tray with the purple vials back into place before he turned his eye to the other trays.

There were two sitting side by side; one held an earlier design of the love potion – the difference being that instead of the victim falling in love with a specific person, they fell in love with the first person they saw. The other held the poisons Revelin has requested. One set was bright red and the other was maroon. He scrutinized the labels, double checking to ensure he pulled out the right set. Had it not been for those tags, he wouldn't have remembered which was which. He'd been worked to death in the past months – from extending the barrier to include at least two ships, to an infertility cure, to creating a portal that would allow safer travel over long distances. As brilliant as Osiris was, Idris wished he'd had more time to prepare all the things his king required.

"Inject the red liquid in the victim and paralysis will slowly set in, eventually making it to the lungs. Once that happens, the individual will suffocate within minutes." He held out the tray, glanced up, and realized Revelin had disappeared. Growling, he turned around, but the troublemaker was nowhere in sight. "Damn it, you charlatan, if you don't quit your pranks, I'll paralyze you from the waist down and use you as a test subject!"

The spy's head dropped down in front of Idris' face without warning and the man jumped out of his skin, losing his grip on the tray.

Revelin caught it in his hands, chuckling. "If you weren't so entertaining, I wouldn't keep tricking you!" He offered a wide grin and suspended the tray in the air long enough to plant his feet on the ground, and then retrieved it to set it on a table.

"Curse you, boy, you'll regret that! You could have killed us!" the magician roared where he was laying on the floor.

"But I didn't!" Revelin held out his hand to help the fairy up.

Slapping his hand away, Idris cussed up a storm as he pushed himself back to his feet. "Get out of my sight before I inject this venom in you!"

"As you wish, captain!" Revelin bowed and disappeared into thin air.

"I know you're just invisible. Get out now, or I swear Osiris will have one less jester." He didn't wait for a reply. If he didn't get the portal working by tomorrow night, the entire plan would go awry. On top of that, he still had to prepare the special drinks the king had ordered for the party, to keep the guests distracted and entertained.

He heard the door squeal open and closed not long after. "Damn joker…" The old fairy retrieved a mouse from another room to test the portal. He would have preferred to use a human instead, but Osiris had forbidden it.

Act III, scene i

"Welcome. It is an honor to have everyone here today."

Hazelle could hear the man that had set up this party, but she was too far in the back of the crowd to see who it was. Not that she cared. The only person she was interested in seeing was Daemyn. She looked for him, but she had a feeling he and Harmony were further toward the front. After all, Harmony's father was Tiernan's friend.

"Due to the radiation beyond the city limits, there will be transportation to the ship where the party awaits. I assure you all that it's safe."

As Hazelle wondered how this man was going to get over a hundred people to a ship across a desert wasteland, she heard a strange whirring start further ahead. Many guests near the front gasped and started talking amongst themselves.

"What is this? Magic?" She could clearly hear Edric's voice protesting already. "How can we trust anything that uses magic?"

"Friends, calm yourselves. Everything is under control." Tiernan's voice rose over the cries of outrage. "You all know how I feel about magic, but times are changing. The king of fairies wishes for a truce between us. This is something I wanted to share with you all firsthand, so you may see that I'm amenable to it."

Someone shouted that this was a trap and they couldn't trust the Fae.

"I understand how everyone feels. Allow me to demonstrate by stepping through the portal myself, to prove that no harm will come to anyone," Tiernan offered.

A hush came over the people and Hazelle assumed he was getting ready to test the transportation device. Various intakes of breath sounded once, twice, and then a third time.

"See? I am perfectly unharmed. Please, I implore you all to support me. You all know I want only the best for everyone. Let's celebrate!"

"So he survived," Lucinda commented bitterly.

Hazelle glanced at her friend before turning toward the people moving in front of her. "Let's go."

They started forward together, halting every few moments as people went through. They didn't see Harmony, Daemyn, or Edric, so she supposed they must have used the portal already. By the time it was their turn, there were only a few left in the crowd. Once the person in front of her disappeared into the whirlpool of purple hues, Hazelle stepped forward. She stared into the vortex, mesmerized. She'd never seen a magical machine up close before, and she wondered if traveling through it would hurt.

She felt a nudge and glanced back at Lucinda, who nodded her head. "Go on."

Hazelle took a deep breath as she twisted around to look into it again. Exhaling, she stepped forward into its depths. She didn't feel any pain; it felt like she had been pushed through. In a blink of an eye, she was on solid ground again.

She was standing on an old, wooden dock. When she looked up, she saw the outskirts of a forest just beyond a sandy beach. The ship was floating on the ocean just behind her, while waves lapped against the shore beyond. This was the forest in which the last of the fairies resided. Beyond it would be the rebel's territory.

Unexpectedly, Hazelle was propelled forward as Lucinda materialized behind her. She fell to her knees just as a wave crashed under the dock, tainted water splashing between the planks and onto her hands. She squealed, pushing herself back on her haunches.

Lucinda crouched down and took her shoulders in her hands to steady her. "I'm sorry. I didn't mean to knock you down. Are you okay?"

Hazelle barely acknowledged Lucinda, her mind racing. Her gut rolled over and she thought she would vomit. Both the man who transported them here and Tiernan had told them they'd be safe, but poisonous water had just touched her! Was she going to mutate into a supernatural creature now, or would it only affect her future children? Would they be doomed to be Fae? How could she marry Daemyn now?

"Fear not, young lady," came the voice of an old man, while Lucinda helped her to her feet.

When she looked over, she realized he was one of the Fae, and he seemed to be checking something on a panel he held in his hand. She wondered if he was one of the magicians overseeing the sci-magic that they had used to come here.

"This entire area is protected by a barrier," he explained. "It's outlined by those electrical posts you see spanning across the beach and on either side of this dock. I oversaw their placement personally. They ensure that the barrier will continue running and that no one can be harmed by the radiation."

Hazelle was speechless, her heart pounding in her chest from the fright. She couldn't help but wonder how they'd managed such a thing; to say she was glad was an understatement.

"Let's find Harmony and Daemyn," Lucinda suggested, steadying her by the arm.

Hazelle nodded and they walked the length of the dock to the ramp that led onto the ship's deck.

Around the railing and overhead, multicolored sparklers floated in the air, keeping the deck alight. Tables of food and drink were set up along the edges of the top deck. Fairies breathed fire, while others danced with flaming hoops in midair in a spectacular display of illusory magic. Hazelle noticed that most of the guests were steering clear of them, though. It seemed Tiernan's words did little to stifle their fear of the unknown.

Many people were milling toward the inside of the ship, where music filtered out beyond the doors in muffled tones. Hazelle wondered if Harmony was inside.

"Would you care for a drink?" a female fairy's voice rung like a bell beside Hazelle.

Both she and Lucinda turned to regard her curiously. The woman held out a tray of spiral shaped glasses filled with neon green refreshments.

"What the hell." Hazelle took one and downed it. The burst of flavor was unexpected, but delightful. It tasted like kiwi and lime, making her tongue tingle while it fizzled all the way down. "Wow." She giggled, nudging Lucinda. "You should try one."

The redhead hesitated and Hazelle rolled her eyes. "Oh, come on. Are you telling me you're in love with the most reckless girl I know and you're afraid to try something new?" She took one of the glasses from the tray and held it out to her. "Try it."

Lucinda glared at her indignantly. "I'm not a coward. I just thought we should concentrate more on finding Harmony and Daemyn and less on getting drunk." She snatched the drink from Hazelle's hand and downed it. Her brows shot up. She'd never tasted anything quite so...high in quality before. Her head was tingling and she wondered how much alcohol had been in that shot. "Happy? Now, come on. We have to find Harmony and Daemyn. We both know he'll be glued to her side the whole time."

Hazelle tossed her head back and laughed. "Not when he sees my dance moves, he won't!"

The brunette ran ahead of her and disappeared into the doorway, Lucinda not far behind. From their vantage point at the top of the stairs, they could see everything. Fireworks crackled overhead, and music blared from a live band. Fairies were walking through the crowd, offering an array of drinks, food, and company. What was even stranger was that some of the guests were taking the fairies up on the last offer. People were dancing with fairies and partaking in rather inappropriate behaviors on the sidelines. The music and noise from the crowd drowned out anything overly scandalous, though.

Hazelle grinned as she took it all in, her heart pounding. "Come on!" She grabbed Lucinda's hand and tugged her down the stairs and into the crowd.

Swaying her hips to the beat, she turned and regarded Lucinda with a look that bordered on inappropriate. Lucinda was slightly discomfited, and let her eyes slide away. She searched for Harmony for a moment, but figured they'd bump into each other eventually. Sighing, she gave up and decided to have fun while she waited.

She closed the distance between herself and Hazelle, following the girl's movements and settling a hand on her hip. The music vibrated through their bodies, filling them with the desire to burn off the energy that pounded through their veins. Their minds traveled far away while lights streaked around them. It seemed like everything was spinning, but slowing down at the same time. All Lucinda wanted to do was go faster.

A hand clapped her on the shoulder and she turned around, blinking in confusion. Once the world stopped spinning, Harmony's face came into view. "Hey!" she said enthusiastically, leaning in for a kiss, but the blonde's hand halted her. Lucinda grinned slyly. "Playing hard to get?"

"What's wrong with you?" Harmony demanded. "We can't be seen like this. We have to escape before Daemyn tracks me down." She glanced behind Lucinda, where Hazelle had started grinding on one of the many fairies roaming around. She pushed past Lucinda and grabbed Hazelle's arm. "Hey, what are you doing? You're supposed to be looking for Daemyn, remember?"

"Oh hey, Harmony." Hazelle giggled. "I just figured he'd find me eventually. Isn't he with you?"

"No, I managed to lose him for now," Harmony replied, furrowing her brows. "You're acting weird."

"Am I?" Hazelle laughed and shrugged. "I feel great. Better than I have since you stole my fiancé." She whirled around, throwing her arms up in the air as she moved her body to the beat.

"Hey!" Harmony grabbed her friend's shoulders and shook her. "Focus. You have to-"

"There you are," Daemyn's voice cut in and Hazelle slipped out of Harmony's grip. "What are you doing? I thought we agreed to stick together." He slid his arm around Harmony's waist and leaned in close to her ear. "We should start getting to know each other if we're to be married, after all."

Harmony had to work hard to keep from grimacing. Her skin

crawled just having his arm around her and Hazelle was distracted with someone else already. "Sorry, I got caught up in the crowd."

Daemyn held out a glass with purple liquid swishing around inside it. "Here's your drink. I downed mine while I was trying to find you. They're quite good."

"Daemyn!" Hazelle squealed, leaping onto his back with a boisterous laugh once she noticed his presence.

Harmony slipped away while Hazelle distracted him. She took Lucinda's hand and backed out of Daemyn's view and the guests swallowed them into the throng of dancing bodies.

Daemyn whirled around, the glass slipping out of his fingers while he attempted to fling Hazelle off of his back. "Hazelle, get off! I don't have time for games."

He felt her arms slip from around his neck only to slink their way around his sides and over his chest. "I've missed you," she said huskily. "Let's go into one of those corners and make up."

Daemyn grabbed her hands and twisted around to regard her with a scowl. "I've told you a hundred times that I'm engaged to Harmony now, and still you have this inane idea that we're a thing. When are you going to accept that we're not?"

Hazelle let out a sound of disgust. "Ugh, how many times do I have to hear that speech, Daemyn? Harmony doesn't want you, but I do. We were perfect together and we can be perfect again, now that she's run away with Lucinda."

"What!?" Daemyn cried. "What do you mean Harmony is running away with that slut? Where?"

"Don't call her a slut. She's my friend!" Hazelle protested before another smirk curved her lips and she leaned in close. "But I can be *your* slut if that's what you're into."

"Hazelle, where are they running off to?" Daemyn repeated flatly.

"To the rebel's territory." Hazelle rolled her eyes. "Can we get back to us now?"

"Get out of my way." Daemyn shoved her away and headed toward the exit.

"Daemyn, wait!" Hazelle pushed her way through the crowd. She wasn't going to let him go again.

Ignoring his annoying tagalong, Daemyn scanned the crowd for any sign of either Lucinda or Harmony. He couldn't see them anywhere. He had to get to the exit before them, so he started making his way through the people blocking his path.

Someone grabbed his arm while he plowed his way through and he glanced back, growling as he tried to pull away from Hazelle. "Let go!" He forcefully pushed his hand into her chest, thrusting her back into the people behind her. Her fingers lost their grip on him and he sunk into the crowd before she could regain her footing. As he neared the stairs, he caught a glimpse of Lucinda and broke into a sprint. He got to the top just as she was heading out the door. Daemyn lunged and managed to grasp her arm before she could escape.

Looking at Lucinda, Daemyn's blood boiled. He'd only just convinced Harmony to accept their upcoming marriage, to let him prove his merit, and this peasant came between them again. He realized that he would never get his chance as long as Lucinda was breathing.

As Lucinda attempted to wrench out of Daemyn's grasp, he twisted her arm behind her back and propelled her over the railing. A deeply satisfied smirk stretched his face as he watched her tumble to the dance floor below.

Distantly, he heard Harmony screaming, but it didn't matter. She would see once this was done; she had to. If only Lucinda was out of the way.

Daemyn descended the stairs. He grabbed Lucinda's shirt, pulling her up before she could be trampled by the other guests. He wanted to finish this himself.

"Daemyn, what are you doing? Stop it!" Hazelle pushed herself between him and Lucinda. "Let her go!" She couldn't believe Daemyn was being so violent. He had a temper, but he had never done anything like this before. He was always such a gentleman.

"Get out of my-" Daemyn started. His fingers dug into Hazelle's shoulder to shove her aside. He felt something prick his neck, and he stopped, staring at her, mouth agape.

Lucinda took the chance to remove Daemyn's hand from her collar, and then his other hand from Hazelle's shoulder. She pulled the girl away to keep Daemyn from harming her further. "Are you alri-" She

141

felt a prick against her neck and slapped her hand over it, gazing blankly at Hazelle.

"I'm fine," Hazelle huffed, rubbing her arm where Daemyn had manhandled her. She kind of liked it when he was rough, but not when he was angry like that. She glanced between the two of them when she realized they weren't moving or speaking. "Hey, are you two all right?"

Harmony bolted down the stairs and burrowed herself into Lucinda, bunching the woman's shirt up in her hands. "Oh my God, are you okay? I can't believe he did that!" She looked up into Lucinda's eyes, her face awash in tears. "I thought he was going to kill you."

Lucinda broke out of her daze and shook her head, bringing a hand up to rub her eyes. "I'm sorry, what?" She looked down at Harmony in bewilderment. "What happened?"

Harmony's eyes widened. "Oh God, did you hit your head?" She pulled away and reached up to feel the back of Lucinda's head, her heart pounding. "Daemyn pushed you over the railing. Are you feeling okay? Do you have a headache?" She moved her hand to Lucinda's forehead.

"I think I sprained my ankle, but otherwise, I'm fine," Lucinda told her, still baffled. "Why are you touching me like that?" She laid her hands on Harmony's shoulders and pushed her off. Then she turned her attention to Hazelle. "Are you okay, Love?"

Hazelle looked at her, furrowing her brows. "Love? Since when have you ever called me that?" She shook her head and turned to Harmony. "Lucinda might have a concussion. She ought to see a doctor." She stepped back toward Daemyn, reaching up to run her finger's down his face. "Daemyn, are you okay?"

He blinked as his eyes started to focus again and he smiled warmly when he saw Hazelle. "I am now." He pulled her to him and leaned forward.

Hazelle stiffened, uncertain of how to respond. Her inhibitions fled as his lips came into contact with hers, her body gradually relaxing. She pressed into him, wanting more. She'd waited so long, but it ended just as quickly as it started.

Lucinda pulled Daemyn away. "Get your hands off her!"

Hazelle gaped at her incredulously before turning her gaze onto Harmony. Her friend seemed just as stunned.

"Have you lost your mind?!" Daemyn wrenched himself away from Lucinda's grasp. "Go scissor with your girlfriend, or whatever it is you do. Hazelle isn't a dyke!"

"Are you kidding me? You're engaged to Harmony, remember? And how would you know Hazelle's sexuality? After what you did to her, you're really surprised she turned to me?" Lucinda's eyes widened in revelation. "I get it. You hate *dykes*" – she said it mockingly – "so you have to ruin my happiness! Is that it? I loved Harmony, so you had to go after her. Then, when you finally got her, I moved on with Hazelle. So now you have another conquest?"

"I've always loved Hazelle! Up until this second, you've always loved Harmony, so why the sudden change of heart? Are you trying to turn Hazelle into another one of your carpet munching whores?" Daemyn demanded. "I won't stand for it!"

It was a miracle they could even hear each other over the music, but no one seemed to notice their argument. The other revelers acted as if the four quarreling youths didn't even exist.

"What the hell do you mean you love Hazelle?" Harmony cut in, shoving Lucinda back from Daemyn long enough to get her attention. "We were about to run away together, and now you're saying you're in love with my best friend? What the hell?"

"I'm sorry, but when you chose Daemyn over me, you broke my heart. Hazelle asked me to come to this party with her and everything changed. Accept it, marry Daemyn, have lots of babies. I don't care." She shrugged and pushed past Harmony to slide a hand over Hazelle's cheek. "Remember when we were dancing together? It was just the two of us, a perfect moment. That's when I realized I loved you."

Hazelle pulled away from Lucinda's touch, disturbed by the way she was acting. "I only invited you so you could run away with Harmony. I've always loved Daemyn and that's never going to change. I'm straight; I'm not even bi-curious. I don't know why you're acting like this, but it's weird, so please stop."

Before Lucinda could reply, Hazelle turned to Daemyn, frowning. "Furthermore, I get that you don't agree with same sex relationships, Daemyn, but that doesn't mean I'm okay with you insulting my friends. Turn me into a carpet muncher?" Her voice arced up, the anger palpable. "If we're going to make this work, we have to respect each other's views."

Daemyn's lips turned upward into a polite smile. "I understand. Anything for you, Beloved." He kissed the back of her hand.

"But you said we could lean on each other, help each other move on!" Lucinda protested, grabbing Hazelle's hands out of Daemyn's grasp. "I thought this was what you meant!"

Hazelle pulled her hands away, exasperated. "No, it was all an act in case anyone heard us! I thought you understood that."

"Well, it doesn't matter, does it?" Lucinda spat as she came closer to Hazelle. "Harmony and Daemyn are getting married alongside Tiernan and Harlequinn. All we have is each other!"

Daemyn grabbed Lucinda's arm before she could touch Hazelle again. "Actually, it does matter, because as of this moment, the engagement is off. I want to renew my engagement with Hazelle."

"See?" Hazelle said to Lucinda. "It all worked out in the end. I knew Daemyn would come back to his senses. Harmony is free to be with you now."

"Well, I don't love her anymore. I love you," Lucinda pressed. "Why would you want to be with Daemyn after the way he treated you? I've been nothing but kind to you. And what about how he treats Harmony and me? He's not going to change just because you want him to."

Hazelle let out a heavy sigh as she glanced between Daemyn and Lucinda. She didn't agree with the way he treated her friends, but she loved him despite that. Harmony had argued with her about this but it hadn't changed anything. She loved her best friend and didn't want Daemyn to slander her or Lucinda, but he was a different person around Hazelle. Her friends just didn't understand because they'd never seen that side of him. "Look, I'm sorry he said those things. He's not normally this vocal about it. I can't change the fact that I love him, though. Just remember that his opinions are not mine."

"The signals I got from you were different when we were dancing earlier," Lucinda protested. "Just admit it – you're into me. There's nothing wrong with that. I'm into you too."

Hazelle rolled her eyes. "I give up. I'm out of here." She shoved

Lucinda out of her way and marched up the stairs, Daemyn following close behind.

"Hazelle, wait!" Lucinda cried, hobbling up the stairs after them.

Harmony stood there, stunned. She couldn't believe what she was hearing. Was there something in the drinks the fairies had been offering? She was pretty certain she was the only one who hadn't had one yet. She'd wanted to keep her head clear for the escape. If they were drugged, though, that meant it would eventually wear off and Lucinda would come back to her senses. Maybe they could still make their escape if it wore off fast enough.

With that in mind, Harmony ran up the stairs in pursuit of her lover.

Act III, scene ii

Isra languished beside Tatiana on a makeshift bed of blankets in a large tent. He assumed it was meant for the king and queen of the supernatural. He had never had to please a Fae woman as part of a contract before, but he supposed there was a first time for everything. He hadn't had a chance to snoop around at all due to how demanding the queen had been. The life of a slave was busy indeed...especially when one's mistress was a nymphomaniac.

Glancing over his shoulder, he couldn't help but feel like he was being watched. He saw nothing out of the ordinary, however, and there were more pressing matters to attend to than his own paranoia. Since the fairy queen was sleeping, this was an opportune time to sneak away and investigate. He felt a pin prick sensation on the back of his neck a breath later. His vision blurred until it faded completely and he felt his body free-falling toward the bed.

Several moments passed before Revelin dared to dispel his invisibility. Their magician, Idris, might be full of complaints, but he knew what he was doing when it came to his potions. Revelin had administered the love elixir to Tatiana first while the "slave's" paranoia mounted. When he'd seen an opening, he'd taken his chance with Isra.

Once he reported back to Osiris, he could watch the rest of the chaos ensue after the ambush was in position. The last bit of this plan had taken entirely too long. He hoped the king wouldn't be cross that he wasn't yet ready to take down Tiernan and Harlequinn.

Pressing a button on his wrist tech, he made the call, glancing toward the two lovers nestled on the bed of linen while he waited.

"Where the hell have you been?" Osiris demanded as soon as the call was accepted. "I've been surveying the party, waiting for your report!"

"Apologies, my lord. The rave made it difficult to set up the assassination attempt, and there was still your wife and her plaything to contend with. Everything has been prepared now. I'm ready to go ahead with the ambush as soon as everyone is in position."

"I'll be right there." Osiris ended the call before Revelin could get another word in.

Revelin shrugged and turned to regard his queen and her new toy. "My, but she does have good taste," he lamented to himself.

"I'll take that as a compliment," Osiris replied as he stepped up to stand beside the spy. He regarded the couple, a look of displeasure apparent on his face. "She's been busy," he said flatly.

"Ah yes, busy enough to unnerve you, it seems." A smile played across Revelin's features.

Osiris ignored him, though he would have preferred to punch the bastard instead. He was quite aware of his humanity. He didn't need reminders.

Before he could ponder it further, however, Tatiana began to stir. Her arms and legs reached outward in a catlike stretch before she opened her eyes and sat up. She looked up at Osiris, almost as if she had no memory of her previous ire.

"Hello, handsome," she rasped. "Did you come to serve me my breakfast?"

Osiris knew she didn't mean food and he couldn't help the smile that spread across his face. "Had I the time, I would. I just wanted to check on you, and make sure you weren't still angry with me."

She collapsed back down on the bed with a sigh. "Will I ever have you to myself again? I'm starting to think you're hiding a sex pixie in your pants."

"I assure you I'm not," Osiris replied. "No one said ruling was easy, Tatiana. You knew what was in store before ever agreeing to marry me."

"Actually, I signed up for a husband that would remain in the background while the elders made all the decisions," she shot back. "Unfortunately, they all had the audacity to die."

"Someone has to secure our future, don't they?"

"Hire someone else to do it," his wife replied, glaring at him.

"I can't ask someone to risk their life in my place. You know that as well as I."

"Blah, blah blah," she mocked, rolling onto her side and closing her eyes. "Whatever. I'll be over here when you're ready to pay attention to me."

Osiris sighed in defeat. He didn't have time to deal with her sulking.

Just as he was about to leave, Isra woke up.

Osiris regarded the shirtless man cautiously. "Sleep well?"

Isra was disoriented when he first woke. He seemed to remember something about a job he had to do, but everything became clear when he heard that voice. He saw Osiris standing proudly, arms crossed over his chest while he stared expectantly at him. He glanced over at Tatiana, before remembering what they'd done not long before.

"Forgive me," Isra pleaded, keeping his gaze level with Osiris'. "I now know my error. You are the one I serve."

Osiris wasn't certain how to take that. Was he referring only to the fact that he'd had sexual relations with Tatiana, or something more sinister? He didn't have time to respond before the man continued.

"I have been keeping secrets from you, my lord. I know that these actions are unforgivable. I am a hired assassin, sent here under the guise of a slave to learn your intentions toward Tiernan." Isra bowed his head, holding his hands out in a prayer. "It was wrong, I know. My head is clear now."

"You were sent here simply to find out if I would betray Tiernan?"

"Primarily, yes. If I discovered that you were planning to betray him, I was to kill you." Isra sat up on his haunches and leaned forward, touching his head to the ground. "Forgive me."

"Are you his only spy?"

"Yes, but there is something else you must know. Something I wasn't certain of before I met you, but that I now know is true."

Osiris arched an inquisitive brow. "What is it?"

"You and Tiernan share the same blood, my lord."

Act IV, scene i

Osiris walked blindly, his head spinning. His mother had died while giving birth to him. His father disowned him and had ordered him to be killed. His brother thought he was dead. They were enemies, leading a war against one another, kings of their respective people.

At first, he refused to believe it could be true, but he recalled those piercing eyes. He remembered staring into them and feeling a shudder run through his spine. Harlequinn had looked between him and Tiernan oddly and then looked at Tatiana, as if to compare their eyes. It made sense now. His jade eyes – the exact color of Tiernan's – had a distinctly human look, unlike Tatiana's.

Isra's mother had saved his life and paid with her own. The spy had kept this information to himself all these years while he was passed off to the assassin's guild and trained in the ways of murder. With one word, he could have changed his fate and doomed Osiris to death as an infant.

"I know this to be true because of your unique physical traits. You were perfectly white, even at birth. They worried you were stillborn until they realized what you were. When they saw the mark, they wouldn't let your brother see you. My mother was the midwife and I was her assistant. I recognized you as soon as I laid eyes on you."

Isra's voice echoed in Osiris' mind, but he still couldn't make himself believe it. How could this be? It was a fate too cruel for any person to endure. How would Tiernan react if he were to learn the truth? Kill him on sight, he supposed, but he still had to try. Tiernan was the only blood relation Osiris had. All of those idealistic goals he'd had as a young king flooded back to him, seemingly in reach for the first time in his life.

He ran for the ship, Revelin at his heels. If he didn't intervene before the poison killed Harmony and her fiancé, he would lose his only chance to know his family and have peace for his people. Now that he knew the truth about his lineage, he had no desire to continue the war between humans and Fae. All he'd ever wanted was a family. As long as Tiernan never learned the truth of his original plans, he might finally be able to have that.

Halting suddenly, Osiris caused Revelin to run into him. The king raised an arm to keep him still. He thought he'd heard screaming.

As if on cue, Hazelle marched through the foliage. "Stop following me, Lucinda!"

"And allow Daemyn to be alone with you? No way in hell."

"But that's what I want!" Hazelle exclaimed, whipping around to glare at her. "Bloody hell, would you snap out of it already? You don't really love me. You love Harmony!"

"I'm over Harmony," Lucinda insisted, crossing her arms over her chest. "I only want you."

"No, you don't, and I don't want you, either." She ran a hand over her face in frustration. "All I want is for you to leave me alone."

"Out here in the middle of nowhere? You're joking, right?" Lucinda scoffed. Besides, I felt the connection between us, and I've seen how Daemyn treats women that aren't all about his manly bits. Do you really want that life? Shut your face, have some babies, put dinner on the table at seven every night," she mocked, her voice taking on gruff undertones as she perfectly mimicked Daemyn's haughty tone. "If I leave you with him, you might start hating yourself even more than you already do."

"I don't hate myself, Lucinda. I *really* am straight! Straight as an arrow." Hazelle made a disgusted noise. "Not that you're *actually* listening," she added and stormed off again.

"Hmm, that's odd," Revelin mused aloud as he and Osiris watched them take yet another path further into the forest.

"What?"

"As far as I knew, Lucinda truly was in love with Harmony…and now she claims she isn't." Revelin rubbed his chin thoughtfully. His thoughts stole back to the visit to Idris' laboratory. The old fairy had complained of his workload, how he had yet to finish with the portal. There were more vials than Revelin could count in that little cubbie, and with the lack of sleep… "Could Idris have given me the wrong vials?"

"I didn't ask you to administer anything to that red-haired woman, did I?"

"No, but it was rather dark in the rave," Revelin told the fairy king. "Perhaps I mistook her for Harmony. Since the woman is alive and well, the only way to know for sure is to find Harmony and make sure she isn't dying or dead already."

As if to answer his question, Harmony came bursting into the clearing next, very much alive. She looked around frantically before following Lucinda and Hazelle's path. Daemyn followed close behind, calling Hazelle's name.

"Daemyn was obsessed with Harmony before today." Revelin watched the humans with mounting amusement, realizing exactly what he'd done.

"It appears you did indeed blunder, then." Osiris laughed.

"Well Fuck Face on a stick." Revelin sighed. "You're not going to let me live that one down any time soon. I'll get the antidotes."

Act IV, scene ii

"Lesbo bitch!" Daemyn swung his fist, landing a hard blow to Lucinda's face and knocking her to the ground. That punch felt great, but he wasn't satisfied. He straddled Lucinda and continued to hit her.

"Daemyn, stop!" Hazelle screamed. "She didn't mean any harm!"

"It was just something she drank. Please don't hurt her!" Harmony pleaded.

Harmony and Hazelle both stood to the side while Daemyn pummeled Lucinda in a fit of rage. They looked at each other helplessly for a few seconds before something clicked. They rushed over, each grabbing one of Daemyn's arms and pulling with all their strength. They managed to get him off the other woman long enough for

Lucinda to regain her feet. While they still held Daemyn's arms, Lucinda started kicking him in the stomach.

"Asshole!" Lucinda held her nose with one hand to stem the bleeding, using the other to balance herself while she continued to kick.

"Lucinda, stop!" Harmony grabbed onto her other arm to get her attention. "There's something seriously wrong with both of you. It has to be whatever you drank at the party!"

"I don't give a shit," Lucinda growled, pulling her arm out of Harmony's grasp. "He made my life hell when I loved you, and now he's doing it again. He's the problem and I'm solving it here and now. Fucker tried to kill me earlier anyway. I'm just returning the favor."

Hazelle pushed her way between Lucinda and Daemyn while the nobleman lay on the ground, attempting to recover his breath. "I'm sorry he tried to kill you and I'm sorry he broke your nose, but I love him. I won't let you hurt him!"

Lucinda stopped and whirled around, throwing her hands up in the air. "What the hell is wrong with you? He's a hateful son of a bitch and you're protecting him! When are you going to open your eyes and see that? He isn't worth it, Hazelle!"

Hazelle glanced away from Lucinda, crossing her arms over her chest. "Because it's so easy to give up on the one person who loved you in your darkest hour, right? He's all I've got. You had Harmony and you threw her away like she was nothing, just like Daemyn did with me. What does that say about you? You're no better than he is," she said defensively.

Disgusted, Lucinda stormed away from Hazelle and Daemyn. She wasn't going to allow herself to be compared to that piece of shit. The throbbing in her broken nose only seemed to get worse. "Damn it, I wish I had some morphine right now," Lucinda muttered before she collapsed to the ground.

The other three stared at her limp body for only a moment before falling one by one.

As soon as they were out cold, Osiris and Revelin dispelled their invisibility.

"Hurry and give them the antidote," Revelin ordered. Osiris bent over Lucinda and healed her broken nose. The sleeping draught they gave them would only last a few minutes, just long enough to make their recent adventure nothing more than a fuzzy dream.

"Only one of them needs it," Revelin informed the fairy king. "Apparently, Daemyn was supposed to marry Hazelle. Unfortunately, he became infatuated with blondie over there.

"Well, give it to whoever needs it and be quick about it." Osiris finished up with Lucinda's wounds and moved to Daemyn.

The fairy spy pranced over to Lucinda like he was putting on a theatrical show for a crowd of onlookers. Osiris could only shake his head and sigh.

Revelin pulled out a needle filled with clear liquid and injected it into Lucinda's neck. "This lady is supposed to be in love with blondie, so if we leave the other one as he is, their issue will be resolved."

Osiris arched a brow curiously. "Why would you care about a mortal's issues?"

"I don't, but since your brother seems to, I figured I was doing you a favor." Revelin jumped up and saluted. "Tiernan offered to marry Harmony and Daemyn beside himself and Harlequinn. He was hoping this peace treaty panned out so he could abolish the uterus selling law."

"How do you know that?" Osiris didn't think Tiernan would have voiced something like that aloud, especially not in front of people like Edric, who would view it as a weakness.

Revelin tapped his chin thoughtfully, and then held his finger up in the air as if he had just figured it out. "I suppose he has similar mannerisms to you, my lord. I could tell that he cared about Harmony's plight, despite threatening her."

Osiris smirked a bit. "I'm surprised you're even using their names."

"I didn't think you would want me to keep calling your brother Fuck Face, although I rather liked it myself," Revelin shrugged.

Osiris chuckled, but their conversation was cut short. Harmony began to stir, so they disappeared from sight once more to allow the youths to sort out what had just happened. The fairy king had more pressing matters to attend to.

Harmony groaned as she sat up in the grass, glancing around. "What happened?" She spotted the other three lying in the grass as well and crawled over to Lucinda. She grabbed her shoulders and shook her, fear slicing through her insides. "Lucinda, can you hear me? Wake up!"

Lucinda's face contorted into an expression of displeasure. She grumbled, rolling over to face Harmony before opening her eyes reluctantly. "What?" When she realized where she was, she sat up, looking around. "What the hell?"

"My sentiments exactly." Harmony pushed herself to her feet and turned her attention over to Hazelle, and then to Daemyn. "Try to wake Hazelle," she told Lucinda as she walked over to the nobleman. She was about to poke him with her toe to wake him when Lucinda halted her actions.

"Wait, shouldn't we go?" Lucinda asked, glancing around. "No witnesses around. Now is the perfect time to make our escape."

"You expect me to just leave my friend and the man she's desperately in love with lying here without making sure they're okay?" Harmony arched an accusatory brow. "As much as I would love for the pompous ass to die in his sleep, Hazelle would be beside herself with grief and I wouldn't be there for her. We're making sure they're not hurt, and then we leave." With that, she pressed the tip of her boot into his side before Lucinda could protest.

Daemyn reflexively stretched before opening his eyes and staring up at Harmony's face. He blinked, utterly confused and somewhat fearful as to the reason he was lying on the ground with Harmony bent over him. "Did we…?"

"Ew, no," Harmony replied, disgust written on her face. "Still think penis is gross."

He visibly relaxed. "Good." He got up and glanced around, all the while completely ignoring the look of confusion on Harmony's face. "Hazelle?" He looked over to where her body lay sprawled on the ground and saw Lucinda bent over her. His blood instantly boiled. "What do you think you're doing?" He marched over and grabbed the woman's shoulder.

"Trying to wake her." Lucinda pulled her shoulder away. "What's your problem?"

Daemyn didn't reply, instead shoving Lucinda aside to kneel beside

Hazelle as she began to stir. He pulled her body against his chest. "Are you alright, Beloved?"

Hazelle reached up to rub her eyes before opening them. She stared mutely at Daemyn for a moment. She'd honestly thought she'd dreamed the whole thing, but there he was. "I am now." She smiled.

"Wait, hold on," Harmony cut in. "You're in love with Hazelle again? Since when?"

Daemyn glanced up at Harmony blankly, clearly no more knowledgeable about his sudden change of heart than she was. "I…don't know. I was more concerned that we'd had drunk sex, to be honest. My priority is Hazelle, not curing you of your unfortunate affliction."

Harmony's eyes shrank into slits. "I'm not buying that. You seriously wouldn't try to stop us if Lucinda and I tried to leave?"

"While Hazelle isn't well, I couldn't care less what you decide to do. In accordance to the law, though, I would have to report you both once I return to the party."

Harmony scoffed. "We both know how that turned out for Hazelle the first time you got engaged."

"Do you want it in writing?" Daemyn said flatly. "Don't get me wrong, I don't agree with homosexuality. You should be marrying a man who can give you children to carry on your family's legacy, not disgracing your father with this nonsense." He grunted when Hazelle nudged him in the side with her elbow, but he ignored it to finish. "However, barring the law that states you are to marry a male and procreate – which, in case you haven't noticed, is extremely important for our generation – I am not interested in anything you or your girlfriend decide to do."

"Fine. I guess that will have to do." Harmony turned around and started walking in the opposite direction. "Let's go, Lucinda."

"Harmony, wait!" Hazelle shouted.

The blond turned to regard her friend. "What is it? We have to go."

"I believe him," Hazelle said. "It's dangerous to traverse through a forest you're not familiar with, even if the fairies don't try to kill you. Why risk it when you might not have to? Your father can't do anything if Daemyn cancels the engagement, right?"

"Even if he is telling the truth, there's nothing to stop my father from finding me another suitor." Harmony sighed. "I want to believe it's safe to stay, trust me. Do you think I want to leave you behind? If he hurts you, who will throat punch him for you?" She smiled, her eyes sparkling with unshed tears. "But honestly, this is our only chance. If I'm going to pass this up, I have to be certain I won't regret it."

"I give you my word that I will cancel the engagement," Daemyn assured her. "Honestly, I could easily discourage every nobleman I know from seeking out your hand. It wouldn't be hard, given your condition."

Hazelle elbowed him again. Harmony regarded him with a doubtful eye before glancing at her friend's hopeful face once more. She sighed again. "Damn it, Hazelle, why do you have to look at me like that?"

Hazelle couldn't help the smile that spread across her face. "I'm sorry, I just...I don't want to lose you. Is that so wrong?"

"No," Harmony groaned. "No it's not." She glared at Daemyn one more time. "I swear to God that if we get home and you take this back, I will make sure you never have offspring. Is that clear?"

"Crystal." Daemyn nodded curtly.

"Now the only question that remains is why the hell we're out here." Harmony put her hands on her hips and took a look around at the unfamiliar landscape. "And how do we get back?"

Daemyn helped Hazelle up, not even bothering to look at Harmony when he answered, "I don't know. I woke up thinking Lucinda was trying to turn Hazelle into a lesbian."

Lucinda turned to Daemyn and looked at him incredulously. "You can't change someone's sexuality, genius." She stopped for a second and thought about it. "Though I think I remember having a similar dream..."

"I remember that too," Harmony replied.

"So do I," Hazelle agreed. "But why would we all have the same dream?"

"I also remember Lucinda and Daemyn wailing on each other. Daemyn broke her nose, but it's not broken now, so..." Harmony turned to regard each of them. "It had to be a dream, right?"

"Yeah, definitely." Hazelle nodded. "Their wounds wouldn't have just...disappeared if it'd been real."

"Well, you did make me drink something strange at the party," Lucinda suggested to Hazelle.

"I drank something too," Daemyn admitted, scratching the back of his head.

"I don't remember drinking anything," Harmony said. "Maybe someone slipped me something, or...maybe there was something in the air at the party?"

"Well, there's no other explanation, right?" Hazelle pointed out. "If it wasn't a dream, they would be in rough shape, but they're not."

Harmony nodded hesitantly. "Yeah, I guess you're right. So how do we get back?"

"Are you all lost?" Nobody was there when they looked around.

"Where are you?" Harmony asked. "Show yourself."

Revelin appeared, hanging upside down from a tree branch. He launched himself into a flip and landed on the ground backwards.

The four youths gawked at him as he turned around and bowed, a smile on his face.

"Revelin's the name, children. How may I be of service?"

"We're lost." Harmony crossed her arms over her chest. "Can you help us?"

"Indeed I can," Revelin replied before disappearing and reappearing behind them all. "This way."

"I think we might still be drugged," Hazelle murmured to no one in particular as they grouped together and followed him.

Act V, scene i

Osiris had prepared the necessary documents, but if he wanted Tiernan to believe him, he needed someone else to back it up. That meant undoing the elixir's effects on Isra and convincing him to confirm the story's truth. How easy that would be depended on how much Isra despised the Fae. There was also the minor detail of Osiris having the love elixir injected into the spy in the first place. Never mind that the man's mother had died saving the fairy king's life and consigned her son's fate to that of an assassin. For all Osiris knew, Isra held all those things, and more, against him.

When he arrived at his tent, Isra was sitting outside the entrance, his legs crossed and arms folded. When he saw Osiris, he immediately stood up straight and then bowed. "Welcome home, my lord."

Osiris scratched his neck awkwardly, waiting for the man to rise before addressing him. He glanced toward the opening of the tent, noticing his wife's absence. "Where's Tatiana?"

"She grew bored and decided to go to the party. I remained here in case you had need of me."

Osiris relaxed, glad that Tatiana was somewhere safe. He didn't want her to be here when he gave Isra the antidote, just in case things got ugly. He made a mental note to have Revelin find her and administer the antidote to her as well. For now, though, he concentrated on the situation at hand.

He regarded the young man standing before him. He wasn't comfortable with Isra's engineered sense of loyalty toward him, though it would allow him to explain the situation without getting gutted, for now at least. "Isra, I'm afraid the adoration you feel for me is falsified." Before Isra could protest, Osiris held up a hand and elaborated. "I had you injected with an elixir. I wanted to ensure that you weren't a threat to my wife or me. I didn't expect to hear what you told me about Tiernan."

Isra remained silent, looking pensive.

"I understand you'll probably be angry with me once I administer the antidote. I won't hold that against you, but I do intend to broach this subject with my brother. The problem is that he won't believe me. I need you to confirm it because he trusts you. I don't intend to harm him or anyone he has brought here, not even you, though your given mission was to kill me. However, I'm hoping your better judgment will help you make the right decision."

Osiris looked away, his hands forming fists as he thought about what telling Tiernan could mean for them both. He had never known his family. When he was a boy, he'd dreamed about what his mother looked like. He'd wondered if he had siblings, what it would have been like to grow up with one.

"I would like to know my family…my mother, my brother. I was told they abandoned me. While that may be true in our father's case, my brother didn't make that choice. I want to give him that opportunity now, even if he chooses not to know me."

Osiris wondered what Isra might be thinking. He was probably denying these things as truth. On the other hand, the concoction would cause him to trust Osiris with his life, encouraging him to believe the fairy.

"We need this peace treaty, Isra." He looked at the man earnestly. "Both the human and magical races will perish if we don't come together and work to heal this planet. Of that much, I am certain. So if nothing else, when I give you this antidote, believe that much. Believe that I want Tiernan to sign that peace treaty so that we can rebuild this world."

Isra faltered, seemingly unsure of how to reply. "If what you say is true, my lord, then I will try to believe you. I do not know for certain how I will react because these falsified emotions, as you call them, feel so real. I expect to feel the same way once you have injected it, but if not, my original orders were to kill you only if you planned to betray Tiernan. If that is not the case, then I have no reason to do so."

He stared up into Osiris' eyes, though the fairy wasn't certain what the assassin was trying to communicate.

"I do not take pleasure in murder; it is only my profession. I hold no grudge against you. I did not even know if you survived until today. I was just as surprised to see you as you were to learn of your history. I had only hoped my mother's sacrifice was not in vain."

"It wasn't," Osiris told him earnestly. "I assure you I want peace now more than anything. Let's do that now." With that, he removed the needle with the antidote from a pouch on his waist and injected it into Isra's neck.

When Osiris pulled away, the assassin regarded him with an unreadable expression. Isra said nothing, but pushed a button on his wrist. The slave's garb he'd been wearing pixelated, enveloping his skin in black numbers. It expanded and solidified, reforming into a black bodysuit. "Part of me is irritated enough by this humiliation to entertain thoughts of slitting your throat. However, I will refrain from doing so."

"Well, you did end up having sexual relations with my wife," Osiris retorted. "Several times, I might add."

Isra shifted uncomfortably where he stood and cleared his throat. "We'll call it even."

"Oh good. Friends, then?" Osiris smiled.

"We'll see," Isra replied. "Let's go."

As Osiris walked down the path that led back to the ship, he was filled with trepidation. His heart pounded against his chest in a way he hadn't felt since his first meeting with Tatiana. He felt an exuberant amount of hope, and a tendril of dread that gnawed its way through his stomach.

He looked over his shoulder at Isra. It made him nervous to have an assassin at his back, but he understood why the man chose to be cautious. After all, the fairy king had arranged for Isra to be injected with a concoction that caused him to say and do things he otherwise wouldn't have. It was embarrassing for the assassin's reputation, not to mention his pride.

"How do you think he'll react?" Osiris asked, unsure if he wanted to hear the answer.

"Truthfully?" When Osiris nodded, Isra continued, "I don't know. The truth of it is that Tiernan blames the Fae for destroying his family. He hates them as passionately as he loves Harlequinn. He takes joy in causing them pain."

He fell silent, trying to gauge how Osiris was taking the information. The fairy's gaze remained glued to the path ahead.

"Not long ago, his greatest aspiration was to wipe magical beings off the face of the planet. He sees it as justice after how the radiation changed humanity. He believes you are dead because that is what his father told him before he drank himself to death." Isra stopped, his eyes closing tightly for a moment. "These are not things I ever wished to revisit, but we remained friends simply because it was not his crime. I don't hold Tiernan responsible for my mother's death any more than you. I didn't believe telling him you might be alive would change the way he felt about your kind, so I never broached the subject."

Osiris met Isra's gaze unwaveringly and nodded his understanding, even if he did feel as if he'd just been punched in the gut. "Well, at least my expectations have been set," he commented dryly before heading up the dock toward the ship.

"For what it's worth, I believe he would be making a mistake if he dismissed your relation to him."

Osiris supposed Isra felt guilty for delivering the bad news that Tiernan may not take the new information well. He'd already known that it was a possibility, considering Tiernan's history with his people. However, there had still been a sliver of hope that the fairy king was wrong. Asking Isra how Tiernan might react only confirmed what he'd already surmised.

"Thanks." He turned his attention toward the door in front of him, which led to the party and his brother. "I'd already guessed as much, but I couldn't help but hope things might be different."

"They still might be," Isra said. "Sometimes things change when a family member is involved."

"Sometimes," Osiris repeated, sighing. "Has 'sometimes' happened with other magical born children?"

"I'm not aware of any others," Isra answered. "But it always starts with one."

A smile slowly crept across Osiris' face as he headed into the dark doorway.

Act V, scene ii

Osiris headed into the bowels of the ship with Isra on his heel. Nobody even bothered to cast them a glance. Tiernan's guests were too caught up in the buzz of the party to pay attention to the odd looking duo. The euphoric concoction he'd had Idris make appeared to be working well. They passed several couples writhing against the walls, but the music was far too loud to hear their interactions. Many others were dancing, grinding, and having fun while the harmless elixir ran its course.

Osiris and Isra combed the crowd, but the dim lighting and the bodies pressed tightly together made their search for Tiernan difficult. Osiris stopped various fairies, asking them to track Tiernan down. Once they had made their rounds, he hung back at the stairs to wait for word.

When word finally came, it was in the form of a skimpily clad Fae woman. She swayed her hips, flirting with several guests as she passed. "I've been entertaining the lord and his companion for hours now, my king. Do you wish to put the plan into motion?"

Osiris shook his head. "The plan is off, but I would like to speak with him."

Her ruby lips pulled up into a half smile. "Of course." She headed northeast with Osiris and Isra following behind.

They found Tiernan and Harlequinn pressed together against the wall. It was strangely vacant on this side, affording the couple the illusion of privacy.

Osiris quickly looked away, raising his fist against his mouth and clearing his throat. He pretended he couldn't make out Harlequinn's vocal responses. It was one thing to find out his enemy was his brother. It was another thing entirely to catch his brother in such a…compromising position.

"Bring me the antidote for this concoction," Osiris told the Fae woman while his back was turned to the couple.

The woman disappeared into the crowd, returning a moment later with two syringes filled with a turquoise liquid.

Osiris took them from her and uncapped the needles, passing one to Isra, who arched a brow. "Administer this to Tiernan while I give the other to Harlequinn. They should have clear heads when we discuss this."

"Another one of your elixirs caused this?" Isra asked, almost as if he was skeptical.

"Amazing what a bit of magic and science can do, isn't it?" Osiris replied in kind. "Though I could have done without the image of Tiernan's ass seared into my mind."

They approached the couple from behind. Osiris moved to Harlequinn's side as she arched her back and let out a moan, squeezing

Tiernan's waist tighter. He injected the fluid into her neck, and Isra did the same with Tiernan.

When the couple opened their eyes to stare at each other blankly, the two men backed off.

"What are we...?" Harlequinn started before she looked down, realizing just what they were doing.

Osiris was certain that she was beet red, though he wasn't able to properly confirm it under the lighting.

Tiernan and Harlequinn hastily separated and pulled their clothes back in order.

Osiris waited for them to look presentable before he cleared his throat and tapped his brother on the shoulder.

When Tiernan turned to regard Osiris, the fairy king didn't miss the quick glance toward Isra first. He looked embarrassed, but curious as well as guarded. "Osiris...how long have you been standing there?"

"Not long," he replied, offering a polite smile. "I just wanted to check that you both are enjoying the party."

Tiernan nodded. "Perhaps a little too much." He chuckled nervously.

"Wonderful." Osiris didn't want Tiernan to think he'd seen anything. Best to pretend it never happened.

"Was there something you wanted to discuss?"

Osiris couldn't blame him for wanting to change the subject. He shared his sentiments for different reasons. "Best to do it somewhere quieter." He held out a hand to guide him to the stairs. Both Tiernan and Harlequinn walked ahead of him while he and Isra followed.

Once outside, Osiris was at a loss for words. His stomach did backflips and his head tingled. He wondered if his brain was trying to numb his panic, or if the panic was numbing his ability to formulate intelligible sentences.

Tiernan regarded both Osiris and Isra anxiously. He wasn't certain what Isra's lack of disguise meant, nor why Osiris wanted to speak with him. It could be as simple as wanting to discuss signing the peace treaty. Or, worse, had Osiris discovered his plan to assassinate him and convinced Isra to side with the Fae instead? If it was the latter, then this might be the beginning of a bloodbath. He could only guess at the implications as he waited for an explanation.

"Please, your majesty. We are on the edge of our seats," Harlequinn chimed in, obviously sharing Tiernan's unease. "Won't you tell us what this is about?"

Osiris glanced over at Harlequinn. He had to find some way to ease the tension, or just get on with it. "Forgive me, I did not mean to perturb either of you. I, myself, am disquieted simply because I have learned something I…was not expecting. This information is sensitive to us all, which is why I wanted to speak to you privately about it." Osiris paused, glancing at them. He saw their confusion.

"Is this about the peace treaty, or perhaps the cure for infertility you mentioned was in the works?" Tiernan asked warily.

"Not directly, no. It does encourage me to push for the peace treaty more now than ever, however."

"Well, I think it's best if you come right out and say it, Osiris," Tiernan replied impatiently.

Osiris noticed Harlequinn elbow him in the side. They shared a glare before Tiernan turned his attention back toward him. "Forgive me, but I dislike subtleties. I'm a leader, not a politician. I've no time to guess at insinuations."

"I understand." Osiris inhaled deeply, holding it a moment before exhaling in a long sigh. "I don't know how to say this delicately. I recently learned that we are family."

The silence only made Osiris' anxiety deepen. He looked first at Harlequinn, who was staring incredulously at Tiernan. When he looked to his brother, his face was unreadable. The lines of his clenched jaw were firm.

"What are you implying?" Tiernan's question was accusative, guarded, even a little angry.

Osiris crossed his arms over his chest, as if to protect himself from the oncoming rejection. "I am implying that the sibling you thought was dead…isn't."

"You never told me you had a brother!" Harlequinn exclaimed. "Much less a brother born of magical origins!"

Tiernan didn't know what to say. All he knew was that it couldn't be true. "I didn't feel it needed mentioning. My 'brother' is dead. My father ordered it." He moved his gaze over to linger on Isra. "And what purpose do you serve by accompanying him, Isra? Have you betrayed me?"

"No," Isra addressed his friend calmly. "I am here because what Osiris says is true. Your brother did not die that night."

Tiernan stared at Isra. He was unable, or perhaps unwilling, to believe what his childhood friend was telling him. "How?"

"It was a long time ago… Perhaps you have forgotten," Isra suggested, "But I assisted my mother with your brother's birth. I knew what he looked like, what he was. I heard your father give the order, and I witnessed my mother disobey it."

Tiernan stared at the assassin for several moments while he attempted to wrap his head around these claims. He still couldn't bring himself to believe it. It all sounded too coincidental, too unrealistic. He knew that Isra had been present, and perhaps even heard his father give the order that the infant be killed. How was it possible that the assassin's mother would also decide to disobey that order? How would she have gotten the baby out of the city? How would Isra even know that Osiris was the same person?

Tiernan realized he was pacing and forced himself to stop. He turned back to Isra, their eyes locking in a battle of wills. "Even if that was true and everything just happened to fall into place, how could you recognize my brother as an adult? The child was a newborn! You cannot simply look at Osiris and decide he must be my long lost brother. There is no proof. Barring that, there could be several supernatural creatures that look similar."

"Not so," came a voice from behind Tiernan.

Osiris saw Tatiana emerging from the doorway, and they shared a look that told him in no uncertain terms that she had not appreciated being drugged. To her credit, though, she did not insist on addressing that now.

Tiernan turned around to regard the Fae woman. "You were part of the audition, were you not? Do you mean to tell me you know what every last supernatural on this earth looks like?"

"Yes I was, and yes I do," Tatiana stated. "There aren't many of us left, thanks to you."

Tiernan's mouth flattened into a hard line as he stared into the woman's silver eyes. "Yes, well, your kind did nearly drive humanity to extinction."

Before Tatiana could reply, Osiris stepped between them, staring into Tiernan's eyes sternly. "Those details have nothing to do with our current discussion." He looked at Tatiana in turn and communicated with his expression that she was to play nice.

Tatiana squinted at him, as if to challenge him, but she said nothing more on the matter. Instead, she pushed past him and stood in front of Tiernan, her hand on her hip. "Tatiana – Osiris' wife, queen of the Fae. A pleasure." She walked past him before turning to regard all three of them. "I can confirm with certainty that no other fairy or halfbreed alive looks quite like my Osiris. His eyes, specifically, are an oddity."

"He does have your eyes," Harlequinn murmured into Tiernan's ear.

Tiernan glanced at his fiancée before turning back to Tatiana and Osiris. He had noticed the similarity and even then, it had disturbed him. There'd been something about the fairy king's mannerisms that had set him on edge. He'd ignored it, passing it off as unease because Osiris had come into his home unannounced and uninvited. He didn't address Harlequinn's comment, though. Instead, he focused on the fact that he'd apparently met the queen of fairies and had no idea. "Interesting how you never introduced us previously."

"We were in what you admitted was dangerous territory," Osiris replied. "Not only was there no need to bring attention to her, but I wanted to ensure that most of the attention was on me. You would have taken similar precautions for your own spouse had you been in my position." He gave Tatiana another look mixed with both adoration and irritation. "She wasn't even supposed to be there, but women are stubborn creatures."

Tiernan had to grudgingly admit that he would indeed have done the same thing. In fact, he would have tried to go without her even knowing. The likeness made him uncomfortable.

"If you wish me to believe this claim, I need proof." Tiernan looked Osiris in the eye. "A DNA test."

Osiris hadn't expected that outcome. It seemed entirely too positive. Perhaps he'd underestimated how important it was to Tiernan to cure the infertility problems humanity was burdened with. "Very well," the fairy king agreed. "How do you wish to proceed?"

"One of mine and one of yours will run the test under the supervision of a neutral party to ensure the results have not been falsified. If we are a match in both tests, we will both concede to the results, whatever they may be."

"And the peace treaty?"

"If I have your word that you will fix the infertility issues your people caused, I will sign it, whether our DNA matches or not."

Harlequinn squealed and threw her arms around Tiernan's neck, which made it difficult for him to look imposing. He finally gave up and cracked a smile. When he looked across the deck, he saw a matching smile on Osiris' face.

Act VI, scene i

Tiernan stared at himself in the full body mirror. He took extra care smoothing the wrinkles out of his white button down shirt. He had combed back his hair, allowing Harlequinn to braid it as she pleased. Even now, he was straightening his belt buckle and Harlequinn laughed at him while she lounged in their king sized bed.

He peered at her in the looking glass and she gazed back, holding her head up with her hand, amusement dancing in her eyes. "What's so funny?"

Harlequinn pushed herself off the bed. "Any idiot could tell that you are stalling, my love." She was wearing his shirt from the previous night and it billowed around her thighs as she came close to nibble on his ear.

Tiernan smiled; she knew him so well. "What of it?"

She twined her arms around his neck from behind, her voice taking on that playful tone he adored. "Stalling isn't going to change the results."

"It isn't easy to face, my sweet." Tiernan sighed. "I'd be lying if I said I didn't dread it. It could change everything I've ever believed…"

"It could force you to face the fact that perhaps our actions against Fae kind were wrong."

Tiernan hadn't wanted to face that truth. He could hide nothing from Harlequinn, though. She'd always been willing to face what he couldn't or wouldn't.

"We can't change the past," she said finally. "The best we can do is try to make amends by building a new future."

Tiernan clasped her hands in his and turned to look at her directly. "Will you come with me?"

"Of course." She stepped back to find herself something to wear.

Once ready, they left their bedroom together and headed for the laboratory located in the basement of his mansion.

Osiris was already waiting for them, along with Tatiana, Revelin and Isra. The magician and scientist had already started the test under Isra and Revelin's supervision. They did their work behind a glass window with all the occupants watching.

Tiernan shook Osiris' hand, and then they turned their attention to Revelin and Isra.

"Is it done?" Osiris asked.

Isra nodded while Revelin bowed deeply for show. The fairy straightened and laid his hand on his chest dramatically. "Yes, my lord."

"You're certain it's been done properly?" Tiernan asked, his eyes directed toward the joker. He found it difficult to take the strange fairy seriously. If anyone had falsified the results, his bet was on Revelin.

"As much as it pained me to do so, yes," Revelin confirmed, his voice taking on a strained tone. "I would never jeopardize anything so important to our people!"

"That's enough, Rev'," Osiris said with a sigh.

Tiernan arched his brows at Revelin's rather odd display. "Is he always like that?"

"Indeed. He's a jester at heart, but he's so damn good at espionage that I can't retire him." The fairy king shrugged. "You eventually learn to dismiss it."

"You're certain he wouldn't falsify the test just to deceive us?"

"He would under normal circumstances," Osiris replied. "But not this time."

"What makes this time different?"

"He knows how important this is to me."

Tiernan looked at Osiris curiously. "How important *is* this to you, exactly?"

Osiris looked at Tiernan, not an ounce of insincerity in his jade eyes. "The only thing that is more pressing to me is the safety of my people." He paused, glancing away. "I have never had a true family. When Revelin brought me back to Oakhart Village, the elders did their best to provide me with what children need. It was no replacement for a real family. I have never known the joy of a father's pride, a mother's love, or a sibling's loyalty. Revelin is the closest I have to that kind of kinship, but still, it is not the same. If the results of this test are positive, I may be able to have that…" Osiris chanced a glance back at Tiernan. "If you choose to give it to me."

Tiernan continued to stare at Osiris even after the fairy king looked away. He hadn't expected such a heartfelt confession. This entire situation was nothing like he'd expected. He would have never dreamed that Osiris would want that kind of relationship with him. Certainly he figured they could get along well enough to make the peace treaty work. However, the fact that the fairy held no ill will towards him after the cruel things he'd done was inconceivable.

"You would choose to forgive me just to know what it is to have family ties?" Tiernan asked. It seemed unreal to him.

"Yes," Osiris affirmed. "Family should come above all else. Don't you agree?"

Tiernan nodded, though Osiris didn't see it. "Yes I do."

The door to the testing area swung open and the magician and scientist came out, one after the other.

"We have the results," Quintin announced, holding out a document to Tiernan, while Idris did the same for Osiris.

Both men took the documents and unfolded them to read the results. Then, they looked up at each other, searching for something from the other's gaze.

Tatiana leaned back against a nearby table, watching Osiris make eyes at his brother. "Could you two speed up the bromance and hug already?"

Osiris hesitated, unsure if Tiernan would want to embrace. He didn't have to wonder once Tiernan himself closed the distance. They patted each other on the back before parting with matching grins.

Harlequinn clapped her hands together, smiling. "Does that mean Osiris gets to be the best man?"

Tiernan regarded Harlequinn almost as if he was embarrassed. "I've already asked Isra, Darling."

"If you don't mind," Osiris interrupted, "I would actually prefer to have the honor of marrying you."

Tiernan looked surprised. "Are you certain?"

"I wouldn't dream of taking his place at your side," Osiris assured him. "We've only just found out we're family. I don't want to cause any rifts."

When Tiernan looked to Isra, the man merely shrugged his shoulders and smiled. "It's your wedding, my friend."

"Well, since you offered," Tiernan said finally, "We would be delighted to have you perform the ceremony, Osiris." He flicked his gaze to his bride-to-be, asking, "Wouldn't we, Love?"

Harlequinn nodded her agreement.

"Wonderful." The fairy king grinned. "I looked forward to it." He turned his attention to Idris. "Be sure to have the infertility cure ready for tomorrow night."

"Then I'd best get back to my lab and get to work," the old fairy harrumphed. He muttered something under his breath about never sleeping again as he exited the lab.

Tatiana followed behind the magician, and Osiris was about to enter the portal when they heard the faint sound of shouting down the hall. Pausing, the fairy king exchanged confused glances with Tiernan and the remainder of the group milled out into the hall to see what the commotion was.

"Get out of my way! I require an audience with Lord Tiernan immediately!"

Tiernan recognized the voice instantly and sighed. "Must be trouble in paradise again."

He approached the doorway that the guards had blocked Edric from entering and waved them aside. "What troubles you, my friend?"

Edric crossed his arms and glowered at Tiernan. "Daemyn has called off the engagement to my daughter. On top of that, Harmony had the insolence to rub her affliction in my face by insisting on parading in public with that peasant woman! This is unacceptable. We had an agreement that Daemyn and Harmony would marry tomorrow. Something needs to be done!"

As he continued to shout, the four youths hurried into the hallway behind him.

"Lord Tiernan…wait!" Harmony implored, panting when she came to a stop. "Please hear us out before you make a decision!"

Tiernan regarded the two couples thoughtfully. Harmony's eyes were filled with desperation as she clutched Lucinda's hand. Likewise, Hazelle clung to Daemyn's arm. The young man held himself with pride, obviously pleased with this new arrangement.

Tiernan shook his head at Edric's absurd expectations and shrugged. "I understand what you and Daemyn had previously agreed upon. However, Daemyn is permitted to change his mind, given that he has his guardian's consent. Since he has chosen another fertile woman to marry, there is nothing I can do."

"This is preposterous!" Edric cried. "I will not allow my daughter to marry a woman! Our lineage needs to be continued!"

"Normally that would be within your rights to decide," Tiernan replied calmly. "But recent events have brought to light a cure for infertility issues. As of today, I am abolishing that law. Harmony will be free to marry whomever she wishes."

The look Edric gave Tiernan made the king feel for his friend. He had always considered the law barbaric, however necessary it was to prevent the extinction of the human race. He understood how difficult it was to adapt to changes that were out of one's control, though.

Coming to terms with his relationship to the magical beings had meant changing his core beliefs, not just in the interests of Harlequinn, himself, or his people, but for the Fae as well. It had been easier to blame them for his misfortunes, to believe his brother was dead so that he wouldn't have to confront the worst parts of himself.

"You will never have my support again." Edric turned on his heel and marched back the way he came.

Tiernan sighed again, stung. He and Edric had been good friends once. Apparently that friendship only went as far as Tiernan was willing to accommodate Edric's wishes. That was no friendship at all.

"Father will come around."

Tiernan glanced up at Harmony, his eyes glazed with sadness.

She stepped forward and reached out to clasp one of his hands in both of her own. "He's just angry that he can't have his way, but he will forgive you." She smiled. "Thank you. You don't know how much it means to us."

Tiernan returned the gesture, and said, "I had promised your father that you would get married alongside Harlequinn and me. I don't suppose you'd still like to?"

Harmony glanced at Lucinda, who grinned at her. She turned her gaze back to Tiernan and nodded. "Hell, yeah!"

"And what of Hazelle and yourself, Daemyn? Looking to get married tomorrow?" Tiernan asked the young nobleman standing in the doorway.

Daemyn shook his head. "I must respectfully decline, my lord."

Hazelle pulled away to stare at him with a heartbroken expression. "You've changed your mind again?"

"Of course not," Daemyn assured her, smiling at her affectionately. "I simply don't wish to get married alongside…those two." He glanced at Harmony and Lucinda briefly, his lips curling in distaste. The smile once more slid into place as he turned back to stare into Hazelle's eyes.

Hazelle was too stunned to reply. Though it was well known Daemyn disapproved of Harmony and Lucinda's relationship, she'd thought it only extended as far as the law was concerned. Now that it was abolished, she had expected him to… She couldn't even think past her shock. Hazelle pulled away from his embrace and walked toward the mansion's exit without a word.

Harmony glowered at Daemyn. "Now I have to fix your mess."

"It's my fault I hold firm to my principles?" Daemyn retorted, glancing around the room for support and finding none.

"Go fuck yourself," Harmony snapped and stormed out after her friend.

Osiris nudged Revelin while the commotion was going on, silently making it clear that they may need an antidote for that love elixir after all. Tiernan and Osiris quickly said their goodbyes. There was still more preparations to be made for the wedding.

It didn't take Harmony long to find Hazelle. She was sitting on the steps in front of the mansion's entrance, hugging herself loosely.

"Hazelle?" she asked. "Are you okay?" She pulled Hazelle into a quick hug.

Hazelle stared at the ground before slowly raising her eyes to meet that concerned gaze. "I don't know. Maybe not."

"That unbelievable asshole," Harmony griped. "I'll rip his balls off and feed them to him."

Hazelle gave a halfhearted smile before a tear slid down her cheek.

"Oh, sweetie," Harmony murmured, embracing the girl once more. "It'll be okay. That idiot will apologize and let you get married alongside Lucinda and me. You'll see."

Hazelle shut her eyes tight and held back a sob, wrapping her arms around Harmony's waist and burying her face into her friend's shoulder. They stayed like that for several minutes before hurried footsteps made their way toward where they sat.

"Love, why are you crying?" Daemyn sat down on the other side of her, pulling her out of Harmony's arms and into his own. "If it means that much to you, we can get married with your friends. We could always have a proper wedding later."

Hazelle pushed away from him and looked into his eyes, searching. "Do you hate them so much that you can't even stand beside them and share a happy moment? What makes you hate them so?"

He looked at her, seemingly unsure of how to answer at first. "It simply isn't natural, Beloved. The unfortunate events that nearly wiped us out were a sign from God that we had sinned. I can't abide it and neither should you. I've always questioned your reasoning for associating with them. They're a bad influence on you."

Hazelle stood and backed away from him, her eyes growing wider with each word. "So what then? You plan to force me to end our friendship once we're married?"

"Honestly, I think that would be best," Daemyn said with a nod. "I didn't want to broach the subject right away, but since you brought it up..."

"You miserable piece of shit," Harmony spat.

Daemyn's gaze moved to Harmony for only a split second, but the coldness Hazelle saw in his eyes was enough to scare her. How had she never noticed that before? "I wasn't speaking to you. When your father disowns you, we'll see how proud you are of your choices."

"Don't you dare talk to her that way," Hazelle intoned, her voice hopelessly uneven.

"You shouldn't address me that way, Love. It's inappropriate," Daemyn chastised her playfully and winked. "It might get you into trouble."

Hazelle couldn't believe what she was hearing. When did he become so despicable? Had he always been like this and she'd just been too blind to see it? "I don't think we can get married tomorrow," she said finally, her hands balled into fists.

"That's fine, Beloved. I only offered because that seemed to be what you wanted. I'm glad we agree that it would be distasteful." Daemyn's tone was honeyed, at odds with the dark light in his eyes when he stood and approached her. He attempted to slip his arm around her shoulders.

Hazelle side-stepped way from him and began walking toward the gates. "Maybe not ever. I have a lot to think about."

"What do you mean maybe not ever?" Daemyn demanded. "Hazelle, don't walk away from me while I'm speaking to you!"

"I will tell you what I mean tomorrow when I know for sure," Hazelle raised her voice as she walked fastest. "I'm going home."

Harmony intercepted Daemyn before he could follow Hazelle. "Let her go. If you truly love her, you can wait one day to see what she says."

Daemyn growled, glancing at Harmony with hatred in his eyes, as if he blamed her. Nothing came of it, though. He simply turned and stormed away.

Act VI, scene ii - epilogue

Pirro had everything prepared for Tiernan and Harlequinn's wedding. The ceremony was to be held outside in the garden, with the reception in the dining hall. Hazelle helped Harmony get ready, tying laces and bows while her friend did her makeup.

"So what's going on with you and Daemyn?" Harlequinn asked. She could slice the tension in the room with a knife. She knew Hazelle was dreading the question – she hated confrontations.

Hazelle paused, holding the laces of Harmony's corset tighter than necessary. She exhaled and dropped them, turning to glance out the window where all of the guests waited. Daemyn would only be there because of her. Telling him she would provide an answer today had been a mistake. She didn't want to ruin the wedding for everyone.

"Hazelle…"

Hazelle sighed and turned back to Harmony, a bittersweet smile on her face. "I spent a lot of time thinking after I went home yesterday. I realized I'd always longed for someone to love me, so much that I willingly blinded myself to Daemyn's faults."

Hazelle went back to lacing up Harmony's corset as she spoke. "When I finally accepted that Daemyn was interested in me, I felt a weight lift off of my shoulders. That weight was the responsibility of not only giving my family an heir, but saving them. We lost everything when my mother died – our reputation, our money. We only have the house because grandmother took over the mortgage. More than that, we lost Mother…and I lost a brother. With Daemyn's support, I could save my family from social suicide."

"I understand," Harmony assured her. "It's a difficult situation to be in and his interest was like a ray of hope."

"Yes, but that wasn't all," Hazelle replied. "I became a social pariah after my mother's death. Rumors were rampant about how I would give birth to abominations and stillborns. I started to believe no one would ever love me. So when I realized that Daemyn really was interested, I thought, 'This is my only chance. If he abandons me, no one will ever love me.'"

"That's not true," Harmony whispered, staring at Hazelle in the reflection of the mirror. "I love you."

Hazelle smiled. "I love you too, but you know what I mean." She took a brush from the table and began working the tangles out of Harmony's hair. "Since I believed he was my family's only chance at a normal life, I overlooked his faults. I even allowed him to insult my friends. Sure, I told him I didn't like it, but what kind of person does it make me if I'm willing to marry someone like that? I never would have forgiven myself if it had ruined our friendship."

"He made it pretty clear that he intended for that to happen," Harmony commented dryly. She started curling her hair once Hazelle had laid the brush aside.

"Yes, he did."

The crestfallen look on Hazelle's face was enough to break Harmony's heart.

"At Tiernan's party, I excused his behavior, thinking that he was only acting like that because of something he drank…but he's always been like that, hasn't he?"

Harmony nodded, unable to say it aloud. She hated seeing Hazelle like this.

"I spoke with my father. He supports me in whatever I decide to do. After what happened to Mother and the baby, I think he realized that he loved the baby, Fae or not, and he would have fought for them both, no matter the consequences. He said he didn't want me to marry someone out of a sense of duty if I might regret it for the rest of my life."

Harmony reached up to squeeze one of Hazelle's hands. "No one should ever have to marry out of duty."

"You're right," Hazelle agreed, returning the gesture. "Now that there's an alliance between humans and Fae, my family might not remain social pariahs much longer." She took a breath, steadying herself. "I'm not marrying him."

"Have you told Daemyn?"

Hazelle sighed. "Not yet. I shouldn't have told him I would tell him today. I'm sorry."

Harmony smiled at her in the mirror. "Don't apologize."

Hazelle plucked a tissue from the box on the table and dabbed at her eyes. "Is it pathetic that it still hurts like hell?"

"No," Harmony said sternly. "You loved that bastard because he only showed you one side of himself. It's understandable that you're hurting. It'll get better." She finished curling her hair and stood up, giving herself one last look over before turning to take Hazelle's hands in her own, a devious smile on her face. "Now, since my father is MIA, I need someone to walk me down the aisle."

Hazelle tilted her head curiously. "Me?"

"Of course!" Harmony laughed. "You don't want to?"

Hazelle blushed. "Of course I do!"

"Good, because that idiot is waiting out there like he's getting married. When we walk down together, he'll be pissed and that's when you tell him." Harmony winked at her friend mischievously.

Hazelle looked pensive. "Are you sure? He might cause a scene."

"I think it's a fantastic idea. Not only will he be embarrassed, but the scene he'll likely cause will probably have a huge backlash on his reputation. It's the perfect revenge." Harmony pulled Hazelle out of the room and toward the back doors that led to the garden.

Once it was time, Osiris donned the ceremonial white robes of the Fae to perform the ceremony. Humans and magic folk alike sat in the chairs provided in the garden. A few of the Fae took it upon themselves to spread fireworks overhead. They sprayed down in colorful sparks that fizzled out before reaching the crowd. Fairy children flew overhead, giggling and dropping freshly picked flowers. Their wings left a glittering trail of light as they passed.

Tiernan stood in his tuxedo, while Lucinda stood laced up in a corset and black leather pants that resembled a tuxedo. She even wore a black choker adorned with a little bow around her neck. They both waited anxiously at the altar. Daemyn stood off to the side in a tuxedo as well, seeming certain that he would be marrying Hazelle today. Harlequinn, Harmony and Hazelle entered from the back doors leading out from the mansion's interior. Tatiana gathered some of the fairies and sang as the brides walked down the aisle.

Tiernan grinned like a fool when he saw Harlequinn in her red bodice that revealed just the right amount of skin. Her face lit up into a brilliant smile as their eyes met.

Lucinda, in a violet dress embroidered with black lace outlining the neckline and bust, strained to catch a glimpse of Harmony. Walking arm in arm with her, Hazelle wore a simple violet dress that complimented Harmony's. Lucinda's eyes never wandered from Harmony's for a second as she awaited her arrival.

Daemyn's reaction was a little less satisfied and a lot angrier. "Hazelle, what are you doing? Shouldn't you be dressed for our wedding?"

As Harlequinn and Harmony took their places beside their partners, they turned their attention toward the big-mouthed noble that was making a scene.

Hazelle held Harmony's hand for strength. "I cancel our engagement, Daemyn."

The silence that followed was deafening. Whispers from the nobles in attendance for Tiernan and Harlequinn's wedding rose from the crowd.

Daemyn's mouth hung open, frozen in that stunned pose until the whispers reached his ears and he let out half a laugh. "Surely you jest, my dear."

"I'm not joking."

A few gasps could be heard from behind them and Daemyn's face hardened into a frown. "This isn't funny, Hazelle. You're embarrassing me."

"And how many times have I let you embarrass me? I'm done sacrificing my integrity and swallowing my pride. My friends are getting married today and I intend to make this one hell of a party. You're not invited."

"I'm not going to stand here and let you belittle me in front of our peers, Hazelle." Daemyn made a grab for her wrist, intending to pull her out of view of the public eye to finish the conversation, but Harmony blocked him.

"Did I hear that right, Daemyn? You're going to drag Hazelle out of sight and teach her a lesson?"

Several more gasps and murmurs came from the crowd.

"I said no such thing!" Daemyn protested. "I simply would prefer to have this conversation in private."

"Well I don't." Hazelle crossed her arms over her chest. "You admitted my friendship with Harmony and Lucinda would be the first thing to go after we got married."

The whispers were louder and Daemyn looked around frantically. "I have no idea what you're talking about! You must be ill!"

"Only when I thought I needed someone like you in my life! Just go. No one wants you here."

Daemyn stumbled backward before regaining his balance, straightening his jacket as he composed himself. "Well, I was right about one thing. They certainly are a bad influence on you." He regarded Lucinda sourly. "I would rethink this whole marriage thing if I were you. It doesn't seem like your bride is being faithful."

Osiris rolled his eyes. "Oh, shut him up, Revelin."

"Can do!" said a voice with no apparent owner.

Revelin appeared behind Daemyn and jabbed a needle into his neck. The man slumped over immediately and Revelin unceremoniously hoisted the man onto his shoulder and walked away.

"Osiris?" Tiernan asked anxiously. "What the hell?"

"Don't concern yourself, Brother." Osiris smiled, attempting to keep his mirth in check. "Just a simple concoction. He will wake up good as new."

"Should I ask where he'll wake up?"

"It might be best if you didn't."

Tiernan let out a groan and Harlequinn patted his back. "There, there, Darling. Let's just get on with the ceremony, shall we?"

Everyone focused their attention on Osiris and the rest of the ceremony went off without a hitch. The fairy king gave each couple their due attention, speaking prose befitting of each from what little he knew of them. Each kiss drew cheers and applause from the crowd.

The reception started out with a bang. Tatiana's band played in the dinner hall while food was served. Dancing ensued once everyone had eaten their fill. They all celebrated late into the night before drunkenly heading to their beds.

It was then that Revelin slipped out of the mansion, rising up into the air and zooming away, down streets and alleyways until he found what he was looking for. Lying on the ground, covered in newspapers and grime, was Daemyn, still dressed in his finest suit. Revelin placed his hands on his hips and regarded the man quizzically. "You *still* haven't woken up?" He sighed dramatically. "So typical of a lazy noble." He poked the man with his toe. Daemyn merely grumbled and rolled over, complaining about stupid lesbians in his sleep.

Revelin crouched down next to Daemyn's ear and whispered. "From this day forth, you will only be attracted to those you despised most."

With that said, he took his leave, heading back to Tiernan's mansion. He crept to Tiernan and Harlequinn's door, which opened silently to allow him in.

"Are you sure the treatment will work?" Harlequinn asked the fairy, her eyes full of uncertainty.

Revelin smiled patiently and tested the needle. A drop slid down the tip. "Our magician assured Osiris that it would work, my lady."

"Will it have any adverse effects?" Harlequinn inquired hesitantly. Part of her didn't want to know. All she wanted in the world was to bear a child. Would it matter to her if the cure harmed her in some way? Even if it didn't, she knew it would matter to her husband.

"There are never any guarantees in this life," Revelin informed her dutifully. "However, Idris did not mention any. Here's hoping the only effect is impregnation with a healthy fetus."

Harlequinn wasn't certain how to take that, but she nodded anyway. She had to believe that this would work. Revelin gently wrapped his fingers around her wrist, stretching out her arm to administer the shot. She winced as the needle punctured her skin. An intense burn overtook her flesh as the liquid entered her bloodstream. When the feeling faded, she opened her eyes, but Revelin was nowhere in sight. Bewildered, she shut the door to retire to bed.

"Are you alright, Love?" Tiernan asked softly.

Harlequin smiled at him, raising a hand to wipe the stray tear that escaped her eye. "I will be," she whispered. "Once I am whole again."

Tiernan wrapped his arms around his wife and kissed her forehead, holding her for the moment. The time for more intimate endeavors could come later. He was in no hurry.

Silently, Revelin stepped away from Tiernan and Harlequinn's bedroom. He truly did wish the best for the couple. He headed in the direction of the guest suites next.

He first visited Hazelle, who was sitting in front of the vanity, brushing her hair in preparation for bed. She watched herself in the mirror with melancholy eyes, thinking about what her friends had and what she now lacked, no doubt. Perhaps he ought to play matchmaker again. He'd have to find someone more suitable next time. Just when Hazelle was getting the pin-pricking sensation of being watched, Revelin slipped out of the room.

He visited Harmony and Lucinda last, tiptoeing about. He watched as they readied themselves for their first clumsy endeavors of intimacy. Once things had escalated far enough, he stepped outside between the two rooms in the hallway, his back to the door, a grin stretching from ear to ear.

"Apologies for the bumpy journey through the woods," he whispered too softly for them to hear. "Live your dreams as your realities and leave the realities you thought you knew...in your dreams."

Dogs Of War

Jeffrey Cook + Katherine Perkins

THE BRUTE, eighty-two tons of armor, firepower, and treads taller than most men, ground its way across the desert floor. They said the monster tank had already been a museum piece, a relic of older days of war, when it had been smuggled across the sea after the days of fire rain. It had tracked the desert again and again before it saw seven years' respite in the enforced 'peace' under the Tyrant – before the tank and its commander had been instrumental in bringing down the last man to try claiming dominion over the whole desert empire. In the generations since, it had seen war, because war was all the people of the desert knew.

Many said the only original part the tank had left was the battered metal plate bearing the name its original crew had given it. In these days, in times of nomads and a transient existence, such a legacy was a thing so rare that every commander of the heavy tank came to share its name – including the quiet and studious man now serving as commander, who seemed ill fit for it, save in record of his victories. He stood proudly, so his torso emerged through the main hatch, that all could see Brian June as his family's inheritance led the procession of his warband into the recently conquered capital.

The capital, so called because it had been the Tyrant's and because it was the only thing truly worthy of being called a town within five hundred miles, had been thought unconquerable, the last invulnerable bastion of Lord Phillip's might, and the key to enough resources to sustain a war. But Jules the Conqueror had done it. He'd built his own army, convinced them of the possibilities, and won victory after victory. He'd gained the allegiance of Marcus's cycle gangs. Others followed, eventually, including the Brute himself, and together, they'd collapsed the last great resistance to uniting the desert empire – to be led by a council of the warband leaders who had made it all possible.

The procession rolled into town, a motley army composed of dozens of the typical trucks and modified armored cars, the monster tank, several cycles, and a single gyro-copter scout vehicle overhead. By now, the crowds had mostly dispersed. The Brute's Force hadn't arrived until well into the afternoon, and the heat of the day pushed all but the most dedicated celebrants indoors.

"Brian," called Stratton from the gyro, "you might want to take a walk, a block to the left. Seems not everyone is celebrating." The pilot had never called Brian by his nickname, nor any rank. He'd long since earned the right. And for his part, Brian just called him friend.

Brian left the Brute under watch, taking with him only a few men on the suggested walk. Down the block was a vehicle lot – Jules's, in fact, with organized rank after rank of armored trucks, jeeps with machine gun mounts, and numerous cars. Marc's cycles, decked out to present a motley appearance in unified colors, sat beside them – a sign of the esteem the Conqueror held for the biker gang leader. Most of the Conqueror's vehicles bore his logo – the wedge-tailed eagle bearing two halves of a wreath of leaves, bringing the signs of life in the desert together in its talons to form a crown. However, many of the most prominent banners had been cut, the golden eagles laying in the dust.

Jules's massive armored command vehicle bore the eagle on top but many other banners adorned the sides, each acquired in the consolidation that made him the Conqueror. Beside it stood two men with volcanoes inked on their bare shoulders. They apparently were not letting the death of their war-leader stand and had just removed the volcano standard, still stained with Phillip's blood, from its new trophy-place on the hood. By way of further vandalism, they were replacing it with the word 'COWERD' in jagged red paint.

Brian gestured for his men to fan out to block avenues of escape, and approached the pair. "That's supposed to be an 'A', not an 'E', there," he pointed out, gesturing to the letters with his saber. As the commander of a tank and a mostly heavy-armor warband, he'd never used the bloody thing, but it was tradition, and, especially with men keeping a watchful eye out, he didn't think he'd need the threat of a gun here. Few people were eager to challenge any of the warlords, and all most people really knew about him was that he owned the biggest tank in the world, and that people called him the Brute.

Both of the pair turned, one of them falling off the hood of the armored carrier entirely. There was a momentary scramble for knives before they recognized him, and efforts at armed resistance abruptly stopped. "Mister... Mister Brute, sir. We didn't mean nothing by it."

"That's right, nothing at all. Just...."

"Just that you didn't think the Conqueror took his trophies seriously? Or maybe you were going to clean it for him?" Brian ventured. "You're lucky I found you, instead of the cycle gangers. Marc's 'college boys' aren't known for being forgiving. Why don't you clean up that paint, and you'll just be arrested without much detail on your vandalism."

"Arrest... like you're putting us in the Pit?"

"Well, I can't say what you fellows did with it under Phillip, but under the Council, it's just going to be what they used to call a holding cell. With Jules in a good mood, you'll be out in a day or two – and can go put on some shirts with sleeves. I'd definitely recommend those."

The two thugs glanced at each other and frantically got to work trying to scrub the red paint before putting back up the Conqueror's eagles, and putting their former commander's banner back where they found it. Brian returned to his procession well before they'd finished, leaving two men to keep weapons on them, and have them arrested when they were finished. He climbed back into the tank and led the way to their lodgings.

"No problems, sir?" came the call over the radio.

"Nothing serious. If a little vandalism is the worst resistance the Conqueror has to deal with, it'll be an easy transition. Let's get moving. I'm sure everyone is hungry, and my wife'll be waiting for me for lunch."

***

"Don't go congratulating me, Jules, I haven't won anything," Marc commented as he was pulling on his gloves, preparing to head for the cycle track in the town's arena. The Brute insisted it had once been some kind of theater or music hall, but the conversion suited Marc fine. His boys would be happier with this new regime if they could spend their time racing, drinking, and brawling a bit, and Marc's relations with the rest of the leaders would be happier if the College Boys could do all of that where it wouldn't spill out into the town.

"Yet, my friend. You haven't won anything yet. Everyone knows you're the odds-on favorite to win the first races. The bookies are all grumbling, rumor has it, because no one will put any money down until they're sure you're done racing for the day."

Marc grinned. "Just the one race, today. Prove to my boys I've still got it. Then I'll stop interfering with your new empire's circus-commerce."

Jules didn't share the grin. "It's not my empire. We have the Council for a reason. And at least your boys only care about your ability to ride. I have a lot more to prove."

"Yet, my friend. It's not your empire, yet. The Council members all have the loyalty of their warbands, but someone has to lead. Your eagle assembled the crown – you just need to put it on."

"My eagles still have talons, mate. Try to snatch the laurels, and all I'm likely to get is bloodied. I can't even lead my band from the front anymore."

Marc made a dismissive gesture and reached for his leather helmet. "Because of injuries you received in battle. Everyone knows you would, if you were able. And you're still the brains that got us all where we are. People love you, and they'll love you more after today, when you praise the Council, call their warbands by name, put on the best event anyone here has seen on your first day in charge – and after I offer you my victory wreath, and you shove it back at me. The crowd will eat it up."

Jules narrowed his eyes. "Not much of an act, when I don't want a crown."

"Let's be honest with each other, mate. You want the crown, and I want you to have it. The Conqueror, Uniter of the tribes, and however many other titles you want to attach – the 'first among equals' thing doesn't really fit with that. Somebody's going to be *more* equal."

"Like you, Marc?"

"Hell no, I don't want the crown. I lead a biker gang. The best of them, sure, but a biker gang. What would I know about leading an empire? I'd rather have powerful friends."

"Powerful friends, and the Queen of New Zealand?"

Marc shrugged. "We both know that boy of hers is really mine. What do I care if she says he's yours? Besides, if it puts a kid of mine in line for the crown, if he wants it, so much the better. I'm not the jealous sort. Especially of Emperors-to-be."

Jules considered, eyes still narrowed while regarding the biker-warlord. "August is the heir to anything I leave."

Marc grinned and mock-sighed. "Well, if you want to go with the kid over *our* son, I'll understand. August has your tactical brains, but rumor has it he can't drive or shoot. Eyes always in a book."

"I have my tactical brains, but can't drive or shoot worth anything, anymore. You see the problem?"

"You proved yourself, and then got hurt. It's different."

"I don't think everyone will see it that way."

"Enough will."

"Enough about my ambition. So, what? You'll be content to sit your time on the Council, then trade your bike and gang for a boat and a Queen?"

"And the two of us will be the Conqueror's strongest supporters. This desert's crown is too heavy for me, Jules. I'm a biker. I need to keep moving, or I die."

"Speaking of honesty and moving fast," Jules tried to change the subject, "at least now you're acknowledging you're going to win the race."

"Of course I'm going to win," Marc grinned, pulling the helmet on. "Someday, one of my boys will beat me, and then he'll think he's all set to lead the band. But today isn't that day."

★★★

"That was a lovely show," Patricia commented, walking hand-in-hand with Brian as they exited the arena.

"I could have done with more sport and less show," Brian returned.

"That was a lot more sport than we've had in ages; though I agree, Marc slowed down near the end to make it at least look close."

"Not the show I was referring to."

"What then?"

"Isn't it obvious?"

"I can't read your mind, Brian."

"That bit with the wreath was a bit overdramatic, don't you think?"

"People know the stories of the Tyrant – they needed to see Jules turning down a crown."

"Turning down the crown, flanked on either side by Eagle banners, the whole place decked out in his colors, and..."

"And what?"

"When Marc did it again on the *third* victory lap, I think Jules kind of hesitated."

"You're imagining things."

"I know the stories as well as anybody. My grandfather worked for the Tyrant."

"And then he led the riots against him. Everybody knows that, dear."

"Yeah, once he saw what kind of man he really was. The Tyrant started out claiming he wasn't some kind of Emperor either."

"And Jules knows the same stories. He was the one who proposed the Council in the first place. You have real power now, Brian. Power that doesn't come from owning the biggest gun. I trust you to keep an eye on things. People trust you. Did you hear how loud everyone cheered? Jules heard it... he named each and every one of your lieutenants. He didn't do that for anyone else."

"Except Marc."

"Marc has two lieutenants."

"That's all he trusts."

"Doesn't matter how he runs things. It's still a very short list."

"I'm sure you're right, Trish, and I'm just too attached to seeing things out of old stories. Unification is the best thing for everyone."

"See? Was that so hard?"

"That was easy. Trying to make rules everyone here will follow is going to be the hard part. This is a collection of nomads and warbands – everyone is used to having their own freedom to come and go."

Patricia tried to offer a comment on this, but Brian didn't notice. "The first Council meeting is tomorrow. I suspect it's going to be a rough one. A lot of people out for the best deal they can get, or trying to trade in what they did to make this possible for favors," he said.

"All the more reason they'll need you there. You actually want to make this work for everyone."

"You make it sound like I'm the only one who does," he sighed. "Which may be more true than I was hoping for, after watching some of the other 'actors' today."

"It was a day for it. They're proud of their bands. You could have been a little more gracious."

"The men and women who fight for me know I value them. I don't need to fling trinkets or make speeches."

"You're going to have to make some speeches eventually."

"Hmph."

"Well, that's one way of preventing broader knowledge of the "Brute's" maturity and thoughtfulness from getting out."

"Let's talk about dinner."

***

"What the hell was all of that?" Clay fumed, pounding a fist on the bar table. He got a few glances from other bar patrons, but not many. Clay, more often known as the Peregrine, was known to be no friend of the Conqueror's. He'd gotten his nickname when it was commented where Phillip's hand pointed, Clay went – and with his fleet of fast-moving hunter-killer cars, it stuck.

"Lower your voice, Per," Casey jumped in, grabbing his friend's wrist. "You're on the Council as a peace offering. Getting drunk and noisy on your first day isn't going to help anyone. You can speak your piece tomorrow."

"After that garbage in the arena today? You heard them. He isn't going to have to reach for the crown, people can't wait to shove it at him. And next time, he won't refuse."

"Phillip still has plenty of support."

"Phillip is dead. I watched the Brute haul off two of his former toughs today, and no one said a word."

"What's anyone going to say, Per? Jules is the big boss, now, crown or no. But if he disappeared tomorrow, people would forget him as quick as they are Phillip."

The Peregrine's expression turned thoughtful. "You might be on to something, Case."

Casey held up his hands. "Wait, wait. I didn't mean we should go back to war or nothing. Your cars are built for speed, sure, but Marc's bikes already lured you out, led you on one chase. And nothing I've got could dent the Brute – and that's not even taking Jules into account. We lost."

"We lost one war, Case. But he let us live, put us on his Council. There won't be any backup in the Council chambers. And without his warriors and that old bus of his, Jules is just a man. Just one, lame, man."

"That's treason you're talking."

"So? Going to report me?"

Casey held up his hands again, shaking his head. "No, of course not," he paused, "It's just, if I'm going to commit treason, I want to get away with it."

"And just what's going to stop us from getting away with it? A distraction, a knife in the back. Not like he can run."

"His pet biker, for one, mate. Anyone who puts a dagger in Jules's back is gonna get Marc's machete to the throat, if he's feeling nice. If he's not, he'll chain 'em to his bike and take them for a long drag."

The Peregrine quieted again, drumming his fingers on the table. "So we'd have to deal with the bikers, true. We could get some of the others in on it. The fighting's been going a long time. The Metal-Head, Decker, Travis – they all hate him."

"But not enough to risk going back to war now. He let them all live, once. Added them to his warband after he beat them. He won't make the mistake again."

"I told you, this isn't about war."

Casey said, "It would be. You heard the crowds, and you know the bikers won't go quietly. We could assassinate the Conqueror, sure. But we'd have a fight on our hands in no time. And we wouldn't win. It'd just be a race to see if we get hung or dragged to death first."

"So we kill Marc, too. His lieutenants spend time bickering over who's in charge, and we're ready for them. One problem solved."

"Doesn't help us put down a riot. You'd have died with Phillip if you hadn't been chasing bikers around the desert when they hit."

"And he'd have your head too, if you'd waited any longer to turn."

"I saw which way the wind was blowing. Phillip was insane, thinking he was going to hold out."

"Plenty of others did, too. They'll twist back, if the wind changes."

"Not enough, Per. It's not enough. Jules has the people where he wants 'em."

"So we tell the people he was setting himself up to be another Tyrant. He just wanted to get all the nomads in one place, so he could control them."

"Right, because people are going to believe a turncoat, and Phillip's huntsman? Not on your life, Per."

"I couldn't help overhearing," came the feminine voice. Both men turned, having failed to notice the eavesdropper. Sin was the house's Madam, invited to the Council not because she had a warband, but because she owned the richest business in town and had outlived not only Phillip, but also two of his predecessors in running the town.

"And I suppose you want to know what we'll give you to avoid turning us in, huh?" asked the Peregrine.

"Yes, but when we're done negotiating that," said the Madam, sliding into a chair, "if I still haven't decided to turn you both in for whatever reward I can get – and you do get the edge that I'll need to be very well paid to do any favors for the College Boys – I want you to deal me in."

Casey looked at the woman suspiciously. "Why would you want that? This is trouble, and you've always liked avoiding trouble."

"Sure, most days," she countered, as one of her girls brought her a drink and another round for the Councilors, on the house, "but the Conqueror is bad for business. I own a piece of every action in this town. The arena books, the fuel smuggling, prostitution, bootlegging, all the locals know it. Phillip knew how to keep me happy, because I kept all the gangs who came through happy. Jules, though, is all about order. And order eventually means regulation. And that's bad for my business."

The Peregrine nodded, encouraging the line of thought. "And if you're on board, you know who's the least happy with Jules, and can get to them in ways we can't. Maybe we can even liquor up most of Marc and Jules's fighters beforehand."

"None of which is a problem, but you're still forgetting two things. Though if you solve one of them for me, I think I know the answer to the other," Sin said.

"Go on," Case urged her, less resistant to the forming idea, now that it had the potential of her help.

"First, you two still need to convince me I should help you. First things first. Put your money where your mouth is, and I'll tell you how to deal with Public Relations."

The men looked at each other, and an unspoken agreement emerged. "Money, and plenty of it," the Peregrine offered, "But that's just a start. You're going to need muscle, with all these newcomers in town. Your businesses start having trouble, we'll get your back. And all of ours will strictly go to your bars, your shops, you name it. And if a few accidents should befall the competition, that'd be terrible."

Sin grinned. "Sold. Keep your money to yourselves right now. We'll talk specific amounts later, when it's quieter, and I'll collect some insurance just in case."

"So what about Public Relations, especially as they apply to our not being lynched?" Casey said.

"The Brute," she said. "If you kill the Conqueror, they'll want your head. If he's in on it, they'll believe the whole story of noble intentions."

"He helped Jules break in here, though," Casey pointed out. "Sure, he's not like Marc where he'd share his *girl*, but they're close. Why would the Brute help us?"

"Because he's paranoid about the same things you are. Just not as ready to resort to murder."

"So how do we change his mind?" Casey asked.

The woman shrugged, standing to go back to tending bar and directing her girls. "That's your problem."

"My problem," the Peregrine said with a grin. "Leave the Brute to me."

***

"I appreciate the drink," Brian said. "But this sudden kindness doesn't make us friends."

"If not friends, then consider it a visit by family," the Peregrine offered.

"That's supposed to make this any better? Because you convinced my half-sister that you could give her a better life around this town than her own tribe could? And then we didn't hear from her for years?"

"The half-sister who has been the envy of your wife for most of those years, as I hear my wife tell it. They're catching up, shopping in the market now. They can get along fine, why can't we do the same?"

"Because I know you too well, Peregrine."

"Sure, we've fought. And you beat me. Sent my cars back in quite the shape both times. And yet I'm willing to let that go. I've changed, and whatever you think of band solidarity, I have, in fact, provided quite well for your sister all this time."

"So you're telling me at some point you've been more than Phillip's bounty hunter, his falcon?"

"And you're going to claim your nickname has always fit you? You've certainly never managed to be rid of it."

"For sake of peace between my wife and my half-sister, and seeing her again… and the fact we need to work together now, say your piece."

"As you say, we have to work together. So hopefully that'll give me a chance to prove my good character. We want the same things out of this peace."

"Out of peace, maybe, but I can't imagine you were too happy about this one."

"I've tried to be. Phillip was going crazy in his advancing years. I got that. And no question, Jules won. And he was more than fair, giving me and some of the others spots on the Council. Not so many as his allies, but that's to be expected."

"But?"

"But I saw your face at the arena; you saw the same thing I did. He hesitated on that last victory lap. He wants a crown. Rule by Council isn't going to be enough for him."

"He turned it down, though. And Jules needs the Council to rule at all."

"Does he? He has us all in one place. He knows where everyone lives. We aren't out in the open desert, with cover and mobility and our own walls to protect us anymore. He has the biggest warband, still. Especially with the bikers' support."

"And combined, we still have more men, more vehicles, more ammunition. He can't rule without the support of the people. And our bands make up a lot of those people. The Council is the best chance to keep the peace."

"Oh, I agree. I agree. But does he see it that way? Or even if he does now, will he see it that way in a month, when our decisions don't match his? Will he see it that way in a year? How about when his injuries slow him down more, when he's looking his mortality in the face and considering his kid's future?"

Brian hesitated, sipping his drink to fill the silence. "We can convince the Council to block any attempt he might make to take power. No one wants a reminder of the Tyrant years right now."

"And you think he's going to let that stop him, if he's really ambitious?"

"What are you proposing?"

"We need to take matters into our own hands, right now. He has most of the people fooled, and he knows it. He has Marc's support. He thinks he has yours. But I can see that you don't want Emperor Jules any more than I do."

"Your eyesight is good, but that's sounding like a call to war."

"No one wants to go back to war. Not now."

"What, then?"

"Jules and Marc attend the Council, too, Brute."

"The tank can keep the name. I'm a politician now, not a warlord. Brian is fine."

"Suit yourself, Brian."

"So what if they do? They'll get our message, loud and clear, I suppose."

"They will. You're a smart man."

"And you're a traitor, if I'm hearing you right."

"Jules is a traitor. I'm a servant of the common good."

"It doesn't look that way from where I'm sitting."

"Look again. You know Jules. You know he won't be content to just have the biggest chair at Council meetings. When he consolidates his power base, it will be impossible to do anything."

"The Tyrant consolidated his power base for years. My grandfather had the biggest gun. It worked out fine."

"Two generations of nonstop warfare is fine?"

"Better than living under a despot's thumb, right?"

"Even better to make sure the despot never takes power."

"You can't be sure of anything, until he makes a move. And I think I trust you even less than I trust Jules. I'll pass, and see what happens."

"And you're going to go report me, now? The way you turned in those other two?"

Brian finished his drink and stood. "Nope. Like it or not, you're my brother-in-law, and my wife and half-sister are out shopping. I want this life for her, and a chance to get to know my blood, again. If Jules makes no move, I won't act against him. You have the same offer. Thanks for the drink." Setting the stein down on the table, he turned, leaving the Peregrine fuming behind him as he watched the Brute walk out the door.

***

"I thought you said you had the Brute handled?" Casey asked, worriedly glancing out the window as if Jules's thugs might come for him at any moment for associating with The Peregrine.

"Relax. I do," the Peregrine assured him, sipping at his wine.

"But he turned you down. You just said so."

"Sure he did. I half expected he would. Murder just isn't in his character. That's half the point, after all."

"We can't do this without him. We'll be hanged for sure."

"We won't be. Because he's going to join us."

"You seem awfully sure he's going to change his mind."

"Not one bit. He said that he'd act when Jules makes his move, right?"

"You said something about that, yes. But Jules hasn't done a thing but consult with his advisors. Hardly proof of anything."

"Proof? Our Brute is a man of the people. He'll act when he hears their pleas, and when he sees them threatened."

"Like Jules is going to make threats that'll ruin his public support."

"Oh, but he already has. Right now, right near where the Brute has his breakfast, there'll be messages scratched onto rocks or raked into the sand. Scared innocent bystanders, worried about the future. Supplanted in their businesses. Some of them, I'm afraid, have already gotten threats, even. Bikers are so unpredictable and prone to violence. There'll be more secret notes tomorrow."

"Marc has kept his people corralled, and Jules has thrown money at half the local businesses."

"Sure, us locals know that. Same way we know most of the names signed to those scratches belong to people who can't write."

"You're forging them."

"He'd recognize my writing too quickly. My drivers, on the other hand, have been kept very busy."

"He'll confront Jules in Council for that. Be the voice for the people, and Jules won't know what he's talking about. You'll be found out."

"You think Jules pretending ignorance will prove anything? Brian is already suspicious of him. Besides, that's only the first half. You know those two vandals he had arrested?"

"I know them, and so do you. They were part of Phillip's guard."

"Which is how I knew where they'd head when they were released. As far as anyone else knows, outside of me, you, and two of my lieutenants, they never made it out of the Pit. They just disappeared. Who knows where."

"I can't believe what I'm hearing. You knew those guys, Per. Sure, they got drunk now and then, a little rough. But they were all right."

"They were going to get everyone into more trouble, and they died for the cause."

"They didn't choose to."

"Don't lose nerve on me now. You want to be rid of Jules, right?"

Casey took a deep breath. "Not like that... but yeah. We need to be rid of him."

"Then it looks like Jules just made his move, eliminating a couple of dissenters. He'll be watching for my people. Have a couple of your folks mentioning it, somewhere some of Brian's band are sure to overhear. It'll get back to him."

"All right, I'll do it. But I don't like this, Per."

The Peregrine took another sip of his drink. "I don't like it either, but drastic times and all. And if your guys do their job, we'll have the Brute on our side when the time comes."

***

"The eggs are good?" Sheila's dark curls bounced as she canted her head nervously.

"The eggs are great, thank you."

"Trish and her husband seem to have a lot of serious conversations at mealtime," she seemed to be grasping for a segue. She wasn't used to this. Sheila was a quiet girl, on the whole.

"The Brute's a serious guy. Always thinking. And Trish is very conversational, I hear."

"Jules, I've been having nightmares."

"Sorry to hear that, Sheila," Jules said simply as he ate.

"About you. And steel and blood and death."

He smiled at his wife. "Yeah, okay, I know we've been through a lot. I think we're done with the worst of the blood and death for a while, though."

"This wasn't of the past, Jules, it was of the future."

"Sheila, I'm sorry for making you nervous, but you need to not dwell on it like this."

"Jules, the day of the full moon, I want you to stay safe."

"You want me to stay home. Maybe the answer isn't for me to go out less, but for you to go out more? Every time we come to any stopping place for a while, whether it's a tent or house, you huddle yourself up." He watched Sheila's eyes go down, fidgeting, and continued hurriedly. "And that's fine, really. If I'd wanted to marry a social butterfly, I had plenty to go with. But maybe you should ask Trish if you can tag along the next time she takes her sister-in-law shopping."

"Jules, you know my mother's people. This is serious."

"Sheila, I can't stay home right now. I can't. The Council is almost half people who fought against me at one time or another. They're looking for any sign of weakness. I can't stay home because of pain, and I definitely can't avoid the Council Chambers because of a nightmare. I've always respected your intuition, but we're on an edge now, and it would be so easy to lose everything we fought for. Be strong for me – a little longer."

"After all you've done, you're saying you can't take one day off? You can tell the Council anything you want."

"Yes, dear. I'm saying that. I've had enough obstacles from having to supposedly hide since my injuries. I can't let my schedule be dictated by fear of bad luck. I know your mother's people put a lot of stock in dreams, and your insights have helped before. But I can't afford to give them even one day right now. When all of this isn't quite so new, I'll let Marc oversee the Council and rest for a few days. We'll finally have some time together."

Sheila sighed, her hand trembling as she picked up her fork.

***

The conspirators huddled in the darkened Council Chambers, staying around to see to late work, gathering again only after a thorough sweep ensured everyone else had left. Brian glanced around at the men and women with him. The Peregrine he still didn't trust in the least, but there were family ties, and something to what he'd said. The notes and the disappearances proved it. Casey was a traitor to

Phillip at the last minute – but that didn't mean any love for Jules. Sin was the most powerful woman in town, with the possible exception of Jules's wife. He hadn't yet gotten a good handle on why she'd object to the increase in the population of the town, or the new growth. It had to mean more money for her. Regardless, he didn't trust her place, or her.

The others he liked better. All of them had warbands of their own, and had ridden with Jules. Most had been beaten first, with their banners hanging from Jules's bus, but they'd still helped him unite the desert empire, joining instead of falling. The Metal-head was the least stable. Some said that the accident that had caused scrap metal to melt to the left half of his face had driven the man, formerly-but-never-anymore called Sam, crazy, but Brian had the sense of history to know that it was Sam's and his gang's own inherent crazy that had led to the accident in the first place. In any case, he respected the raider band's daring, if not their sanity. The man had made for some interesting Council meetings.

Decker was a lot like Brian – smart, tactical, and loyal to his men. Decker's trucker brigade was rough, but that wasn't unusual, and they were at least consistently hard workers.

Travis ran a mixed fleet of vehicles, with a bit of air support. Brian had fought him a few times over various resources out in the desert, with a mixed record. The man had an answer for everything, somewhere in his arsenal, but couldn't say they were particularly great at anything. Despite their conflicts, he'd shown no hard feelings – but then Brian had to consider that he'd said just that to Jules, too, and yet here they were.

Cal's band was the smallest, but the kid was a quick study. Somewhere or other, he'd found or built a tank. Nothing like the Brute, but a five-man, fifty-five ton armored vehicle with a big gun still inspired comparisons. He made no bones about admiring Brian, and Brian had to wonder if his participation may have come about with the Peregrine assuring him that the Brute himself was on board with the plan.

And finally, Pauline. The woman had held her own warband together for longer than most in the room had been alive. She'd certainly survived more fights than any of them, and maybe any two of them. And nothing in the rules or any disapproving glances stopped her from smoking her giant cigars in Council chambers.

"So, we're all agreed, then. Something needs to be done about Jules and Marc." The Peregrine brought the discussion into focus.

"You're assuming too much," Brian responded, "I agree that Jules is going too far. Marc's done nothing wrong, and has no claim to leadership we don't let him have. This is bad enough. We can kill a tyrant-to-be, but this can't be a murder of convenience."

"Brute, we have to do this all the way. Marc will go nuts if Jules dies, and he lives. He can fight, he has a huge warband, and he'd collect a lot of Jules's too," Casey stepped in. Several sets of eyes moved back and forth, following the conversation without offering anything.

"You want me to tell the people that we prevented a new Tyrant from arising, fine. But I'm only going to tell them the truth. If Marc dies, count me out. And if you try and trick me, say one thing and kill him anyway, you'd best kill me, too."

"Be reasonable, Brian," the Peregrine started, before Brian cut him off.

"No, be honest, Clay. This isn't about seizing power. We're all equals here, and that won't change. The College Boys may be a bit of trouble, but that's it. Odds are, if Jules dies, Marc'll just be off to New Zealand, anyway."

"E's right, mate," Travis cut in. "If'n Marc is on yer hit list, I'm out."

The Peregrine was about to say more, but Sin put a hand on his arm, and spoke up. "All right. So he lives. But that means that we need to make sure he's nowhere in the area when things go down. He can't have any chance to try and stop anything, or get revenge. He'll be fine, if he has to think things through, first. If it's first gut reaction, though, he'll fight, every time."

Travis spoke up again. "Leave 'im to me, mates. I've been drinkin' with 'is boys. I can lead 'im off to talk. Suits me better'n stabbin' anyhow."

Sin stepped back in. "So now we need someone Jules trusts to put him in the right place, and a distraction."

Half of the Metal-head's face smiled. "Distraction."

Decker nodded. "I'll get him where he needs to be. I'd prefer to face the man, anyhow."

Pauline took a deep drag from her cigar. "I'm on crowd control. Make sure no one panics. They'll believe an old woman better'n you boys with blood on your hands."

"We have a plan, then," the Peregrine began, before looking pointedly at Brian, "or I think we do. I've been corrected once. Where are you going to be?"

Brian looked his brother-in-law in the eye, "Cal and I will take up the flanking spots and make sure he doesn't escape. You know, if you screw up."

***

"You keep your ears open in the meeting. I need you to get the hang of this so you can just handle it for me eventually, and I can take days off."

"You're thinking of taking days off, Dad? That's new." Sometimes August didn't seem like he'd grown more than an inch since the day Jules'd taken the desert brat into his track, but runtish or not, he really was growing up.

"Tactical Lesson #1555: A wise man doesn't turn down repeated requests from his wife unless he has to. As it stands, I have to, but she was really bothered again this morning before I left."

"She's not bothered easily," August remarked. "She's never seemed bothered about New Zealand. Of course, neither do you, when Marc goes."

"What happens in New Zealand stays in New Zealand, and you're not supposed to know about it until you're older." Jules was grinning more than scolding, though. The kid really was growing up, and he did keep his ears open.

"Dad, where's Marc?"

Jules was surprised. Marc had immediately picked up the habit of meeting him at the doors. Much as Jules believed the biker had no interest in a crown, or at least this one, he certainly liked associating himself with power, and escorting the Conqueror into the chamber each day certainly did that.

"Weird," he said, looking around. Something felt wrong about this. He wasn't a superstitious man. He'd trusted his wife's instincts when he had the leisure to, because she tended to have good points however much she couched them in magic nightmares, but he believed in making his own luck. That didn't necessarily mean ignoring a bad feeling, though. "August, go in the alley over there and keep an eye out for Marc. Whatever's delaying him, I can't wait, but you stay."

Someone did come to the door, but it wasn't Marc. Instead, he was met by one of the warlords. Decker had another question about trading posts and supply routes. Jules could understand the interest, given that Decker had more shipping trucks than anyone, and the town afforded the united empire a chance to start expanding. Most of the specifics of the questions were lost on him, though, as he struggled with balance on the swollen joints of his injured leg.

Suddenly, the Metal-head moved past in too much of a hurry. That wasn't unusual, but the man rarely was so careless as to bump his shoulder into people when the way was wide open, but now he crashed into Jules's side, setting him stumbling into Decker and nearly falling. Decker managed to hold him upright, if barely, and the jarring bump sent a new wave of pain through his leg.

Recovering himself, Jules was about to thank Decker when he realized that his first effort to pull back was unsuccessful, and the trucker had hold of his arms. He couldn't turn to face the voice that snarled "Die, tyrant!" from behind him, couldn't do anything about the stabbing wound to his neck. The sudden gout of blood, however, startled Decker enough that Jules was able to wrench himself free. Backing away, however, ran him right into both Sin and the Peregrine's knives, two more wounds to his back.

Jules was going for his own survival knife and starting to turn when Decker drew on him, stabbing him to the chest before he could get his weapon free. Jules spun away, stumbling away from his attackers – and right into the reach of the man with half a grin. The Metal-head's dagger plunged into his shoulder, preventing him from getting his blade free.

Surprise finally gave way to soldier's instincts, and he fought back. Despite the wound, he crashed his lead shoulder into the metal-faced man, sending him sprawling into the path of other pursuers. Half-limping, half-running, Jules rushed towards the nearest people, calling for help – and came up short to see Brian pointing a sawed-off shotgun with a pistol-grip at him.

"...Brian?" The older man's eyes were no longer darting around, analyzing. They were frozen on him.

"Jules." Brian did his best to look him in the eye. On Principle.

"Brute, what in hell are you doing?" Casey called, seeing the gun. "Something a little less noisy, please?" Jules's weak cries had gotten a little attention, but not nearly what gunshots would draw.

"Assassins keep things quiet. I told you, fellas, no murder. We're the good guys," Brian said, firmly and pulled the trigger. Jules took the shot to the chest, launched backwards. He hit the ground heavily, and went still, with one last breath.

The streets erupted, with panic causing some to flee the scene and curiosity leading others, often hardened veterans, to race towards it, weapons drawn.

Pauline was true to her word, taking full advantage of the respect she'd earned in at least half-a-century at the head of her own warband, calming the crowd and assuring them that if no one attacked, no one else needed to die.

There was a period of threats and glaring between warbands, but the old woman, when backed by sufficient force of arms, proved up to the task. Even Jules's own command staff decided it wasn't worth dying when there was nothing to be done for their leader. Following Jules's own example, Brian quickly offered up Jules's seat on the Council to August, so long as everyone set aside any further efforts at violence for the day.

It served, at least until Marc arrived, much of his gang in tow. Despite greater numbers all but Brian backed away from Jules's body, still on the ground, as the bikers approached.

"What the hell?" Marc snarled. "The person who brought the tribes together gets murdered, and people are just standing around? Who do we need to throw into the Pit to rot?"

"No one today, Marc," Brian offered, looking him in the eye. "He wasn't murdered. His own ambition brought this on him."

Marc eyed the shotgun. "You killed him! But you fought beside us!"

"I did. I still believe in peace. But not at the cost of all of our freedom. He wasn't going to be content at the head of the Council."

"And that was so terrible that you had to kill him in the streets? You saw what kind of leader he was."

"This is still a nation of nomads, Marc. We need to be free. He was a general – victory at any cost. What would have happened to those who disagreed with him in politics? That's not hypothetical. There's evidence you'll need to see."

Marc stood, hands clenched and shaking, then stilled. "I'll look at your evidence. But you can understand why I'm not taking this well." He spread an empty hand and reached it towards Brian, who shook it.

"I know. He was my friend, too. But we did what we had to do. I'll give you a moment."

Marc knelt next to the body, moving it to a more dignified position, crossing the arms over his chest. More of his gang surrounded him. With that done, the biker spoke quietly, for none to hear save the Conqueror's ghost. "They did what they had to. They ask for peace, but their actions cry havoc. They've slain the huntsman… but the dogs of war will answer. On this, my friend, you have my word."

***

"So to get things over and done," Clay said. "We'll just give the body to his mixed-blood girl and let her take it out in the woods and paint herself white or whatever, as long as it's all done away from everyone, so the whole sorry business can be forgotten."

"No," Brian insisted. "There's a way to do things, and we'll do things right. A fellow like Jules gets a proper send off. Drinks, speeches, a good pyre. It's an opportunity to explain what happened to everyone, and why. That seems like my job. I did what needed doing, but I was his friend."

There was just the slightest cough, but not an indignant one, from Marc, standing on the edge, looking forlorn.

"Marc, I can only let you in on this if you can promise me you'll be reasonable about it. If you help everyone understand what happened, too. The Consolidation was bringing us closer to before the riots my grandfather started. And riots happen for a reason."

"I'd really, really appreciate being able to see him off, Brian. And I promise. I'll help everyone understand that riots happen for a reason."

***

Brian had never seen so many people in one place. The town square was packed, with more people on top of all the surrounding buildings. The funeral procession had drawn the entire local population, and now everyone had crowded as close as they could get to the small stage. He took a deep breath, stepping forward as the chosen spokesperson for the conspirators, and began. "Brothers and sisters… and yes, I consider you all my brothers and sisters now. We have peace. We have peace in large part because of the man being buried today. I fought against him in another time, and learned his genius firsthand. And then I fought at his side. I learned from him, and called him brother-in-arms. He was leader and teacher. And in my own fashion, let no one say I didn't love him like a brother.

"It's not that I hated him, or was jealous. I'm here today to honor his legacy. Ultimately, the problem was that, much as I did consider him like a brother, I love freedom more. We're free men now. He fought for peace, that we could have a future free of constant warfare and fear. And then he betrayed his own dream. We're nomads, people of the deserts, people of the wastes – born to freedom, and we'll die free. Now people can know where they stand and feel safe – in their movements, with their families, and at their trades. I mourn for Jules the Conqueror, even as I honor all he claimed aloud to stand for. Look around you. Be proud of what we've achieved together. Honor the Conqueror, mourn him as you will, and respect his legacy. But never forget: all we've gained, this fragile peace, this freedom; it comes with a cost."

Brian took a deep breath, looking out over the crowd. Then he gestured Marc forward, addressing the crowd one last time. "If any loved Jules more than I did, it may be this man. I leave you now, but he speaks with the Council's permission, to tell you of the Conqueror's past glories, acknowledging the man who brought us here."

The Brute stepped off the stage, moving to join some of the others of his company, feeling somewhat ill-at-ease among his chosen allies, but not so much so as he'd felt under Marc's scrutiny while he spoke.

The biker stepped up, looking out at the crowd. "I'm friends with some of you, while some of you maybe have grudges. Whatever else, though, today, we're countrymen. This is our land now, all of ours. So, from there, I guess I'm supposed to make a big speech about how we all got here, right? Well, I'm not gonna.

"They called Jules the Conqueror, and I guess that was right. He rolled over everything in his way. And then whoever that had been, he put their banner up on his bus. Sounds like ambition to me, right? The Brute says he was an ambitious man, and the Brute's family used the very same tank to put down the last tyrant we had. So I guess he'd know from ambition.

"And every time he rolled through somewhere, over someone else, Jules's advisors and lieutenants, they'd tell him to just cut his enemies' throats and be done with it. Maybe put their top men in chains. And sometimes he did. Look at Phillip. His damned banner still has the man's blood on it. But Jules, no, that wasn't his way. It wasn't enough to win. He couldn't just win, he needed to hear his enemies swear loyalty. And if they did, then they'd ride with him. His army grew and grew – because of all of these warlords he made swear an oath. I mean, can you imagine – a shame worse than death for proud men, right? But they did it, because they loved their fellows and families. Sounds like ambition to me, turning proud men from enemies into some kind of sworn soldiers. The Brute and his fellows say that was ambition, and they'd know. Half your councilors, the leaders of the city, had to endure all that shame and humiliation to end up where they are."

The crowd started to stir, a murmur rising in a few places. A couple of the conspirators noticed, looking between each other.

"And apparently, the Conqueror's ambition was making him a threat to the rank and file and the civilians here. The Brute's shown me scratched out messages from, for instance, the gentlemen of the corner repair shop over there. Frightened and intimidated, they were. I'd never heard of anything happening there, but I'm sure they must know. None of these guys would make something like that up."

Comments of confusion started to spread through the crowd. Brian waited for the shouts of affirmation, of clarification, which did not come, and part of his blood went cold.

"It wasn't so long ago that the Conqueror wasn't afraid of anyone," Marc continued. "And then he took a bullet that shattered his hip. We've all known pain, right? So what did the Conqueror do? No, he didn't lead from the front. No one saw his face in the field anymore. They had to rely on calls through the radio right up to this fort falling to him. Other men had to do his fighting for him, and what kind of man did that make him? Someone willing to gain from the pain and sacrifice of other men. The Peregrine, Casey Longrider – noble men of the Council have accused him of ambition. And surely people who worked for Phillip recognize ambition when they see it?"

Brian started towards the steps back to the platform, finding some of the bikers in the way. Thinking better of it, he headed quietly the other direction, working through the crowd to reach the Brute. A couple of the others likewise started working away from the stage.

"Once upon a time, Jules was a warrior. Got his old saber bloody a couple dozen times. But what point would a duel be now? That was then, now he was a cripple. If you could see the body right, you could still see the old scars that broke him, along with the stab wounds, and a gunshot." He mimed firing a pistol. "One shot, and no more tyranny. The town's all ours again, no worries."

Marc started to turn away, moving towards the steps, as the crowd went silent. Then he paused and turned back. "Speaking of the town being all yours, Jules shared some information with me. No harm in anyone knowing now, I guess. We got to talking after the games, back after that whole show with the victory crown and all. The one he didn't want... only because it wasn't the real thing, I suppose." He paused, reaching under his jacket to draw out a sheaf of folded papers. "But he told me where to find his will, in case. He wanted to make sure his kids got what was coming to them. Because that's what ambition is all about, right? Legacy. Who you leave what to. Whole bunch of stuff, cars, gas, guns... going to August, and some kid in New Zealand.

Great, right? What's that leave for you folk, who worked for him, bled for him, fought for him? Well, I guess he didn't totally forget you. Seems each warband gets a bunch of land in here. And trade rights. And a share of the town and its take. But, you know, it's all desert out there, right? What's that worth?" He flipped the paper open to the third page, and crouched, handing it off to the nearest hands in the crowd. "Whole lot of nothing. Miles and miles of wide open nothing. Enough nothing for everyone. And who knows if this town is worth anything? People sure fought for it, but what does that prove?

"So, you know – Jules the Conqueror is dead. People say he died because he was ambitious. Good, honorable men and women just out for the greater good. Men and women like the Peregrine, Casy Longrider, the Metal-head, Decker, Travis Nova, Grandmama Pauline, Madam Sin, Cal Forte, and the Brute. I'm done with praising Jules the Conqueror. Let's just be done with it and bury him. He's paid the price for his ambition. So, you know, keep in mind all the nothing he did for you, all the nothing he left you with, and thank the people who put him under if you see them, will you?"

For a few moments, silence reigned. Then the crowd erupted.

***

A dozen gravediggers and four undertakers were chosen to deal with the bodies before the desert sun made the town unbearable. A mass grave had been suggested and rejected. In the manner of the Conqueror, Marc declared that each man, whatever his warband, should have a funeral. Though mourners of different factions were asked to stay to opposite sides, Jules's loyalists nearer town and the conspirator's allies to the desert, all would be permitted to attend in peace. And every set of three bodies, until they were buried, would have a child assigned to them, to keep the buzzards away.

Three days of truce were given for these arrangements, and then there would be war.

***

Three factors had, in the end, held the town together, still able to be called a town, despite being in rough shape. August controlled the largest warband, composed of all of those whose oaths of loyalty to his father had meant something to them. In the chaotic scramble without leadership, most of the vehicles, or tactics, sheer numbers were often the rule of the day.

The bikes and veteran riders were the most readily able to make use of their vehicles in the riot situation. Mobility and being at home in the chaos helped, and their own leader had inspired the riots in the first place, giving them a fierce morale no one could match.

Next most suited to mobility in the cramped quarters was Leland Miller's cavalry. Most thought desert horses and camels were a waste, but it had meant that Miller's scavengers hadn't had to compete for all the same resources, and no one else needed the dry grasses of the scrublands. Miller, one of Jules's loyalists in Council, had also distinguished himself in the fight. By chance, his warband had been able to block Cal Forte from reaching his tank and following the Brute. The young conspirator was killed in the process, and a Molotov cocktail had landed inside the open tank. The armor had held when the shells detonated but it burned for two days, and the wreck remained where it had stood. Leland himself had run into another of the conspirators, and while Leland had been injured in the fight to the death, Casey Longrider's car keys, stained with their owner's blood, jangled from his belt as he limped towards the meeting of the new three-man council in charge of the town.

"We think most of the escapees are following either the Brute or the Peregrine," Marc pointed out, gesturing to the map on the table. "Our scouts lost them here, in the hills."

"Then why are we waiting? We need to get after them, before they escape," August insisted, gesturing to the lands heading for the coast.

"They're not trying to escape. They're just buying time to get organized," Marc answered, nodding to Miller as the horseman entered and sat at the table in what was left of Sin's bar.

"How can you be so sure?" the young man asked, glaring at Marc.

"Where are they going to go? They need supplies, and they know

209

one way to get them. Besides, we ruined their plans. They'll want revenge."

"They'll want revenge? They're the murderers!" August said.

"Doesn't stop them from being pissed off. They tried for power, and they lost."

"And took my father, and half the town down with them."

"Might any of them negotiate?" Miller tried. "The Brute, perhaps?"

August glared at the horseman, who went silent. "There'll be no deals. Anyone who followed them back into the desert is a traitor."

Marc sighed. "We're not going to be able to hunt down every last man out there. A lot of them were confused. And riding with a warlord long enough will…"

August cut him off, "Then we'll give them the choice. Surrender, and there'll just be some time in the Pit. Stand with traitors and die."

"No one is going to trust that. I wouldn't," Marc answered.

"I suppose you have a better idea?"

"Cut off the heads of the serpent, and anyone in the direct way. Then do what your father did, and offer to let the next man up swear an oath, in order to let the bands back in. Some will take it."

"Decker's men, given half a chance…"

"My father's way got him killed."

"Your father's way saved a lot of lives, and made him a lot of friends," Marc said.

"Who weren't there when he needed them. He was expecting to meet you, Marc."

"And Travis made sure I was distracted. Part of their plan."

"It certainly didn't take much effort on their part."

"He was an ally – we were both part of the Council. "

"You were awfully close to some of the murderers."

Marc gestured to the damaged town. "Does it look like I have any friends there? Be careful, kid. I'd hate to think you were questioning where my loyalties lie."

"I'll be more careful when I'm more sure of my allies. And I believe your loyalties lie in New Zealand, with one of my father's women, and my little brother. That's certainly less tangled for you now, isn't it?"

"So that's what this is about? Your father had no problems with that arrangement, why do you?"

"Because my brother gives you a claim to the crown, and you've already ruined the town once. For good reasons, but I have no assurance that you're planning to stop with the traitors."

"I could care less about the crown. My fiancee has one, and if that's what he really wants, my best friend's son can have one when this is all said and done. Or are you forgetting who was offering it to your father in front of everyone?"

"For show. You're useful, but trust that you'll be watched, warlord."

"Watch all you like. All you're going to see is me winning a war for your benefit before I decide this place isn't worth the trouble anymore and go visit your father's girlfriend."

Leland started once again to say something, and thought better of it.

"You'll be winning the war? I have the biggest warband, by far. I've been preparing for this from my father's lessons. Your help is appreciated, but…"

Marc cut him off, standing from the table and preparing to leave. "Tactics from books and lessons isn't the same as having seen a fight, kid. I'm going to go meet with my damned scouts. Let me know when you're ready to meet with someone who actually knows what they're doing in the damned field."

***

Leaving the city had been hard, but at least he'd had the good sense to see it coming. People filtering out after the riots didn't always have it so lucky, and good portions of the conspirators, and their forces, hadn't made it out at all.

Now, for good or ill, they were one giant warband, led mostly by Brian and the Peregrine. Those who had followed the Brute out escaping in its wake, and all of Cal's forces, swore fealty to Brian, while many of those of the town were added to the Peregrine's band. And everyone present, except Brian, wanted to kill Marc and the College Boys for what had been done.

Brian couldn't help but question his allegiances now. The Peregrine had lied to him, no question. A fight between their bands, however, could easily ensure none of them survived. Had the split been over anything less, he might have been able to go back and ally with Marc and August. But while Marc might see a way to compromise, if it meant the super heavy tank was with him instead of against him, he was sure Jules's son would never see reason.

"You too, Brute?" came the voice from behind him.

He whirled, at first seeing no one, amidst the early morning of the camp. "Who's there?"

"Wondering if you were having trouble sleeping, too," came a voice, now just a bit to his left. Turning again, he saw Jules, sitting on a rock, looking at him.

Brian blinked, and rubbed his eyes, trying to clear them. "Jules?"

"What's left, yes. Apparently there's something to my wife's superstitions after all."

"You can't be real."

"Unfortunately, untrue. I have to be real, at least until my murder is resolved. Then, hopefully, you're right, and I can rest."

"You had to be stopped. You were lying to all of us."

Jules sighed heavily. "True, this time. The next time the crown came up, I wasn't going to push it away. I did want the Council's advice, but there were too many grudges. Someone had to lead if there was ever going to be real peace."

"You, Jules?"

"I was to be a place holder. Warming a seat. It's true my son can barely drive. He certainly can't shoot. Because I always wanted it that way. I wanted to unite an Empire that could be passed on to someone who ruled from books and wisdom. Not at the point of a gun. Yes, I was ambitious, but not the way anyone thought."

Brian sighed, looking down at his gun. "And now we're back to war. This isn't what I wanted, Jules. This isn't what any of us wanted."

"This isn't what you wanted, I know. Some of your allies would rather watch the world burn, if they can't control it."

"They lied to me. I see that now. Without that, I never would have..."

"I believe you. You're a better man than most in this day and age. A better man than I was. But I'm afraid the chance for peace is lost. I see a bigger picture now. Soon, we'll both have a chance to rest."

"Wait... what... how, when?"

"A great deal of that is still in your hands. But you'll see me two more times. And after our third meeting, you will die. It's not my choice, Brian. But it is what it is."

Brian stammered, trying to find the words. By the time his mind cleared enough to ask another question, Jules was no longer sitting there, but two of his guards, Claude and Vance, were approaching. "Did you see the man sitting here?" he called to them.

"Man, sir? You were all by yourself. Muttering and talking to yourself, sure. You feeling all right?"

"Yes, yes, thank you, Vance," he answered, "Just not enough sleep. Too much to do."

"All right, well... get some sleep, sir. We've got watch for a couple hours still. It'll be all right."

***

Feeling very much not all right, and not at all like sleeping, Brian sat in his tent, trying to convince himself the ghost had been a figment of his imagination. When the rest of the camp started stirring, he joined the Peregrine for breakfast. "You brought this on all of us."

"Blame Marc, not me. And blame yourself. You insisted that he be allowed to speak. For that matter, that he be allowed to live."

"And I'm glad for it. I'm having a hard enough time just being a murderer once over."

"Liberator. I may have forged some details, but Jules was going to take over, one way or another. That part was always true."

"Which upset you only because it wasn't you being offered the crown."

"This is getting us nowhere. Talk and trouble yourself all you want. We have to deal with right now. You can accuse me of anything you like when we retake the town and form a new Council."

"With you at the head?" Brian asked, an eyebrow raised.

"Stick with me, help me win this war, and you can have the big chair, for all I care. I'll sign anything you want to that effect, in front of my own people if you like. We stand little enough chance of surviving. But if we're united, we can still win."

"All right, so I assume you have a plan?"

"I do. The town is going to be impossible to assault, but we can starve them out. We know where they are, and where any of their people will be coming from and going to. We hit their supply trucks, destroy their scavengers, and keep moving. And when they come out in force for us, we choose the ground. You engage August's forces, and I'll get my revenge on the College Boys and whoever comes with them."

"Just personal, or do you have some other reason for who takes on whom?"

"Strategy. You have more armor, you can take on the heavy trucks, and buses, and cars. August's numbers would crush me, but you have a chance. But against Marc? They'd be on you before you could fire a shot. And if they ran, you'd never catch them."

"I don't seem to recall you catching them on your last chance, either."

"I have five times the troops I did then, and he won't call too many others. Anything remotely heavy would slow down his precious cycles. And this time, he's chasing me down, not the other way around. I've got this."

"And when do we meet again?"

"In town, once it's fallen. Send your pilot up. I'll mount a red flag when Marc is dead. You run up August's blue eagle banner when he falls. Without them, we can take the town and meet in the middle. We'll start over, without the Conqueror, this time."

***

August attacked at dawn, his main force coming from the east. The bright desert sunrise shimmering off the desert floor masked his approach until they were all too close to the Brute's forces. The scouts in the towers built onto the top of one of the buses gave the first warning. "Incoming and moving fast! The kid's bus, and plenty of friends!"

The camp, mostly prepared to move or launch into war, became a flurry of action. Individual camps flung into the backs of trucks as drivers and gunners raced for their stations. The noise of engines drowned out everything else, as Brian and his tank crew raced for their stations in the Brute.

As soon as he reached his driver's station and his radio, he gave the command. "Straight at them, guard the supply trucks, heaviest armor at the front, faster vehicles stay behind the armor until we engage." He didn't know a lot of his new troops, or how they'd react. His own people would take to his standard formation fine. The rest, he just had to give the commands and hope for the best.

The radio crackled to life. "Towards their charge, sir?" One of his new lieutenants, wasting time.

"Towards them, follow me, and stay behind the damned heavies 'til I say so!"

There was a moment of silence while the tank roared to life and started the crawl forward, before the radio crackled again. "That's right into the teeth of their guns. August has a lot of cars out there, sir."

"He would. A lot of cars. When they get closer, take a very close look. It'll be a lot of cars, bikes, and other fast-and-lights, with the bus and its guards as big, shiny, necessary distractions. He'll have everything that can come up on us quick in one big line, to kick up dust and look like there's even more than there are – and everything with heavy armor and anti-tank weapons behind us, waiting for when we scramble to high ground. Go towards them, boys and girls. Right at the line, and no one fire a shot 'til I do. Cars and jeeps, just guard the supply trucks. Don't let them get around you."

One more pause, and, drawing a sigh from Brian, one more question. "The spies don't see nothing, sir. How do you know where his big guns are?"

"Because that's what all the books say to do, Lieutenant. As soon as Stratton gets airborne, he'll verify."

Machine-gun fire kicked up clouds of dirt and rattled off the tank's armor, and the heavy-plow guards of Brian's first wave of armor. There were some panicked shouts over communications, but the line kept going. "Target the Conqueror's bus, sir?" asked the spotter, as a two-man crew loaded the first heavy shell.

"And waste a shot on the heaviest armor? Find anything with a big gun mount or a missile launcher, take it out. Then do it again. Anything anti-armor, put a hole in it. Because by all the gods, I can't trust anyone else in this piecemeal army to do it. And don't fire 'til you have a sure shot. We don't have ammo to spare."

At the very least, the gangers in his new army followed the order to just drive into the machine-gun fire and whatever else August's army could throw at them, until the tank's main gun fired. One of August's jeeps took a hit, launching into the air and flying backwards, forcing cars around it to skid to a halt veer out of line. Seconds later, Brian's machine-gunner popped out of the main tank and to his station, the veteran gunner picking his targets and firing salvos into lead cars.

There were shouts and damage reports, but Brian kept his voice calm, insisting people stick to the pattern. Too many parts of his new warband were more used to evasion and high-speed dogfighting, not enough used to heavy armor. Smelling blood, some of the cars – parts of the Metal-head's former forces, he thought – broke formation, launching themselves out in front of his road-graders. After the first shout to get back in line, there was nothing he could do The cars blew apart under concentrated fire. August had too many guns on hand – the biggest force Brian had ever seen in one place, and he knew this was less than half of what was out there.

Seeing some of their own in flames, more cars and a few cycles broke ranks, trying to speed out and away off the flanks. A few more broke off and raced backwards, away from August's charge. After the first shouts Brian shook his head, and called, "Stay in the damned line, and quit firing at the shiny bus. Cars, get the cars!" A few more of his forces broke off, but all of his own band and plenty of the veterans of other warbands followed orders, and more and more gaps started to show in August's line.

Without giving the opponent even a second of a break in his armor-line, Brian went right over one of the flaming wrecks of cars that had broken formation, gritting his teeth and reminding himself that by the time he reached them, if they were alive and hadn't gotten out already, he'd saved them burning to death.

They hit August's line, heavy trucks with plow attachments, APCs, modified battle-vans, and the tank crashing directly into the lighter, faster vehicles that couldn't get out of the way in time. True to Brian's prediction, nothing heavy met them aside from the central bus, covered in banners, and the two heavy trucks flanking it, playing bodyguard.

As the heavy armor line broke holes in August's line, the trailing cars, trucks, and bikes altered course to break through the blockade. Another call came over the lines. "We have an opening. Are we running, sir?"

"Hell no, Lieutenant. All armor, twenty more yards, and all-stop. Give our guns some cover, and let the supply trucks get past you. Cars, jeeps, anything faster than a truck, get past the armor line, let the kid think we're making a run for it, then come about. Do as much damage as you can – two passes, and two passes only. Ignore the bus and kill anything designed for pursuit."

"Two passes? We have them confused. We ought to go for the kill while we've got it," came the answer.

"Kid is green, but he won't stay confused forever. Their armor will be moving by now, and I don't plan to be around when it gets here. Trust me, target pursuit vehicles only. Two passes, and we're gone. Stratton, can you get me confirmation? Are they moving?"

The sound of the gyro's blades came through in the background as the old pilot called back, "Damned right they're moving. Looks like he finally figured it out – they had you totally surrounded. I'm getting out of missile range, and heading to scout the next camp, sir. I'll firebomb their lines when I pass you."

Brian and the tank hit the twenty-yard mark. "All armor, stop. Boys, bring the big gun around and put a round up their tailpipes. Supplies and supply escorts, full throttle. Get beyond us so we can cover your backs. Everyone else, let's do some damage."

He lost men and wheels he couldn't afford in the exchange, as the lighter cars engaged one another, and a couple of his heavies finally took too much gunfire, one of the trucks rolling, another just exploding as an armor-piercing shell found the gas tank. Some of his people broke position, and they lost a supply truck when its cover bugged out. But for all the damage he took, August's confused forces took more. The tank's cannon fired true again and again, eliminating the heaviest guns, and dozens of August's fastest, lightest vehicles were left flaming wrecks.

"That's our firing runs. Move it, now!" Brian finally called, just as the Conqueror's bus was finally coming about, all of the banners glaringly obvious even amidst the dust clouds. Most of his forces followed orders, while some, focusing on August's forces in disarray, remained engaged, destroying everything they could. "Move it!" he shouted one more time. The call pulled a few more vehicles from the fray, but not enough. "Armor line is moving. Anyone who can't get in front of it gets left behind. We're out of time."

It grated against his instincts to abandon anyone, but he knew the kind of numbers closing on them. Even the Brute wasn't going to stand up when the big guns showed up. He still had a warband, and the people left had seen him get them through at least the first battle. He'd exposed August's lack of experience, and the kid's army was in worse shape than the Brute's, at least in terms of losing a lot of speed. He was going to call it a win – an expensive one, but a win.

It got slightly more expensive when he saw Jules standing in the tank's path through his viewscreen. He was about to ask if anyone else saw that, but there were no shouts of alarm, and he thought better of it. By the time the tank ground over the earth where the Conqueror had been standing, Jules was gone.

***

"Cut them off, cut them off! Bring the guns around!" The Peregrine was shouting into the radio, working on coordinating his own hunter-killers with the mishmash of units he'd picked up from other warbands. On first contact with Marc's forces, he'd hit the bastard hard. The Peregrine's personal band's own cars were elite, with veteran drivers. Phillip had let him take his pick of men, mechanics, and vehicles to get the job done. Marc had picked up a bunch of trucks, both from vehicles left abandoned in the city, and from volunteers to serve under his command instead of the kid's. Problem was, the biker wasn't used to commanding the heavy vehicles, and it showed. Clay's mixture of sports cars and modified hot rods made them look like they were standing still, and the escort cars with the armor division hadn't been much help. Quick passes with machine guns and light rockets had shredded the tires, leaving most of the big rigs sitting ducks, while the Peregrine's armor and big guns closed in. They'd mostly had to limit themselves to taking out the tires, not the more heavily armored sections or personnel. But they'd remedy that when their own bigger guns closed in.

Under heavier fire, the gun nests on the trailers stopped firing back as gunners abandoned their stations, and the armor started to buckle. That was when half the trucks popped open, and the motorcycles poured out the backs, engaging the cars, while the Peregrine's scouts starting calling in something about more waves of Marc's own cars closing in.

The trucks were little more than cover now, but that cover was providing the perfect environment for the motorcycles. The Peregrine's heavy guns couldn't draw a bead on them, especially with the hunter-killer cars trying to chase them around the armor; fast and maneuverable as the cars were, the cycles were even quicker. The fact that the tiny vehicles could fit under the trailers, appearing out of nowhere to cut off pursuing cars, gave them more of an edge.

With most of his big guns rendered useless, the Peregrine turned them in the direction from which the scouts said more of Marc's army was approaching. Amidst the confusion, having enough trouble with the deadly game of tag around the trucks, with an unknown number of enemies closing, some of the units in the Peregrine's army broke, ignoring his calls and threats.

He was sure, any moment, there'd be explosions and gunfire, and shouts over the radios from the retreating units, but there was nothing. Marc was letting them flee. All that news did was encourage a few more cars to break ranks and run for open ground, abandoning the Peregrine and the rest of his forces.

Now, the Peregrine wasn't sure how many troops were closing in, exactly, and the bikes were making a fool of his best men. If he didn't act decisively, he'd keep losing people. When faced with a decision, the hunter chose the aggressive one. "Charge the bikes!" If he filled the area with enough metal and guns, there'd be nowhere for them to run to. Better, when the rest of Marc's forces arrived, the Peregrine and his men would have the heavy cover of the biker's own armored division.

Clay's joy was short lived, putting the plan together only when he saw the cycles coming at him, Marc's most elite troops weaving through oncoming traffic and ignoring everything except the lead vehicle. They let his troops go, because Marc wasn't after them. He had no designs on killing the Peregrine's warband. It was all to get him to commit, and get close enough to them that they could engage without coming under a rain of gunfire themselves. The first crowbar cracked his reinforced windows. The baseball bat caved it in. The Peregrine started to wheel around, calling a retreat, but it was too late. The third cycle tore past, flinging the bottle and flaming rag through the broken window, and amidst a charge turning into a chaotic retreat, the Peregrine's world went up in flames.

***

As soon as they'd left August and his men regrouping and licking their wounds, Brian had been able to set camp. They'd circled the supply trucks and set up gun emplacements, then sent lighter vehicles out to scavenge for food. After two days of rest and repairs, he would start preparing for the next battle, gathering his warriors and leading a column to high ground where they could see the dust rising from the desert if anyone came their way.

Right now, though, Brian was approaching the radio. "Any message transcripts?"

"Just ... just one. From our guys in town, hiding some of the civilians."

"What did they say?"

"Well, sir, there was ... something happened... and they found a note, and they read it, and I wrote it down, but ..."

Brian sighed and just snatched the sheet from the man's hand.

Dear Brian:

So that's what it was really all about.

You killed Jules. For Freedom.

For some of us, Jules's Consolidation wasn't about losing Freedom. It was about gaining it. I never thought we were on an inevitable slide to being dominated by Bureaucracy or any other Tyranny. I thought that a lot of us could look over our shoulder less, not live in fear of being made into some macho statement by a guy showing one set of colors who thought we 'belonged' to a guy with another set of colors. I thought people's coming together with a few more ground rules gave plenty in the community the freedom from total subjugation on any random thug's whim.

For just a short time, I had slow breakfasts with a good husband. I won't go back to only ever smelling blood, gas, and fear. I won't.

I'd have been happy to tell you my thoughts on the subject before, if you'd ever been willing to talk about it like we were both grown adults.

I love you. Know that. But I am going out on my terms, not as some trophy for the enemies you made for yourself.

Trish

Patricia was gone. He was just absorbing the shock of the note when the call came through on the radio. He didn't even need to answer before Stratton relayed the news.

"Mate, the Peregrine is dead. His boys have scattered. Half of 'em are coming your way to join up, the others are buggering off or surrendering. Marc is on their heels. He's coming for you. Be ready."

***

"Can't, Brian. I can't be the guy that did that." Ericson had been his

221

gunner for five years. Brian trusted him but understood. He'd have a hard time had the request gone the other way.

Brian had gotten the battle report from the stragglers of Clay's band who showed up to join him. It hadn't been a battle. It had been a hit. Marc had sacrificed the trucks and feigned a mass charge, just to lure the Peregrine into striking range. And when they had him, they assassinated him, rescued their personnel from the trucks, and ran. Far more of the Peregrine's troops had survived then anyone would have expected, and Brian figured it sent a clear message to most of the veterans with the experience to recognize what had happened.

Jules would have done the same in the situation. Brian might have too, if he thought slightly more like a sniper and less like an armored division commander. Still, he had to appreciate the attempt to spare lives, even if he was pretty sure it would bring Marc and August into conflict. The boy definitely hadn't intended to show any mercy.

With Marc leading the rush at them, after Brian had left most of the kid's faster troops crippled, he knew what he had to do.

"You don't understand, fellas." Brian clutched the note. "This *has* to be the last word. They can't find me bleeding and gibbering – or locked in myself because my aim was just a bit off. They need to get a corpse and a note, because if I'm anything that could be called 'alive,' they can fight through people to get to me, and we've lost enough. We really have."

"I can't, mate," every man of his tank crew said, one by one. "You're my brother."

Brian was breathing heavily, panic setting in. And it happened again: he thought he saw Jules. He thought he saw Jules staring up at the sky.

Brian looked – and watched the little gyrocopter come in for a landing. He went to meet it, holding the note in one hand and the saber in the other.

"They're coming, Brian," the little guy said as he unhooked himself.

"Stratton," Brian said. "This is important. They have to get a corpse and a note. I need you to kill me."

Stratton took off his goggles and looked Brian in the eye. "Of course, mate," he said, reaching for the cavalry saber. "You're like a brother to me."

***

"You want to forgive all of these traitors, just let them drive back into town like nothing ever happened, because he left a note?" August was fuming as he paced, glaring at the biker and his lieutenants. Marc had decided it wasn't wise to hold these meeting entirely privately.

"Dying wish, both to us, and his men. And a chance at the peace your father wanted. If we don't then they find new leadership, and this fight goes on a very, very long time. And I don't guarantee we'd win. I don't even guarantee I'd be on your side. Let it go. You have your revenge on your father's killers."

"These people just fought against us, Marc. Tried to kill us. We can't trust them."

"Your father protected you from a lot, August. And he spent a lot of money and favors doing it. But this is reality. If I could only drink with people who'd never been my enemy, I'd be drinking alone a lot. And some days, knowing the things I've done, even that wouldn't work."

"And I suppose you think I should offer their elected commanders spots on the Council, right?"

"I'd strongly suggest we do that, yes. But I think people will understand if you keep bodyguards."

"I'll take it under advisement."

"I ain't your advisor, kid. We formed a three-way alliance. I respected your father. He was a great leader. He should have been Emperor. You haven't earned that yet. We're tearing out the high council seat and putting in three. 'Til we do, and until you quit acting like you're already running everything, all these people who rebelled out of fear of someone calling themselves the Emperor are going to be real edgy. And you'll actually need those bodyguards."

"I still have the most warriors, the most cars, and the most guns. Don't threaten me or tell me how it's going to be."

"And the Brute made you look like an idiot. You're a smart kid. I see a lot of your father's brains in you. Be smart. We won. Take it and walk away."

August glared at the biker for a few more moments, then answered, "Fine," before turning and walking back to his command staff.

Marc nodded to his men, then walked to where Brian June, the Brute, lay atop the body of the tank, clothes rearranged to cover the wounds, appearing more at peace than he ever had in life. Marc sighed.

"August won't be happy when he finds out about the part of the note I didn't read. But I'll do it. You'll be cremated inside your tank. When the shells all go off, it'll go with you."

He leaned against the tank, continuing to talk to the body. "I know you're hoping it'll be a symbol to some, that maybe we can try peace now, and put the weapons away. Even now, you're the best of us, my friend. Killer, yes. But not a murderer. I finally believe that you always did what you thought was right for the people, no matter what it cost you. I wish I could say the same, but I'm not that good. Soon enough, the three-man alliance will fall apart. One corner is too angry, another is too weak, and the third... the third has his heart across the sea already."

Marc pushed away from the tank, turning in the direction of the coastline as if he could see it, hundreds of miles away. "I'll run from one of the Conqueror's sons to another. I'll finally see her again. And when war follows me, we'll fight, and we'll see whose son ends up inheriting a crown. And when he does, I'll hope he's a better man than me."

And he called his boys and the tank crew to load the body into the tank, and arrange it among the shells. They waited until August was on his way back to the town, with most of the forces in tow. Marc had the opportunity to light the long fuse after the speeches were done, but passed the torch instead to the old pilot, the most loyal of the Brute's men.

As the relic burned, Marc could only think that an era, one of warfare and bloodshed, was passing. Then the shells detonated, one by one. The ground shook, and fires climbed high into the skies. Everyone's ears were ringing too loud to hear him say, "And its death throes herald in a new one."

After all, war was all the desert people ever knew.

Clockpunk Sonnets

127

In a time no longer asserting youth

Your bodice'd form would have claimed no eyes,

And those it did would be quickly shielded.

But now in the Victorian sway of your hips does attraction lie

And the drapery that passed for dress in the era past has died.

For even the poorest of street urchins can don the flowing clothes

And pass for young royalty of Georgian nobles.

Beauty seems to be erased from the earth

And resides no longer in its special place.

The turn of time has cheapened its worth,

Leaving a broken heart in its place.

But you, with your eyes so dark

That they pierce the night as you sail along in airships flying through the sky,

Are a contradiction of beauty without the delicacy that is a common find.

Yet it is beauty that those which look into your piercing eyes behold,

Such that every tongue says beauty should look so.

HANK

Carol Gyzander

CHAPTER ONE

THE RED GLOW of the dim security lighting barely illuminated his path as the door of the man-trap closed behind him; his small beam of light scanned the research lab as he got his bearings. Keying the access to the storage vault, the red-haired man pocketed a small, flat package, then turned to the screen next to it and inserted a tiny data storage unit from his pocket. When it beeped, he passed his wrist display over the scanner to enter his ID badge; another beep, and he withdrew the unit.

Moving about the lab, the man placed three small incendiary devices, setting each to trigger mode as he did so. One last look around, and he pressed his ID badge to the door mechanism of the security man-trap. After the door cycled and he passed through, it closed behind him; he again showed his ID badge to open the second door.

The man smiled and his shoulders relaxed a little as he walked down the hallway. Once outside the building, he reached into his pocket and pressed a button; he headed down the London street between a few other late night travelers, counting in his head. Others around him jumped when a deafening boom filled the air. He started to whistle, heading to the transit stop.

CHAPTER TWO

"Jesus. There's nothing left of this place." Hank rubbed his face with his hand while the two men stood and surveyed the destruction that had been the research lab. The young, wiry man grimaced. "I don't even know how to get any information from this wreckage, Bardolph." *I've been back a month and this happens?*

Although about the same age as Hank, the other man had scars on his cheek and a more haggard appearance that added years to his age.

"Hank, my friend," said Bardolph. "That's why you brought me up out of the Underground when you came back to work here. There are actually a number of clues available; judging by the direction of the displaced wall materials, and the size of the holes in the floors and ceilings, I'd say there were two... no, three pocket devices that were likely triggered at once. And they were placed inside, by someone with proper access who is probably a novice, as the lab was destroyed but the doors to the man-trap are still intact and no security alarms were triggered by a fake access ID. Probably Class 3 incendiary devices, which means there is a French component to our little scene here."

Hank shook his head. "You can tell all that...?"

Bardolph smiled. "Seriously, Hank, you would know this if you hadn't lived such a sheltered youth. Tsk, tsk, growing up at daddy's knee here in EngCorp."

"Come on, man. I left that behind. And you know my forte has been accessing financial systems, not bombs. I can't help it if you like destruction."

"Heh. I like to get into systems AND blow them up. What can I say? I'm multi-skilled."

"Seriously, Bardolph, don't let security or Uncle Exeter hear you say that. I had enough trouble convincing them that I wanted you on staff now that I'm back."

"Right."

"OK, I'm ready to ask the Head of Research what else he knows about this; he's coming to give me the report I asked for on the Doomsday Project anyway." *Finally I will get some information about what brought me back from the Underground.*

"Doomsday Project? You're going to take on Agincourt? Those French bastards are the biggest arms manufacturers in the world. I wouldn't be surprised if the incendiary devices that blew this place came from them."

"Come on, you know what I've been working toward the last five years. I just need to get more trust from Uncle Exeter and the EngCorp board, but this kind of maneuver gives me good backing for moving ahead. Jesus, Bardolph, Agincourt chooses to manufacture weapons when ninety percent of the world's population has trouble finding enough safe food to eat."

Hank looked his companion in the eyes. "I've done as much as I can from outside the system; I came back to EngCorp to harness the power of these corporations to help people instead of dominate and destroy them. Maybe I can do it from inside."

"Yeah, yeah. Wanna hold my hand while you step down off your soapbox, Hank?"

"Ah, shut up. Be in my office in fifteen minutes. And be on good behavior."

CHAPTER THREE

Hank sat with his back to the ornately carved wooden desk, one foot propped up on the window ledge. The rest of the furniture in the huge corner office was sleek and streamlined, and a wall of display screens covered one side of the wall in addition to the one on the desk. Two men sat on couches by the bar at the far end of the room.

Hank's hands were clasped in front of him as he stared out the window over the city, pointer fingers tapping on his lips.

"Do you really think the French are never going to release this Doomsday weapon, Arlo? And it is only going to be used for intimidation purposes?" Hank asked, his chin on his chest. *I can't believe this is my corporation's official opinion on Agincourt's project: not to worry about it.*

Hank looked out over the city from his office viewpoint at the top of the largest building in the city. From there, he could see the shining, clean apartments and offices of the corporate world, but little of the dark, twisted alleys of the lower levels of the city where the majority of its residents struggled to make a living. The Underground, an area where he was quite competent, and which had until recently been his home.

"Well, yessir, that is the opinion of the research committee." The chubby, balding man standing in front of the desk clutched a thickly bound sheaf of papers as he spoke.

"Come on, Arlo. I asked *your* opinion, not that of the paper goons. And don't call me sir." Hank turned the chair to look at the man, noting the shift of weight from side to side and the refusal to look in his eye as Arlo hugged the report tightly to his chest.

"Yessir, I mean Henry."

"Hank. Call me Hank. I stopped being Henry when I left the President's mansion and moved to the Underground. And now that my father has passed away and I'm back, I'm still Hank."

"Yessir, um, Hank."

"Come on, we're doing this all wrong. Sit down and let's just talk. This is important stuff we're discussing, and you're the Head of Research. We want to know *your* opinion, Arlo, on this and the other important subject of the day." Hank walked around to the front of the desk and gestured to the pair of chairs in front of the desk. He flicked a glance at his Uncle Exeter, a distinguished man with an impeccable haircut, sitting on the couch at the side of the room next to Bardolph, who slouched with his head on the back of the couch. Hank settled into one of the chairs, and Arlo perched on the edge of the other chair without sitting back, the report held primly in his hands.

"Can we get you something? Coffee? Maybe something a little stronger?"

Arlo shook his head quickly, then looked up and nodded a bit. "Could I try a glass of juice? The real stuff? I've never had it before."

"Fine, Arlo, that's good. Gentlemen?" And Hank looked again at the pair at the side of the room. Exeter glanced at Bardolph, who smiled and put his feet up on the coffee table. Exeter stiffened for a moment, then got up, poured several glasses from the sideboard and brought them over. He returned to the couch, smoothing his expensive suit as he sat down.

"Thank you, Uncle. Here, this is better – we can sit together and talk." Hank suppressed a smile as he sipped his drink, then placed it on the edge of the desk and smiled at Arlo. *Hey, let's put this guy at ease. He'll talk more.*

Hank said, "You're the expert on this stuff. And I'm going to review the report, and then we can talk in more detail later. So let me tell you what I know and then you can tell me if I have it right, okay?"

Arlo nodded, sipping his drink. "Oh, my." He gulped some more and smiled.

"OK, so this report spells out for me the details of this new Doomsday weapon. Agincourt is using it to intimidate us into letting them take the lead in various economic forums, because we're afraid to provoke them into letting it loose on the world. The corporation feels that it is too risky to oppose them, and you agree with the report. Correct?"

"Yes. That is what the report describes. Sir, if I may turn your attention to the first three pages..."

"Arlo. It's OK, I can read the report on my own. Now that I know you support it, I will look at it tonight. In the meantime, I want to review something else of more immediate importance with you – last night's theft of the moddy chip research and destruction of the chip lab."

Arlo paled. "I... I have not prepared anything on that..."

Wow. I've been dreading this kind of bureaucratic thinking. Why wouldn't he assume that would be important enough to discuss?

Hank continued, "I know that EngCorp has been working on these moddy chips for a long time, and that they promise to be good options for communication and security, but the communication aspect is the current problem – how to make them transmit reliably over long distances. Right?"

Arlo nodded again, carefully settling back in the chair a bit with the glass tightly gripped in both hands, the report balanced on his knees. He took another gulp of the sweet juice. "Yessir, that is the gist of it. If we can get these moddy chips to be more reliable, we can use them across the corporation for controlling what kind of access people have to facilities, logging reports, and sending messages to someone wherever they are." Arlo moved his hands apart to indicate the transmission of data across supposed vast distances, slowing his hands as the precious juice threatened to spill on the report in his lap.

"Then we will not be dependent upon someone losing their cell phone or running out of battery power...and will not suffer communication interruptions due to power breakdowns or electrical storms. And, in the event that Agincourt releases whatever form of destruction this Doomsday weapon takes, with the chips, we won't be likely to be isolated without communication."

Hank had been watching Arlo intently as he spoke. "So the key issue is that we need a reliable communication method that is not dependent upon an external, continuous power supply? That's why they're placed inside the body?"

Arlo's eyes brightened and he leaned forward, patting the nape of his neck with his empty hand. "Exactly! When the moddy chip is installed in the base of the neck, it can use the electrical energy of the neural system for a never-ending source of power…at least while the person is alive. Perhaps for a little while after." He drank more juice and his foot started tapping rapidly on the floor.

"I see." Hank nodded. He looked at Bardolph who was grinning as he watched Arlo twitch. *This guy is getting high on the sugar in the juice!*

"We also have information that Agincourt has been working on this same technology for a while?" Hank said.

Arlo nodded vigorously and would have sloshed the contents of his glass if he had not already emptied it.

"Bah, Agincourt! Those French bastards. I think they stole the idea from us six months ago – but maybe they got stuck. We had a working prototype of a moddy chip, and I would say they broke in and took it. A classic case of corporate espionage! Well. OK, it wasn't exactly a working one, but that line was really promising. They took it and all the records and destroyed the lab where it was being developed. Now the head developer for that line of moddy chips is gone. Maybe they kidnapped him."

Arlo shrugged and held out the empty glass, looking in Exeter's direction. The distinguished man raised his eyebrows, then rose to pour another glass. Hank raised his hand and his uncle paused before pouring.

"So, Arlo, we have other labs that are also developing these moddy chips? The thief didn't get them all?" *I really hope that is true.*

Arlo smiled. "Oh, heavens yes. Our most promising line of moddy chips was not even touched; that lab is in another, more secure location. And this juice is wonderful – I don't know how you can get the real thing. I swear, the stuff you get in the store is just appalling. Nasty stuff. Thank you." Exeter resumed pouring at a gesture from Hank.

Hank nodded and smiled, and raised his glass to Arlo, having only had a few sips of his own drink. Arlo drank again.

"So, Arlo, do we have any proof that it was Agincourt who took the prototype?"

"Proof? I know it was them! Those nasty French bastards." Arlo scowled.

"Yes, you said that, but if we want to get the prototype and plans back, it would help if we had some proof; then I could get our corporate lawyer – Uncle Exeter, here – to make a legal claim against them for the return of our equipment."

Arlo frowned and looked down at the report in his lap. "This is not what I thought we would be discussing. I, uh, did not prepare a report on this."

"It's all right, man, just tell us what you know. Is there any proof that they were the ones who took the prototype?"

"Proof? No… uh, no, I do not have any proof. I personally think it was Smith, the young guy who worked doing cleanup in the lab. He was about your age, sir… uh, Hank. And he had a French accent." Arlo's words began to come more rapidly.

"We just thought he was one of the guys who came in to work from the Underground and went back to the city at the end of each shift. He passed the security scan. But he should have been on cleanup duty when the accident happened, and – except for the developer – he was the only one who did not come back to work afterward. I mean, who would give up a good job like that? There are so many people who need work."

Hank held out his hand. "All right, then. Thank you, Arlo, we'll be in touch. And I'll look your report over tonight."

At Hank's curt nod, the research chief fumbled with the empty glass and the report as he handed them to Hank, managed to shake hands as well, then stood and headed out.

When the door had closed behind him, Exeter came over to join Hank by the desk. "So, what are you thinking, nephew?"

"Bardolph and I need to do some investigation. But I think that this may be our best chance to do two things at once – get our plans back, and take over Agincourt so they don't destroy the world."

"What?" Exeter's voice was shrill. "You're serious?"

"Come on, Uncle, you knew there was a reason that I agreed to come back to EngCorp after my father died. Contrary to what most people think, it wasn't just because I wanted to make money. I've been living in a world most of the board members here have no concept of. That's why I told you I wanted him." Hank gestured with his chin at Bardolph, who gave a little bow.

"And," Hank continued, "that is the problem. All of these corporations dominate the world based upon profit – not what is good for people or the environment."

Exeter stared at him for a moment. "So. You want to go after Agincourt?"

Hank nodded. "Dauphin's father forced a split from our corporation ten years ago to set up Agincourt and focus upon arms development; they sell nasty weapons to anyone who ponies up the cash. It can't go on. And we both know his son, Dauphin – remember he and I grew up together – he's too full of himself to be trusted with something like this."

An image of young Dauphin's face flashed through Hank's mind, the blond youth sneering as he won a card game by cheating. Hank's fists clenched and he shook his head to clear the image and forced himself to relax.

He paced around the office. "Since I left to go Underground, I've been looking for a way to force them back under our control and turn things around before it's too late. Now we have a Doomsday machine at our throats... The only thing offering comfort is that the nuclear disarmament has been completed. At least they can't nuke us."

He turned back to face the other two men. *God, I hope Uncle Exeter is on board with this. He's my best chance for support from inside EngCorp, because the official report doesn't seem to be too worried about Agincourt's Doomsday project at all.*

The three looked at each other for a beat. Exeter nodded and sat in one of the chairs in front of the desk. "Let's get busy."

Hank smiled. *Bingo.* "Better pour yourself some juice, gentlemen; we have some planning to do here."

"Right," said Bardolph, moving toward the desk. "Anyone believe for a minute that Agincourt walked into the lab, took the moddy chip prototype, and whisked away the head developer without his agreement? No? OK, let's see who actually had access and was in the building at the time, and what the deal is with this maintenance guy Arlo mentioned. Smith, right?" He sat down at the desk and brought up the security reports on the wall displays.

CHAPTER FOUR

"Let's be alert here." Hank walked the aerial walkway in the Underground, next to Bardolph. Parts of the handrail were missing.

"Yup. Never know around here."

The sign on the door of the run-down building read, "Room Available." Turning the knob, they entered a dingy lobby; the front desk was protected by metal bars and a dirty plexiglass screen and was unmanned. Looking around, Bardolph gestured to the bell on the desk. "You do the talking."

At Hank's ring, an aging person of indeterminate gender emerged from the back room behind the desk cage.

"What?" said the desk clerk.

What is that smell? "Smith. He in?"

"How the hell would I know?"

"Well, he lives here, doesn't he? He didn't come in to work today." Hank smiled.

"Since when does anyone care about that guy? He owes me back rent. Owed. Are you coming to pay his debts after the accident?" The oldster cackled.

"Accident?"

"Yeah, don't you know? He was flattened by a falling cargo bin. Yesterday morning at his job. I'll have to sell off anything of value to pay his back rent." The clerk spat on the floor behind the desk.

"He was working two jobs?" *And yet he lived here.*

The desk clerk snorted. "Who isn't working two jobs? There's no money to be made these days unless you work on supporting the computer shit that took all the jobs. Myself, I'm a fashion model on the side." The oldster preened and then snorted.

"Mind if we take a look at that room?" Bardolph asked.

"Sure, 210. Here's the key card. You might like it – window view."

The two men looked through the door of room 210 and grimaced. Bare metal bed frame; filthy, lumpy mattress partially covered by a torn sheet. Dirty clothes covered the floor. A rusty sink dripped constantly in the corner and apparently served as the toilet as well.

"Ugh. This is what two jobs pay for?" Hank's lips were tight. *I wouldn't let a dog live here.*

"Yeah, man, this is why I do computer hacking for a living. This is what two non-tech jobs pay for. Check out the window view." Bardolph moved the drapes aside to reveal the brick wall of the neighboring building, three feet away.

They drew on gloves and began searching through the meager belongings for anything of interest to their investigation. Finding nothing, they headed back down the stairs. The clerk was at the desk, dozing behind the cage; Hank slapped the card key on the desk, and the oldster jumped.

"Wha – ? You want the room or not?"

"Oh, hell no, thanks."

Outside the dingy hotel, they tossed their gloves in a dumpster. Rats scurried away momentarily then decided the men weren't a threat and returned to foraging. Hank rubbed his face with his hand.

"Well, that cuts it. According to our friend there, the cleanup guy who worked in the chip lab was killed before the chips were even stolen. We can take a look at the accident, but I suspect it's what we figured all along; the missing developer, York, was the only other one who could get in and then actually get the chips out of the building. Let's head over and see his place. It's above the edge of the Underground."

On a higher-level aerial walkway, with sunlight falling around them, they came to a well-kept apartment building and buzzed the door showing the developer's name. A woman with reddened eyes opened the door a few inches.

"Yes?"

"Ma'am, I'm Hank, the President of EngCorp. This is my security advisor Bardolph. And you are…?"

"Oh! I'm Chelsea. York's wife."

"Is your husband home, ma'am?"

Tears started to roll down her cheeks. "No. He didn't come home last night. I don't know where he is. I don't know what to do." She started to sob. "Come…come in." She opened the door, allowing them into the small, though clean, apartment. Furniture with simple, clean lines was arranged into a seating area and an eating area, with an opening for a kitchen space and a door at the opposite end that led to the bedroom. Unlike Smith's miserable room, sunlight came in through the window and brightened the room.

"Won't you sit down?"

"Chelsea, I'm so sorry. Has…has York been different recently? Like, has he been seeing any new people or going to new places?"

"Why…yes, we went out to dinner the other day to a restaurant. I've only been to a fancy restaurant a few times, so I was excited and ran a vidcording the whole evening. And while we were there, a blond man called him over to talk to him. When York came back, he told me the man had paid for our dinner! Then last night I thought it was odd…" She paused and started to tear up again. "I thought we'd be able to work everything out…"

Hank's hand tightened into a fist until he forced it to relax. *A blond man…*

"Yes? You thought what was odd?"

"I saw my husband walk by last night – his red hair was really clear in the streetlight. He should have come in, should have been coming home. But I saw him out the window and the same blond man was waiting at the end of the aerial. York left with him. And…he hasn't been back. And I can't afford to call for a security investigation."

"Chelsea, I'm so sorry. But tell me; you said you took a vidcording at the restaurant. Is there a chance you got a picture of this man? It's important – it may help us find your husband."

She wiped her tears and fumbled on her wrist display for a minute. "Here. Here's the whole thing."

Hank held out his wrist display unit and bumped it to hers, capturing a copy of the recording. "All right, thank you. You've been very helpful. And I'll keep in touch and come to see you again. Please let me know when you hear from your husband." He bumped her wrist again, passing her his contact information. *Or if you do.*

Outside the apartment, the two men reviewed the vidcording at high speed. It started with York and his wife entering the restaurant and being seated; Hank stopped it at a picture of a blond man, hair slicked back from his forehead, lazily waving his hand for York to come over.

"You know who this is, right?" Hank looked at Bardolph, who raised his eyebrows.

Hank continued, "Dauphin. Son of the President of Agincourt. Trust me when I say Dauphin is an asshole – he's two years older than me, and I used to have to play with him whenever the families got together. He convinces people to do things for him, and he thinks the sun twinkles out his backside." Hank's lips tightened.

"So what do you think this means?" asked Bardolph.

"I'd say Dauphin took a personal interest in our friend York, the chip developer. Paid him to do the job, then lured him away. And now Dauphin has the chips, the plans, and the developer – if he's not dead already. I'll show this to Uncle Exeter, but I believe he'll agree we have the beginning of a legal case to petition to get our equipment back." *And maybe York. If he's still alive.*

Hank looked at Bardolph. "And in the meantime, I'm going to visit some of our compatriots and ask if they're willing to help."

CHAPTER FIVE

Standing on the corner behind a crumbling pillar, Hank watched people jockeying for position in the long food line at the building across the street until he saw a young man approach and dodge nimbly through the line to a side entrance. Crossing the street, Hank tried to follow but proved to be much less adept at negotiating through the crowd.

"Hey! No cutting!" A heavy man put up an arm to block Hank's progress.

"Sorry, man, just passing through." Hank ducked under the arm and kept going.

He heard some yelling from the front of the line; the corporation's food distribution center had scanned one man's armband and turned him away for having an invalid band. "Come on, I know it will work if you just try it again!" cried the man. "Please!" People in the crowd pushed him out of the way.

A child of about eight years old pulled her mother's arm as Hank passed. "Mum! We've been waiting so long, and I'm so hungry."

Her mother made shushing noises and helped her suck on her thumb. "It's OK, sweetie, I'm pretty sure they won't run out of food this time."

Hank tightened his lips at the child's words but kept going. Reaching the side entrance, he slipped inside the vestibule, then scanned the names on the list of buzzers.

Emperor of the Known Universe: 412. And a security camera over the door. Hank gave a wry smile. *OK, that has to be my old buddy Alexander's buzzer. Modest.*

He looked back out the window of the door and noticed another man wearing a heavy coat trying to cut through the crowd; watching him out of the corner of his eye, Hank waited until the man passed the door without a glance.

Hank rang the bell, three short and two long rings, then turned to face the security camera until the door buzzed and he slipped through. Heading up the steep stairs and avoiding the damaged steps, he counted four flights and then turned down the long, darkened hallway until he came to the door labeled 412. Three quick knocks brought the door open an inch and an eye peered at him through the crack.

"Hell's bells, Hank, it really is you. Hold on." The door closed and Hank heard the sound of the chain scraping across the lock, and then the door opened and he slipped inside before it closed again behind him.

"You've got a lot of nerve. It's been months! I was wondering why somebody used the old code for ringing the bell. But then the camera showed you on my doorstep, man. How the hell are you?" said Alexander.

The young man held out his arms and they hugged, clapping each other on the back.

"OK, Alexander, I'm OK. Have you finished your scan now? And give me back my wristband. How many times did you check me?"

The young man grinned and sheepishly held out the hand that had been half hidden at his side, holding the wristband. "Yeah, you passed. First level at the door, second on the stairs. Third at the doorstep. And I've got a new scan shirt that works from about ten feet away, with a second level that works up close. Because you can never be too sure. Oh, yeah, here's your wristband. I was just having fun with you."

Hank broke out laughing. "Ah, Alexander, how I've missed you."

"Well, hell, Hank, you're the one who left to go back up to rich daddy's company. Was it so bad down here?"

The laugh slid off Hank's lips. "Not so bad – but not so good, either. Are you so used to the line downstairs that you don't even see it? All those folks waiting for food? I heard a little girl crying because she was hungry and the distribution center ran out last time they were here. That's crazy, Alexander."

Alexander also quieted. "Well, they may be hungry, but they won't get nuked in the next war. At least we managed to pull that thing off, Hank."

"That's the kind of job I'm here to see you about, Alexander. You heard about the explosion at my company's lab?"

"Oh, yeah, crazy. Any idea who it was? What did they get?" asked Alexander.

"Well, my best guess right now is that it was Agincourt; and it's not so much the idea of what they got as it is that they feel they can just walk into my company's lab and take what they want. They've overgrown their position and they are too bold."

"Too bold? We hacked into corporation databases and planted memos that helped support the anti-nuke movement. That's not bold?" Alexander held his arms wide apart as he spoke.

"Well, yeah, but we had a good goal – we convinced the corporate decision makers that all of the other high-level managers also supported the anti-nuke treaty. The vote went our way." Hank paced back and forth across the room.

"Seriously, Hank, that was a genius move. I would never have known anything about how these corporations work on the inside. Turns out they're all a bunch of worry-wart bureaucrats trying to keep their jobs."

Yeah, you learn a lot growing up inside the biggest corporation in the country.

Alexander paused and looked at Hank across the room. "So. Now that you've gone back to EngCorp, you think Agincourt is invading your corporation? Those arms dealers are unscrupulous. They'll sell anything to anyone."

Hank turned and strode rapidly back. "Yeah. And can you believe this Doomsday project is in their hands? Crap. The report I just got from my research department shows that it's worse than we ever thought when we were working against the nuclear program, Alexander."

"Huh." The young man leaned against the kitchen counter behind him, arms crossed. "And?" His head tilted to one side as he looked at Hank.

"What do you mean, 'and?'"

"*And*, what are you planning to do about it? I know you, and you're not likely to let this go unanswered."

"Heh. Well, yeah, that's why I'm here. EngCorp is going to take them over. If the lawsuit we are pursuing doesn't work, then I have other ideas. Wanna help? I only have a general plan, but I think I'm going to need a number of hackers with your...particular skills. I'll probably need people to access their system remotely."

"Standard payment?"

"Oh, yeah, standard payment – plus the knowledge that you might just make the world safe for another generation."

"Bah. Who's going to live that long?" Alexander snorted.

God, that *was a scary sound.*

"How about if we bring in Erpingham? Gower? We can message them now." Alexander held up his wrist display and smiled slyly. "I have them on a private channel."

Hank nodded. "Now you're talking. This is why I came to you first, buddy."

Hank and Alexander headed outside after their meeting, with the promise of help from half a dozen hackers. The crowd outside had mostly dispersed, except for small groups who stood about muttering to each other, and the ground was littered with torn wrappers and debris, but not a speck of food was to be seen. The window of the food distribution site was bolted shut. The mother and daughter whom he had overheard earlier sat on the curb, empty-handed. The little girl stared at the ground.

At the end of the block, Hank stopped and looked back at them. *Jesus.* He paused, then went back and spoke to the mother. "How long since you've had anything to eat?"

She startled, and drew back with her arm around the child. "Who's asking?"

"Sorry, just trying to help." He started to turn away.

"Oh! Um, wait. Please. Wait?" The mother roused her child and started to get up.

"We're going to get some food now. Can I get you something to eat? What would you like?" Hank spoke gently.

"We're not fussy. Right, sweetie?" The little child looked up at Hank and shook her head. Hank and Alexander exchanged glances, and Alexander shrugged.

"OK, come on, we always go to the place down the block. It's not fancy, but it's got decent food. You can take whatever you don't eat along with you." Hank smiled at them and they headed off down the street together. *What on earth am I doing? I have important stuff to do… It's just this kid…*

The four entered the little hole-in-the-wall cafe and stood in front of the counter. "Go ahead, order whatever you want. This is my favorite place around here. Everything is pretty good, but I always order the chicken pieces."

The small space was crammed with tables and chairs that were mostly empty. A counter divided the eating space from the cooking area, and a dirty curtain partially covered the storage area behind the stoves. The cook and the counter person were huddled near the storage area but came forward when the four approached the counter.

Hank and Alexander ordered their usual meals and guided the other two through their order. After ordering, the two men sat down at a table, and the woman and child stood at the counter waiting for the food; Hank saw them watching the workers cooking behind the counter with eager interest. When some of the food was put on the counter while she was waiting, the little girl snuck bites of it off the plate until her mother noticed and pulled her hand back.

Once all the food was ready, the girl held tightly onto the tray holding Hank's meal as she carried it over to the table and carefully placed it in front of him. Hank smiled at her as she went back to help her mother carry the rest of the food.

Hank looked down at his plate and chuckled as he realized that about a quarter of his meal was missing. He picked up a fork and speared a bite of chicken, and it was almost in his mouth when he detected a strange aroma. Pausing with the fork up to his lips, he frowned. *This doesn't smell right.*

"Alexander, hold on – I think there's something wrong with the food." Even as he spoke, the little girl stumbled and dropped the tray of food she was carrying. She fell to the ground and started writhing convulsively; foam came from her lips.

"Oh my God." He gestured to the mother. "See to her." Hank scanned the cooking area, then sprang over the counter as a man in a large overcoat emerged from behind the dirty curtain and started to slip out the back door; Hank grabbed his arm and spun him around. "Cambridge! What the hell?"

Hank punched the man in the face, and he fell against the wall as Alexander came up behind them. Hank held him up by the throat.

"What the hell did you think you were doing? Why did you do this? That poor little girl! Isn't she even a person to you?" Hank nearly screamed in the man's face.

"Sorry...sorry, Hank. I needed the money. Lost my job when my company got bought out." Cambridge sagged in Hank's grip.

"You did this for money? Who paid you to poison everyone here?"

"Not everyone, Hank – just you – Dauphin paid me to poison just you. You ordered your favorite meal. I didn't know she was going to eat your food."

Hank snarled and his grip tightened so much that the man scrabbled at the hand encircling his throat. Then Hank straightened up and slammed the offender against the wall, releasing the man into his companion's grip.

"Alexander, hold him. I'm calling for EngCorp security. Nobody down here is going to do anything to arrest this piece of scum."

CHAPTER SIX

A month after their meeting with Arlo, Hank and his uncle sat together once more on the couches in the large office that overlooked the city. Each had a glass in his hand of something stronger than juice. The two were reviewing a court document on the tablet that Hank held.

"So this is the final answer from the International Courts, then, Uncle Exeter?"

The older man nodded. "I'm afraid so, Hank. I'm sorry. We spent weeks developing the petition and arguing it through the highest levels of the court system – or what's left of it these days. I took it as far as I could, but each time it was rejected. Agincourt has presented convincing-looking legal documents that indicate the separation from EngCorp took place legitimately ten years ago, and they deny any involvement in the theft and destruction of the chip lab. I don't really trust the integrity of the legal system anymore, and I don't know for sure if there was collusion involved, but we are out of options."

Hank shook his head and tossed the tablet onto the coffee table. "Well, I can't say as I had any great faith in this attempt, anyway. The government and the International Courts are a joke. I came back to EngCorp when father died because it's the corporations who run things now. France doesn't even have a military force anymore; they rely on Agincourt."

The older man nodded his head. "The President of Agincourt gave us a courteous reception at the pre-court hearing, which was the least he could do after the years we worked together. But I can't say much for the way Dauphin behaved. He as much as said that he has no respect for your leadership, and that he still thinks of you as a frivolous and inexperienced youth."

Hank's eyebrows went up. "He actually said that? He has a lot of–"

Exeter cut him off. "Yes. However, from what I've seen since you've been back, you have an exceptional set of skills and perceptions – which I don't think you would have if you had stayed here living as your father's son. Your father may not have been happy with the way you left to go into the Underground, but it has made you the president that EngCorp needs."

Hank inclined his head. "Why thank you, Uncle. But now that the court ruling is done, and the body of the chip developer, York, was discovered in France, we don't have much in play at the moment."

Exeter drank deeply from his glass. "There is, however, something of interest that was delivered today from France, addressed to you personally. It seems terribly convenient that it arrived on the same day the decision was proclaimed. Do you want to see it? Security is bringing it up once they have finished scanning it."

Hank drank as well. "Sure, why not? And thank you, Uncle. I know you did the best job anyone could have done with this court case. It's not your fault the international court system is a joke."

He put his drink down as a knock came at the door. "Come in!"

One uniformed man opened the door and held it open for another, who was pushing a cart with a large box on it. The security man looked at the older man wearing the elegant suit, and the younger man in the modern jumpsuit, and turned to speak to Exeter. "Sir, we've scanned the contents and it is safe." Exeter shook his head slightly and gestured to Hank, and the security man flushed.

Good God, sometimes I just want to give up. Don't they even know that I'm the president now? "Open it up. Let's see what's inside."

The security agent deftly slit open the top of the carton. "Sir, there's a letter inside," he said, holding out the paper.

"What's it about, Uncle?" asked Hank, gesturing for the security man to pass it into Exeter's outstretched hand.

The lawyer motioned the security men out, and once they had left, he read the document aloud.

To Hank, the young president of EngCorp.

I have not seen you since you left your father's home for a life of debauchery. In the meantime, I have been working hard as a responsible businessman.

You have recently attempted to take over our corporation and obtain some of our property through a legal proceeding that we have blocked at every turn. You are acting like the shallow youth I know you to be.

There is nothing in our corporation that can be obtained by one such as you – with your background of dancing, partying and carousing. So here is a gift that is more appropriate to your habits and abilities.

You never won when we played anything as boys; you will not win now.

Signed,
Dauphin of Agincourt

"Oh, this is going to be good," murmured Exeter, pulling open the carton to reveal a case full of tennis balls.

"Bastard," said Hank, looking into the open box and standing very still. "He tries to poison me and then sends me...tennis balls?" *At least some things don't change. He's still an asshole.*

He turned and stalked across the room, arms rigid and his step fast and hard, then returned to face his uncle with his hands still clenched at his sides. "So you say we have exhausted all of the legal means at our disposal to get the moddy chip prototype back?"

Exeter nodded.

"I'd say it is time for us to turn to the less-than-legal methods...the ones in which my friends and I excel. I'll be putting together a team to–"

"Hold on," said the older man. "The less you tell me, the less I have to deny. Just tell me what my part is."

"All right, Uncle. I'm going to set up a communication system for us, as I expect to be out of the country for a period of time – as soon as I make some arrangements." Hank smiled. "And select some traveling companions." Seeing him, Exeter shivered.

CHAPTER SEVEN

Exeter rode the EngCorp private train toward the remote moddy chip lab, watching the countryside pass by the window as he neared the smaller English city. *I can't believe Hank's reaction to this poisoning attempt. Two more conspirators discovered, and he insists on holding them to the corporation standards of death for attempted murder. I would have thought he would have more leniency. Perhaps there is even more to him than I originally thought.*

The train pulled into the private underground station, interrupting his musing.

"Sir? We're here." A guard guided him off the train and toward the security scan. Exeter followed the guard, looking around with interest. The guard led him to a secure room, where they scanned his whole body and performed a rather invasive personal search.

Hmmm. All the years with EngCorp's legal department, brother and advisor to the president, and I've never been here before. Now I never want to come back here. I can't believe Hank talked me into having this done.

At the end of the security scan, a lab technician in a white coat met

Exeter, escorted him into the elevator, and entered a code. Exeter started when they began moving down and not up; he counted ten levels going by on the display screen. They exited the elevator to see Arlo waiting to greet them; the lab technician smiled and headed through a nearby door, leaving the two men alone.

"Ah, yes, hello. Thank you so much for joining us here, Exeter. Would you like the tour before we get busy?" Arlo rubbed his hands.

Well, I certainly wouldn't mind putting this off for a few more minutes. Good God, all these years with EngCorp – how could I not have known this was here?

Exeter sighed and shook Arlo's hand. "Of course, Arlo. I apologize that I have been remiss in not coming out here before. This is, shall we say, outside of my usual area of expertise."

"Not a problem, sir – I can certainly understand that. Let me show you around. We are in the secret, remote facility of EngCorp, where we have both our secure storage facilities and our most promising labs. We will wind up at the moddy chip lab at the end of our tour and finish our business."

Exeter shivered. *Great. Our business.*

Arlo led him across the hall, and they got into a motorized cart. "Come, buckle in – we cannot emphasize safety too much. Come now, yes, that's it."

Once Exeter was safely ensconced in the cart, Arlo drove off at a rapid speed down the long hall, occasionally beeping and waving hello to technicians they passed in the hall. They went past a number of cross corridors, and Arlo beeped a warning and then veered sharply around one of them.

"See, down here – we have the largest storage bay. We keep all sorts of vehicles down here, and a large array of parts to keep them running."

The cart stopped in front of a glass-windowed door, and Exeter got out and peered inside.

"But...these are all old cars and trucks. Why on earth would we keep so many outdated vehicles?"

"Ah, sir, there are certain advantages to old vehicles. Most of these have non-electronic systems in them. They are easier to maintain, easier to fabricate parts...and, to put it plainly, they are resistant to EMPs."

"EMPs?"

"EMP. Electromagnetic Pulses. They can short out the electronic circuits of most of our modern technology. But vehicles and machines like these are not affected by the EMP force and will continue to run when modern machinery would be quite fried. Totally out of commission."

Exeter pondered this information. "But if that happens, wouldn't you be stuck down here?"

"Oh, no, sir. We had all the electronics in this facility made of specially-hardened circuitry that should resist an EMP. I just hope we never have to try it out."

"Tell me, Arlo, who designated that all of this be set up here?"

"Uh, well, the president of course. I mean, before he died. I mean, Hank's father, the previous president."

My brother! Exeter's eyebrows lifted and he whistled softly. *Well. I suppose this means my brother listened to his son more than he let on if he was actually worried about some of the things Hank had been complaining about for so many years – and that caused Hank to leave the corporation and work against the nuclear arsenals. Damn.*

They continued, with Arlo showing Exeter the extensive food stockpiles and holding tanks for water. At the end of the tour, Arlo stopped at one of the lab doors and motioned for Exeter to follow him inside. *Oh God, here we go. This must be where I get the moddy chip.* Exeter paused, then braced himself and went through the double doors after his guide.

He was greeted by a well-lit room full of lab tables and stools, each covered with a dizzying array of electronic equipment. A window at one side opened onto what appeared to be an environmentally controlled clean room, filled with racks that contained Petri dishes under lights.

"What is all that?" Exeter peered through the window.

"Oh, just the room where we grow things. Here, come right down this way. Nothing to see there." Arlo half escorted, half pulled him by his elbow down the center of the room. At the far end, they passed through a door into a brightly lit, sterile-looking room; two technicians were waiting by a console next to a specially designed chair with a face rest attached to the front of it.

Exeter glanced around. *Well. This looks like an operating room of sorts.*

"Exeter, these are our top technicians. They are going to install your moddy chip. Here, let's get you changed."

The two shook hands with Exeter, then donned surgical gowns. They went to a clean station and washed their hands, then held them under a blue light for several minutes. Arlo gave Exeter a gown to put on and waited while he changed behind a curtain. When all were ready, Arlo gestured to the chair and had Exeter sit, then stood facing him.

"Now, you understand what we're going to do, right? We're going to install one of the moddy chips in the back of your neck. It will only take a few minutes and should be relatively painless. After the procedure, we'll have you rest quietly for a bit, and the chip will start to meld into your neural system. You can go about your regular business, and it should be online in just a few days; I'll come by and test it out for you in your office."

Man, oh man, the things I have previously done for this corporation are nothing compared to this.

"Yes, I understand," said Exeter. His voice was mostly firm, with only a mild quaver.

Arlo looked at him for a moment. "I want to be sure you do understand. Do you have any questions?"

Exeter sighed. "OK, yes, I do. This is the other moddy chip that we're installing, right? From the line that was even better than the one the Agincourt agent got? What makes it so special? And please, remember I'm a lawyer – not a technician."

"Let us put it very simply, then." Arlo held up his little finger for Exeter to view. "This is a tiny device, smaller than your fingernail. It is made of carbon nanotubes, an organic, non-silicon material that will escape most current scans for electronic devices – and, it is resistant to EMPs. The chip is inserted into the back of your neck, where it interacts with the microtubules in your cells' organelles."

At Exeter's blank look, he added, "It works with your cells to draw energy from your neural structure. And it can transmit audio messages a long distance. We are working on further capabilities as well. This is, of course, a prototype. But no worries; we all have one here. So does Hank, now. It allows us to communicate much more directly when needed without being tracked."

Exeter nodded slowly, then nodded again. "OK, I get it. What do I do?"

The lead technician stepped in. "Just lean forward in the chair, sir, until your face is comfortable on the resting pad. Yes, that's it... OK, now we're going to swab your neck and administer a local anesthetic. The whole process will only take a few minutes. Would you like to listen to some music?"

Oh, God, here we go.

CHAPTER EIGHT

Hank walked down the dirty, narrow street at ground level, underneath the entwined roads and walkways that criss-crossed the space overhead. *Creepy, as usual.* The street was dim due to the small amount of light that managed to filter down through the overhead structures. He had to step carefully to avoid garbage and holes in the street. He stepped over and around the sleeping forms huddled by the edge of the walkway and in doorways of abandoned buildings.

Neon light flickered from some of the storefronts as he passed, with lights showing through security bars on the grimy windows; many more were boarded up. His target was one of the open buildings at the end of the street, with blinking lights in the window advertising beer and harder drinks.

Slowing his pace as he neared the front, he scanned the street one more time for any sign of movement, then turned and slipped through the door. Suppressing a smile as the familiar sour smell of stale beer and sweat reached his nose, he waited a moment for his eyes to adjust to the even darker gloom inside.

Strange how I've missed that smell.

Several groups of men huddled at tables, with a few individuals perched on seats at the bar; none of them looked up as he entered, but the bartender flicked a glance in his direction. Hank inclined his head towards a door at the back of the room, and the bartender nodded just slightly.

Hank walked to the back and went through the door, glancing at a slender man in a baggy, hooded jacket who occupied a stool at the bar; as Hank passed, the man slid off the barstool and followed him into the back room just as the door was closing.

At the click of the latch, the two turned toward each other and smiled. Hank held a finger to his lips, and the other nodded. Each pulled a small device from his pocket and proceeded to scan the room – and each other. When the scan was complete, both grinned and fell into a bear hug. The baggy jacket was removed and tossed aside, revealing a young woman in a black jumpsuit.

"Nim! It's been a while. You look good for a low-life such as yourself. Pretty good camouflage, there."

"Hey, Hank, I was really surprised to hear from you! I thought you were off living the high life and ruling the world. Why are you slumming around down here? Not busy enough running the biggest corporation in the world?"

"Ah, Nim, sometimes I think the corporate world isn't much different from down here; they just dress nicer. But I have an expedition that requires some of your expertise in physical defense – and I need to keep it quiet."

"Well, yeah, pretty much everything we've ever done has had to be quiet. I don't think many people outside our group even know we're connected, Hank. Are the others coming in on this? What's the story?"

They turned as a soft knock came at the door. Hank scanned the area through the wall, then smiled and opened the door to let two men through before closing the door behind them. The mutual scans were repeated, and the noise level in the room increased greatly as they all greeted each other.

"Bardolph. And Pistol! Glad you got my message. Nim beat you here." Hank was smiling from ear to ear.

The older man had a graying ponytail and a pot belly; he nodded as he pounded Hank on the back and then pointed his finger at Nim. "Now, don't go trying to break my hand again, missy."

Nim smiled to hear his brogue. "I didn't try to break your hand that time, Pistol; I just applied pressure at the correct point. I would have stopped before anything actually broke." Pistol held out his hand for a shake but snatched it back out of her grip, smiling a bit, and hugged Hank.

"Ah laddy, it is quite delectable to receive a private communiqué from the President of EngCorp on my personal channel," said Pistol. "I did not expect to hear from you again once you went back to the land of the suits and enterprise."

"I know, Pistol; I thought I had left this all behind me as well. It turns out that I need the group's expertise for something that can have far-reaching effects. Bardolph," said Hank, extricating himself from Pistol's embrace and shaking hands solemnly with the other. "Glad you're here, as always."

Nim nodded. "Well, we've been through some amazing things these past five years. The arms dealers aren't shut down yet, but at least the nuclear disarmament inspections have been completed. We can take some credit for that."

"That's certainly the truth," Hank agreed.

Pistol brushed dirt off his jacket as he spoke. "Did you see me? I wasn't sure that it was a real message, even though you used the regular codes and added the one for extreme caution. So I watched from outside to see you all come in."

Hank wrinkled his nose at the smell. "You were one of the street sleepers. I probably stepped right over you."

A smile formed on Pistol's lips without reaching his eyes. "Can never be too sure. What's all this talk I've heard about the three who were executed this week?"

"Ah. Cambridge, Scroop, and Grey. I've worked with them all at various times – and I would never have suspected that they would turn against me. Yet Cambridge tried to poison me when I was traveling down here in the Underground, and we found that Scroop and Grey were paid off as well. I tried to not believe it...but a little girl died in my place. They had to face the penalty."

Hank's shoulders sagged.

"But, why?" Nim gasped. "Why would they turn against you? Is it because you're the president of EngCorp now?"

"They said Agincourt put them up to it."

The four looked at each other for a moment, then Pistol shook his head and spoke up. "In my youth, a corporation could never have executed someone; there would have been a trial, and the government would have been in charge. Now courts are only for economic issues. Or, thank God, for overseeing the nuke treaty."

He fell silent again for a moment, then shook himself and grasped Hank's arm. "But how are ye, laddy? It is terrible that little girl died – and those you trusted turned against you. How are ye holding up?"

"I don't even know, Pistol. Sometimes I feel as though I can't trust anyone anymore."

The older man nodded. "So that explains the scans when we came in. Fair enough. Cannot be too careful. So why are we here?"

Hank straightened up and moved to the table in the corner, and the others followed him.

"Pull up a chair, people, we're going to be here for a while. We need to figure out how to hack our way into Agincourt's computer system and get back some stolen plans from my company. Once we get this missing information back, I plan to take over Agincourt. They can't be allowed to be in charge of such dangerous technology as the Doomsday project. This break-in is just one more example of how they act without taking the human component into account."

Pistol whistled and then smiled. "Aye, laddy, that's a daring plan if I ever heard one."

"I wouldn't be a responsible president of EngCorp if I did not take over and become president of Agincourt as well." Hank smiled, but the smile didn't reach his eyes.

"Here's what I have in mind to do," he continued. "Usual jobs. Bardolph is our hacker, Nim is physical security, and Pistol gets us through any security systems we encounter. The usual payment applies, plus the satisfaction of helping the world. We have to get in touch with that guy who works at Harfleur – the warehouse company owned by Agincourt. What's his name? Montjoy, right?"

CHAPTER NINE

Montjoy keyed in the access code through the window of his truck, leaning out over the rusted sign at the warehouse gate that proclaimed "Harfleur – a division of Agincourt" in French. The system automatically scanned his partially loaded truck, and then the gate opened with a groan of mechanical gears. Before he drove through, Montjoy pushed the button that opened the back of the delivery truck, and the four waiting outside the gate swiftly jumped inside and closed the door; the truck pulled forward, and the gate swung shut behind them.

Driving into the automated compound, he called over his shoulder in heavily accented English, "So? Are we all okay?"

Keeping low, Hank crept up behind the driver. "I can't believe that really worked. How stupid can they be to run their security that way?"

"It is as I tell you, yes? They don' expect anyone to come into a warehouse that holds only obsolete equipment, spare parts, and broken machines. So why bother with the security? It is the same with the computer station inside. Last time I was there, the office door was even unlocked. People rarely even go inside."

Montjoy pulled the truck around the side of the warehouse, heading for the row of giant freight doors. As he pulled up to one of them, it automatically opened, and he backed up to the loading bay. Opening the back door, he spoke over his shoulder again.

"Just head down corridor and turn left. You will find office at the end. No lock, I think. You should be able to get inside no problem and then use code I gave you for the computer. But once in there, I don' know what you think you can do."

"We've got it from there, Montjoy. Thanks. The list of user names you gave us should get us what we need. Half the credits are in your account now; the other half will be in your account in a few days. After we've gotten out intact."

Hank clapped him on the shoulder, and the four conspirators slipped out the open door, wearing backpacks, as the automated system started unloading boxes from the truck. They headed down the corridor past robot units that ignored them.

"Look, no electronics. I wonder if the door is unlocked, just as he said." Pistol stowed the scanning device and twisted the knob; when it failed to open, he dropped to one knee and worked at it for just a moment with a slender tool from his belt. Looking at the others, who nodded, he turned the knob and the door swung open.

Nim stopped him with a hand on his arm, gestured to the rest to wait, and then moved to the door ahead of him. Stepping through, she lit a small flashlight and trained it around the room. After a moment, she beckoned the other three to come inside.

The others followed her with their own lights. After checking the rest of the room for electronics and spy devices, they dropped their gear along the wall with a thud; a week's worth of food and water was heavy.

Several windows were covered by drooping blinds that let in some of the glow from the security lights outside. One end of the room held couches and what appeared to be a small break room with a kitchenette and three tables with chairs; a door at the end opened onto a washroom.

Nim checked it and came out with a disgusted look. "Clear – and the best I can say is that it works."

Hank thumped one of the couches and a cloud of dust rose into the air. "Well. This may be home for a number of days, folks, assuming that nobody shows up and throws us out." *That's what Nim is here for, of course.*

Pistol shook his head. "Dibs on one of the couches."

The rest of the room was lined with file cabinets and filled with dusty rows of desks, with five old-style computers.

Bardolph sniffed. "These things are obsolete, but I think I can use them. They obviously just left the old stuff in here since so much is done with automation these days – why bother making life easier for the few remaining people who might need to come in and check anything?"

Bardolph turned one of the computers on; he sat at the desk and flexed his fingers over the keys. "All right, let's see what we can do to get further inside this baby."

"What are you going to do?" asked Nim.

Bardolph didn't look up as he typed. "Since Harfleur is a business partner with Agincourt, we should be able to find a way to get inside Agincourt through their Virtual Private Network if we get the right level of user access. Look out, VPN, baby, here I come."

The others moved around the room to make it more secure and review exactly what equipment was on the site. Pistol set up a series of scanners to alert them of anyone – or anything – that approached, then went back out and dodged the automated machines to set up the same scanners in the warehouse area and outside. Nim took up a station looking through the window in the door, down the corridor, in case something should elude the scanners, and Hank did the same at the window of the office that opened to the outdoors.

"How goes it, buddy?" Hank asked Bardolph after many hours had elapsed. Enough time had passed that the others had exchanged guard positions several times. Pistol stifled a yawn.

"Well, I guess I do owe you a status report," said Bardolph.

The others perked up.

"The passwords for the user ids Montjoy gave us had all expired. So I tried all of the regular access methods – open ports, passwords they foolishly left as the default value. Like the admin who uses 'admin' as his password." Bardolph rubbed his tired eyes.

"Yeah, yeah, we *all* know how to do that part. What have you found?" Nim snapped. Her fists clenched and Hank put a hand on her arm.

She's used to physical action – looks like she wants to hit something.

"Patience, my friend," said Hank. "Bardolph is here because he's the best at this stuff. He's just reviewing his actions so we know where we stand."

Bardolph ignored the interruption. "Well, as I said, I worked through the list of user ids that our French friend gave us. My hope was to get in as someone with high enough security that we could put in some keystroke loggers at different points. And then we'd capture someone logging in."

Nim rolled her eyes, and Hank looked at her with his eyebrows raised. Nim plastered a smile on her face.

Bardolph continued, "I didn't get any immediate access, so I hooked up an encryption buster to see if it could figure out some passwords. But it's taking way longer to run than I expected. Even though the rest of the physical security here is very low, I suspect that Agincourt has them using a much longer encryption code than normal. So there are many, many more options to try. That's what's been taking so long."

Hank ran a hand over his face. "Well, I guess it's a good thing that the world's biggest weapons manufacturer has better security than it first looked like when we got here – even if this is a remote, affiliate location."

Pistol called from his post by the door. "So where does this leave us? Come on, we've been here for hours and we're not even through the first level yet!"

Hank looked at the team around him. "I know it's taking longer than we expected. And every minute we're here increases the chances of being detected. But I know we can band together and figure this out; we've done much harder jobs than this. Let's think about what we know of this place. The main computer system connects with Agincourt, and therefore it has some tight security – witness the enhanced encryption code. But at this location, the physical layout and access look very lax. How can that help us? All we need is one user's access, and Bardolph can get us the rest of the way into the system."

They all sat and pondered, looking around the room. Then Hank sat up straight in his chair. *Wait…no, it couldn't be that simple.*

He leaned over and opened the desk drawer to the left of the computer station Bardolph was using. Taped to the side of the drawer was a paper with a user id and password written in pencil, alongside a fairly current date.

Turning to the hacker, Hank said, "Once more unto the breach…of security! We're as good as in, now – the game's afoot."

Bardolph clapped a hand across his eyes and moaned. "Really? That simple and stupid – and I missed it? Let's see if this password is still valid."

Getting back to work, he keyed the user id and password into the system. He was rewarded with a change on the screen and a low ding that indicated that he was now logged into Harfleur's system and could use the VPN connecting them with Agincourt's system – his ultimate goal.

Fingers moving rapidly, he employed some hacking exploits to gain additional authority for the careless user who had left the password; next he created a remote user id and logged into Harfleur as that user. Submitting a command which ran across the VPN to the Agincourt system, he pulled up a list of Agincourt user ids and their associated system authorities. He signed in as the highest authority he found, repeating the action and accessing more logins until he came across one with "all object authority." This allowed him to create an even higher level user id, giving him access at a level where he could embed his own code in the system.

It was a matter of only an hour until he looked up at the others. "I'm in, and I've gone as far as I can for now. All we can do is wait for this high-level user to sign in. They will actually activate the code I inserted in the Agincourt system – which will utilize that user's privileges to hijack authority. This will trigger the download of the research information that they stole from EngCorp, back to your company, Hank, and then delete it from their system. And the login will also trigger software that lets you begin to take them over."

Quiet cheers arose from the other three. "Way to go, buddy!" said Pistol.

Nim raised her arms over her head. "I never doubted you!"

Bardolph rolled his eyes. "Yeah, right."

"Excellent job, man. Congratulations." Hank rubbed his hands together and leaned forward. "But we're not done, of course. We still have to make sure the target user goes onto the system to activate the inserted code when he signs in. Who is it? Whose login path were you able to access?"

"Um, about that... Well, I took the only high level one I could get access to. Dauphin. But he doesn't seem to actually sign into the system all that often."

Hank sat back, his jaw slack for a moment. A low sound started in his chest, became a chuckle, and then a louder laugh. "Oh, seriously, Bardolph, that is perfect. Jesus. I'm not surprised he doesn't sign in very often. He always tried to get people to do his work for him." He leaned back in the chair, wiping his eyes.

The others had been watching him with frowns, but then also began laughing. Finally, their laughter ran down, and all four grew silent, one by one.

"Good God, Hank. How are we going to get Dauphin to sign in if he doesn't do anything for himself?" Pistol shook his head.

Hank stared into the distance. Minutes passed. Then his eyes focused upon his companions again, and a smile played across his lips.

"I've got it. It's blatant and subtle at the same time. First, I need to contact Alexander to have some of the remote hackers simulate a cyber attack against EngCorp. And we need to contact Arlo and have his lab build a present for Exeter to take to Dauphin. Agincourt stole our chip. Well, maybe Dauphin'll be happy to get one more."

CHAPTER TEN

"Alexander, we're ready to use some of our resources." Hank spoke into his wrist device.

Immediately, he heard a response from his long-time colleague. "Hold on, starting double encryption." A series of beeps sounded, and Alexander's voice came again.

"OK, shoot. What do you need?"

"Well," said Hank, "this is going to sound pretty stupid, but I need some hackers to pretend to try and get into EngCorp."

"Yeah, you're right. That does sound stupid. What's the point?"

"After the lab break-in, we confirmed that Dauphin had York add some tracking software onto the EngCorp system, and they're watching what goes on. Now I want them to think that someone else tried to access EngCorp to steal some data, but it doesn't need to actually work – just show access attempts against the system. I'll give you the areas to focus on."

Hank could hear Alexander laughing. "OK, buddy, this may be the easiest job we've done in a while – *not* breaking into someplace. Go ahead and send me the specs of what we should do."

As Hank prepared the data to send to Alexander, he caught sight of Nim at the guard post by the hallway door. She waved to get his attention and held her finger to her lips, then gestured to the light blinking on the scanner monitor by the door. Hank cut the connection with Alexander, then tapped Bardolph on the shoulder and indicated quiet; they looked over and saw Pistol asleep on one of the couches.

Hank moved to the couch and placed his hand over Pistol's mouth, waking him silently. Pistol roused to see Hank holding a finger to his lips and came alert instantly, rolling off the couch and moving to the scanner screens.

"One truck approaching. It's through the gate and pulling up to the warehouse section now." Pistol's voice was low. "Appears to be a maintenance truck with one person in it."

Bardolph looked up from his console. "Yup, I see a repair request for the automatic conveyor belt at Truck Bay 3. Damn, I should have thought to check these. Says it's expected to take an hour to fix it. I imagine he'll close out the repair request when he's done and leave. I'd say our biggest problem is if he has to use the bathroom while he's here."

"Agreed," said Nim. "If he finishes and leaves, he won't even know we're here. But if he comes down to this end of the building, I'll have to take him out. And I don't even intend to let him get that close. Bardolph, I assume you could fake the completion of the repair request, if it comes down to it?"

At Bardolph's slight sneer, Nim smiled and put her hand on the doorknob. "Right. I'm going to get into position before he gets inside. Pistol, we'll do the same thing we did at the bank that time, OK?"

Pistol gave her a loopy grin and staggered a bit as he walked towards her. "Oh yesh, shertainly, you can count on me." She smiled as she opened the door and they slipped through.

Hank watched the two head down the corridor and split up at the warehouse area, then he and Bardolph watched their progress on the monitors Pistol had set up to view the warehouse. Pistol took a seat hidden behind a large storage bin near the corridor and settled in to watch the display on his wrist.

Nim moved so quickly that they almost missed her. She scrambled silently up the near-vertical side of another storage bin and leapt lightly from bin to bin toward Bay 3, either jumping across the spaces between the rows or leaping up to grab the support beams on the ceiling and swinging across wider spaces. In a matter of moments, she had settled into a concealed position that overlooked the area needing repair, before the bay door had even opened to allow the repair truck to back in.

"Damn!" said Hank. "I didn't know she could do that! Bardolph, I wasn't there that time – what were they talking about – something that happened at a bank?"

"Seriously scary, man. The three of us were accessing a system and bank security showed up – three huge guys with machine guns. Pistol distracted them for a moment by acting like a drunk in the middle of the bank, and Nim did the same thing she just did – got up high. She jumped them from above and took out all three guys in under twenty seconds, using just her legs. They didn't even have time to aim."

"Wow, she disabled three guys that fast?" asked Hank.

"Oh hell no, Hank. They were all *dead* that fast."

Good God.

Hank continued to watch the warehouse monitors as he got the EngCorp access information together for Alexander and sent it off; he breathed a silent thanks when he saw the maintenance guy complete the repair and step outside to urinate against the building. Then the repairman got into his truck and drove away.

CHAPTER ELEVEN

Thirty members of the Agincourt risk assessment team were assembled in the conference room at the headquarters of the French weapons company. The president's son, Dauphin, sat at the head of the table facing the computer experts. All were leaning back in their chairs and laughing.

"So," said Dauphin, "We have stolen the plans for their chips, blown up their lab, killed their lead developer, and the best they could do was to take us to court...and lose." He snickered and the others again joined him.

"I don't think Hank and EngCorp are going to be any kind of major players in this world. He thinks he knows everything, and he certainly doesn't. He doesn't even know we are in his system." The others nodded at his words.

"But Dauphin, we're tracking EngCorp and see they're experiencing more than the usual number of cyber-access attempts," said the one member of the risk assessment team willing to speak up. "What if they turn on us in retaliation?"

Dauphin waved his hand to dismiss the words. "I told you, we have nothing to fear from them. I grew up in their facilities. And this new president of theirs is a playboy prince, a vain, giddy, shallow, humorous youth. I have been beating him since we were boys."

One of the security analysts blurted out, "Yes, sir. From what you say, they are sadly outnumbered by the risk assessment team we have in our corporation. What can such a small force do against our vast resources?"

Another spoke up. "I propose a wager that, if it comes to a full-on electronic assault by their computer personnel, we will take them out with a minimum of trouble." He looked around the room. "Who will bet with me? How many of their people do you wager that we would capture trying to break into our system?"

The others joined the wagering while Dauphin looked on with amusement.

CHAPTER TWELVE

"All right, Pistol, Dauphin still has not signed in yet. Are the other players in place?" Hank surveyed the team at Harfleur; they looked haggard but determined.

Four days is a long time to hide out here. We sort of stink.

"Yes, Hank, the first wave of fake attacks against EngCorp went exactly as planned. Indeed, we now have a small but dedicated array of users all set and primed to launch an assault against the Agincourt mainframe. I strongly suspect their security force will not know where to look first." The older man rubbed his hands together. "We are just waiting for final confirmation. Our players are ready, but they seem to be nervous."

"I can understand that. Agincourt is probably the biggest and most dangerous target they've gone up against. Hmm…let me think a bit. Do we have a private communication channel set up with the team?"

"Yes, Hank, of course," said Bardolph. "They're logging in as they get set up. And it's extremely secure. That way we can all talk if needed without any chance of a trace."

"Good. Let me get on there. Set me up a secure user id named…Leroy. And Pistol, please let me know when everyone is ready to get to work."

"Consider it done, boss." Bardolph turned back to the screen.

Hank opened a channel on his private communication device, and – at a signal from Bardolph – signed in as Leroy. He chatted with the various users who were anxiously awaiting the start of the computer assault, pretending to be a fellow hacker, calming each and making them feel more focused.

When Pistol signaled that all the computer assault team members were in position to begin their access, Hank signed off as Leroy and turned to the other three in the Harfleur office.

"So it looks like we're ready to go. Everyone feel comfortable with what we're going to do? Our remote team players are going to simulate a foray against the Agincourt computer system as the next step. If we're lucky, this will insult Dauphin enough that he logs into the system to check things out. If not, then Exeter is going to deliver the gift we had Arlo's lab put together directly to Dauphin. Exeter can be very persuasive. One of these is bound to make him log in."

Bardolph shook his head. "I know the plan, Hank, but I can't help but wish we had more than just the four of us and six other hackers scattered across England and France."

"Ah, I look at it differently, my friend." Hank smiled and gripped his arm. "Think of it like this: We ten are going to do something that nobody would imagine we could do – take over the biggest arms manufacturer in the world. Imagine the glory that's going to land at our feet when this is done! I don't want to share this with too many people, so please don't wish for more – the fewer people, the greater our share of honor. You know me. I don't care about money or elegant clothing. But if wanting honor is a problem, I am the biggest pain in the ass around."

Bardolph nodded and gripped Hank's arm in return, then clapped him on the shoulder. "All right, then!" They sat back.

Hank continued. "There's something else I've been thinking about. Tomorrow is going to be a great day in history. We're taking a huge risk as we go up against Agincourt, and our success will make a story that parents will teach their children; from this day until the end of the world, we will be remembered every year."

Hank paused, his eyes tearing up. "We few, we happy few, we band of brothers; for you that does this with me, shall be my brother."

There was a momentary silence as he stopped speaking; then the others smiled, and hugged each other, and clapped each other on the back.

"We are ready!" cried Pistol.

Nim had tears in her eyes as well. "I'm happy to be your brother, Hank."

"Indeed," replied Hank. "Let's do this! Signal them to start accessing the Agincourt system. I assume Agincourt is watching us now; I don't care if our hackers really get into either system or not, as long as the systems people at Agincourt think that someone has broken into our lab again, and that they are under attack as well."

The four Englishmen settled in to watch the progress of the six other hackers remotely. Reports came in periodically as one or another of the hackers gained minor access or got shut out.

"Ah, Williams says he was able to access the ventilation system at the main headquarters building before they closed him down. Heh." Bardolph chuckled.

Hank smiled. "Yeah, imagine what they probably thought he was trying to do to them."

"And Bates had to bug out of his physical access site. He says he felt that they were going to defeat the site forwarding system he had set up and find his actual location."

Hank nodded. "OK, that means he was keeping them busy and making them aware of the potential of system access. That is, of course, why we're not hacking from here; I don't want to call attention to the changes that Bardolph has already made from this location. But this all makes Exeter's package seem even more legitimate. Dauphin hasn't logged in yet – he must still be having his lackeys check things. I think it's time we sent Exeter in. Let's get in touch with Arlo at the lab."

Nodding, Bardolph connected to another communication channel and brought up an image of the EngCorp Head of Research on the screen. They saw the research lab in the background.

"Hello, Arlo. All's well with you?" Hank asked with a smile.

"Uh, yessir, uh, Hank, I mean this is all quite unorthodox. I feel really quite unusual to be taking part in something like this."

"Not a problem, Arlo. Exeter's already in France; we need you to get in touch and signal that we're ready for him to take the package to Dauphin. I just didn't want him to have any history of communication with our location on his wrist device when he gets to Agincourt, much less an open channel to us when he gets there. I assume he has his moddy chip covered already until he gets through security. But it's quite all right for you to contact him through regular company channels on his wrist device."

"OK, will do, I mean yessir..." Arlo rolled his eyes. "I will get in touch with him directly, Hank."

"Good man. When he gets into the Agincourt offices, we'll have this channel open so we can watch when you hear anything back from him."

The four settled in to rest before the next phase, taking turns on guard.

CHAPTER THIRTEEN

That afternoon, Exeter waited in the huge reception room at Agincourt, his hands carefully folded in his lap. He looked up as the large wooden door opened at the end of the room and a young woman came out and walked over to him. A security guard was with her.

"Sir, I've been instructed to take you for an additional security screening before you enter Dauphin's office." The young woman gestured to a small alcove at the side of the reception room.

Well. This is new, thought Exeter. *I wonder if we've been making them feel more vulnerable already.*

Exeter inclined his head with a small smile and followed her through the alcove and into a small room with a body scanner and two technicians; the security guard followed.

"I'll be just outside," the young woman said, and left the room.

"Please step up here, monsieur," said one technician, gesturing to a platform with an attached screen. "This will only take a moment."

Exeter walked into the scanner. The other technician watched the screen light up with an outline of his form. Several spots lit up in red.

"Sir, I need to check what I see in your jacket pocket and what is on your arm," said the technician at his side.

Good. It didn't detect the moddy chip in my neck.

"Of course." Exeter started to reach into his jacket, and the security guard's hand came up with a weapon pointed at him.

Exeter smiled. "It's just a prototype to show Dauphin. Of a moddy chip design he has shown interest in recently." *Now that's an understatement.*

The technician took it from his hand and scanned it with a small device. "Looks OK. I'll assume nobody would be brash enough to actually plug this into our system." He placed it on the table and the guard relaxed. "And the other?"

"Ah, this is just our corporate communication system. You'll see that our Head of Research is online with me now." Exeter held up his wrist communication device for them to view. When they gestured, he took it off and passed it over to the technician who performed another scan.

The technician examined the screen and saw Arlo's face.

"Yes?" said Arlo. "Exeter?"

"It checks out," said the technician, passing it back to Exeter. "All clear."

Exeter spoke into the wrist device as he put it back on. "No problem, Arlo, I've finished an additional security scan and am heading in to see Dauphin now."

He pocketed the moddy chip again and nodded to the security guard, who escorted Exeter back into the reception room. The young woman guided him into Dauphin's office, and the security officer took up a station just inside the door. Exeter saw a large, expensively furnished room with a desk on a raised dais, with two small chairs on the floor facing the desk. The result was that anyone sitting in the chairs would feel dwarfed by the person at the desk.

Are we making up for something here? Lack of daddy love? Personal inadequacies?

The blond man at the desk looked down at him. "Ah, Exeter. To what do I owe this unexpected visit?" He shook his head at the two accompanying Exeter. "That won't be necessary. I am sure that I have nothing to worry about from our friend at the lesser corporation, isn't that right, Exeter? That is, assuming he passed the security scan?"

"Yes sir, he passed, but I would caution you..." the security guard said.

Dauphin held up his hand, then pointed toward the door. "If he passed, I'll be fine. I have known him since I was a child."

The two left the men alone, closing the door behind them as they left. As Dauphin watched them go, Exeter quickly peeled off the cover that hid the moddy chip on his neck and pocketed it.

"Have a seat, please. May I get you something?" Dauphin's hand gestured lazily towards the full bar at one side of the room. "Some English beer, perhaps?"

"No, thank you, Dauphin. Thank you for seeing me on such short notice." Exeter turned on the full force of his smile. "I know we've been at each other's throats for a while now – EngCorp and Agincourt. But I have a definite idea that I know who's going to come out on top of this corporate struggle. And I want to be on the winning side." *From what I know of him as a youth, he will assume I mean his side.*

Dauphin watched him for a moment, a small smile on his lips. "Indeed. And you feel the winning side is mine."

Exeter folded his hands one over the other, his wrist screen pointing towards Dauphin. "Why, yes, of course. I watched you in our court dealings over this chip nonsense. You know what is going to happen to EngCorp with Hank at its head. He has no experience in business, no finesse. And I can tell that you are the future of Agincourt…and the world. I wouldn't be surprised if your father stepped down soon, leaving you as president."

Too much?

Dauphin sat up straighter in his elaborate chair and lifted his chin. "Why, yes, that does indeed seem probable to me as well. I am delighted to hear that you are still a perceptive individual, Exeter. My father has just not yet determined that the time is right to turn the corporation over to me." Dauphin leaned back, lacing his fingers behind his head.

Exeter frowned a bit and tilted his head. "Yes, as someone from the same generation as your father, I can understand the cautious approach. I suspect he's simply watching to see whether you can innovate and create new possibilities for Agincourt. At least, that's what I would be doing were I in his shoes."

Dauphin's eyebrows rose. "New possibilities. Keep talking."

"Well, for example, the moddy chip plans that were…lost from our lab."

Dauphin smiled. "Lost. Yes, of course. They seem to be a promising avenue of approach, shall we say?"

Exeter shook his head. "You wouldn't believe how much you'll be able to do with these moddy chips once they are fully developed. But I'm afraid any information that you may have, uh, *acquired* about them, is not quite complete."

"Indeed. Just exactly what do you mean?" Dauphin leaned forward in his chair.

Heh. Now I've got you hooked.

"Not all of the moddy chip prototypes and plans were obtained from the EngCorp lab. Some of the best ones were under development at another location. A location that I have recently accessed, shall we say?"

"Well. This is indeed an interesting development, Exeter. I have received reports of various break-in attempts to the EngCorp systems. As well as some minor attempts against Agincourt. Is it fair to assume that these were your efforts at obtaining the most up-to-date moddy chip designs?"

Exeter inclined his head with a small smile. "At your service. May I show you?" At Dauphin's nod, he reached into his jacket pocket, brought out the small chip that the security officers had previously scanned, and attached a cable that could connect it to a computer. He held them out to Dauphin but stopped just before passing them over.

"I would only suggest that you be very careful when you plug this into your system, Dauphin. I've been told that it contains some very powerful code. I'm not sure that your system is capable of handling it. Perhaps you should consult with some of your technicians if you don't know how to do this."

Dauphin snorted. "Seriously, you think our system is inferior to yours? That I don't know what I'm doing?" He turned to the computer on his desk and logged in, fumbling over the cable connection for the moddy chip. Exeter suppressed a smile, and then turned so that his wrist communicator showed Dauphin at the computer.

He's logged in. It doesn't even matter if he plugs in the moddy chip or not!

CHAPTER FOURTEEN

"OK, he's signed in! Dauphin is on the system!" Bardolph jumped up and his chair went flying out from beneath him.

"Great. Finally. Is our code being triggered to run?" Hank picked up the chair and peered over his shoulder. *Got my fingers crossed on this one.*

Bardolph sat down without even noticing. "Yes. Uh. Yes, our code is running to access the various systems and take control, just as we planned. But…uh…something *else* is running, too."

"What do you mean, something else is running?" Hank stared at the hacker.

"Not sure…hold on. Wow. Oh, wow. A lot of other systems are coming on-line," said Bardolph.

Hank's hands clenched tight. "Any idea what they do? Or what areas they're running?"

Bardolph went pale. "Well, it looks like…it looks like signals are heading out to all the various military sites that Agincourt controls. I'm seeing activity as systems come on line."

"Oh, no. This can't be good. Get Arlo on the screen," said Hank.

Nim turned the screen around so they could see the Head of the Research Department at the underground lab facility. The man was looking over his shoulder, flinching at dull noises that came periodically from overhead, outside the lab. Red security lights reflected off the sweat on his bald head.

"Arlo! Are you okay? Is something happening there?" Hank raised his voice to be heard over the background sounds at the lab.

The man shook his head. "*No!* I mean yes, this is entirely out of the ordinary. I'm down in the computer system bunker, under the city. And there are explosions going on above us. I cannot get a feed from most of the external cameras anymore. They just went dead."

"Who else is with you? Are you secure?"

"Yes. There are a dozen techs down here at all times, and enough food to last for a year. I just never thought we would be needing it." Arlo mopped his head with the sleeve of his lab coat.

"All right. Stay where you are. Can you still access Exeter's wrist device?" said Hank.

Arlo's face brightened a bit. "Oh! Yes. Yes, I can. Hold on. Exeter? Can you hear me?"

The four in the Harfleur warehouse office watched Arlo as he turned to the adjacent screen. "What's going on, Exeter? We seem to be under attack here."

The bald man waited a moment, then turned back to the Harfleur screen. "I don't get an answer from him, but I can see his feed. He's still in Dauphin's office and they're at the computer. They look worried. Or scared. Or something. But have you seen the EngCorp system security monitors?"

"Ohmygod, ohmygod!" Bardolph's fingers frantically worked the keyboard, bringing up various monitoring screens and maps. "Oh, Hank, this is bad." He stared at the screen. "Look."

"What does this all mean?" Hank's fingers pressed into Bardolph's shoulder.

"These lines in red show incoming missiles from France to England. It looks like our system changes triggered Agincourt's Doomsday system," said Bardolph.

They must have been even more paranoid than I ever imagined.

Bardolph's voice continued. "And the blue lines show our EngCorp defenses attacking them in response. Now look at what else is happening."

The four watched in horror as the lines spread across the entire map of the world, with additional colors joining the pattern as different corporations' defenses joined the fray one after another. They heard the sound of explosions in the distance, far outside their building, yet remained relatively unaffected at their remote location in the Harfleur warehouse in the countryside.

My God. What have I done?

Nim turned back to Arlo on the secure channel. "What's your situation?"

The screen showed the research chief in dim light, with a red light flashing behind him.

"Well, we are now on generator power. The best I can tell from our remaining sensors, the city above us is mostly leveled."

Hank gripped the desk in front of him. "Can you still see Uncle Exeter, Arlo? And Bardolph, patch through his voice from the moddy chip so we can hear him. Even if the rest of the power is out, that should still work. We need to know what's going on at Agincourt!"

Arlo made a few adjustments, and Pistol's screen filled with the transmission from Exeter's wrist device. They saw Exeter's view as he moved through the reception room behind a pair of men carrying the limp form of Dauphin, with security people on each side and ahead of them. One of the walls had collapsed, and smoke and dust filled the room.

Bardolph triggered a speaker on the desk to access the moddy chip frequency, and Exeter's ragged voice filled their ears as he jogged along.

"Hank? I don't know if you can hear me, boy. But this looks bad. We took a direct hit and it's a wonder we're not dead yet. The president of Agincourt was killed, and Dauphin is seriously wounded. The only good thing is that at least everyone has given up nuclear arms. But there are chemicals in the air here."

"Oh, no! Oh, no, Uncle, can you hear me? I'm so sorry! What have we done?" Hank's voice cracked.

Another explosion hit near Exeter, and the image spun wildly as he ducked and covered his head as a reflex. The image went black, and they could only hear his voice coming through the moddy chip connection.

"EMPs, I'd say. Totally wiped the electronics here. More gas. Hank. There's not much left here – I saw the images from outside on Dauphin's screen. I assume you're in the system, if there's anything left of it – you have to take control."

He coughed. "You are the person that is needed to bring this together. Hank, I said it before, and I still believe it. You may not be the president that your father wanted, but you're the person the world needs now. Oh God, I hear another–"

An explosion hit, and his voice went quiet.

The four sat in stunned silence. Pistol had tears running down his face, and Nim buried her head on his shoulder. Hank and Bardolph sat slumped in their chairs.

I am worse than the biggest pain in the ass around; I prompted the destruction of the world as we know it. We certainly will be remembered every year on this day. But...for what?

After what seemed an eternity, they roused themselves and looked at each other. Hank rubbed his face with his hand and finally spoke. "There's not much left; but Arlo's team is in the EngCorp lab, and we're here. We can at least try and rebuild the world the way we would like it to be. Brothers, I believe we have some work to do."

Appendix
Play Summaries

I could a tale unfold…

Stories in this volume were inspired by Shakespeare's plays. While each punk story reads well on its own without knowing anything of the Bard's play that inspired it, we thought you may appreciate a short synopsis of each play – followed by a hint of how it is interpreted in punk fashion.

As You Like It

(which inspired "As You Like It"
by Katherine Perkins and Jeffrey Cook)

Play Summary from Wikipedia[1]

The play is set in a duchy in France, but most of the action takes place in a location called the Forest of Arden. This may be intended as the Ardennes, a forested region covering an area located in southeast Belgium, western Luxembourg and northeastern France, or Arden, Warwickshire, near Shakespeare's home town, which was the ancestral origin of his mother's family – who incidentally were called Arden.

Frederick has usurped the Duchy and exiled his older brother, Duke Senior. The Duke's daughter, Rosalind, has been permitted to remain at court because she is the closest friend and cousin of Frederick's only child, Celia. Orlando, a young gentleman of the kingdom who at first sight has fallen in love with Rosalind, is forced to flee his home after being persecuted by his older brother, Oliver. Frederick becomes angry and banishes Rosalind from court. Celia and Rosalind decide to flee together accompanied by the court clown, Touchstone, with Rosalind disguised as a young man and Celia disguised as a poor lady.

Rosalind, now disguised as Ganymede ("Jove's own page"), and Celia, now disguised as Aliena (Latin for "stranger"), arrive in the Arcadian Forest of Arden, where the exiled Duke now lives with some supporters, including "the melancholy Jaques," a malcontent figure, who is introduced to us weeping over the slaughter of a deer. "Ganymede" and "Aliena" do not immediately encounter the Duke and his companions, as they meet up with Corin, an impoverished tenant, and offer to buy his master's crude cottage.

Orlando and his servant Adam, meanwhile, find the Duke and his men and are soon living with them and posting simplistic love poems for Rosalind on the trees. (The role of Adam may have been played by Shakespeare, though this story is said to be apocryphal.) Rosalind, also in love with Orlando, meets him as Ganymede and pretends to counsel him to cure him of being in love. Ganymede says "he" will take Rosalind's place and "he" and Orlando can act out their relationship.

The shepherdess, Phoebe, with whom Silvius is in love, has fallen in love with Ganymede (Rosalind in disguise), though "Ganymede" continually shows that "he" is not interested in Phoebe. Touchstone, meanwhile, has fallen in love with the dull-witted shepherdess, Audrey, and tries to woo her, but eventually is forced to be married first. William, another shepherd, attempts to marry Audrey as well, but is stopped by Touchstone, who threatens to kill him "a hundred and fifty ways".

Finally, Silvius, Phoebe, Ganymede, and Orlando are brought together in an argument with each other over who will get whom. Ganymede says he will solve the problem, having Orlando promise to marry Rosalind, and Phoebe promise to marry Silvius if she cannot marry Ganymede.

Orlando sees Oliver in the forest and rescues him from a lioness, causing Oliver to repent for mistreating Orlando. Oliver meets Aliena (Celia's false identity) and falls in love with her, and they agree to marry. Orlando and Rosalind, Oliver and Celia, Silvius and Phoebe, and Touchstone and Audrey all are married in the final scene, after which they discover that Frederick also has repented his faults, deciding to restore his legitimate brother to the dukedom and adopt a religious life. Jaques, ever melancholic, declines their invitation to return to the court preferring to stay in the forest and to adopt a religious life as well. Rosalind speaks an epilogue to the audience, commending the play to both men and women in the audience.

Dieselpunk story: "As You Like It" by Katherine Perkins and Jeffrey Cook

An exciting boxing match pits Orrie against his brother's interests. Will his powerful truck with the refitted engines stand up against his pursuers with nitrous injectors? When Rosie is thrown off Factory property by her best friend Cecily's dad, Boss Frederick, will her disguise of being a boy work out when the two women run off past the last way station? And what will happen when they all get together in the forest?

Coriolanus

(which inspired "The Tragedy of Livingston" by Janice Stucki)

Play Summary from Wikipedia[2]

The play opens in Rome shortly after the expulsion of the Tarquin kings. There are riots in progress, after stores of grain were withheld from ordinary citizens. The rioters are particularly angry at Caius Marcius, a brilliant Roman general whom they blame for the grain being taken away. The rioters encounter a patrician named Menenius Agrippa, as well as Caius Marcius himself. Menenius tries to calm the rioters, while Marcius is openly contemptuous, and says that the plebeians were not worthy of the grain because of their lack of military service. Two of the tribunes of Rome, Brutus and Sicinius, privately denounce Marcius. He leaves Rome after news arrives that a Volscian army is in the field.

The commander of the Volscian army, Tullus Aufidius, has fought Marcius on several occasions and considers him a blood enemy. The Roman army is commanded by Cominius, with Marcius as his deputy. While Cominius takes his soldiers to meet Aufidius' army, Marcius leads a rally against the Volscian city of Corioli. The siege of Corioli is initially unsuccessful, but Marcius is able to force open the gates of the city, and the Romans conquer it. Even though he is exhausted from the fighting, Marcius marches quickly to join Cominius and fight the other Volscian force. Marcius and Aufidius meet in single combat, which only ends when Aufidius' own soldiers drag him away from the battle.

In recognition of his great courage, Cominius gives Caius Marcius the agnomen, or "official nickname", of *Coriolanus*. When they return to Rome, Coriolanus's mother Volumnia encourages her son to run for consul. Coriolanus is hesitant to do this, but he bows to his mother's wishes. He effortlessly wins the support of the Roman Senate, and seems at first to have won over the commoners as well. However, Brutus and Sicinius scheme to undo Coriolanus and whip up another riot in opposition to his becoming consul. Faced with this opposition, Coriolanus flies into a rage and rails against the concept of popular rule. He compares allowing plebeians to have power over the patricians to allowing "crows to peck the eagles". The two tribunes condemn Coriolanus as a traitor for his words, and order him to be banished. Coriolanus retorts that it is he who banishes Rome from his presence.

After being exiled from Rome, Coriolanus seeks out Aufidius in the Volscian capital of Antium, and offers to let Aufidius kill him in order to spite the country that banished him. Moved by his plight and honoured to fight alongside the great general, Aufidius and his superiors embrace Coriolanus, and allow him to lead a new assault on Rome.

Rome, in its panic, tries desperately to persuade Coriolanus to halt his crusade for vengeance, but both Cominius and Menenius fail. Finally, Volumnia is sent to meet her son, along with Coriolanus's wife Virgilia and child, and a chaste gentlewoman Valeria. Volumnia succeeds in dissuading her son from destroying Rome, and Coriolanus instead concludes a peace treaty between the Volscians and the Romans. When Coriolanus returns to the Volscian capital, conspirators, organised by Aufidius, kill him for his betrayal.

Nanopunk story (in play format): "The Tragedy of Livingston" by Janice Stucki

CJ Livingston, the Governor of New Jersey, is in the midst of debates during the presidential primaries against his strongest rival, Don Whist. Influenced by his belief in the class system, his strong-willed mother, and by the nanobots that the higher class inject to produce superior performance, will CJ listen to the voices of the common people and help to preserve their way of life? Or will his misplaced alliances and abuse of nanobot technology aid in his downfall?

A Midsummer Night's Dream

(which inspired "Blast the Past: Fae and Far Between" by Rozene Morgandy)

This play is filled with many characters both human and faerie, and many cases of mistaken identity. A short video that covers all the characters and their interactions can be found at:
http://www.sparknotes.com/shakespeare/msnd/

Play Summary from Wikipedia[3]

The play consists of four interconnecting plots, connected by a celebration of the wedding of Duke Theseus of Athens and the Amazon queen, Hippolyta, which is set simultaneously in the woodland and in the realm of Fairyland, under the light of the moon.

The play opens with Hermia, who is in love with Lysander, not wanting to submit to her father Egeus' demand that she wed Demetrius, whom he has arranged for her to marry. Helena meanwhile pines unrequitedly for Demetrius. Enraged, Egeus invokes an ancient Athenian law before Duke Theseus, whereby a daughter must marry the suitor chosen by her father, or else face death. Theseus offers her another choice: lifelong chastity while worshiping the goddess Diana as a nun.

Peter Quince and his fellow players plan to put on a play for the wedding of the Duke and the Queen, "the most lamentable comedy and most cruel death of Pyramus and Thisbe". Quince reads the names of characters and bestows them to the players. Nick Bottom, who is playing the main role of Pyramus, is over-enthusiastic and wants to dominate others by suggesting himself for the characters of Thisbe, the Lion, and Pyramus at the same time. He would also rather be a tyrant and recites some lines of Ercles. Quince ends the meeting with "at the Duke's oak we meet".

In a parallel plot line, Oberon, king of the fairies, and Titania, his queen, have come to the forest outside Athens. Titania tells Oberon that she plans to stay there until she has attended Theseus and Hippolyta's wedding. Oberon and Titania are estranged because Titania refuses to give her Indian changeling to Oberon for use as his "knight" or "henchman," since the child's mother was one of Titania's worshipers. Oberon seeks to punish Titania's disobedience. He calls upon Robin "Puck" Goodfellow, his "shrewd and knavish sprite", to help him concoct a magical juice derived from a flower called "love-in-idleness", which turns from white to purple when struck by Cupid's arrow. When the concoction is applied to the eyelids of a sleeping person, that person, upon waking, falls in love with the first living thing they perceive. He instructs Puck to retrieve the flower with the hope that he might make Titania fall in love with an animal of the forest and thereby shame her into giving up the little Indian boy. He says, "And ere I take this charm from off her sight, / As I can take it with another herb, / I'll make her render up her page to me."

Hermia and Lysander have escaped to the same forest in hopes of eloping. Helena, desperate to reclaim Demetrius's love, tells Demetrius about the plan and he follows them in hopes of killing Lysander. Helena continually makes advances towards Demetrius, promising to love him more than Hermia. However, he rebuffs her with cruel insults against her. Observing this, Oberon orders Puck to spread some of the magical juice from the flower on the eyelids of the young Athenian man. Instead, Puck mistakes Lysander for Demetrius, not having actually seen either before, and administers the juice to the sleeping Lysander. Helena, coming across him, wakes him while attempting to determine whether he is dead or asleep. Upon this happening, Lysander immediately falls in love with Helena. Oberon sees Demetrius still following Hermia and is enraged. When Demetrius decides to go to sleep, Oberon sends Puck to get Helena while he charms Demetrius' eyes. Upon waking up, he sees Helena. Now, both men are in pursuit of Helena. However, she is convinced that her two suitors are mocking her, as neither loved her originally. Hermia is at a loss to see why her lover has abandoned her, and accuses Helena of stealing Lysander away from her. The four quarrel with each other until Lysander and Demetrius become so enraged that they seek a place to duel each other to prove whose love for Helena is the greatest. Oberon orders Puck to keep Lysander and Demetrius from catching up with one another and to remove the charm from Lysander. Lysander returns to loving Hermia, while Demetrius continues to love Helena.

Meanwhile, Quince and his band of six labourers ("rude mechanicals", as they are described by Puck) have arranged to perform their play about Pyramus and Thisbe for Theseus' wedding and venture into the forest, near Titania's bower, for their rehearsal. Bottom is spotted by Puck, who (taking his name to be another word for a jackass) transforms his head into that of a donkey. When Bottom returns for his next lines, the other workmen run screaming in terror, much to Bottom's confusion, since he hasn't felt a thing during the transformation. Determined to wait for his friends, he begins to sing to himself. Titania is awakened by Bottom's singing and immediately falls in love with him. She lavishes him with attention and presumably makes love to him. While she is in this state of devotion, Oberon takes the changeling. Having achieved his goals, Oberon releases Titania, orders Puck to remove the donkey's head from Bottom, and arranges everything so that Hermia, Lysander, Demetrius, and Helena will believe that they have been dreaming when they awaken.

The fairies then disappear, and Theseus and Hippolyta arrive on the scene, during an early morning hunt. They wake the lovers and, since Demetrius does not love Hermia any more, Theseus overrules Egeus's demands and arranges a group wedding. The lovers decide that the night's events must have been a dream. After they all exit, Bottom awakes, and he too decides that he must have experienced a dream "past the wit of man". In Athens, Theseus, Hippolyta and the lovers watch the six workmen perform *Pyramus and Thisbe*. Given a lack of preparation, the performers are so terrible playing their roles to the point where the guests laugh as if it were meant to be a comedy, and everyone retires to bed. Afterwards, Oberon, Titania, Puck, and other fairies enter, and bless the house and its occupants with good fortune. After all other characters leave, Puck "restores amends" and suggests to the audience that what they just experienced might be nothing but a dream (hence the name of the play).

Elfpunk story: "Blast the Past: Fae and Far Between" by Rozene Morgandy

Harlequinn and Tiernan are planning their royal wedding and are surprised by a sudden contact with an albino from the faerie world, who turns out to be Osiris, the king of the faeries, with a wedding gift that will take the humans across the toxic wasteland between their lands and into the Fae world. Much trickery, mistaken identity, and magic potions follow. Will the humans overcome their personal issues, where two women in love are not allowed to marry due to fertility problems among the humans? And, most importantly, will the humans and the Fae resolve their long-time feud?

Julius Caesar

(which inspired "Dogs of War" by Jeffrey Cook and Katherine Perkins)

Also see http://www.sparknotes.com/shakespeare/juliuscaesar/ for a short video that covers all the characters and their interactions.

The play opens with the commoners of Rome celebrating Caesar's triumphant return from defeating Pompey's sons at the battle of Munda. Two tribunes, Flavius and Marrullus, discover the commoners celebrating, insult them for their change in loyalty from Pompey to Caesar, and break up the crowd. They also plan on removing all decorations from Caesar's statues and ending any other festivities. In the next scene, during Caesar's parade on the feast of Lupercal, a soothsayer warns Caesar to "Beware the ides of March", a warning he disregards. The action then turns to the discussion between Brutus and Cassius. In this conversation, Cassius attempts to influence Brutus' opinions into believing Caesar should be killed, preparing to have Brutus join his conspiracy to kill Caesar. They then hear from Casca that Mark Antony has offered Caesar the crown of Rome three times, and that each time Caesar refused it, fainting after the last refusal. Later, in act two, Brutus joins the conspiracy, although after much moral debate, eventually deciding that Caesar, although his friend and never having done anything against the people of Rome, should be killed to *prevent* him from doing anything against the people of Rome if he were ever to be crowned. He compares Caesar to "A serpents egg/ which hatch'd, would, as his kind, grow mischievous,/ and kill him in the shell.", and decides to join Cassius in killing Caesar.

Caesar's assassination is one of the most famous scenes of the play, occurring in Act 3, scene 1 (the other is Mark Antony's funeral oration "Friends, Romans, countrymen.") After ignoring the soothsayer, as well as his wife's own premonitions, Caesar comes to the Senate. The conspirators create a superficial motive for coming close enough to assassinate Caesar by means of a petition brought by Metellus Cimber, pleading on behalf of his banished brother. As Caesar, predictably, rejects the petition, Casca grazes Caesar in the back of his neck, and the others follow in stabbing him; Brutus is last. At this point, Shakespeare makes Caesar utter the famous line "Et tu, Brute?" ("And you, Brutus?", *i.e.* "You too, Brutus?"). Shakespeare has him add, "Then fall, Caesar," suggesting that such treachery destroyed Caesar's will to live.

The conspirators make clear that they committed this act for Rome, not for their own purposes and do not attempt to flee the scene. After Caesar's death, Brutus delivers an oration defending his actions, and for the moment, the crowd is on his side. However, Mark Antony, with a subtle and eloquent speech over Caesar's corpse – beginning with the much-quoted *Friends, Romans, countrymen, lend me your ears* – deftly turns public opinion against the assassins by manipulating the emotions of the common people, in contrast to the rational tone of Brutus's speech, yet there is method in his rhetorical speech and gestures: he reminds them of the good Caesar had done for Rome, his sympathy with the poor, and his refusal of the crown at the Lupercal, thus questioning Brutus' claim of Caesar's ambition; he shows Caesar's bloody, lifeless body to the crowd to have them shed tears and gain sympathy for their fallen hero; and he reads Caesar's will, in which every Roman citizen would receive 75 drachmas. Antony, even as he states his intentions against it, rouses the mob to drive the conspirators from Rome. Amid the violence, an innocent poet, Cinna, is confused with the conspirator Lucius Cinna and is murdered by the mob.

The beginning of Act Four is marked by the quarrel scene, where Brutus attacks Cassius for soiling the noble act of regicide by accepting bribes ("Did not great Julius bleed for justice' sake? / What villain touch'd his body, that did stab, / And not for justice?") The two are reconciled, especially after Brutus reveals that his beloved wife Portia had committed suicide under the stress of his absence from Rome; they prepare for a war against Mark Antony and Caesar's adopted son, Octavius. That night, Caesar's ghost appears to Brutus with a warning of defeat ("thou shalt see me at Philippi").

At the battle, Cassius and Brutus, knowing that they will probably both die, smile their last smiles to each other and hold hands. During the battle, Cassius has his servant Pindarus kill him after hearing of the capture of his best friend, Titinius. After Titinius, who was not really captured, sees Cassius's corpse, he commits suicide. However, Brutus wins that stage of the battle – but his victory is not conclusive. With a heavy heart, Brutus battles again the next day. He loses and commits suicide by running on his own sword, which is held by a soldier named Strato.

The play ends with a tribute to Brutus by Antony, who proclaims that Brutus has remained "the noblest Roman of them all" because he was the only conspirator who acted, in his mind, for the good of Rome. There is then a small hint at the friction between Mark Antony and Octavius which will characterize another of Shakespeare's Roman plays, *Antony and Cleopatra*.

Dieselpunk story: "Dogs of War" by Jeffrey Cook and Katherine Perkins

The Brute, a monster tank left over from earlier days of war, rolls into the desert town at the head of a motley army of modified armored cars, cycles, and a gyro-copter overhead – provoking a round of back-stabbing and double dealing amongst those who would take power from Jules the Conqueror. But will the competition on the cycle track spill over into all-out battle on the desert sands?

Henry V

(which inspired "Hank" by Carol Gyzander)

Play Summary

Young Henry V, the new King of England, needs to overcome his dubious reputation from his early wild days. Laying claim to parts of France, based upon some legal technicalities, he winds up invading the country when the son of the French king, the Dauphin, sends a case of tennis balls as an insulting response to Henry's claims.

The common people who are affected by his decision to invade France include Bardolph, Pistol, and Nim – common lowlifes he abandoned when he took the throne. King Henry learns of a conspiracy against his life, led by a past friend Scropes; in an action that shows a marked maturation from his earlier youthful behavior, Henry condemns the three to death.

The English invade France, and at the battle at the town of Harfleur, Henry gives an impassioned speech that motivates his much smaller force to continue the battle – the source of the well-known phrase, "Once more unto the breach." (Act III sc I). After the English victory at

Harfleur, the French messenger Montjoy travels between the two kings to convey ransom and surrender negotiations, to no avail. Later, the French are depicted as frivolous noblemen, wagering on how many English lives will be lost in the upcoming battle of Agincourt. But Henry goes among the English soldiers in disguise, raising their morale and strengthening their dedication. He then delivers a stirring St. Crispin's Day speech, where he exhorts them to not be disheartened by their small numbers against a larger army, as each will have a greater share of the honor of the victory.

We few, we happy few, we band of brothers.
For he today that sheds his blood with me
Shall be my brother… (Henry V, IV.iii.60–62)

At the end of the battle of Agincourt, the English have won and the French king offers his daughter as bride to Henry.

Cyberpunk story: "Hank" by Carol Gyzander

Hank is now the president of EngCorp, and trying to overcome his reputation from youthful days in the gritty Underground. When a break in results in plans for EngCorp's new moddy chip being stolen by the French company of Agincourt, an insult from his childhood nemesis Dauphin provokes Hank into a cyber attack against the French. Will the moddy chip help their efforts? Will Hank be able to lead his cyber troops once more unto the breach?

Excerpts from Wikipedia are included here; the work is released under CC BY-SA as described at http://creativecommons.org/licenses/by-sa/3.0/

Carol Gyzander

1. https://en.wikipedia.org/wiki/As_You_Like_It
2. https://en.wikipedia.org/wiki/Coriolanus
3. https://en.wikipedia.org/wiki/A_Midsummer_Night's_Dream
4. https://en.wikipedia.org/wiki/Julius_Caesar_(play)

SOUND & FURY

Shakespeare Goes Punk

SOUND FURY

Shakespeare Goes Punk

Did you like
Once More Unto The Breach?

You will probably also enjoy our first volume, *Sound & Fury*.

Would you like to see news of the next volume coming out? Upcoming volumes may include *All's Well That Ends Well, Hamlet, King Lear, Romeo and Juliet, The Merchant of Venice, The Rape of Lucrece, Twelfth Night…*

Readers love books by Writerpunk Press.
YOU WILL TOO.

Visit the link below for information about other books by these authors, and follow us on Twitter for news of the next volume!

Visit NOW: www.punkwriters.com

Twitter: @punkwriters

"Know your place, Caliban," Prospero shouted as the tips of his fingers released a pulse of electricity. Instantly the nymph's breathing became labored as power was cut off from the enhancements that kept Caliban alive...

SOUND & FURY

Shakespeare Goes Punk

See the Bard reimagined in punk style.
www.punkwriters.com

Sound & Fury is available on Amazon

WHATEVER AN AUTHOR NEEDS

FreeYourWords.com

Covers
Print Book Layout
Ebook Formatting
Author Merchandise
Displays + Adverts

38939113R00179

Made in the USA
Middletown, DE
13 March 2019